CW01558792

ABOUT THE AUTHOR

David Evered's professional career has been in academic medicine and research. He has published numerous papers in peer-reviewed medical and scientific journals, postgraduate level books and made many contributions to multi-author texts. He has been a consultant physician in Newcastle Upon Tyne, the Deputy Head of the UK Medical Research Council, a Special Adviser to the International Agency for Research on Cancer (World Health Organisation) and a Trustee and board member of Macmillan Cancer Support. David is an enthusiastic amateur historian. He published his first novel in 2018, *Beyond the Arch*, with Troubador Publishing.

David has lived in Newcastle, London and France. He is now retired and lives on the Berkshire/Hampshire border.

THE LONG SHADOWS OF WAR

DAVID EVERED

Troubador Publishing Ltd
Unit E2 Airfield Business Park,
Harrison Road, Market Harborough,
Leicestershire LE16 7UL
Tel: 0116 279 2299
Email: books@troubador.co.uk
Web: www.troubador.co.uk

ISBN 978-1-83628-363-8

British Library Cataloguing in Publication Data.
A catalogue record for this book is available from the British Library.

The manufacturer's authorised representative in the EU for product
safety is Authorised Rep Compliance Ltd, 71 Lower Baggot Street,
Dublin D02 P593 Ireland (www.arccompliance.com).

Printed and bound in Great Britain by 4edge Limited
Typeset in 11pt Minion Pro by Troubador Publishing Ltd, Leicester, UK

In memory of my father – Thomas Evered

The past is never dead. It's not even past. All of us labour in webs spun long before we were born, webs of heredity and environment, of desire and consequence, of history and eternity.

William Faulkner – Requiem for a nun

What we call the beginning is often the end. And to make an end is to make a beginning. The end is where we start from.

T.S. Eliot – Little Gidding, Four Quartets

1

21 October 1989

'Come on, Ellie – for God's sake, get a move on,' Mark shouted from the bottom of the loft ladder. 'Is that everything or not?'

'I think so.' A muffled voice came back through the hatch. 'No, I'm not sure. Hang on a minute. It's bloody dark up here.' There was a pause. 'There is something else – right at the back. Looks like a trunk. I'll have to crawl on my belly (not to mention my boobs) to get to it.'

Mark waited as Gisela manoeuvred herself across the loft floor.

'I'm there,' she shouted. 'It's heavy. I'll shove it across.'

Mark could hear the trunk scraping over the boards as Gisela pushed it towards the hatch. She levered it over the edge. 'It's heavy. Catch!' He staggered back under the weight losing his balance. It fell with a resounding thud.

Gisela's face appeared a moment later. She brushed her hair to one side leaving a dusty smudge on her forehead. 'I'm coming down. That really is the lot. It's mucky as hell back

1

there.' She grinned. 'Perhaps it contains a priceless heirloom. Then we can retire and live in luxury in the south of France!'

'Dream on, Ellie.'

Gisela shrugged. 'No harm in dreaming. Probably just more of your old toys. I need coffee.'

They were interrupted by three loud knocks followed by an imperious voice from below. 'What the hell are you two still doing up there? I haven't got all day.'

'Martina, we're coming. There was a lot more up here than we thought.' Mark gave a rueful smile. He turned to Gisela and said quietly, 'That bloody stick of hers always comes into play when she wants to enforce her diktats. I hope she's organised coffee.' They carried the trunk down and added it to the items awaiting distribution or disposal. This was the third weekend they had met to clear their mother's house following her death earlier in the year. Sorting through the relics and detritus of a life was a necessary, if melancholy, activity. For Martina and Mark this had been their childhood home.

Martina was waiting in the kitchen, hands on hips. They sat on two of the packing cases and she handed them mugs of coffee. 'We need to get on. I must be back in Birmingham by six. I can't leave anything to Paul. He's useless.' Mark chose not to react. He had heard more than enough about the perceived shortcomings of his brother-in-law over the earlier weekends. He had accepted that his sister would take control. It had always been so. She was the elder by two years and had transitioned seamlessly from bossy older sister to assertive and occasionally stroppy adult. It was generally not worth the effort of challenging her. Her assertiveness had found a natural outlet as a hospital consultant of more than ten years standing. In an unguarded moment she had once admitted she was sometimes known as the Martinet. 'How appropriate,' Mark had muttered at the time.

Martina looked down on them. 'There's still a load to do.' She picked up a clipboard from the counter. 'Furniture's sorted. Now we need to go through the paraphernalia of Mum's everyday life, and make sure there are no loose ends in the paperwork.'

'Your baby, Marty.'

She turned away for some moments, gazing out of the window, before turning back and rapping her stick on the floor. 'No, it's not just up to me. You're an executor too.'

'Okay, but you know all about the finances. You had Power of Attorney after her stroke.'

'And it's time you did your bit. You didn't do much back then.'

'It was difficult because of Ellie as you know – always was.'

'You didn't make a lot of effort.'

'Be fair, Marty. We were never particularly welcome. I tried but her efforts amounted to the square root of bugger all. Ellie was only half accepted after Michael was born.'

'Mark's right. It wasn't easy.'

'You should have understood. You know there was a lot of anti-German feeling then, especially for Granny and Grandpa's generation.'

'Yes, they used to have a go at me too. It was bloody ridiculous. Ellie was only a kid in the war. Mum was just a living confirmation of Philip Larkin's verse.'

'Who he?' asked Gisela.

'A poet. He wrote: "They fuck you up, your mum and dad. They may not mean to, but they do. They fill you with the faults they had and add some extra, just for you." She even managed that as a single mum.' Gisela laughed.

'Come on,' said Martina sharply. She gestured towards the pile of boxes stacked in the hallway. 'Let's just get on with it. There's still a load of personal papers and hundreds of photos to go through.'

Mark shrugged. 'Okay, but how about that trunk?' He grinned. 'Perhaps Mum had a secret life. Possibly a Mosley supporter or had a hot Latin lover.'

Martina sighed. 'Not even you could think that's likely. Alright, but just get on with it. And don't get rid of anything without checking with me. I'll sort the paperwork.'

'Alright, but it'll probably be pretty boring – minutes of the Parochial Church Council or notes on Women's Institute lectures. No sex, no scandals, no violence.'

Mark left Gisela sorting photographs and carried the trunk into the lounge. This was the room where he and Martina had listened to children's hour, read their books and played endless games of snap, snakes and ladders and Monopoly on winter evenings. The faded patches and indentations on the carpet marked where the furniture had been – the chintz covered three-piece suite and coffee table grouped around the fireplace, the bookcase and the Pembroke table where their graduation photographs had stood. The mantel shelf above the rustic brick fireplace was bare and dusty. It had been guarded at each end by a pair of Staffordshire dogs, already sent to auction together with the collection of Clarice Cliff pottery which had been displayed in a corner cabinet. The wallpaper above carried the dusty footprint of a reproduction of Constable's "The Haywain" which had hung there throughout their childhood. Mark walked over to the bay where the Christmas tree had stood each year. He paused before opening the French windows. This was where he had stormed into the garden after a monumental row with his mother and grandparents when he had announced his intention to marry Gisela. Every inch of the room ignited a memory.

He opened the French windows and walked slowly to the rear of the garden. New houses had been built on the field beyond and were now concealed by a dense leylandii hedge. It formed a dark and oppressive backdrop to the once immaculate but now overgrown garden. He glanced up at the broad horizontal branch of the large oak in the corner which had supported a swing erected by his father. The autumn sun slanted across, highlighting the tints of the remaining foliage. Leaves swirled around, stripped from the trees by sudden gusts, adding to those already carpeting the lawn and the patio. Weeds sprouted in the earthenware pots and between the flagstones. Smoke drifted across from a nearby bonfire adding to the sense and smell of autumn. The garden furniture was in disarray. Two chairs had blown over in the previous week's storm adding to the air of abandonment – the end of a life.

He looked back. An indefinable air of sadness surrounded the silent villa – the hallmark of an empty house. Yet this house could never be entirely devoid of life for him. It was a crucible which encompassed the memories and experiences of his earliest years. Faint echoes of laughter, of anger, of sadness and of past tensions reverberated within its walls and resonated down the years. This might no longer be the place to which he belonged but it had left an indelible imprint on his mind. He remained tethered to this house by his past.

The sky suddenly darkened and there was a brief flurry of rain. He carried two of the garden chairs into the empty room. He opened the trunk. Inside were two large boxes. One was inscribed "Joan Brown – Personal papers" and the other "George Brown". The name of his father had been heavily underlined, as if in anger, by a ball-point pen which had scored deep grooves into the cardboard. The flaps at the top were sealed with yellowed tape. It had evidently lain undisturbed for many years. He sat on one of the chairs and placed his father's box on the other. He knew almost nothing of his father – gone from his life before his fifth birthday. When asked, all his mother would say was that his death had been a tragic accident – a consequence of the war. She would never elaborate, saying it was too painful to discuss. The only photographs he had ever seen were in an album. There had never been a framed photograph on display. His mother's grief and sense of loss had clearly made it too painful for her to face daily visible reminders of his father. She must have been devastated to be widowed in her early thirties, particularly as he had survived the war but then died two years or so later.

He opened the box. On top were various official papers – his military service record book, documents marking his educational attainments, his Membership of the Institution of Civil Engineers and details of his employment by London and North Eastern and then Southern Railway, as they were known in pre-nationalisation days. Beneath were two small boxes. Four medals and their ribbons fell out of one. The ribbons were stapled to a letter which listed them as campaign medals for the 1939-45 war. The other resembled a jeweller's box. It contained a cross surrounding the motto "For God and Empire" on a pink ribbon with pearl grey edges and stripe down the centre. There was a card inscribed with his father's name showing that this was a military OBE. There was a citation which read "For services to the British Military Government in Germany". He was stunned. Why had his mother never said anything about this? Why had she not put it on display? It was an amazing honour. He put it to one side.

At the bottom of the box were two large files. Attached to each was a sheet on which was written "The contents of this file are to be destroyed unread." These were signed formally "Joan Brown". Mark hesitated. Sod this, he thought. This was his father. He was damned if he was going to be controlled by his mother from the grave. It was not a binding legal instruction. Marty would probably disapprove but, what the hell, she was busy elsewhere.

He opened the first file, placing the paper to one side. There were two booklets on top. The first was a dark red school notebook with George Brown RE inscribed on the cover and dated 28 February 1944. The handwritten pages were covered in an elegant cursive script broken up by numerous line drawings. The first page was headed "Bomb Disposal Course". Mark thumbed through the notes. They detailed various devices, high explosive, incendiary, kopfring and flash bombs and various anti-personnel and anti-tank mines. He was stunned to discover there were so many ways of packaging explosives and blasting one's enemies to perdition. These were accompanied by details of various fuses, together with procedures for isolating, lifting and defusing devices or detonating them safely. The notes were very detailed and the drawings meticulous. Mark reflected that if you were going to be required to clear explosive devices, you probably wouldn't let your attention wander in lectures.

A buff file followed. It was marked "179 – Mine Clearance Service Group, Düren". The first page was inscribed in Gothic script, "Illustrated Report – To Captain George Brown, the helpful protector of the Mine Clearance Service Groups, to remember the time of his successful activities as boss of the Mine Lifting Office, Aachen." His newly acquired knowledge had evidently been put to use. There were cuttings from a German newspaper, "Rheinische Zeitung", and a number of photographs. These showed his father instructing and overseeing mine clearance and disposal. Much seemed to have been carried out by Germans and the record had been put together by German personnel. It was more of a tribute than a report. There was a discharge notice dated March 1947. His father had been in Germany for nearly two years after the war ended in Europe and until less than a year or so before his death.

Mark opened the second file. It contained numerous diaries, invitations to official military events, photographs of his father with fellow officers and other soldiers, and some of him with a family. Presumably he was billeted with them. Mark flicked through the pages. The diaries filled fifteen or twenty thick notebooks recording his activities, observations and thoughts over the years of his marriage, his wartime service and the post-war period. The entries were all dated. Some covered consecutive days but there were long intervals between others. The handwriting was immaculate and very small. He would have to read these later.

Mark turned to his mother's box. This carried the same injunction, that the contents should be destroyed unread. It contained family photographs, some loose and some in albums. He opened one and scanned the small, grainy black and white images mounted on coarse black pages with legends below in white ink. At the bottom of the box there was a dark blue leather writing case enclosing a cache of handwritten letters and poems. He was about to explore further when Martina put her head round the door. 'Anything I should know about? I must be off soon.'

Mark dropped everything back in the boxes. 'Nothing you'll need. Just old family records.' He hesitated before adding, 'But there are some surprising things.'

Martina came right into the room. 'Tell me.'

'There are various official documents – certificates and so on. It seems Dad was trained in bomb disposal. There are records of his doing that in Germany after the war. Did you know about that?'

'Not a thing.'

'It's a bit odd. He was a civil engineer. Presumably his work was construction. What's even odder is that he was awarded an honour – an OBE. It's strange Mum never mentioned it or put it on display. Why hide it?'

'I agree, it's odd. But I guess we'll never know now. What else?'

'A load of diaries.'

'And the other box?'

'I've only just opened it. Mainly photos – family outings with Mum, some with Grandpa and Granny, some with that awful friend of hers, Edna Calvin – Auntie Edna. She was always around at one time but then she just vanished. I couldn't stand her. I wonder what happened to her.'

'She wasn't that bad. She could be stroppy but she was good to me when I was ill.'

'Maybe, but not to me. And there's a load of old letters. I'll take them all home and look through everything later.'

Martina shrugged. 'Okay. I don't have time to do any more today. I must be off.' She bent down and picked up a sheet of paper which had fallen to the floor and turned it over. 'What's this? You shouldn't be doing this. You can see Mum wanted this private stuff destroyed. Put it all in my car and I'll get it shredded.'

Mark shook his head. 'No, Marty, these are family records.' He was damned if he was going to relinquish them. 'If I hadn't seen them, I wouldn't have known about Dad's war. I need to know more.'

'You don't need to,' she said emphatically. 'It's just curiosity. We're Mum's executors. We're here to carry out her instructions.'

'Only what's in her will.'

'Don't be so bloody legalistic. We should respect her wishes. Give me the box.'

'No, and they're not just her papers. They're Dad's as well. She controlled our childhoods – she's not going to bloody control me now she's dead. I want to know more about my dad; about both our parents.'

Martina bristled and thumped her stick on the floor. 'You're talking like a fucking journalist now. This isn't an item for your bloody newspaper. This is family.'

'Yes, it is. And it's for me – for us.'

'It's the past, it's irrelevant.'

'How can you say that? The past isn't irrelevant. For God's sake, you're a doctor – a paediatrician. You should bloody well understand that.'

'This is history – forget it.'

'Well, it's important to me even if it isn't to you.' He paused and looked hard at Martina. 'I'm beginning to think you know what might be in these papers. What are you trying to hide? What was Mum hiding?'

'Don't be ridiculous. I didn't know they existed until today.'

Mark looked at her suspiciously. 'Maybe not, but I think you've guessed what might be in them.' He got up from the chair and stood protectively over the boxes.

'For God's sake, stop behaving like a kid who's scared his toys might be taken away.'

'I'm not arguing, Marty. It matters to me. I'm taking all this home and I'll go through everything there. I'm going to do it whatever you think and you can just stuff it.'

She looked at her watch. 'God, I must go. I don't have time to argue. Alright, but promise you'll shred any personal letters.' Mark nodded. Martina looked coldly at him. 'I'm not sure I trust you.'

'And I'm not sure I trust you. I think you know more than you're letting on.'

'Absolutely not.' She left without a further word, slamming the door behind her.

Gisela came in a moment later. 'I heard you arguing. What was that all about? What did you say to piss her off? She scarcely said goodbye. She just shoved past and marched out.'

'Don't you start. It was she that pissed me off.' He pointed. 'It's those boxes. They're personal papers of both our parents. Mum left a note saying they should be destroyed unread. Marty was insisting we should do so.'

'Well, shouldn't you?'

'No, this is about family. I know next to nothing about my dad. My instincts tell me there's something odd about all this. I'm not letting Marty destroy them.'

'Okay, so was your mum a soviet spy or your dad a closet communist?'

'Nothing like that – least not so far. There's a lot here, some surprising stuff too.'

'And?'

'Dad's story is intriguing.' Mark picked up the red school notebook and the buff file.

'What are those?'

'It's about his war service. It seems he was in Germany for nearly two years after the war. He was supervising the clearance of mines for which he received an honour. And there's a tribute here from some German soldiers and, look, there are newspaper cuttings. Perhaps you'd translate them for me. There's also a load of diaries and photos.' He handed over one of the cuttings.

'There's a lot here. It'll take some time. This one starts, "Death still lurks in the Hürtgen Forest". It goes on to say that, after three months of fighting, the forest was destroyed and the unburied dead, Americans and Germans, were everywhere. It talks about Mine Clearance Service Groups and their dangerous work.' She paused. 'That's just scanning it. It's a long piece. Your father's name is there. That bit reads, "The central management and administration of action plans and the management of the area in the districts of Köln and Aachen is the responsibility of the English Captain Brown, whose energetic support of all mine clearers is gratefully acknowledged".'

'Do you know anything about this area and the Hürtgen Forest?'

'Not really. I recognise the name, but that's all. It can't be too far from Cologne, or Köln as we call it, if it was close to Aachen.'

'What do you remember from back then?'

'A lot, too much. As you know, I don't much like talking about it. What else have you found?'

'Not a lot so far. I never really knew my dad. I'm beginning to wonder if the accident that led to his death occurred in Germany. The answer may be here. Would you help me find out a bit more? Would your mother help?'

Gisela put the box on the floor and sat on the chair, leaning forward, head down. She was silent for several minutes before looking up. 'I don't think I can,' she said slowly.

'Why not?'

'It could be painful. It could bring back a lot of memories. There are things I don't want to talk about or be reminded about. I think Mutti would feel the same.'

'Ellie, this is important for me. I really would be grateful.'

'Mark, I'm sorry. I just can't do it.' She paused. 'And there's something you should just think about.' She shifted uneasily on the chair. 'And I'm not quite sure how to say this. Your dad might have been a hero – but he might not.'

'What do you mean? The work was obviously bloody dangerous and he received an honour. And look at this tribute. It's from Germans.'

'I know. But it may not be as simple as that. We were lucky, I was lucky. We got to the British Sector. It was better than the others, but still no picnic and some Brits behaved very badly. They behaved as if they were the victors, and yes, I know they were. That was annoying sometimes but not so important. But with some it was far worse. Some abused women and some set up scams, often with German spivs. And don't tell me every barrel has, how do you say it, "a bad apple or two". It wasn't most of them, but it was more than just a few. If Germany had won and occupied Britain, Germans would have behaved just as badly – probably even worse. But it didn't happen that way round. Your dad may have been a hero, but just possibly he might have been an absolute bastard.' She paused. 'He might even have been both. You might just find out things you'd prefer not to know. Maybe that's why your mum wanted those papers destroyed. I really think you should pause before doing anything and building up a particular image of your father.'

Mark was finding it difficult to accept that his father might have been less than a hero. He had risked his life to help make the place safe for German people to go about their everyday business. He restrained his instinct to respond angrily. After a few minutes he just said, 'I hadn't thought of that, but I'm going to find out about him. I'll just have to take that chance.'

'That's up to you but you must leave me out of it. Anyhow, as you know, I've got a lot on, but I will translate the newspaper cuttings.' She hesitated. 'Or perhaps Michael might help if you're going to go ahead. This is about his grandfather.'

2

22 OCTOBER 1989

Mark poured himself a beer, put on some music, upended his father's box and spread the contents over the kitchen table. He looked again at the tributes. His father had clearly been highly respected. But how was he recruited for this? And how was it that he had emerged from the routine of everyday life and, in challenging circumstances, carried out such remarkable feats? A cool head, an analytical mind, a steady hand and limitless supplies of courage would have been required although he must have been shit scared at times.

Mark could remember all too little of his father. He believed he had come from the north-east. His mother had once referred to him as a Geordie. He vaguely remembered a couple of visits to the area and an older sister, Aunt Alice. Probably she was no longer alive. There were also some cousins but he couldn't remember their names nor his aunt's married name. It was odd they had played no further part in their lives. Could they have died young? Had they become estranged? Or were there other issues which had made contact difficult or impossible? Might his father have been adopted and had no contact with his birth parents? If any of his family could be traced, they might have additional records. A visit to the General Register Office would be the first step.

'Oh, you're back from Gran's.' Mark's musings were interrupted by Michael. 'Everything sorted?'

'Yes, but there were some surprising things there.'

'Dad, can we turn that schmaltzy music off?' Mark's fondness for sentimental country and western music was a family joke.

'It's Hank Williams – country music royalty. Better than your hard rock stuff.' As a concession he turned the volume down.

'So, what did you find?'

'My old dinky toys and my Hornby Dublo train set. I'll have fun with them.'

Michael groaned. 'Oh God, second childhood kicking in? Is that all?'

'No, it's not. I'll get you a beer. You might be interested.'

Michael looked suspiciously at his father's glass. 'Is that one of your evil home brews?'

'Yes, but this batch is good.'

'Makes a change. I'll risk it. What's all this?' He pointed at the table.

'This was all hidden at the back of Granny's attic. This lot's about my dad. He did some amazing things in the war.' He held up the medal. 'By the way, it's late. Shouldn't you be getting back?' Michael was starting his second year reading history at King's.

'It's okay. No early lecture tomorrow. I thought I'd stay tonight. Mum's doing some washing for me.' He took the glass of beer and tasted it cautiously. 'Hmm, almost fit for human consumption.' He sat down. 'Tell me about it.'

As Mark began to speak, he began to wonder where this quest might lead and what further might be revealed.

'So what do you think happened to your dad?'

'Haven't a clue.'

'How do you feel about it?'

'Not sure.' Mark could only remember regretting the lack of a father intermittently. Occasionally, he had envied friends when he saw them doing things with their fathers; kicking balls around, playing cricket on the beach, going to sporting events and being supported in various ways. He had experienced a fleeting sense of regret from time to time that he hadn't had a father to do such things with him. One or two friends, but not many, had also lost fathers in the war and been in the same position. But his had survived despite the hazardous nature of his military role. It seemed a cruel irony that he should have died in an accident so soon after discharge.

But life had been the way it was – the way it had always been. His nuclear family had consisted of only three people, with the close involvement of one set of grandparents. That had been the totality of his family. He had had too little time to experience or develop a sense of closeness to his father. He had a few memories but there had never been a major sense of deprivation or dispossession – more an occasional awareness of absence rather than a feeling of loss.

Then there were questions about his death. What was the

nature of the accident? Was it a result of injuries sustained while clearing mines? Or was he psychologically damaged and in a psychiatric hospital or might he have committed suicide? Where was he buried and why was there no death certificate with the papers? Why had his mother erased all overt traces of his presence? Above all, why had she kept these records if she had intended they should be destroyed unread? It made no sense. Perhaps, Gisela was right. Perhaps his father had behaved dishonourably or illegally either in Germany or after returning to England. That could have led his mother to expunge all traces of his presence as completely as possible. Did Martina know more? The more Mark thought about her reaction, the more likely it seemed that she might know something discreditable about their father. It would explain her resistance to his intention to discover what was in those diaries and letters. Mark hesitated. Was this a quest he should undertake? He was certain it was, even though it might reveal some uncomfortable truths.

He looked at Michael. 'I really don't know how I feel just now. Might this interest you?' he asked tentatively. 'I'll need someone who reads and speaks German to help me follow this up. Would you translate for me?'

Michael had been thumbing through some of the diaries. 'These aren't diaries. They're more like journals or chronicles. They're very detailed. This could just fit with my course.'

'How come?'

'War studies and the cold war are a big thing in the department – and there's a lot of emphasis on personal testimonies. Yes, I'll help.'

'Good. I'd hoped your mum might but she's worried

that it might revive difficult memories. I've only looked at some of the earlier diaries so far. I've highlighted a few about your grandparents meeting and the early days of the marriage. Have a look at them.'

***

14 May 1937
George

All day overseeing bridge repairs on the East Coast mainline with Bob. Saw a fantastically pretty lass at King's Cross. Sprained her ankle badly. Sir Galahad there like a flash. Helped her home. Met her parents. Want to see more of her (in all ways!!!). Need to play my cards (and my pieces) right.

George had just finished work for the day. He was strolling across the concourse at King's Cross to take a bus back to his room in Highbury when he saw a blonde woman struggling with a large bag and a violin case. He nudged Bob. 'She's gorgeous. I'm going to give her a hand.'

'Looks like posh totty to me. Go on, but I reckon she's out of your class.'

'No harm in giving it a go.'

'Alright for you bachelors. I've a home to go to. See you after the bank holiday.'

George headed off in the direction of his quarry. He was getting close when she slipped and fell awkwardly giving a small cry. He ran over and helped her up. She put her right foot gingerly to the ground and winced. She was in pain. The ankle was swelling rapidly.

'Where are you going?'

'Cambridge to stay with a friend.' She took a tentative step holding onto his arm but was scarcely able to place any weight on the leg. She looked lost and was almost in tears. 'I don't think I'm going to make it.' She was right. She wasn't in a fit state to travel, nor go anywhere much, with or without a large bag.

'Can I help you to get somewhere? Where do you live?'

'Putney.'

She took another step or two, stumbled but steadied herself, putting a hand on George's arm.

'I'd be really grateful if you could help me to a taxi?'

George carried her case and supported her elbow as they headed out to the taxi rank. There was a long queue and few vacant taxis rolling up. She stood keeping her right leg off the ground holding George's arm for support. As the minutes passed, she looked more and more dejected. 'This is going to take an age. If only there was somewhere to sit.'

George hesitated. It was entirely the wrong direction for him. But what the hell, he had nothing better to do. 'You might do better on the tube. I could carry your stuff and see you home.'

He was right, she might be standing there for half an hour or more. There was a long pause as she looked around vainly hoping that some alternative would occur to her. Finally she turned to him, 'Would you really? Are you sure it's not out of your way?'

'It's no problem.'

She was more comfortable when seated on the underground. 'Thank you so much. I'm not sure I could've coped if you hadn't been around.'

'I'm sure there would have been any number of knights in shining armour to help. I just got there first. My name's George.'

'I'm Joan – Joan Watts.'

'Will there be someone at home to help you?'

'Yes, my parents.' She smiled slightly. 'They'll be surprised to see me back again so soon. I was looking forward to my weekend away.'

'So what do you do when you're not going away for the weekend?'

'I teach in a primary school. Piano mainly, but also some general teaching. I get together with college friends every few months to play chamber music.' She pointed to the case. 'I play the violin as well.'

'And there was I thinking you were one of Al Capone's mob.'

She smiled wanly. 'Do you play an instrument?'

'I learned the piano for a bit as a kid. I wasn't much good. But I enjoy music. I go to choral concerts sometimes.'

'We had to have two instruments at college. The violin was my main one but piano's more useful at school.'

George discovered she was an only child and that her parents owned two haberdashery shops in Kensington and Chelsea. It was evidently a small business but one with a moneyed clientele. Joan was very tidily and, to George's inexpert eye, expensively dressed. Bob was right; she was way out of his league.

The house was about half a mile from the station. It was a slow walk. Joan leant heavily on his arm while he carried her suitcase in his other hand. The detached Edwardian three-storey house was close to the Upper Richmond Road and set back from the street. The front garden was immaculately laid out with regimented rows of bedding plants behind neatly trimmed privet hedges. A Rover 16 was parked on the gravel to one side.

Joan's parents, Helen and William, were politely grateful and hoped that George's good deed had not taken him out of his way. When they discovered he lived in North London, they hesitated for a moment and then invited him to join them for a meal. George was about to decline but Joan insisted this was the least they could do to thank him. Helen Watts rang a bell and a maid was instructed to lay two further places at the table. It quickly became apparent to George that his hosts considered themselves to be his social superiors. He suspected they harboured some of the innate suspicion which many Londoners have towards those from the north, particularly those with northern accents. It had never been entirely clear to him where Geordie stood socially amongst the hierarchy of northern and midland accents – Brummie, Tyke, Lancashire, Scouse and so on. It was probably fairly low down the pecking order. Nevertheless Joan was very pretty and, encouraged by the enforced intimacy of their walk, George was keen to see her again. He was, however, far from certain this would be regarded as acceptable by her or her parents.

Quite unashamedly, George set out to impress. He let it drop into the conversation that he had won a scholarship to the Royal Grammar School but quickly sensed that boasting about his educational attainments was getting him nowhere. He then added that he had been a member of the school chess team. William Watts responded positively to this and suggested they played once the meal was over, saying it was difficult to find other good players locally. He proved to be no more than averagely competent and, determined to impress, George won the game very quickly. He immediately realised this had been a dumb thing to do and stressed that his success had been due to luck. He suggested a return match to give Joan's father the opportunity to exact his revenge. He won the second game but managed to spin it out for over an hour and a half. 'Nearly had you there,' William said at the end. 'I'd like to have another go at taking you on.' This was exactly the outcome George had been hoping to achieve.

'How did you make out?' asked Bob Burgess three days later.

George grinned. 'Good, I've got a foot in the door – maybe even a whole leg!'

It became an established routine that George would join the family once a month for Sunday lunch and play chess with William through the afternoon. He would ensure William won every third or fourth game.

***

12 SEPTEMBER 1937

Arrived early for lunch today. They were just back from church. Mrs Watts sent me to join Joan in the drawing

room. Could hear her playing the violin. Went in very
quietly.

Joan was standing by the bay window looking out over the
garden quite unaware of George's presence. He sat quietly just
inside the door. She was playing without music with a faraway
look on her face. The light and lilting refrain of Dvořák's
Humoresque filled the room. As the last notes faded, she
paused for a few moments and then raised the violin again. The
tempo slowed with the Meditation from Thaïs. She lingered
over the sensuous phrases, the slow vibrato creating a sense
of romance tinged with melancholy. She put the instrument
down on a small side table and George clapped gently.

She turned abruptly. 'You made me jump. I was miles
away. I didn't know I had an audience.'

'That was amazing. How about an encore?'

'Alright.' She lifted the violin once more and the strains
of Elgar's Salut d'Amour flowed out and, as the final plaintive
note faded, they remained still for a few lingering moments. 'I
love that. I nearly always finish with it if I'm playing for myself.'

***

10 October 1937

Arrived early again, hoping to hear Joan play. The
sound of the piano drifted through to the hallway.
Stopped outside for a moment before going in. She
was playing music from Fred Astaire films and singing
along quietly: "The way you look tonight", "Putting

on the Ritz" and "Dancing cheek to cheek". She was
totally immersed in the music.

Joan sat back and moved the sheet music around. She was
suddenly aware of a presence and turned. 'You've done it
again, George. How long have you been there?'

'Quite a time.'

'Do you know the films? I love them – specially the
dancing. Mum and Dad say they're frivolous. Perhaps, but
I still love them. I'll stop now.'

'No, don't. I love hearing you play. You're so good.'

She shrugged. 'Good enough to teach but not good
enough to be a professional performer. I'll play what I'm
going to play for the kids tomorrow.'

She swivelled on the piano stool and started to play, singing
along with the music. After a moment George went over and
stood behind her with a hand on her shoulder and joined in:

Happy days are here again
The skies above are clear again
So let's sing a song of cheer again
Happy days are here again

Joan turned on the piano stool and put her hand briefly on
his. 'You've got a nice tenor voice. How about trying "On
the sunny side of the street"?'

'The kids love that.' She stood for a moment, lifted
the lid of the stool and pulled out the vocal score of The
Mikado. She opened it on the music desk. 'Now try this.'
She started to play "A wand'ring minstrel I", leaving

George to sing solo. She turned when he came to the end, clapped quietly and looked directly at him. 'We could do with you. We're short of tenors in our choir. You'd be great.'

It was tempting and it would provide an opportunity to see more of Joan. And her parents could scarcely disapprove of him singing with her in their church choir. But it was difficult to envisage himself in a surplice. 'I'm not sure. I'm not really much of a churchgoer.'

'It's not a church choir. It's a local choir. We sing for fun and put on concerts occasionally in the winter – light music. I'm the accompanist for rehearsals but I sing along as well. Give it a go.' She smiled. 'You can't say no now you've auditioned successfully.'

'Alright, you're on.'

***

9 JANUARY 1938

Regular lunches with the Watts – now fortnightly. The choir is good and I get to see much more of Joan – and away from her parents. Rehearsals on Wednesdays. Pub afterwards. Two concerts this winter, Novello and Coward, Cole Porter, Irving Berlin with a bit of Gilbert and Sullivan. Carols in an old people's home on Christmas Eve. Took her to two concerts. Dream of Gerontius and The Messiah.

***

26 JUNE 1938

Walking with Joan most weekends, South Downs and the Chilterns. Joan is great on wildflowers. She collects huge bunches for the kids. She's a bit like an Edwardian lady – botany and music.

***

11 SEPTEMBER 1938

Henley today. Campion, cow parsley, lady's bedstraw, clovers, spurges, mallow and a Chiltern gentian. Getting quite good at this. Picnic in a field near Hambleden. I proposed tentatively. She asked if I had spoken to her father. I had. Approval given rather cautiously. She said "yes" – hooray. Engaged. Back to Putney for a drink with her parents.

***

15 JANUARY 1939

Date fixed. April 22. Joan's parents making a big contribution to the purchase of a house. They insist it's Joan's house and her name will be on the deeds. Guess that's fair. Sometimes worry they think I'm a chancer out to enrich myself. Can't say anything without appearing ungrateful. Will live with Joan's parents for first three months until purchase complete.

***

AUGUST 1939

Our first home, Wimbledon. Not the posh bit up the hill or near the tennis. Just up from Alexandra Road, close to the station, the dogs and the football ground. Wimbledon is an amateur team. Not bad but not in the same class as the Magpies. Now with Southern. Not much different from LNER. Same routine; oversight and maintenance of the infrastructure. Best part is Bob is now at Southern too.

Good news. Joan's pregnant – expecting in March. Still singing but cutting down on weekend walks. Her mum and dad are in and out a lot. They keep repeating that irritating rhyme – "a son's a son 'til he takes him a wife, but a daughter's a daughter for all of her life".

My mum and dad here for the weekend to see the new house – first visit since the wedding. Joan's parents came for lunch. Not entirely comfortable. Kept pointing out the financial contributions they had made. Dad said over a pint in The Plough that he didn't warm to them. Maybe, but they've been very generous.

***

21 JANUARY 1940

Icy cold. War has come. What a world for a kid to be born into. Joan's pretty large – needs to rest a lot. Not much sign of war so far. People are talking about a phoney or "bore" war. Signed up as an Air Raid Precaution Warden and volunteer ambulance driver. Trained in first aid and gas decontamination. Not much to do yet. Mainly enforcing the blackout and checking people have their gas masks. Most very relaxed. They'll be more careful once the bombing starts! I guess Newcastle will be hit. Jerries are bound to go for industrial centres – the shipyards, the coalfield and Vickers-Armstrong where Joe works. And the railways!

***

4 April 1940

It's a girl. Joan was sure it would be a boy. A friend persuaded her to try the ring test. You suspend your wedding ring on a thread over the bump. If it swings to and fro it's a boy and if in a circle it's a girl. It's obviously bollocks. Her mum kept saying it was best if the first was a boy. I wasn't fussed. Joan had decided he should be called Martin – so Martina it is.

Alice has arranged for her boys to be looked after by Mum and Dad and came to help. Joan's mum has been around a lot and a friend of Joan's has been in and out. Some tensions. Helen tends to delegate the muckier tasks to Alice. Came close to challenging her but Alice shot me a warning glance. Later said I should bite my tongue in the interests of family harmony.

Bob caught up with George as they were leaving work one evening. 'How about a pint?'

'I should get home.'

'Come on – you said the house was full of women and you were generally in the way. Time to wet the baby's head.'

'Okay, Alice did suggest I might be better coming home a bit later while she's holding the fort.'

'There you are – permission granted. So, how's it all going?'

'Knackering. Joan has to get up to feed Martina twice a night. It wakes me each time. I'm just glad I haven't got tits!'

'You muttered something about too many women. What's all this? Your fatal charm?'

'No such luck. There's Alice and my mother-in-law and this friend of Joan's who's been around a lot.'

'Oh yes?'

'Edna, she does some teaching at Joan's school, the flute.'

'What's the problem?'

'Mainly her manner. She seems to see Joan as a sort of protégée. She tends to organise and is brusque almost to the point of rudeness, except with Joan.'

'Have you talked about it?'

'I have but it's a no-go area.'

'What does your sister say?'

'She doesn't take to the woman, nor does my mother-in-law.'

***

15 JULY 1940

Phoney war's over and how! Bombing has started. Newcastle badly hit. Quite a number killed. Aidan has been injured. Won't be long before they hit London.

Chamberlain had been replaced by Churchill in May, much to the disapproval of Joan's parents. They considered him a warmonger and a particularly bellicose one at that. An aerial battle was under way with the Germans attacking shipping and air force bases in the south-east. George's worries about the bombing had been realised. The first major attack on Newcastle came early in July.

'I should go to Newcastle this weekend to see Alice and her family.'

'What's happened?'

'Aidan was injured after a raid last week.'

'I thought you said the house wasn't hit.'

'It wasn't. But he was playing in the back lane the next day and a wall collapsed on him. It broke his leg. He's in hospital.'

Edna was with them that afternoon. 'You can't go up there. You should be here with your family to make sure they're safe.'

'Of course. But Alice and Joe and their boys are family too,' he said sharply.

It was far from clear what exactly he could do personally to keep the family safe. If their names were on a bomb that was coming their way there was not much he or anyone could do about it. They just needed to make sure they maintained the blackout and headed for the shelters when the siren sounded. One of the dottier ideas suggested in a letter to the papers was that falling bombs should be sprayed with rubber solution so they would bounce!

***

George could see the damage as the train crossed the High Level Bridge. He walked up to Joe and Alice's house. They had been lucky. A number of bombs had fallen on the West End and some nearby houses had been damaged. George guessed they had been aiming for the Elswick Steel Works or possibly the Tyne bridges. Aidan looked cheerful enough in the ward at the Wingrove.

Alice said they were planning to evacuate the boys once Aidan was mobile. They would stay in the city. 'Joe's work is essential,' she said, 'like yours. And what about you? Are you going to evacuate Joan and Martina? You must have talked about it.'

'We have. But Joan's parents say that they'll not be forced into leaving their business or their home by Herr Hitler. I'm not sure how long that'll last once the bombing starts.'

Alice laughed. 'And what then?'

'Haven't a clue, but it's bound to happen. It's the capital and there are the docks and the railways.'

'I hope to God you keep safe.'

'Me too, I've got too much to lose now. But it can't be long. The Jerries have already tried to take out the air force. Unsuccessfully, thank God.' He laughed. 'When they do focus on London, I don't think the All England Lawn Tennis and Croquet Club will be an important target.' He hesitated, 'Though, I'm not sure I would rely too much on the accuracy of their bomb aimers!'

***

NEW YEAR'S DAY 1941

There it is. Resigned to a semi-bachelor life in Wimbledon. Weekends in leafy Farnham. Not wonderful. Missing Joan and Marty. One bonus – no more Edna. Horrendous attack by incendiaries on City two days ago. St Paul's hit. Papers calling it the Second Great Fire of London.

George's predictions had proved correct. A large air raid on Berlin in early September had led to massive retaliation starting a few days later. Initially there had been large scale daytime raids targeting the docks and, from early October, huge aerial attacks directed at central London nightly for the next eight weeks. The damage was immense. The Centre Court was hit in October and on one night in early November more than sixty incendiaries fell on Wimbledon, several close to the house. Helen and William Watts' spirit of defiance had crumbled. They had decided to leave. They held Churchill partly responsible, claiming that if Halifax had been the prime minister he would have come to an accommodation with Hitler.

Joan's parents had been emphatic that she and Marty

should go with them. George felt he could not reasonably disagree. They had rented a house in Farnham and moved in December with Joan and Marty. George would have to stay in Wimbledon. His nightly duties as a warden and ambulance driver and his daytime responsibilities on the railway were essential. He would join the family whenever he had time off. He took the train to Farnham on New Year's Eve.

Joan met him at the station. 'You'll love the house. It's great for Marty and the garden will be wonderful for her when it's warmer. And she's started to crawl since you last saw her. I'm having to watch her like a hawk.' She took his hand and led him up the hill. Ten minutes later they turned into a road of substantial traditionally built properties. The houses were set well back from the street, fronted by broad driveways and surrounded by large gardens. George looked round before going in. He had to concede it was a great environment for a kid, although far from ideal for him. He was going to miss seeing his daughter grow and develop day by day.

***

'Well, George, what are your New Year resolutions?' asked William cheerfully over breakfast.

George hesitated. 'I've made one.'

'What, only one?'

'Yes, but it's a big one.'

'Are you going to tell us?'

'I've talked to the local recruiting office. I've decided I must enlist.'

There was an uncomfortable silence. It was broken by his mother-in-law. 'I can't believe you could even think of doing that. It's irresponsible. Think of Joan and your daughter.'

'Mrs Watts, I have. I think of them all the time but we have to win this war. I can't imagine how awful it'll be if we don't – for Joan and Marty and you and all of us.'

'But you're doing essential work.'

'Yes, the recruiting officer did try to discourage me.'

'He was right.'

'Partly. Of course, the network's essential for transporting troops and armaments; and Southern was hit hard in November. We've been working endlessly – clearing and relaying lines, rebuilding bridges, ensuring viaducts are safe, shoring up embankments.'

'There you are. It's your duty to stay.'

'Yes, but those things can be done by older engineers just like they're bringing retired teachers back into the schools.'

'But think of your responsibilities here. Think of all those who never came back from the last war.'

'I do. I have thought about it very carefully. I'm not sure I'm that safe in my work or as a warden in London.' That was undoubtedly true. The railways were very exposed to the destructive efforts of the Luftwaffe. Many daytime rail movements were reserved for troop and ammunition trains to minimise the risk of attacks. Repair work often had to be done at night. That required illumination and that provided an ideal target for the bombers. 'I know the war's being fought far away just now and I certainly don't want to go far from home. I'm joining the Home Guard for now. But there'll come a time when we'll have to invade to win. I must sign up then. Engineers will be needed.'

3

3 NOVEMBER 1989

Mark had retreated to a quiet corner of the gallery in Cork Street nursing a glass of lukewarm cava. A bar had been set up at one end. Assistants were busy dispensing drinks while others distributed pigs in blankets, honeyed sausages and canapés with slithers of smoked salmon topped with cottage cheese and dill. He was not taking much interest in the proceedings when his reverie was interrupted. 'You're looking pretty gloomy.'

He looked up to see Michael in front of him. 'I didn't know you were going to be here.'

'I wouldn't miss Mum's big night. Why are you looking so down?'

He shrugged. 'Oh, various things. Work, other things.'

'How are you getting on with the stuff about your dad?'

'Nowhere much. Went to the Register Office this afternoon. It's going to be more difficult than I thought. There are between three and four hundred deaths a year of people called George Brown. The guy there said it's always a problem with common surnames. It would be easier if I knew when and where he was born. And I'm not absolutely certain of the year he died and I haven't a clue where he died. The guy suggested I come back when I have more details.'

'I thought you said he died in 1947.'

'I think so but I don't know for sure. It could have been the next year or possibly later. He could have been ill for months before he died.'

'Could he have died in Germany?'

'Possibly – that would make it even harder.'

'What next then?'

'I need to go back to those diaries and look for clues.'

'I've read the early ones now. It looks as if his pursuit of Gran was a fairly low-key affair.'

'Perhaps – or maybe he just wasn't much of a romantic.'

'It was interesting about Gran. She used to play the piano for me to sing along.'

'I bet that didn't last long.'

He laughed. 'It didn't once she'd heard my voice. I didn't know she played the fiddle as well.'

'She didn't very often. Sometimes she would go to her bedroom and play. It always sounded very mournful. I think she was good, but I'm no judge.'

'Sounds as if her musical tastes were a lot more upmarket than yours.'

'And yours.'

Michael waved his hand around. 'Cheer up, Dad. This is awesome.' Mark looked round the spacious exhibition space – the subdued wall lighting, post-impressionist paintings adorning the walls, overfilled sofas and the artfully lit randomly placed pedestals supporting the bronzes. The gallery had filled up quickly after six. Overloud voices and stridently false laughter filled the space. He observed the ebb and flow, the variable geometry of clusters of guests, endlessly assembling, disassembling and re-assembling to form newly configured groups. Two small coteries stood resolutely apart, seemingly defying others to break into their private caucuses. Others moved ceaselessly around greeting real or imagined acquaintances with a word, a wave or brief physical contact. A few loners wandered hesitantly, champagne flute in one hand, catalogue in the other, looking at the bronzes on display – whether critically or uncritically it was impossible to know.

'Well, I'm off to get some of that fizzy stuff. I'll get you a refill. It's bound to be better than your home brewed potions.'

'Not so sure about that.' Mark handed over his glass.

Michael was back a moment later saying excitedly that a couple of the bronzes already had "sold" stickers on them.

'Oh, don't be fooled by that. Our arts guy says galleries put them on a few items before opening to persuade punters they're selling fast.'

'I'd have thought that was self-defeating – and devious. Bit like journalists.'

'More like bloody politicians.'

'Well, I'm off to look round. I'm going to pull rank as the artist's son and ask that assistant to guide me.' He headed for a willowy blonde and a moment or two later she was leading him round the exhibits.

Mark was wondering how soon he could decently beat a retreat. He was heading back to the corner when he was waylaid by a tap on his shoulder. 'Did I overhear you utter that canard that politicians are occasionally less than straightforward?' He turned. Sandy Scott was standing in front of him smiling, immaculately dressed as ever – Savile Row suit, bow tie and silver-topped cane. All part of the public image he had nurtured so carefully over the years.

'Hi, Sandy,' he said disconsolately.

'That's not much of a greeting for one of your key sources. Anyway, what are you doing here? I wouldn't have thought this was your natural milieu. Or is your paper so short of staff that you've been deployed to report on the arts as well?'

'God no. I'd be useless. Anyhow, I wouldn't have thought this was for you either.'

'No,' he smiled, 'and yes – and possibly.'

'That's a politician's answer if ever I heard one. So why are you here?'

'The arts minister passed the invitation on to me. He's Welsh and the house is debating Welsh business this evening. That's not for me. Anyway, we politicians never pass up an opportunity for a free drink – even cava. Not much different from you lot.' He grinned. 'More seriously, he knows I collect bronzes, though I generally give private views a miss. I can't stand the people who hang around at these events.' He glanced quickly over his shoulder. 'I assume we're off the record?'

'Don't worry. After two or three glasses of this cat's piss, I couldn't report anything accurately.'

'Do you journos ever?'

Mark grinned. 'Occasionally, but the odd inexactitude keeps you politicos on the hop and our willingness from time to time to be a little economical with the truth sometimes saves your bacon.'

'And is your editor equally charitably minded?'

'Don't talk to me about Mike Willis. He's a shit. I've never understood his mind and, candidly, have absolutely no wish to or to get too close to that arse-licker.'

Sandy laughed. 'He really has pissed you off. What's he done to provoke this? You can tell Uncle Sandy.'

'You should be pissed off too. The op-ed piece I wrote after interviewing you yesterday was good but the fucking editor spiked it.' Sandy had always been good for a catchy phrase and his waspish comments garnished with a little malice always added spice to the copy. He was a persistent thorn in the flesh of the Thatcher government. He had never made it beyond the lowest of ministerial ranks. He knew he never would and he certainly didn't care. He was in his early sixties and independently wealthy. But his political instincts were good and his sharp insights invaluable. His comments on the deteriorating relationship between the prime minister and the chancellor who had resigned a few days earlier had made good copy.

'I can live with that. After all, I'm only "sources close to the government", though that's a bit of a joke these days.'

'Willis fucking idolises Maggie – probably fantasises about her too.'

'God help him then.'

It occurred to Mark that Sandy's presence might provide

a pretext for an early exit from the gallery. 'I've had enough of this. How about a drink in the pub?'

'Alright. The Burlington is just up the road.'

'You go ahead. Get me a pint. No, cancel that, get me a whisky and start a tab in my name. The least the editor can do is stand you a drink or two for spiking your pearls of wisdom even if he doesn't know he's doing so. I just need to tell my wife and son where we are. I'll ask her to join us later. She'll be a bit yet.'

'I didn't realise you were here with your dearly beloved and your son. Shouldn't you stay?'

'Probably, but I've had more than enough. I'm just a spare part here. I'll explain in the pub.'

Mark looked around. Michael was now ensconced on a settee in a corner with the assistant. 'Dad, this is Izzy. We're going for a drink when this is over.' It was clear that his father did not feature in his plans for the rest of the evening. Gisela was talking animatedly to a tall, flamboyant, well-upholstered character with a monocle wearing a bow tie and a flowing cape. Mark walked over. She introduced him as a dealer from Paris. She looked disappointed when he said he was off to the pub but nodded in acquiescence, saying she would join him later.

***

Sandy had cornered a quiet spot. The highly polished wood of the bar, the distinctive carnelian signature wall, the art deco style lighting, the brass footrail and the heavy lined curtains defined it as a retreat for traditionalists.

Sandy pushed Mark's drink across the table towards him. 'So, what were you doing there? You looked fucking miserable.'

'It's my wife's exhibition. The gallery has sold one or two of her pieces before, but this is her first solo show.'

'Gisela Schafer is your wife? But she's German. I spoke to her for a few minutes.'

'It's alright, the war's over. I'm not bedding an enemy alien. The gallery insisted she used her maiden name. Said it sounded more exotic than Brown!'

'Well, they're right about that. Tell me more.'

'She's been creating bronzes for some time. They started to sell a year or two ago.'

'They're good. I'm impressed.'

'Me too. I never knew she had this talent and she never thought it would take off. She says it's a bit like alchemy, even if the result is bronze rather than gold.'

'I reckon some gold will head her way after this.'

'The gallery has insisted on strictly limited editions. Supply and demand. Simple Thatcherite economics!'

'I'll go back later in the week and look more closely. I might invest in one.' He looked up. Gisela was edging her way through the crowd of Friday evening drinkers looking around as she did so. Sandy stood, waved and pointed to the empty chair at the table. He helped her out of her coat and pulled the chair out for her. 'I'm not sure I introduced myself properly when we spoke earlier. I'm Sandy Scott. It's an amazing show. I'm really impressed. You must be over the moon.'

Gisela looked up at him. 'I am now. I was pretty edgy earlier.'

'I think this calls for champagne.'

Gisela raised her eyebrows. 'That would be wonderful.' She whispered to Mark while Sandy was at the bar, 'Who is this guy?'

'One of my MP contacts. He's a collector as well.'

Sandy rejoined them a moment later with a wine cooler, a bottle of Bollinger and three flutes. He raised his glass, 'To your continued success.'

'Thank you – I can't quite take it in just now.'

'Did Mark tell you I collect bronzes? One of my many vices.' Gisela nodded. 'I was fascinated by the symbolism. It's challenging, and I was intrigued by some of the titles.' Sandy opened the catalogue and flicked through the pages. He pointed at "Heimat?", "Flight" and "Encircled 13/8". 'The copy in the catalogue is enigmatic to say the least. It only hints at the emotions and experiences behind the pieces.'

'That was deliberate – the titles are my own but some guy at the gallery wrote the text. To be frank, I was a bit embarrassed by his hype. But he insisted it was essential to excite interest.'

'He was right. It does. I'd love to know how you plan and visualise your work.'

'You'd probably be disappointed.'

'I'm sure I won't.'

'Well, I really can't explain adequately how I go about it. I wish I could. I go through dozens of versions in clay before I get to a structure I really want – even then I'm never entirely satisfied. I'm never sure if version twenty-seven was better than version eight or twelve or whatever.

In the end I reach a stage when I just have to go for it. The whole process, from the first positive through to the final casting, is emotionally draining. It was just a hobby and just for me, but now I have to wonder if what works for me will work for others.'

'It does. Don't change it. Enjoy your success – and the champagne.' He raised his glass again and turned to Mark. 'So how did a disreputable journalist like you get hooked up with such a talented artist?'

'Oh, it's a long story.'

'That's alright. I've nothing much to do until it's time to get back for a division at ten.' He looked at Gisela. 'Mark told me he'd picked you up at Piccadilly Circus.'

She laughed. 'That's so far from the truth. I picked him up but not in the sense you use that phrase.' Sandy looked at her quizzically as he sipped his champagne. 'Are you sure you really want to hear this?'

'It's bound to be much more interesting than anything going on in the Commons.'

She shrugged. 'Alright, if you're really sure. We met just after I'd got here in August 1961. I'd come as an au pair to improve my English. The family said I should get out and see the city on my second Saturday here. I was feeling very low. It was the last thing I wanted to do. The Wall had just gone up in Berlin and my aunt and cousins were trapped in the East. I was very close to them. I wandered around the West End for a bit and then went into a news cinema. I watched the footage through twice and came out feeling thoroughly miserable. I bought copies of Bild and Die Welt from a newsstand and found a corner in a coffee bar. The editorials were very critical of the west for doing nothing. It was all extremely depressing and it made me feel a load worse, so I decided to go back to my room.'

'Ellie's right – she did look bloody miserable.'

'I went down to the station. Mark was sitting against one of the walls. He was a mess. Mostly people were ignoring him. It's that thing you Brits do when you're embarrassed. You pretend nothing's happening and look the other way. I thought he was ill and helped him up – held him up too. He muttered something about Brahms and Liszt. My English wasn't bad but not so fluent then. I asked if he was on his way to a concert. He laughed and laughed and said he was comprehensively cockeyed and totally tipsy. I hadn't a clue what he was talking about but it was obvious he was pissed. I didn't know that word then.' She glanced at Mark. 'Being married to a journalist, I do now!'

'That doesn't sound like a very promising start!'

'It wasn't a start at all.'

'So what next?'

'He hugged me and then backed off, saying he was sorry and hoped I'd forgive him. One of the staff came over and said soliciting wasn't permitted and told me to bugger off. I didn't know those words either. I tried to say I was just helping. He muttered something about bloody foreigners and told us to fuck off. My vocabulary expanded a lot that afternoon!'

'What then?'

'Ellie, I'm quite sure Sandy doesn't want to hear all this.'

'Oh, I do. This is the best entertainment I've had all day.'

'Well, he was very apologetic and asked if he could buy me coffee. I felt it might be better than going back to my room and being on my own, so I agreed.'

'So what were you doing in London, pissed in the middle of the afternoon?'

'I'd been with friends to celebrate our A level results but I'd lost them somewhere.'

'He also said it was his birthday. I discovered later that wasn't true.'

Sandy laughed. 'All the necessary aptitudes for his career. What next?'

'I really think we should give Sandy a break.'

'Not at all. You've spent your career getting the lowdown on me. This is my chance.'

'We went back to the coffee bar and he talked and talked. He was very funny about living in England. Eventually, he said he was sober enough and should get home. He'd been worried he would get an earful from his mum if he was even a little pissed. He said goodbye and kissed my hand. Then he asked if he could see me again and show me London. He was the first English boy I had ever spoken to properly and he'd cheered me up a bit, so I said yes. We arranged to meet the next weekend at Piccadilly Circus. I wasn't sure he'd pitch up, but he did.'

'And were you in reasonable shape when you got home?'

'Just about – the big row came later.' Sandy raised his eyebrows. 'I told my mum I was going to London the next Saturday to see a girl. I'd been dumb enough to say we'd met at Piccadilly Circus. She thought I'd picked up a tart. I said I'd offered to show an overseas visitor around and then added she was German. That was when the shit really hit the fan. She became quite vitriolic saying that all Germans were brutal and sadistic killers, and they'd caused two world wars and they were all Nazis. I kept saying Ellie was far too young to have been a Nazi. But she wouldn't listen. She just said the Nazis might be dead but all Germans were fascists and if they weren't fascists they were Prussians and if they weren't Prussians they were Jews or maybe all three. Thank God, I didn't know then that Ellie's family had come from East Prussia. I tried to say it was a country that had produced great music and literature and not all Germans should be tarred with the same brush. That got me nowhere. She was adamant that I wasn't going to London.'

'So how did you get away?'

'My sister came to my rescue. She said she'd planned for us to go to the coast that day. That was news to me. When we were alone, she said, "I'll cover for you. Go and see your fraulein but give me your swimming trunks so I can dip them in the sea and drag them along the sand to provide some corroborative detail." It was pure self-interest. She'd been planning a day out with a boy. It took a great deal of subterfuge to go on seeing Ellie. It was a long time before I dared ask her home.'

'So, where did it go from there?'

'Mark was fun. My only previous experience of the English was as a kid during the occupation. They were very upright or uptight, how do you say it, or maybe both – mostly but not all of them. And London was fun. You've no idea how different it was. You all complained about the bomb sites that hadn't been cleared but it was a paradise by comparison.'

'How much more did you see of Mark?'

'Not a lot at first. He went on to Cambridge and we saw each other three or four times before I went back to Germany.'

'But you kept in contact?'

'Vaguely. He was having too good a time in Cambridge to spend much time writing letters – or thinking about me. I could only write during term. He said his mum would go ballistic if she saw a letter with German stamps. Two years later I came back to teach at a girls' school and wrote again. This time to his home. I had no longer term intentions and he certainly didn't. As a cub reporter he was busy enjoying life in London. By then I'd decided I wanted to live in England but it was some years later that we got married.'

'And were you accepted then?'

'Not really. Mark's mum refused to come to the wedding in Germany. She came to a party we organised in London for friends and family, but Mark's grandparents refused. Mutti, my mother, and Willy, my stepfather, came.'

'It would have been better if Mum had stayed away. She was scarcely polite to Gisela's parents. Most of the evening she looked about as happy as Banquo's ghost at the feast.'

Sandy laughed and then glanced at his watch. 'You'll have to excuse me. I must get back for a division. I do congratulate you. I'll go back and have another look next week. I'd love to talk more to you about your work sometime. Perhaps I can contact you through the gallery?' Gisela nodded.

Mark topped up their glasses after Sandy had left. 'Nice guy – charming and perceptive.'

'Too charming by half.'

'What's that meant to mean?'

'Just you should watch your step with him.'

'Come on, Mark, he, at least, was taking an interest. But why did you have to lurk in the corner getting pissed and then just clear off with your mate?'

'Ellie, don't start. I'm sorry. It's been a lousy day. Mike was his usual stroppy self and spiked a good piece I'd written supporting Lawson's plan to shadow the mark. He's been undermined at every turn by Maggie's advisers. No wonder he resigned. Mike won't hear a word against her. He keeps bleating that my views don't sit well with the proprietor's views and values. That's a joke. The proprietor doesn't have values.'

'I'm sorry, but couldn't you leave all that behind at work?'

'Easier said than done. Anyhow, you know I find the types at these arty events get my goat. That frog was typical.'

'That frog, as you call him, is interested in selling some of my works in his gallery in Paris.'

'So that's good. I said I was sorry. Give me a break.'

'Mark, we can't go on like this. You're so tied up in your unhappiness about the situation at work and, at home, you've got your head buried in those family papers. You've no time for me and not much for Michael except when he's helping you. It would be good if you were to show your support a bit more visibly. I have to put up with some of your political events which can be pretty tedious for anyone who's not a political nerd.'

'Alright, but you're doing well enough without me.'

'Come on, I've had enough of this. I'm not going to have a row with you in a pub, particularly when you've been drinking. Let's go home.'

4

NEW YEAR – 1 JANUARY 1942

GEORGE

Life has developed a pattern but it's a bit of a semi-detached marriage – me in Wimbledon, Joan and Marty in Farnham. Get there when I can. Ten days off for Christmas. It was good – in parts. Marty is a delight – walking and into everything. Talks non-stop, tho' not everything makes sense yet. She was fascinated by the tinsel and fairy lights and the parcels under the tree. It was fun watching and playing with her. Joan played carols. Tried to get Marty to sing along. All a bit of a laugh.

Matters had started to go downhill after a traditional Christmas lunch. They were sitting comfortably in front of the fire with a glass of port after listening to the King's speech when Joan's parents dropped a bombshell. They announced they were buying a house for Joan in Farnham and the Wimbledon house would be sold as soon as a buyer could be found. George was dumbfounded. He had assumed Farnham was just for the duration of the war. Joan had said nothing when he had arrived for Christmas two days earlier. None of them had even hinted that this had been in any of their minds. He was furious that such a major family decision had been taken without any discussion. He was about to vent his feelings but managed to contain himself. He got to his feet, saying he needed to walk off his lunch. He took a torch and was back long after dark.

He confronted Joan as they were preparing for bed. She said it was a wonderful house and it would be ideal and safe for her and Marty. It had just come on the market and they hadn't wanted to risk losing it by delaying. George was frustrated that Joan didn't seem to understand why he was so piqued. She repeated that it was the right thing to do saying he wasn't around much and he hadn't been there to discuss it. 'That's bollocks. It's not that difficult. I'm in London – not Outer Mongolia.' She added she was sure he could rent a room for himself after the Wimbledon house had been sold.

Joan led him up the hill on the south side of the town on Boxing Day to see the house. An immaculate gravelled drive led up to the traditionally built, tile-hung villa, set well back from the road. It was surrounded by a spacious garden backing onto open fields. George had to concede that it would be a great family home and the garden would be ideal for Martina. Joan rounded on him saying she couldn't understand why he had been making such an issue of it, particularly when her parents were being so generous. She then added, 'He who pays the piper'. That really got under his skin. Her parents had indeed paid a large deposit for the house in Wimbledon but he paid the mortgage and the bills. Who was calling the shots in this marriage, he asked himself. He immediately recognised it was a stupid question. It wasn't him.

There was a further confrontation the next day when George repeated his intention to enlist. That ratcheted up the tensions. Joan said pointedly that he was just as prone to making unilateral decisions affecting all of them. 'I'll have to make all the decisions for the family if you join up.' She paused before adding, 'Particularly if you don't come back'. George had to admit that there was something in what she said. The atmosphere had soured to such a pitch that he invented a pretext for leaving early. He decided to spend a few days in Newcastle. Sometimes it felt more like home.

He took the train north to spend the New Year with his parents and Alice and her family. He and Alice went for a walk on the Moor during the afternoon of New Year's Eve. The grass, touched by the previous night's frost, glistened in the late afternoon light. George, shielding his eyes against the glare, looked up the slope towards Cowgate where the grazing cattle were silhouetted by the last rays of the setting sun. They walked companionably in silence for fifteen minutes or so before Alice turned to him. 'George, do you want to tell me what's troubling you?'

'It's nothing.'

'That it isn't.' George hesitated, unsure if he should unburden himself.

'It's up to you but I'm here to listen if it would help.'

'I know – it's just that, well, whatever we do, Joan and I don't seem to get very close these days with me mainly in London and she in Farnham. And there are tensions – the house, her parents and that friend, Edna. She's now moved to Farnham as well and lives close by.'

'Oh God, I remember her – much too well.'

'I thought we were shot of her.'

'And?'

'I know all couples have rows sometimes. But even when we're not at odds, we don't seem to get as close as we did. Mostly we don't have rows. If we do, Joan simply turns away or retreats to her parents. I hate to say it, but it's often easier for me when I'm away from Farnham. The problem is I think it's easier for her too. And I'll be away a lot more. I'm joining up.'

'Perhaps things will be better when you're all together full time.'

'God knows when that'll be.' He looked at her. 'As for me, I guess I've made my bed and now I must lie in it.' He paused after using that well-worn phrase. 'And,' he added ruefully, 'I don't so often get to lie in it. But that's enough of my moans. It's so good to see you and the family.'

Alice squeezed his arm, then looped hers in his as they headed back to her house for the New Year celebrations. A neighbour had been lined up as the "first-foot", bringing a coin, coal, bread, an evergreen twig and a drink to the door to offer prosperity, warmth, sustenance, long life and good cheer. Would 1942 bring all these things or were they all on hold until the war was over – or would they ever come? George hoped Alice was right and it would be different when he was back permanently – or would it? She had urged him to write to Joan as soon as he was back in London and extend an olive branch. He knew she was right.

***

3 January 1942

My dearest Joan

It was wonderful to have time with you and Marty over Christmas and enjoy the creature comforts of home!!! I'm really very sorry the last few days did not work out so well for us. I do understand and go along with the plan to sell the Wimbledon house and buy in Farnham. It will be wonderful for you and Marty – and safe. I just wish we could have discussed it before you and your parents made the decision. I shall stay on here until the house is sold. I know your mum and dad have been very generous. I really am grateful and I know their support is important to you.

I also know there are tensions about my joining up. I have thought about this endlessly and have discussed it over and over again with Bob. He's a good and sound friend. We both feel we must do this. Our work on the railways is essential, but it could be done by older engineers. The army doesn't have enough engineers. There will be loads to be done and we will have a critical part to play. Bob and I will sign up in April. I've been having a meal with him and Mo once a week. She supports Bob's decision. This is something I feel I must do. I do hope you understand.

My love to both of you – a big kiss for Martina.

***

20 APRIL 1942

Wimbledon house sold in March. Living with Bob and Mo when I'm working. To Farnham whenever possible. Letter from Joan. Pregnant again. Wrote to say how happy I am. All well. Due mid-September.

***

14 MAY 1942

Final shift as an ambulance driver. Off for basic training on Thursday.

George reported for his final shift three nights before heading off for basic training. The supervisor was on the telephone when he got to the control post. He looked up as he finished the call. 'Thank God you're here. It's not a good night. In fact, it's a bloody awful night. I've just sent two out. I need you to go straight out too. I've only one attendant to go with you. A pub's been hit up near the Angel – sounds bad.'

George drove through the darkened streets but when he turned into Upper Street his way was illuminated by a fierce blaze ahead and to his right where a stick of bombs had carved a line of destruction across three streets. He was directed around the debris by a warden to the site where a cluster of incendiaries had fallen. Two other ambulance crews and a fire tender were already there. He dismounted from the cab and was instantly enveloped by a cacophony of sounds – sirens, shouted commands, the loud hiss as water from the hoses made contact with the flames and cries of pain and panic. Sandbags had been placed in doorways and locals were frantically operating stirrup pumps to add to the efforts of the professional firefighters. Police were shepherding residents away from the scene towards the shelters. The dead and injured had been laid out on stretchers in ranks with military precision on the opposite pavement – men, women and two children. Some were in uniform. The faces of five had been covered. A warden was walking along attaching a label to each. Local people were providing blankets for the wounded and offering tea to stunned survivors. The most severely injured were being lined up and loaded into the ambulances. George and his attendant had lifted two into his vehicle when he heard a plaintive cry from an adjacent ruined house. He ran over. A warden tried to stop him saying the building was unstable. George pushed past. 'I'm going in. There's a bairn in there.' He clambered over the rubble. There was dust everywhere and a strong smell of gas. He tied a moistened handkerchief over his mouth and nose. Through the gloom he could make out a small girl trapped by a beam which had fallen across her legs at the base of the remains of the staircase. She was whimpering softly.

George knelt. 'We'll soon have you out of here, pet. Where's your mam?'

'She fell over by the door. She was holding Emmy. Some men carried her away. Emmy was crying.'

'What's your name?'

'Lily.'

'Let's get you out, Lily, and then we'll find your mam.' George cleared the fallen plaster carefully by hand and slowly eased the beam off the girl's legs. One was badly broken. A shard of bone was protruding through the skin below the knee. The other seemed uninjured. There were some ominous creaking noises. Part of the banister rail fell to one side. George held Lily protectively. 'We must keep very still,' he whispered. They waited motionless – silence. One, two, three minutes passed and then he called softly to one of the crew looking on anxiously from the doorway to throw him some strapping. He gently bound the girl's legs together. He leant down. 'I'm going to carry you out, Lily. It'll hurt a bit so I want you to be very brave.' George carried her slowly out to the street and placed her on a stretcher. He looked down. She was about seven years old. An image of Martina came unbidden to his mind. Thank God she was safe in Farnham. He crouched close to Lily and whispered, 'You're a very brave girl.' He kissed her on the forehead. 'These guys will help you find your mam and make your leg better.'

There was a shout from a warden, 'Who's the driver of this bloody ambulance? It's time it was off.' George walked over. 'You! You're here to drive a fucking ambulance and get these folk to hospital not to play the fucking hero.'

George was about to say something but decided against it and slid into the driver's seat. He made two further journeys that night to carry others to hospital. The first grey light of dawn was filtering through an early morning mist as he drove slowly back to the depot. Plumes of smoke were rising from still smouldering ruins and the acrid smell of charred timbers mixed with escaped gas assaulted his senses. God, what a war. Even those at home were on the front line. Were Lily, her mother and baby sister ever reunited? Had they all survived? Would he and Joan and Marty survive? There was no way of knowing any of these things.

***

27 May 1942

Basic training. Letter from Joan urging me to seek immediate discharge on compassionate grounds. Says my support needed – busy with Marty and tired carrying number two. No chance of that after two weeks! There must be dozens of pregnancies resulting from home visits on leave. One of my new mates said some wives were making "alternative procreative arrangements" – most don't put it quite like that! Had to tell her it's not possible – in for the duration. I write regularly but only hear back occasionally. Joan says she's too tired to write more often. She's given up the choir – and trying to predict the gender of the baby.

***

24 JUNE 1942

That's it. Basic training at Tidworth over. Six weeks – quick march, attention, at ease, stand easy, present arms, order arms, ground arms, shoulder arms, port arms, about face, left incline, dress right and, best of all, dismiss. Now we're soldiers. Not sure the RSM agrees. "You engineers are a bloody shambles," he shouts across the parade ground. "You can't walk in a straight line even when you're sober, let alone bloody march. We need to win this fucking war. We'll never do it with the likes of you." A final dressing down at the end. "You're fit for cannon fodder but not much else. I wouldn't risk a pussy cat on a Bailey bridge you lot have built and I wouldn't land from a row boat on one of your Mulberries. You'd do more for the war effort if you built for the fucking Jerries."

Bob and I were encouraged to apply for commissions. Both accepted. Must have been on the basis of our engineering qualifications. Certainly not our military aptitude. Mo had a laugh when we told her we were to be Second Lieutenants. Asked how we thought we would fit in with posh eighteen-year-old officers fresh from Officers Training Corps at their public schools. 'University of life,' we told her. Anyhow we had the last laugh. Promoted to Lieutenant a month later due to our age and expertise. Told Mo that if we continued to be promoted at this rate we would be Major-Generals by the end of the war and she'd have to salute us.

***

1 JULY 1942

Seventy-two hours leave after basic training. Wangled a travel warrant for Newcastle to see the family. Spun a bit of a line saying parents were old and frail. Powers that be have no way of checking. When I told Dad, I thought he was going to knock my block off, but he calmed down. Great weekend. Saw Alice and Joe. She's a volunteer nursing assistant at the Wingrove. Joe's doing hours and hours of overtime at Armstrongs. Bus to Hexham at the weekend to see Ian and Aidan – very fit and enjoying life on the farm. Ian says he's going to be a farmer.

Alice recruited George to help wash the dishes one evening. 'It's good to see you but shouldn't you be spending your leave with Joan and Marty, especially now there's another on the way?'

'I do feel a bit guilty,' he admitted, 'but mostly I feel like a spare part in Farnham. Everything's so well organised. I feel I just disrupt the smooth running of the house when I'm there. Possibly not – but that's how I feel.'

'Much better to know everything works well and they're safe, away from the bombing.'

'You're right.' He laughed. 'Better than finding chaos whenever I get home. I guess I'll only be a guest as long as I'm in uniform.' He shrugged. 'Not sure I'll be a lot more after I've been demobbed.'

She laughed. 'George, you must forget you're a red-blooded Geordie and leave things to those on the home front.' His sensible older sister was right.

***

28 July 1942

Posted to a TBRE or Training Battalion Royal Engineers – yet another bloody abbreviation. In Elgin in Scotland. It's further from Farnham than Hamburg or Leipzig and almost as distant as Berlin. Not told Joan that. We're having some fun here. There's a battalion football team – tho' the side is never settled as guys come and go. It's been impressed on us that the Royal Engineers have form – losing finalists in the first ever FA Cup Final and won the cup once – beating the Old Etonians. That bit of intel gave Bob and me a lot of pleasure. A lot more from one of the instructors who's keen on the history of the corps. Apparently RE officers designed the Albert Hall and Pentonville Jail.

Now using our engineering skills. There's so much to prepare for the invasion when it comes. Now the Yanks have joined we'll definitely win.

***

20 September 1942

A son. Ten days' privilege leave. Good. He's to be called

Mark after Joan's grandfather. That's alright. It was my grandfather's name too.

Joan's parents were around the house a lot. 'It's wonderful to have a grandson and you must be over the moon to have a son and heir.' Joan said she was happy with a pigeon pair. This was not a phrase George knew. She said it just meant one of each sex. His father-in-law thought it referred to the fact that pigeons generally only lay two eggs and the myth is that one is female and one male. George wondered if, by implication, Joan was making it clear that she was not up for increasing the size of the family.

Joan was busy with Mark and George spent much of his time with Marty. He took her for a walk each day in her buggy, gas mask slung over his shoulder. 'Which way, Marty?' he would ask as they set off. She revelled in issuing commands – "big field", she would shout, or "cows" or "berries" or "woods" or "bridge". They collected great bunches of wildflowers to take home and Joan would name them and show Marty how to press them. They gathered late blackberries from the hedgerows. There was a Bramley apple tree in the garden and Joan made apple and blackberry crumble. Marty became fascinated by a wide rail bridge over a sunken lane nearby with a tremendous echo. She insisted George took her there several times. She soon got the hang of shouting and waiting for the echo to come back. It was often difficult to get her to leave and go back in time for tea. It was beginning to feel more like home.

George was sitting with Marty on his final day as she was having her tea. Edna was standing to one side leaning against one of the kitchen cupboards, a cup of tea in her hand. Marty was pushing her food around her plate. 'Are you going away again, Daddy?' George nodded. 'I don't want you to go.'

'I don't want to go, sweetheart, but sometimes we have to do things we don't want to. Eat up quickly and then we can play before bed.'

Marty continued to toy with her food.

'Martina, get on and eat up. You're forever messing around with your food,' Edna muttered.

Marty looked round. 'I'm talking to my Daddy.' She scowled and turned her back on Edna.

'That can wait. You can talk after you've eaten up.'

Marty looked at her. Her face crumpled.

George put his hand on her shoulder. 'It's alright. Auntie Edna didn't mean it like that.'

'She needs to understand food's rationed and Joan wants to get on with the washing up.'

George was angry. He said firmly that it was none of her business to supervise or discipline his children. She became quite stroppy and muttered that Joan needed her help as he was an absent father. That really hacked him off. He said Joan's parents provided support and her input wasn't needed. She left in a huff saying she would be back the next day after George had gone. Joan had remained silent, back turned at the sink, throughout this altercation. George was concerned she had not supported him. He challenged her after Edna had left. All she would say was that Edna meant well.

***

6 JUNE 1943

*Ten days' leave. Good to be home again. Takes time
to adjust and feel it really is home – tho' it's the only
one I've got. Sometimes feel like a stranger. Have to
ask where to find everyday things. Guess it'll be like
that until I'm demobbed. God knows when that'll be.
Who knows when this bloody war will be over?*

*Marty's everywhere – in and out of the garden, talking
non-stop and with great urgency. The words tumble
out – as if she's worried she won't meet some deadline
for communicating all her thoughts. Didn't take long to
reconnect. Went to the echoing bridge. She remembered
immediately. 'This is my Daddy's bridge,' she announced
to a bemused passing dog-walker. 'He made it to talk back
to me'. She took the opportunity to exhibit her vocal range
and insisted we sing "Twinkle, twinkle little star" at the
tops of our voices over and over again. Took Mark twice
in his buggy. Encouraged by Marty he got the hang of
learning to shout and wait for the echo.*

*Great leave. I keep imagining the things I'll do
with the kids when the war's over. I'm missing seeing
them develop month by month. But I guess seeing them
occasionally, I'll be amazed by their progress each time
I'm home.*

*Edna not much in evidence. Suspect she was
encouraged (warned?) to stay away while I'm home.
Marty says she's been around a lot.*

***

JANUARY 1944

Parting company with Bob. He's back in Wiltshire preparing AVREs (Assault Vehicle Royal Engineers) for the invasion – converted Churchill tanks with a spigot mortar, "flying dustbins". Others carry demolition equipment – "carrots", "goats" and "double onions", devices for mine clearance and bobbins, box girders and fascines for beach landings, bridge building and crossing soft ground or ditches. These tanks look extraordinary. They're calling them "Hobart's funnies" or "Churchill's toys". We've all been trained to assemble Mulberries, Bailey bridges and skid Baileys from components to be towed across the Channel and to put them together at great speed and under fire – essential to establish a bridgehead.

***

FEBRUARY 1944

In Winchester – course on lifting, defusing and clearing mines. Not told Joan. Didn't dare say I'd volunteered, albeit after some persuasion from the CO. He said my engineering skills, attention to detail and analytical abilities provided the right skill set. Wasn't sure how he made that judgement. Asked why he thought I had good analytical skills. He grinned and said he'd noticed I would corner the mess copy of The Times and knock off the crossword quickly. Thanks, Dad. You taught me the knack of doing cryptic crosswords. Apprehensive but looking forward to the challenge. I wondered, thinking of the kids, if I should be signing up for this. Decided that thoughts of them would make me meticulously careful. Having to be careful about keeping my diary. Writing it up a few days ago while having a pint in the mess was spotted by the CO. He spoke quite sharply about security. Must be careful about what I write and only do so when I'm in my billet.

5

9 November 1989

Mark was home early. Only Michael was in. He was stretched out full length on the sofa watching Countdown. There were the remnants of a cheese sandwich, an open packet of bourbon biscuits and an empty mug on the coffee table. 'Where's Mum?'

'Haven't a clue. Not seen her since this morning.'

'Oh, she said she would be in her studio all day. Anyhow, what are you doing here? It's a Thursday. Shouldn't you be in college?'

'I thought I'd work at home today.'

Mark pointed at the television set. 'Doesn't look much like work to me.'

Michael directed the remote at the set, muted the programme and pointed at the empty plate. 'Late lunch break.' He got slowly to his feet. 'Okay, back to the grindstone. By the way, I've been thinking more about your dad's journals. I talked to my tutor earlier in the week about my final year dissertation. He agreed that some aspect of post-war Germany would be a good subject. Your dad's stuff could be useful.'

'How come?'

'It gave me the idea – Germany at the end of the war, particularly the fate of "displaced persons". Have you done any more with the journals?'

'Not a lot. I've been busy. You've already seen the earliest ones.'

'I've dipped into a few of the others. The later ones will probably be more relevant. I'll ask Mum to help with some of the background.'

'Go carefully. She may not be too keen. She doesn't much want to be reminded of that part of her life. Any idea where she might be?'

'She had a call when she was in her studio after I got back this morning. She went upstairs, changed and went out. Said she needed to go to the gallery. Haven't seen her since.'

Mark made himself a coffee and settled on the sofa. He switched off the television, thumbed listlessly through the paper and then nodded off. It was getting dark when he awoke. There was still no sign of Gisela. Surely, she couldn't still be at the gallery.

It was after six when she got home. 'Sorry,' she said, slurring her words slightly, 'Been out to lunch.'

'Must have been a hell of a lunch.'

'Business as well.' She steadied herself and flopped heavily into a chair. 'I think, I just think I might have had a little too much wine.'

'Who the hell were you lunching with?'

'Your friend Sandy Scott.'

'How come?'

'The gallery rang. Said they had a major buyer who was going to buy two of the more expensive pieces and he wanted to meet the sculptor. They asked me to go over if I was free. I was, so I did. It turned out to be your mate Sandy.'

'Not my mate, just a contact. Not the same thing.'

'Well, you seemed pretty matey in that pub.'

Mark shrugged. 'And you had no idea who you were going to meet?'

'None at all.'

'Typical devious politician, particularly as he'd met you.'

'Well, he reckons he's a friend of yours. He said he really liked my work and might buy more in the future. Then he said he would love to take me out to lunch if I had nothing on.' She giggled. 'I told him I never accepted invitations to lunch in the nude but I'd enjoy it if I could remain fully clothed.' Mark gave her a thunderous look. 'Don't look like that – that was a joke.'

Mark had been listening with a growing sense of disquiet. 'As I said, it must have been one hell of a lunch.'

'It was. He took me to Le Caprice. It was fabulous. He's a serious collector. He's very knowledgeable and he's charming.'

'That much is only too well known – and he's obscenely rich.'

'No need to sound like that. At the end he summoned his driver who dropped him off at the Commons and then told him to drive me home.' She stretched her arms out expansively. 'So here I am – the renowned and highly collectable sculptor Gisela Schafer.' She paused. 'I really feel a bit woozy. He's also asked me to go down to his place in Kent some time and give him my opinion on his collection.'

'And?'

'I said I would. Don't look so bloody surly. It might also help your contact with him as well.'

'Don't pretend you're doing this for me.'

'I'm not.'

'I've warned you about him.'

'I don't need warning,' she said sharply. 'Anyhow, I'm going to go and lie down for a bit until the effect of that very expensive wine wears off. Not that I want it to if you're going to be so bloody grumpy.'

***

Later that evening Gisela and Mark were drinking coffee at the kitchen table after a silent supper. 'Mark, don't go into a major grump. The lunch was quite innocent and Sandy might just be useful to me in the future.'

'But why did you agree to go to his place in Kent?'

'I was flattered. I told him I was an artist.' She spread her arms. 'Me, an artist. Did you know that?' Mark looked at her stonily.

'He's a lecher.'

'Maybe, but if he is, he was having an afternoon off from leching. And if he is, I reckon he'd be pretty good at it.' She looked across at Mark's surly expression. 'Mark, for God's sake, stop being so bloody negative. His behaviour was entirely proper. I'm well able to look after myself and I'm not looking for amorous adventures. Just trust me – as I do you,' she said pointedly. She paused for a moment before adding more gently, 'Look, I know things are not good for you at work and you keep having run-ins with Mike Willis but it won't help anyone if you bitch at me.'

Mark grunted. This tetchy interchange came to an abrupt end when Michael burst in. 'Mum, Dad, come and look at the television. Something unbelievable's going on.'

'What's that?'

'Just come and look,' he repeated urgently. They followed him into the lounge. Their eyes were immediately drawn to the screen which showed crowds on both sides of the Brandenburg Gate and the Berlin Wall. These were intercut with scenes of jubilant people standing on top of the wall while East German guards looked on impassively. Crowds were forcing their way through to the west.

'What's this? Is it real?'

'It's real alright. I've been watching for about fifteen minutes. The border controls have been overwhelmed.'

Mark leaned forward to get a better look at the screen. 'This has been building for weeks,' he said. 'Huge numbers are leaving the DDR and there've been big demonstrations in Leipzig for the last two months.'

'They just said that. And there was a shot of a huge demo last weekend, Alexanderplatz I think it was called. Thousands on the screen were chanting "Wir wollen raus" and "Tor auf, Tor auf".' Michael looked across to his father. 'That means "we want out" and "open the gate".'

Gisela sat on the arm of the settee, transfixed by the

images on the screen. It was difficult to process what she was seeing. 'We thought that wall was for ever,' she said shaking her head in disbelief. 'I can hardly believe it.' This was the wall that Reagan demanded should be torn down and which Maggie and Mitterand had hoped Gorbachev would retain.

'This has been happening right across the Warsaw Pact countries.' They all sat, mesmerised, slowly taking in the scenes. 'It was bound to happen but nobody thought it would happen this quickly.'

Incredulity was being replaced by elation for Gisela. 'I never believed I'd see this. It's a Kennedy moment.'

'What do you mean, Mum?'

'Oh, almost everyone says they can remember where they were and what they were doing when they heard Kennedy had been assassinated. It was unbelievable. We both cried.'

'So, where were you and what were you doing?'

Gisela looked at Mark. 'We were in my digs. It was early evening here.' She smiled. Her landlady had stipulated that tenants should not entertain guests of the opposite sex in their rooms after eight in the evening. That suited them well. They would go to bed together while still feeling fresh and frisky and then go to the pub for a relaxed drink without any sexual tension between them. Well, not too much – they were still young. They had been in bed and had put the radio on after sex.

'So, what were you doing?'

'As you would say, on a need to know basis, you don't need to know.'

'Mum, I think that's an answer in itself.'

Mark looked at Gisela. 'I'm not sure.'

'What? You're not sure you were in bed with Mum?'

'No, you idiot. I'm not sure about the comparison. That was all about one guy, more mourned for what it was thought he might have achieved than for what he did achieve. He was an icon for our generation. Some people acquire that status, like Princess Diana. This is of far greater significance.'

'Kennedy was a hero for us when he said "Ich bin ein Berliner" outside the Schöneberg Town Hall.'

'Dramatic, but it didn't change anything.' Mark laughed. 'Anyhow, I was told the way he said it meant that he was claiming to be a doughnut.' Mark turned to her. 'This will really reshape the politics of Europe. I must go into the office. It's too late to do much for tomorrow's paper but we'll need to have quite a spread for Saturday with a lot of analysis.'

The telephone rang after Mark had left. Michael passed the receiver to his mother. 'It's German granny. I can't make out what she's saying. She's crying. She sounds very upset.' Gisela said she would take the call in the kitchen. Michael sat fascinated. History was playing out in front of his eyes, in real time. The cameras switched repeatedly from images of thousands of ossis to those of East German border guards with impassive faces standing impotently to one side at the east-west crossing points, Bornholmerstrasse, Invalidenstrasse and Friedrichstrasse (Checkpoint Charlie). Only a trickle of people had passed through at first. They were told they would not be permitted to return – ever. This edict was quickly forgotten and the VOPOs were finally overwhelmed by sheer weight of numbers chanting

"Open the gates, open the gates." People and vehicles were pouring through. The trickle had become a flood. At first, many tried to get their identity documents stamped to show they had crossed the border on such an historic date. Then, as the crowds grew, the imperative to reach the West, even if only temporarily, became ever more pressing. The limited access was insufficient for the crowds and more and more clambered onto the wall. Some jumped down into the West to be greeted with cheers, hugs and champagne. Growing numbers were gathering on both sides. Fireworks were set off throwing multi-coloured stars in the shape of exotic flowers into the night sky. Children were shouting, dogs barking and thousands of voices were coming together to sing the Deutschlandlied. Some had brought tools to start the process of demolition of the wall and obtain fragments as souvenirs. The sound of clubs, sledgehammers and chisels being struck against concrete by these wall woodpeckers, or Mauerspechte, provided a cacophonous background to the clamour building on both sides. The racket of horns of innumerable Trabants and Wartburgs on one side and Mercedes on the other formed a discordant and anarchically happy orchestra. Many from the East were happy to simply walk around revelling in their newly found freedom. Others headed for the city centre lights, unconstrained by their lack of Deutschmarks. Friends, relatives and strangers were only too ready to share or buy drinks. Ever-increasing numbers converged on the Brandenburg Gate where a spontaneous and unrestrained celebratory party had developed. Everyone from East and West wanted their own small part in history.

Gisela came back into the room. Michael looked up and saw she was crying. 'It's alright, everything's alright. Mutti was crying because she's so happy.' She smiled. 'I see people on the box handing round champagne. Stay there, I'm going to get some. Let's join them.'

Gisela sat lost in thought, glass in hand. A multiplicity of memories and emotions clustered in the forefront of her brain. Her life, her family was here in England – in suburban Kew. It was a world unimaginably different from that of her childhood. Images of her lost father and her widowed mother, of the chaos and trauma of their flight and the privations that followed arose unbidden and colonised her mind. Was she and would she for ever be a captive of her German heritage and her German past? Would she ever be able to break free entirely from the emotional shackles which were the legacy of her youth? Would it ever be possible to confront and face down the demons which lurked in the recesses of her brain? Demons which would ambush her unawares from time to time, gliding stealthily into her consciousness, appropriating her thinking and disrupting her peace of mind. Was it possible that the march of history might reconcile her to her homeland? Michael had turned away from the screen. His eyes were focused on the conflicting emotions passing over his mother's face. He walked over and sat on the settee beside her. He put a hand gently on her shoulder. 'Do you want to talk about it?'

'I'm not sure. It's a long story. The main border was closed in the early fifties though Berliners could still move pretty freely between the East and West of the city. Thousands did so every day to work and see relatives and friends. It was more difficult for us in the Federal Republic. My Aunt Ulla lived in East Berlin, in Prenzlauer Berg, close to her mum and not far from the wall. It was difficult to meet her and her boys. We only managed to do so twice in West Berlin. Then the wall went up. There was no warning. It left people without jobs. I never saw Aunt Ulla again. She died two years later from cancer. People were told the wall was for their protection, an anti-fascist rampart, an Antifaschistischer Schutzwall. They were told it was essential to stop westerners from crossing and benefitting from the advantages of living in the east, but it wasn't. It was to keep people in.'

'Surely nobody believed that crap?'

'Mostly not – but some did. The DDR wasn't all bad. Most accepted it. People had jobs, their kids went to school, sport and cultural activities were encouraged.'

'You're making it sound idyllic.'

'It wasn't. But after the war people just wanted stability and peace. The DDR gave them that.' She paused, 'Just like some accepted Hitler after Weimar. He offered discipline and jobs and scapegoats: Jews, Romanies, communists.'

'But you've always said East Prussia suffered horrendously?'

'Only towards the end. It was a rural backwater – a long way from Britain. The first big bombing raid on Königsberg wasn't until the summer of 1944. It all changed at the end of that year. We can talk more when Oma comes for Christmas. She might tell you more.'

'I hope so. Her story would be great for my dissertation.'

'Michael, go gently. This isn't a history project for us.

Remembering hurts – like hell sometimes.' He nodded. 'I'll ask Oma. Tonight has brought back so many memories – it's difficult. I can't talk any more right now. I just want to sit and watch and enjoy.'

***

It was almost four in the morning before Mark returned. Gisela was still awake. He whispered, 'Sorry to disturb you. The office was a hive of activity. A lot of us showed up. I see you and Michael have been at our champagne stock.'

She switched on the bedside light and grinned at him, slightly drunkenly. 'I'm so happy just now and if you tell me that you've not had a drink or three, I shan't believe you.'

He nodded. 'We did get hold of some for the newsroom. I've also spent hours in the library looking through back issues so I can draft an opinion piece for tomorrow's paper. There's so much to analyse and even more as we speculate on what might happen next.'

'I've hardly been to sleep. I keep thinking about it all and everything that happened back when I was a kid. I'm just so happy.' She looked at him and pulled him towards her. 'Come here, you grumpy sod. There's one more thing I need to round off a night of celebration.' Five minutes later he rolled off her. She whispered in his ear, 'Tonight would not have been complete without a grand climax.'

Mark laughed. 'Ellie, I must sleep. I've shot my bolt. I need to be back by ten for an editorial meeting and I'll have to spend most of the day researching and writing.'

'I've lived here almost all the time the wall has been up.

Mostly, I've not wanted much to go back to Germany – though, of course, I did to see Mutti and Willy while he was still alive. Now, I do want to go back to Berlin. And I'd like to go to Dresden to see Ferdinand.'

6

28 November 1989

Magda

Mein liebster Michael,

I so look forward to seeing you at Christmas. The last weeks have been so wonderful. Your Mama asked if I would tell you something of our family from all those years ago. The fall of the wall has brought so many memories back to my mind. I thought it might be a little easier for me if I put them down on paper – but even that was difficult.

This is our family's story – how we had to leave your grandfather and our home. I have never tried to write about those times before. I often think back to them and that can make me very sad. Several times I have had to stop as it has been so painful. The ink is smudged in places – you will understand why. Your Mama will remember much of this but perhaps not all. She may tell you more.

Alles liebe, Oma

January/February 1945

The eighteenth of January 1945 is a date in my life I shall never forget. Everything changed for us that day – for ever. It was very cold. Winters on our farm in Braunsberg were always cold. Winters in East Prussia were always cold. The winds would sweep over the flatlands from the east and that winter was even more arctic than most. I was awake very early, long before five – earlier than usual and colder than usual. Holger's comforting warmth was no longer by my side. It was not unusual for him to be up early in spring and summer but this was January. It was inky black outside. I pulled a blanket round myself and went to the kitchen. Holger was sitting with his elbows on the table and his head in his hands. He didn't hear me at first. I went and stood behind him and put my hands on his shoulders and rested my head on his. He turned and looked at me. He was crying. I had never seen Holger cry before. He took both my hands. For a long, long time he said nothing. Then slowly he said, 'It's over, it's all over for us, for me, for you and for Gisela.'

I was frightened. I pulled a chair over and sat beside him. I put my arm over his shoulder and pulled him close. I didn't understand. I asked him what was all over. He said our lives on the farm and maybe even our lives. He said we had to go. He said it again and again. He said it would be our only chance. I didn't want to understand. It was our farm, our home. It always had been. I believed it always would be. The war was coming to an end. I knew it would be hard but I was sure we would get through.

Holger held my hands tightly. He kept saying over and

over again that it wasn't safe. That there was no future for us on the farm and that we had to go. I was scared. We had seen reports in the Völkischer Beobachter and on Die Deutsche Wochenschau. We had read of the killings in Nemmersdorf. We knew the Russians were coming in huge numbers and had heard they were killing everyone in their way. We had seen refugees from further east and heard their stories as they passed through. They were running west as far and as fast as they could. They'd told us how bad it was: women raped and then crucified on barn doors; children's heads crushed. It didn't bear thinking about. We knew the Russians were close. We'd heard the rumble of guns. We'd felt the ground shake with the heavy thump of artillery.

I felt sick. Our whole life was being dismantled and destroyed. I didn't want to accept it. I couldn't bear to think of a different future. Holger said we must be strong. He had talked to his brother Konrad through the night. They were sure there was no other way. Ulla would leave later that morning with Friedrich and Ferdinand. He said we must go too. He said it would be safer if we went together.

Slowly it dawned on me that Holger and Konrad would not be coming with us. All men between 16 and 60 had been ordered by Gauleiter Koch to join the Volkssturm; a final effort to hold fast to the soil of the Heimat. A futile effort. A citizen army with almost no uniforms or weapons or ammunition. There was no way they could stand up to tanks and heavily armed soldiers. Would they survive? It seemed unlikely. But there was no way of knowing.

The Gauleiter had said there should be no evacuation. Posters everywhere ordered everyone to stay. But everyone was running – running westwards. We knew it was unlikely women and children would be stopped. It was a risk but it would be a bigger risk if we stayed and greater still if Holger and Konrad came with us. I tried to persuade him to come disguised as a woman. He smiled and said that, at nearly two metres in height, he would quickly be exposed and it could endanger everyone. Flying courts-martial had been set up. Summary executions were taking place. He would be shot as a deserter.

My mind was in turmoil. There were so many questions. Where would we go? How would we get there? What should I take? What would happen to our stock? We had heard of abandoned cattle wandering freely and untended near Insterberg. There were no answers – only questions. Holger stood and pulled me to my feet, putting both his hands on my shoulders. He was speaking with ever-increasing urgency. He kept repeating that he just wanted Gisela and me to be safe and this was our only chance. That we must go west as far and as fast as we could – and we must do it for him.

I was numb, scared, overwhelmed, daunted. I can't describe all my feelings at that moment. Deep down I knew I had to do it, but I was in a funk. I didn't think I had the strength to save Gisela without Holger's support.

Holger and Konrad had planned everything. We were to take the horse and cart and a handcart. There were two possible routes. One was to go to Pillau and try to get on a boat to take us west to Lübeck or Kiel or even to Sweden. But to get there we would need to head back towards Königsberg and towards the Russians. And there were thousands trying to board boats. The other was to go west along the coast. Holger said he'd heard there was a land corridor open. He thought we should go for that. If we could get to Elbing or beyond we might find a place on a freight train. There were almost no passenger trains. Most had been requisitioned by the Wehrmacht. Holger kept saying whatever we did we must get away from the Russians. He and Konrad would try to join us when they could. He said they would find us wherever we were. He repeated over and over again we must go west and keep going west. Anywhere, but somewhere where we would be picked up by the Americans or the British.

I went to the small bedroom where Gisela was sleeping. She didn't stir. I knew Holger was right. We had to go. There was no alternative. But it would break my heart to leave the farm – our home for fifteen years. We would be leaving for an unknown destination and an uncertain future. My life, all our lives were dissolving, hour by hour, minute by minute. Everything I loved, everything that was most precious to me was there on the farm. I felt sick inside. And I was angry. I raged at the disaster which had been inflicted on Germany but, most of all, on us as a family. I could not see how we could ever be a family again. I could not see any way that Gisela could have a future. We had sympathised and sorrowed with friends and neighbours whose husbands and sons had been lost, many on the Eastern Front. I had tried to comfort inconsolable children at the school where I taught who had lost fathers and brothers. But now the war had come into the heart of my own family. I had to go. Somehow I had to find the strength to do so. I was not sure I was up to it, but I had to do it – for Gisela and for Holger.

***

Holger's brother, Konrad, was at the door at daybreak. The news was getting worse. He said Ulla and he would be back with the boys two hours later and that we should take the tractor, although we'd probably have to abandon it when it ran out of fuel.

I wandered round the cottage. I was numb. It was all happening so quickly, too quickly. I didn't know what to take or what I needed to take. I dressed Gisela very warmly. We planned she should travel in the cart for part of the time as she wouldn't be able to walk as far or as fast as Friedrich and Ferdinand. Holger had collected what food there was and all the money that was in the house. He said I should divide the money up and hide it in different places about my body and we should travel with a group for safety. I was sure we would be back after the Russians had passed through. Maybe after two weeks, possibly three. There had to be somewhere we could hide. The Russians would be pushing on to Berlin. Surely, they wouldn't be interested in a backwater like ours. At the last minute I picked up our wedding photograph and placed it in the cart. It seemed like an acceptance of defeat, the end of a life – almost an act of betrayal.

We were ready two hours later. I hugged Holger tightly. I whispered that I was sure I could find a place to shelter near the coast and come back after the troops had passed through. Holger was close to tears. He shook his head. He said it wouldn't be safe. He made me promise to keep going west. He gripped my hands firmly. I'll never forget what he said. 'Please, please do this for me and for Gisela. You and Gisela are my life. I need to be as certain as I can be that you're both safe.' He hugged me and then Gisela and turned away to hide his tears. Konrad put an arm round him. I was empty, overwhelmed by a sense of desolation. I sensed this would be the last time I would ever see Holger, the last time I would ever see our farm, our home.

Ulla came up and hugged Gisela and me. She whispered urgently that we should go. The boys were playing around as if this was an adventure. Ulla drove the tractor, towing one cart. Friedrich led the horse hitched to another and I pulled the handcart. We made it to the highway running alongside the Frisches Haff and headed west towards Elbing. We were not alone. This was a mass migration – a great trek. Thousands were heading west, women, children and a few older men. There were carts and prams, bicycles, even a funeral carriage. One or two were on horseback. Others were pulling sledges over the frozen fields. Every conveyance was piled high with food stocks, cases, paintings, toys, musical instruments.

It was a silent trek. People walked heads down – each isolated by their own sense of desolation and hopelessness. From time to time we had to scatter as Wehrmacht vehicles came through, heading for Königsberg and the front. We were strafed by Russian planes and forced to shelter in icy water in the ditches with the bodies of animals and people preserved in death by the cold. There were abandoned goods by the roadside – picked over and looted. Items considered worthless had been discarded in nearby fields covered with snow which glittered in the pallid winter sunlight. Some walked over the ice of the Frisches Haff only to be strafed from the air. At night we slept in barns or churches or under hay ricks. Sometimes we slept in the open in temperatures of minus twenty degrees, huddling close for warmth. The finger-like beams of searchlights scanned the night sky which was punctuated periodically by flashes from anti-aircraft guns.

There were rumours everywhere, growing and multiplying. Mass killings, women raped, breasts cut off, the old slaughtered, children crushed, communities rounded up into barns and burnt to death. News filtered through. We tried to persuade ourselves that the rumours were over-sensationalised, spread by Goebbels for propaganda purposes. But everything seemed to confirm Holger's worst fears.

We had to abandon the tractor at the end of the second day. There was no fuel. We loaded what we could onto the other two carts. It took us four days to reach Elbing. The old town was in ruins from the bombing. There was no chance of a train. There had been a disastrous crash the night before between two trains packed with refugees at Grünhagen only twenty kilometres away. We heard later that the Russians moved in the next day and killed many of the survivors. It seemed we were only a day or so ahead of the Russians, although we learned later that Elbing held out until March.

We set off for Danzig. Gisela was huddled in the cart. I made her walk a bit to create some warmth. 'Why has

Papa sent us away?' she kept asking. 'When will he come to us? Where are we going? How will he find us? When will he come to take us home?' I had no answers. I kept saying Holger would find us. What else could I say? We didn't even know if any of us would survive to the next day, the next week or the next month. The waysides were littered with bodies of people of all ages. Some older people propped up against trees, dead from hypothermia. The nightmare was overwhelming. It was no longer an adventure for Friedrich and Ferdinand. This was about survival and nothing else. We trudged on. There was no help to be found in villages and towns on the way. Local people were resentful and often hostile. Many were preparing to flee. Provisions were increasingly scarce. Such as were available were being conserved by the locals. It was another six days before we reached Danzig. We sold the horse. We knew it would be slaughtered for food. Food costs were rising astronomically. We still had some from the farm. At least it had remained fresh in the icy conditions. The Reichsmarks we got for the horse would come in useful for the next stage of our journey.

Ulla and I agreed we needed to rest for a day or two, ideally under cover. Late that afternoon we found a shed behind the ruins of a grand town house close to the centre. Ulla said she would go into the town to see what might be possible for the next stage of our journey. Danzig had a reputation for violence. I was anxious and worried for her safety, but she insisted she should go. She was right. We were not safe where we were. We were not safe on the road. We knew we would probably not be safe anywhere until we reached the British or Americans. Perhaps not even then.

She turned back as she was leaving and whispered, 'If I don't get back, look after my boys.' Ulla had been a rock.

She'd been gone a short time when the door of the shed was pushed open violently. I shrank back into the corner with my arms around Gisela, the boys at my side. A tall man stood in the doorway blocking out the waning light with a hunting rifle in his hand. I was unable to make out his features in the dusk with the setting sun behind him. 'Get up,' he commanded in German, sharply gesturing with the rifle, 'and out – now.'

I pushed ahead of the children to say we were tired and cold and had nowhere to go. I pleaded that we might stay for one night. I promised we would cause no problems and would leave in the morning. He relaxed a little. 'So, you're German. I thought you were Polish or Russian.' He shifted his position a little. Another figure had walked up behind him. 'What's going on, Hans?'

'It's alright, Marthe. These people are German. It's only a mother and her children.' I relaxed hearing this. The woman moved her husband to one side and asked where we were from. I explained we had left Braunsberg more than ten days earlier and had walked from there. I begged them to let us stay for a day or two, until we were ready to go on and the children were stronger. He lowered his rifle and said we could stay. His wife said the streets were dangerous. Troops were retreating and deserting and many Poles were seeking revenge. She said it would be safer if we joined them in the cellars of the house.

We were led across the devastated garden to the ruins of the house and down an outside stair to the cellars. We pulled the carts over, unloaded them and left them close to the house. I left the children with Marthe and went back to the shed to leave a note for Ulla. The cellars were extensive and provided a far more secure shelter from the snow and wind. We were given one of the underground rooms. We were fortunate. Hans and Marthe were to be our saviours. She was very comforting to the children. They had had two sons, both killed on the Russian front. They shared some of their food and produced a bottle of brandy from their cellars.

By ten that evening I was anxious and the boys were worried. Ulla had not returned. She had been gone for more than five hours. There was no way I could leave and search for her. I didn't know where she had gone. Hunting for her in a devastated city I didn't know in the blackout would have been pointless. She finally returned an hour later and stumbled through the darkened garden to the cellars. I looked at her in the candlelight. She had been drinking, and a great deal more than the modest tots of brandy we had drunk to warm ourselves in the cellars.

'Where the hell have you been?' I muttered angrily. 'I've been worried sick and the boys were scared.'

Ulla had been to the docks first. There was no chance of a passage. People were fighting to get onto boats, hoping to get to Sweden. She had then gone to the rail station. There were very few trains and the timetables were useless. She had met two soldiers – a Leutnant and a Hauptmann returning to the eastern front. They had insisted on buying her a drink. She said she had been about to refuse but decided they might be a useful source of information. 'And were they?' I asked tartly. I was still angry.

They had already had several drinks and were quite indiscreet. She learned that we had left just in time. The Russians had taken Allenstein and Königsberg had been almost surrounded. They had reached the shores of the Frisches Haff and were moving close to Braunsberg and Elbing. They confirmed that all men had now been enrolled in the Volkssturm, so we really were on our own. We had to make sure we survived for the children and for Holger and Konrad.

It seemed our best chance would be to leave by train – if we could. The soldiers had suggested we should not head for Berlin but use local trains and aim for Stettin and then on towards Hamburg. I asked Ulla if we could rely on their advice. She couldn't be sure – but she didn't think they were trying to mislead her. They'd drunk a lot and were speaking very freely. She admitted she had flirted a bit and led them on and sensed they were expecting certain favours in return. When they became more amorous, she left to go to the toilet and escaped through the back of the station bar. We decided to consult Hans and Marthe in the morning.

We didn't sleep much. There was a bombing raid, fortunately not too close. Gisela snuggled up to me saying she was frightened and wanted to go home. She wanted her Papa to keep her safe. I pulled our wedding photo out from my bag and we looked at it together. 'You look happy there,' she said. I hugged her and we both cried. There was nothing I could say. I tried to explain that Papa had gone away to fight for her and we would all go home once he had beaten the enemy. Would I ever be forgiven for such lies, I wondered? The war was going to be lost very soon. The sooner it was over the better for us and for Germany – or so I hoped and prayed. And I prayed that Holger and Konrad would survive unharmed. I suspected this was a forlorn hope.

***

Marthe came into our cellar room in the morning with warm drinks for the children. She looked at Ulla. 'It was very foolish of you to go alone into the city – particularly to the docks. There've always been tensions and often violence between Germans and Poles here. Things are much worse now.'

Ulla nodded looking suitably penitent. Contrition didn't come readily to her. Marthe said the information Ulla had received from the soldiers was probably as good as any. She suggested we stay another night to recover our strength before travelling on. We agreed – it was dry there and our hosts had managed to retrieve some bedding from the ruins of their home for us. We needed that extra day.

Marthe and Hans appeared the next morning. They said cautiously they had been thinking about their future. They had been planning to leave since the house was bombed but had not been able to motivate themselves to do so. They had not been able to see any future after losing their sons. But Hans said he had a sister who lived in Köln and although they had not been able to get in touch with her, they had finally decided to try to go there. They believed the Americans were close as they had already taken Aachen. Köln had been bombed repeatedly and there had been three massive attacks, most recently the previous October. They didn't know if she or her house had survived. They then asked if they might travel with us. They said they could help us get out of Danzig and might be able to help later as Hans spoke English. Marthe said it would help them too. It would give them a sense they had a family to care for.

Ulla and I looked at one another. It was a time for instant decisions. Without hesitation, we agreed and Marthe gave both of us a hug. Our adoptive family plotted our journey by rail to Stettin and on to Rostock, Hamburg, and finally south towards Münster. The journey took twelve days. There were many changes and diversions and much walking between towns carrying what we could. The rail journey was hellish. Three times we were evacuated from trains as they were requisitioned for military use and once to escape strafing. We were simply abandoned by the track. Even when we were on trains it was ghastly. They were packed. There was only room to sit or lie on the floor. There were almost no toilets and the carriages stank. Fights broke out all round us for space, for food and for seats. Everywhere there were signs of devastation. We couldn't see how it could ever be possible to re-create a normal life. In some ways it was good we were so tired and had little time to think. We just needed to keep going. We needed to make sure the children were safe.

We had hoped to find refuge in Münster. It had been heavily bombed. Hans told us to stay on the outskirts while he sought an old business associate. He came back and said the centre had been almost entirely destroyed and the Prinzipalmarkt area was totally flattened. Nearly nine-tenths of the houses in the city and many of the barracks had been severely damaged. Later we heard that only one thousand houses remained undamaged out of more than thirty-three thousand. Hans couldn't find his former associate.

Münster was not the place to stay. Panzer and infantry divisions were garrisoned there. Fighting would be fierce as the Americans and British advanced. But it was difficult to go much further. We were getting close to the front line and the border. We decided to walk further west and find a place close to the Dutch border and wait for the American and British forces. We were lucky. We came to an isolated farm twenty-five kilometres from Münster near Burgsteinfurt. We could see a woman herding twenty or twenty-five cows into a barn. She closed and barred the barn door as she saw us approaching. I went forward alone. As I reached the yard, the gate was swung shut. She had a shotgun at the ready. I stepped back a few paces and raised my hands. She was plump and a little older than me. I said cautiously we were not there to cause trouble; we just needed a place to rest for a few nights. The children could take no more. I asked if we could stay in one of the barns.

She raised the shotgun a little higher and said sharply that she had no room for refugees. I could see that the yard and some of the equipment looked neglected. I took a deep breath. I said it seemed she could do with some help and that my sister-in-law and I were both from farms – and my husband was a dairy farmer. She looked at me suspiciously and asked if that was true. I nodded.

She told me to stay where I was and went back into the farmhouse. She returned after a few minutes. She said reluctantly that she couldn't deny that she needed some help, as her husband had been taken away. 'Show me what you can do,' she said. 'Go into the barn and start milking. The stools and pails are there. If it turns out you're all talk, you can get off my land.' I suggested I should go back to the family and bring Ulla back with me as she could help too.

They had all been watching anxiously as the woman had raised her shotgun, even though she had not pointed it directly at me. I reassured them and said I had suggested that Ulla and I had skills which would be useful around her farm. The two of us went over and set to work milking with the woman standing behind us still cradling the shotgun. After we had each milked six, she said she could see we knew what we were doing. We learned later that the forced labourers who had been sent to her had all run off. She said we could stay in one of the barns and she would expect help in the fields, not just with milking. We both nodded. 'And if any of those kids start messing around, you're out,' she said. 'And who are those old folks?'

'They're godparents,' Ulla interjected quickly. And in many ways they were.

She nodded again. 'Well, get on and finish the job and when you've finished you can take a couple of litres for yourselves. You'll have to make your own arrangements for food,' she said curtly as she turned on her heel and headed back to the farmhouse.

Not long after, we discovered how fortunate we had been in deciding to travel overland. Two ships, the Wilhelm Gustloff and the General von Steuben, had been sunk in the Baltic in early February with the loss of fourteen or fifteen thousand people. Holger's final words of advice to me had been good.

7

10 June 1944

George

Invasion underway. Won't be long before I'm off. Date unknown. Bob was posted to the RE Fifth Assault Regiment. Went in on D-day with 79th Armoured Division. They knew it would be one hell of a job breaching Hitler's Atlantic Wall. Building harbours, breaching defences, maintaining firm access routes over the sand and removing knocked-out vehicles. Telegram from Mo two days later. Bob badly injured assembling a Mulberry. Repatriated to Netley. Got permission to visit. He was remarkably cheery but he's lost a leg and has some internal injuries. His war is over. Said he might be transferred to Leeds after surgery. Hatfield House another possibility. He fancies a stately home with beautiful aristocratic volunteer nurses. Easier for Mo to visit. It will fuel his romantic fantasies. Said I would visit Mo if I could get a twenty-four hour pass.

***

14 June 1944

Day pass to go to London to see Mo.

George knocked. He waited – no answer. He knocked again. He was about to turn away, certain Mo must be out when he heard footsteps shuffling towards the door. The flap of the letter box was pushed open. What was going on? Mo's voice came haltingly through the opening. 'Who's there?'

George crouched. 'Mo, it's me – George. What's wrong?'

She opened the door. She was in a dressing gown and slippers, her hair askew. She looked at George for a moment and then put her arms around him. 'Thank God you're here. I don't know what to do.'

He looked at her aghast. 'What's happened?'

She stood back. 'Oh God, you don't know. I thought that was why you were here. Come in. I'll get some tea.' She took his hand and led him into the kitchen. He looked around. 'I know it's a mess, I'm a mess. A telegram came. Bob's dead.'

It was impossible to absorb, to comprehend Mo's words. It couldn't be right. It was as if he had strayed unwittingly onto the set of a play and was merely the detached observer of a scene. It couldn't be true. Bob had been so well a few days earlier. They had been laughing and joshing each other as usual. He had been so sure he was recovering. Slowly reality hit. He sank into a chair with his elbows on his knees and his head in his hands. He felt physically sick. What could he say? No words would come. There were no words which could describe his feelings at that moment.

Mo put a hand on his shoulder. She stood silently behind him, tears rolling down her cheeks. 'It seems awful to say this, but in a strange way I was happy he'd been wounded. It would mean his war was over and he'd be safe and home. He wrote every day from Netley. He was so chipper after you'd seen him. Then that telegram came. The worst thing is I never got there to see him. There was a letter today. I'll show you.'

It had been written by the CO at the camp. It was evident he had not known Bob personally. It said he had suffered further internal bleeding and had needed emergency surgery but they had been unable to control it. This was followed by the usual platitudes about his commitment to his men and his willingness to lay down his life for his country. Was anyone really willing to do that? The words jarred. Bob and George and the thousands, millions of others knew they ran the risk of being wounded or dying. They knew it was a possibility, but willing – no.

George sat with Mo for more than an hour holding her hand, their mugs of tea untouched. For a long time she didn't want to talk – she just wanted to be with someone who had known and loved Bob. It had never occurred to George previously that he might have loved a man, but it was the only word which fully expressed his feelings. They had done so much together – as colleagues on the railways, when he had lodged with him and Mo, drinking in the pub, playing football and all through their training.

Finally, he turned to Mo. 'I don't know what to say. To say I'll miss him doesn't even begin to describe how I feel. I don't have the right words. Bob was simply the best mate I've ever had.'

'George, I don't know what to do now.' Mo paused. 'Do you remember those neighbours, Sarah and Tommy? We went to the pub with them once or twice. He was a flight engineer on a Lancaster.' He nodded. 'He was on a mission early this year and didn't come back. Nobody on the flight saw the plane after they had dumped their payloads and scattered for the return. She doesn't know what to think. She doesn't know if he's alive and a prisoner or if he was killed. The not knowing is destroying her. She swings between believing he'll walk through the door one day and surprise her or hearing he's a prisoner – or that he's dead. Nobody can answer her questions. I don't know if it's better for her to keep thinking he might come back or if she should accept he might not. I've tried to help, but I can't now. It'll be too painful. She's been round. She didn't say so, but I suspect she thinks it's better for me as I have certainty. I don't know if that's true. Now I've got to arrange Bob's funeral. I've never been to a funeral. I have nightmares about seeing that box going into the ground and being covered with earth. I'm scared it will be all too much for me. I'm frightened.'

She hugged George. Some minutes later she sat back and said hesitantly, 'I've lost the only man I've ever loved. Now I've only got memories. And there's something that makes me even sadder.' She was sobbing uncontrollably. 'We decided to put off trying for a child until the war was over. We got that so bloody wrong. We agreed it was sensible. Bugger being sensible. If only, if only we had thought that possibly Bob might not make it. But it didn't cross our minds. Maybe we just didn't want it to. To have had a child would have made this a bit easier. It wouldn't and couldn't have been a substitute for Bob. But a kid would have been a part of him here with me. Something to hold onto – something to live for.'

There was nothing George could say. They stayed sitting in silence.

She hugged him again. 'You've no idea how much your being here has helped. Thank you so much for coming. Please keep in touch and, for God's sake, make sure you come home safely from this ghastly war. Bob told me what you'll be doing – please, please take great care. You have kids and you're a link with Bob. I couldn't stand losing you as well.'

Mo's last comment had hit a nerve. George's last leave had been tense at times. They all knew he would be posted overseas. The invasion had stalled, to an extent, and was making slow progress in Normandy. It was unlikely he would be sent to France until things were moving forward again. Joan had pressurised him relentlessly to find a way to stay in England and he had had to reiterate endlessly this was not possible. He would have to go wherever he was posted. She had echoed Mo's final words, saying again and again that he must not forget he had responsibilities to all of them and particularly to Martina and Mark. He knew he never would, but their conversation had left him wondering what would happen if he didn't come back.

Probably Joan's parents would step in. They would ensure they were all cared for and provide support as they were doing already. It was galling at times to find himself sidelined, but it was a comfort to know they'd all be looked after if he was no longer there. He hoped Alice and Joe would play a part if that became necessary. He sat down that evening and wrote a "just in case" letter to his sister.

***

15 JUNE 1944

Restless night. Can't stop thinking about Bob and Mo. He was an amazing friend. They were amazing together. We've never managed to get that close. What does Joan want from me? I'm not sure I know. I'm not sure I've ever really known. She pressures me to try to get a discharge. There's no doubt she wants me home as a father and husband – our own family unit. As a lover? Not so sure. But we were closer when we first knew each other. We shared things. Has she changed – have I changed? I don't know. Perhaps we both have. Maybe Mo and Bob's marriage was exceptional and most of us will never be able to match it. Will we get closer when I'm home again full-time? I don't know. Whatever we do manage, I know I must settle for what I have. A home and two wonderful kids. It's more than many have.

***

3 September 1944

We're off. Exactly five years from the declaration of war. The invasion troops broke out from Normandy some weeks ago. Our guys are now moving rapidly north and east across France with the Germans in retreat. We're following.

***

18 September 1944

Got to Brussels three days ago. The men thought it was a bit of a joyride. No resistance. Sure as hell it'll all change when we hit the German border. We roared through the farmlands of northern France and into Belgium. Nothing slowed our progress. Our route ran close to the Western Front of the last war – past cemeteries and signposts to places with names we knew so well – Arras, Vimy, Ypres and, a little further away, Mons and Le Cateau. Difficult to believe these fertile fields were once the devastated landscape I remember from photographs of twenty-five years ago. The macabre thought crossed my mind that they had been well fertilized by the bones of our predecessors.

Greeted warmly in France but like heroes in Belgium. Belgian, British, American flags everywhere. Crowds went mad, waving and blowing kisses. Bands playing. Flowers thrown. The trucks looked like mobile florists when we got to Brussels. Whenever we

*stopped women climbed onto the trucks hugging and
kissing us, handing out food and beer. I suspect some
of the men were offered the opportunity to indulge in
a little more. I'm sure some took up that offer.*

The Guards Armoured Division had advanced four
hundred miles in nine days, the last seventy-five in a single
day. Brussels had been liberated on the day George had
landed. His troop was attached to the Guards and caught
up with them in Brussels. He was unsure how the toffs in
the Guards would adapt to a jumped-up Geordie officer.
He was even more apprehensive when he discovered
they would, at first, be sharing their officers' mess. He
was relaxing with a pint that first evening when he was
approached by a Guards major who looked closely at his
collar badges. 'Oh my God, you bloody grease monkeys
get everywhere.'

George looked directly at him. He may have been a
major but that riled him. 'You should be grateful we do.
The full motto is "Ubique Quo Fas et Gloria Ducunt" –
everywhere that right and glory lead.'

'Ah, a Geordie scholarship boy.'

That really got up his nostrils. He broadened his
Geordie accent. 'You wouldn't have got this far without our
lot providing landing facilities and clearing obstacles. The
race through Belgium might have been a picnic but that'll
change. You'll need us again. The Siegfried Line for sure has
no bloody washing on it. And another thing, you'll need my
mine lifting expertise if you're not to be blasted to buggery.
No more grouse moors if that happens.' He hesitated before

adding, 'Sir.' He had been about to address him as "mate" but thought that would be pushing his luck.

The major looked at him hard for a few moments before laughing. 'Alright – point taken. I'll get you another drink for services about to be rendered.'

***

24 MAY 1945

Eight months on. War in Europe may be over but nothing much has changed for us. Still sitting on the German border. Life was grim in the southern Dutch provinces but far worse further north and west. They had been deliberately starved by the Germans. Thousands died in the "hunger winter" that's now over. Some relief from Operation Manna, when food dropped by Lancasters, and Operation Chowhound, the Yank mission. The locals had to wait for the German surrender before they were liberated – only three weeks ago.

The advance had stalled towards the end of 1944 and the ambition to reach Berlin before the end of that year, ahead of the Russians, had come to nothing. Plans to establish a salient by taking the bridges across the Maas, the Waal, the canals and finally the Rhine at Arnhem in Operation Market Garden had failed. The Americans had taken Aachen after a bloody battle in October – the first German city to fall. But progress towards the centre of Germany had then come to a halt. The strategists had insisted that the Roer River Dams to the east of the Hürtgen Forest should be taken before advancing further, to prevent the Germans breaching them and flooding allied troops downstream. It was planned that the approach should be directly through the Hürtgen. It was an abysmal area through which to advance. The forest was riven by deep, heavily wooded valleys with broad upland plateaux and few tracks and roads. The terrain was difficult for tanks, challenging for artillery and impossible to achieve adequate air cover. The area had been well prepared by the Germans with bunkers, minefields, barbed wire, and booby-traps. The small number of routes and clearings had allowed German machine-gun, mortar and artillery teams to pre-range their weapons. The weather was atrocious that autumn and worse still in the winter, with sleet, snow and mist. The battle had been a German defensive victory.

It was February before the Roer Dams were finally taken by the Americans, only to find that the retreating Germans had left the sluices open, further delaying the advance. They finally reached Cologne in early March, just forty miles east of Aachen. They got there two days before the capture of the Ludendorff Bridge at Remagen further up the river. Attention had been diverted away from the Hürtgen by the German last ditch Ardennes offensive – the Battle of the Bulge. The Hürtgen might have become a forgotten battle but the forest was to become all too well known to George.

***

26 August 1945

Summoned to Divisional HQ near the German border to see the CO.

'I've work for you, Brown. No more loafing around in the mess now the boundaries of the occupation zones have been agreed. We're responsible for mine clearance in our Zone. That means you.' George nodded. 'You'll be in command of the Mine Clearing Office in Aachen. It's a large area.' He unrolled a map and pointed with the stem of his pipe. 'Your area will be from the Belgian and Dutch borders here in the west to Euskirchen, Düren, Julich and Roer in the east and from Monschau and Schleiden in the south up to Geilenkirchen and Erkelenz in the north.'

George looked at the map. 'Good God, that looks to be about 1800 square kilometres. What resources will I have?'

'I'll come to that. This area is very heavily mined and there are all too few of you trained in mine clearance.' He gave a sly smile. 'I wonder why so few of you signed up for it.'

'I'm beginning to wonder that as well, Sir.'

'Well, you did and that's all there is to it. Here's the plan. Most of the clearance will be done by Mine Clearance Service Groups or Dienstgruppen. These will be groups of German POWs, mainly from their Pioneer Corps. Some, possibly many, will need training. We're planning on six groups to be supervised by the Aachen Office, each led by a German Arbeitsleiter. Each will consist of 100 to 150 men. Recruiting them will take some time. Training will be shared by your team and the Germans with the greatest expertise. They should, after all, know about their own bloody devices and it'll be in their interests to co-operate. They'll be as keen to survive as you are. You'll be responsible for planning and overseeing operations, meeting group leaders daily, setting targets and ensuring all areas have been fully cleared and details recorded.'

George gulped. This was a massive job both in terms of the enormity of the task and in man management. 'What men will I have in my team at base and how many will I be able to deploy in the field to supervise operations?'

'Many of our lot will be going home soon. The most we can give you will be a SQMS, a sergeant, both regulars, and fifteen other ranks, including three experts. A number of vehicles will be allocated to you. I can't give you an exact number just now. Two other things. First, a deadline has been set for the clearance of all mines by the end of July 1947. Second, the plan was that each Mine Clearing Office should be led by a major supported by a junior officer. We just don't have the personnel for this. You'll be promoted to Captain. This, I imagine, will see you through until you're demobbed.' There was a pause as he lit and drew deeply on his pipe. 'Unless you enjoy it so much that you choose to take a regular commission.' George smiled and raised his eyebrows. 'I thought you might not leap with joy at that suggestion. Your posting starts next month. We've taken over a school building. Your unit will be based there. There's room in the grounds for a secure area for your vehicles and gear and temporary accommodation for your men. There's one other unit there providing admin staff for the city.'

'I guess that's the next question: how do I liaise with the civil administration?'

'There is no civil administration. It's us. Monty has made it clear that he only wants to hear good news, or even better, no news at all. And our political masters in London don't want to hear anything either. They're too pre-occupied with issues at home.'

'How about liaison with German personnel? I know almost no German.'

'Your NCOs are good and your sergeant speaks German fluently. We'll try to ensure that each Arbeitsleiter speaks English. If not, it'll be one of the senior members of the group.'

'I wonder if it might be sensible for me to learn some German. I'd feel uncomfortable not being able to talk directly to the men.'

'We don't have the time or the facilities to organise a crash course for you.'

'Perhaps, there's a local German teacher I could approach?'

'Not a good idea, Brown. There's a strict edict against fraternisation. Our masters insist that all contacts with locals must be strictly professional and formal. And formal means organised and overseen by the military administration.'

'I don't want to fraternise, Sir. I simply want to learn some of the lingo to make it easier to manage the teams. I'm sure no German teacher will have particularly warm feelings towards us.'

'Brown, you never know. Some are wanting to ingratiate themselves with us and some have questionable motives.

There are a lot of chancers and opportunists out there. The powers that be worry that contact could lead to socialising with possibly disastrous consequences.' He paused as he relit his pipe. 'We've also been warned that the Nazis trained some assassins in the last months of the war. They're called werewolves. They're meant to be the core of a resistance movement and breathe new life into the Reich. It hasn't come to much but there are still some fanatics and loonies out there. They've assassinated the Bürgermeister of Aachen we'd appointed. Some may still be hanging around.' He paused again. 'But I see your point. If you find someone suitable, you can make preliminary contact. But you mustn't make any arrangement until they've been screened and approved. You have a little over three weeks while we assemble the rest of your section, the Dienstgruppen, equipment and vehicles. You should spend two weeks in Aachen with the SQMS and the sergeant. They've been tasked with getting everything together. Then you can take ten days' home leave. You won't be getting any more for some time.'

George met the sergeant the following day. 'Redpath, Sir,' he said. The surname was a local one and the accent was familiar.

'Good to have a fellow Geordie on the team.'

'With respect, Sir, not a Geordie. I'm a Wearsider – I'm from Sunderland.'

George grinned. 'I guess I can overlook that. I'm sure the Magpies will be back in the first division to sort you lot out once the League is up and running again.'

'Not so sure about that, Sir.'

'We shall see. Tomorrow 0600 – we'll set off to recce our patch and find our base and billets.'

The next morning they picked up the SQMS, Thwaites, who was a Lancastrian. He and Redpath had served together before and knew each other well. They commented later they were pleased that the officer-in-charge was "one of them" and not a toff.

The trio with their driver headed over the border and south-east towards Aachen. They stopped as they reached the Siegfried Line. They left the truck and edged carefully around the anti-tank "dragon's teeth", five rows deep, of varying heights, a metre and more high, and reinforced by forts, bunkers, pillboxes and barbed wire. They walked a short distance along one of the cleared tracks. Their driver had brewed some tea and handed them mugs as they leant back against the concrete "teeth". It was an awe-inspiring sight as Hitler's "westwall" stretched out towards the horizon and on for nearly four hundred miles to a point close to the Swiss border. They took photographs of themselves by the line and then drove on silently in a sombre mood. They crossed over the Roer Triangle. The damage resulting from the clearance of the area was all too plain – ruined houses, burnt out vehicles, abandoned weapons, discarded backpacks, derelict homesteads and the stench of the decaying bodies of livestock.

The challenges were formidable. The first tasks would be to map the area in one kilometre squares, decide what equipment and transportation would be required, establish a method for record keeping and agree arrangements for effective communication between the Office and the Clearance Groups.

They drove into the city and located the school building which would be their base. They decided to orient themselves by walking to the centre. Aachen had not initially suffered the same level of bombing as many cities, but that had changed in the six weeks in which it was encircled before and during the battle the previous October. They were stunned by the extent of the destruction. There were few people on the streets. Only eleven thousand civilians had remained at the end of the war, from a pre-war population of over one hundred and fifty thousand. Many had fled but residents were slowly returning – though to what?

The ancient centre had been almost totally razed to the ground. The cathedral was still standing although badly damaged. Four-fifths of the city had been reduced to rubble. Few houses were undamaged. Many remaining buildings were unstable and open to the elements. Walls had been ripped away leaving rooms with only two or three sides remaining, exposing the sad detritus of families whose homes, and probably lives, had been abruptly and violently destroyed. The ziggurat imprint of staircases was visible on exposed walls. Few were fit for human habitation although many were occupied. People were living in derelict buildings without water, heating or light and little protection from the weather. Washing was hung out on protruding spars. The smells were all pervasive. The acrid stink of sewage mingled with the odours of food being prepared over open fires fuelled by combustible materials scavenged from damaged buildings. The fetid stench of decay and putrefaction permeated everything. Fragments of brick and concrete crunched under foot. A pall of gritty dust hung in the air. It was difficult to conceive how Aachen or any city could ever rise from such ruins and live again.

George and his colleagues were watched impassively by women looking out from their stopgap homes. Those on the streets walked past, heads down, staying close to the sides, some carrying pails of water filled from water carts. Others were shifting rubble by hand. Mangy dogs were foraging in the wreckage. There were few men. The major signs of life came from the children – ragged, many of them barefoot, skinny and some with missing limbs following their peers on makeshift crutches. Some were scrambling over the ruins, scavenging or playing adventure games. Others surrounded them, hands held out: 'Tommy, Tommy – chockies, ciggies, food.' They gave what little they had and were surrounded by ever-increasing numbers. Redpath explained they had no more to give. He turned to George. 'They reckon we're a dead loss. They said the Yanks were much more generous. Bloody Yanks. One of the kids even offered me his sister in exchange for food.' George was increasingly concerned that he knew nothing of the language. Redpath spoke it fluently but it would not be a good use of his expertise if he were to monopolise his time as an interpreter. And it was essential that he remained with the team and was not appropriated by some other unit with a more senior officer-in-charge.

The next day George left Thwaites to make a preliminary assessment of equipment and their logistic needs. He and Redpath set off in the truck to delineate the areas they would be required to map and clear. It amounted to 1789 kilometre squares – close to George's original eyeballing estimate. George then made contact with the local administration which was in the hands of a harassed infantry major. It was no more than a courtesy call. He was struggling to establish some form of civil administration and organisation which would meet the urgent needs of people for water, food, fuel, power, sanitation, transport, education and medical facilities. As he said despairingly, 'This was not a job I was trained to do.' George was tempted to say that the sappers had the necessary skills to face many of these challenges, but he had a different job to do.

***

29 AUGUST 1945

The destruction is unbelievable. The damage in London from the Blitz is minor by comparison. I was close to tears when I saw those skinny, hungry, ragged, maimed kids. How lucky I am to have Marty and Mark. Thank God they're safe. Things may be difficult at home with rationing but they can look forward to a future. Can any of the kids here look forward to a future? Can this country ever recover? I keep looking at the snap in my wallet of Joan and the kids which I took last June. How happy they look. That was my last leave – how they will have grown. If only I was in control of my life and could get home and be a father and a husband again.

8

3 December 1989

Mark had arrived home to an empty house a few minutes before four. It was almost dark. He had been at the paper since early that morning. He was sitting disconsolately at his desk. He leant back in his chair staring vacantly at the computer screen. The room was almost in darkness. His face was dimly lit by the spectral glow of the screen. A little additional light filtered in through the window from a nearby streetlight. He drummed his fingers idly on the desk. There was nothing he could do until the text of the official communiqué from the summit was phoned through. He heard the front door open. 'Ellie,' he called out, 'I'm in here. I was wondering where you were.' Michael stuck his head round the corner of the door. 'It's me. Why are you sitting in the dark?' He flicked the switch and closed the curtains. 'I've just popped home to get some clean clothes. Where's Mum?'

'Haven't a clue. I think she said she might be out for

the day. I'm not sure she said where. To be honest, I wasn't paying a lot of attention.'

'Well, I'm going to have a cup of tea.' He grinned. 'Still drying out after last night. You want one?' Mark nodded. 'Biscuit?' He nodded again.

Michael was back a few minutes later and sat in the leather armchair, putting his feet on the coffee table. 'You're not exactly a bundle of fun today. What's up?'

Mark shrugged. 'Nothing in particular. Just waiting for the newsroom to phone through.'

'Why not listen to the news?'

'I will. But I need the exact wording of this communiqué. The words of these things always require decoding – reading between the lines.'

'Suspicious?'

'Have to be. As George Orwell said, "Journalism is printing what someone else doesn't want printed – everything else is public relations".'

'Will Germany have been on the agenda?'

'Bound to.'

'Have you read what German Granny sent?' Mark grunted. 'Is that a yes?'

'Yes.'

'It's awesome – bit like a scenario for a film. I'd no idea how bad it was. What did Mum say about it?'

'Not much. She read it twice the other evening and then handed it to me. She sat for a long time looking very down. I read it and tried to talk to her but she said she couldn't talk about it and went off to bed.'

'Do you think she'd talk to me? And how about Oma

when she's here? It would be great for my dissertation, especially if they can write some more about their time after the end of the war.'

'I don't know. Tread carefully.'

'Okay. So how's your Daddy project going?'

'Alright. I've got to the point where he's arrived in Germany. That's only about a quarter of the way through. I guess I'll learn more from the rest. It's slow going. There's a lot of it and some's quite technical.'

Two hours later Michael left to go back to his digs and Mark was getting anxious. He pulled the curtains back from time to time and peered out. It was getting misty. It was after seven when he finally saw Gisela getting out of a car he didn't recognise and wave to the occupants as they drove off.

Mark walked out to the hall. 'Where have you been and who the hell were those people?'

Gisela looked at him, taken aback by the accusatory tone. 'Out,' she said briefly and started to go upstairs.

'Hold on. Is that all you've got to say? Obviously you've been out – but where?'

'Mark, this is our home. I don't interrogate you when you come home late. Which you often do.'

'That's inevitable with my job. So, where have you been? It's a Sunday, you can't have been at the gallery.'

'I don't feel much like telling you anything if you're going to be so bloody aggressive.'

'Okay,' he said grumpily. 'Where have you been? I was worried.'

'If you really want to know I took up your friend's

invitation to visit his house and see his bronzes. They're impressive. So is the house and the estate. And my bronzes are very prominently displayed.'

'Why didn't you bloody tell me you were going to see him?'

'Because you simply didn't bother to ask. You obviously weren't interested when I said I might be out for the day, so I saw no reason to tell you. Anyway, I knew you'd make a fuss. I decided I'd prefer to put up with your stroppiness afterwards.'

'God, you can be bloody devious. And I keep telling you Sandy's not my fucking friend and I hope he's not yours either. He's a contact.'

'For me too. You said on Friday you'd be working over the weekend because of this Malta summit and you went out very early. I didn't want to sit around on a wet Sunday, on my own at home. So, I rang Sandy and he invited me for lunch. As it happens, I had an enjoyable and interesting day. He's a very good host.'

'Ellie, I've warned you about him – he just wants to screw you.'

'Maybe he does want to fuck me – is that such a strange thing for someone to want to do? But he certainly made no move to do so. Anyway, there were others there for lunch. One was a senior lecturer in modern European history and there was another backbencher and a journalist, Sebastian something or other, from the Telegraph. Said he knew you.'

'Sebastian Morris, he's a creep.'

'For God's sake, stop being so bloody negative.'

'So, what did you talk about?'

'A lot about Germany and reunification. The historian guy asked if I would put some of my memories in writing. And there was a lot about this summit. Sandy also showed them my bronzes and enthusiastically talked up my work.' Mark grunted. 'The others were there with their wives. There were eight of us altogether.'

'Well, Sandy must have loved it when you invited yourself so he had a woman as well. You were just Sandy's bit of skirt.'

Gisela coloured. 'That's bloody insulting.'

'I keep telling you he's a lecher.'

'I've had more than enough of this. Why are you being so fucking antagonistic? Is it because I'm doing my own thing or is it tensions at the paper? Even when there aren't rows, you have your nose in your parents' papers and scarcely notice me. You're bloody impossible at the moment.'

Mark stopped, then said a little more quietly, 'Sorry, but that guy worries me.'

'How about a little trust? Just remember I learned very early on how to look after myself, much earlier than you ever had to. And remember I'm an independent person. It was good to talk to people who wanted to hear my views and to talk about Germany's future.'

'Well, you didn't seem prepared to do it for me.'

'That's not fair. You know why I didn't want to be involved. You've read what Mutti wrote. Have you no idea how tough that must have been for her to write and painful for me to read? I'll put some of my memories on paper now for Michael and you. It may make you a bit more understanding.'

The row was brought to an abrupt end by a ring on the doorbell. Mark opened the door to find his sister standing outside with a small suitcase. 'I've a meeting in London tomorrow,' she said without preamble. 'Can you put me up for the night? I'll go to a hotel if it's not convenient.'

'No, that'll be fine.'

Gisela was standing behind him. 'Come in, Marty. You've come at a good time.'

'Why's that?'

'Never mind. We were a bit at odds about something. You don't want to hear about it and I certainly don't want to hear any more about it.' She gave Mark a sharp glance and then looked more closely at Marty. Her sister-in-law was looking very tense. 'What's up?'

'I'm not sure I want to talk much either. I was going to come down early tomorrow but I needed to get away. I need to work out what to do to get us out of the mess Paul's got us into.'

Gisela put her arms around her. 'Go upstairs, Marty, and dump your bag in the spare room. We'll get you a drink.'

'Large G and T please.'

'Ice and lemon?' Martina nodded.

Mark looked at Gisela. 'She looks shaken. She's normally so under control. I know she worries about Paul's drinking but there must be something else.'

Gisela handed Martina her drink when she came down twenty minutes later. She sank into an armchair, head down, nursing her glass with both hands. It was clear she had been crying. Gisela sat close by and put a hand on her arm. 'Marty, we all have tensions in our marriages from time to time.' She looked at Mark and raised her eyebrows. 'Do you want to talk?'

There was a long pause before Martina looked up. 'I don't much, but I should. What's happened may affect you as well.'

'How come?'

'I don't quite know where to start.'

'We know you've been worried about Paul's boozing. Has that got out of hand?'

'No, well no more than usual. It's only part of the problem.'

'Go on.'

'It's not only drinking. Paul gambles. It was trivial at first and seemed harmless enough. He would say it was just a little flutter. But it's become much more than that. I stupidly don't check our joint bank account very often but I did last week. He's almost entirely cleaned us out. When I confronted him, he admitted he had been gambling more heavily and had lost extremely heavily.'

'Do you need financial help?'

'Yes, but I can sort that. I've tried to be sympathetic.' She took a drink and shook her head. 'Difficult when he's been so bloody stupid.'

'Presumably you can arrange counselling and professional help.'

'I was starting to do that but everything came to a head on Friday. He didn't get up for breakfast. Said he was taking a day off. I was surprised as he'd not mentioned it before. Said he needed time to think. That's not like Paul.'

'What then?'

'A couple of hours later I got a call at work from a

neighbour. She said there were police and reporters at the house. I got a colleague to cover and shot home. The neighbour said Paul had been taken away in a police car. I went to the station and they let me see him. It seems he's not only been using our money but he's been helping himself to clients' funds at work. He was suspended by his partners four days ago.'

'What now?'

'He's been charged. He's on police bail. Some of the funds he filched are from Mum's estate.'

'Oh God, how much?'

'I don't know. Nobody knows yet. His partners are working on it.'

'But what was he doing on the earlier days after he was suspended?'

'Gambling with the little he could get his hands on. He stupidly believed that one big win would put everything right and he would replace the money and nobody would ever know. You don't need to be a genius to guess how that worked out.'

'How can he have been so dumb?'

'I'm so sorry.' Martina put her glass down, leant forward and put her elbows on her knees. Mark took the glass and mixed her another drink.

'Here, you need a top-up.' He placed the glass on the side table. 'What will you do?'

'I'm not sure. The marriage hasn't amounted to much for some time. It started to go wrong when we found out we couldn't have kids.'

'We'd assumed that was your choice.'

'No.' She hesitated. 'I've never said any of this before. We'd been desperate to have kids but it didn't happen. When we were investigated, it turned out that the problem was with Paul. He was devastated. I think that was the tipping point. I couldn't say anything to anyone. It would have destroyed him.'

Gisela went over and sat on the arm of her chair. She put an arm round her. 'Marty, I'm so sorry.' She kissed her gently on the cheek.

'I don't know what to do. I can't turn him out. He's nowhere to go – and no money.'

'What'll happen now?'

'He'll appear before magistrates in a week or so. I don't know if this can be dealt with by them or if it'll go to a crown court. And I don't know what'll happen or if he'll get a custodial sentence.'

'What about the money?'

'I think his firm will have to make good. Fortunately the losses aren't enormous. And they're partly at fault for not having better controls in place. Whatever happens, his legal career is over. I don't know what he'll do.'

'Oh God, that's awful – for both of you. Our little spat was trivial by comparison.' Mark nodded.

'I just wanted to be somewhere other than home.'

'What's Paul doing now?'

'I don't know and I don't care. He was out so I left a note saying I'd be back in a couple of days. I should have asked – would it be alright if I stayed a second night after my meeting tomorrow?' They nodded. 'I'll get the early train back on Tuesday.'

Gisela looked at Martina. 'Don't you think you should call? It's just possible he might do something foolish. Whatever he's done, it might be better if he knows where you are.'

'Not Paul,' she said dismissing the implication that he might self-harm.

'Marty, it is possible he might do something stupid after a few drinks. Would you mind if I called him?'

'Ellie's right.'

'I suppose not. Anyhow, I can't stop you.'

Gisela was back a few minutes later. 'Paul's alright, just. He's more than a little pissed. It was worth calling. He's feeling very sorry for himself.'

'Are you surprised? But you were right. I'll call him tomorrow.'

Gisela put small bowls of nuts and crisps beside Martina. 'I'll organise something to eat in a few minutes – this'll keep us going for now.'

'For God's sake, let's talk about something else. Mark, what's happening in the big world out there? What's this summit all about?'

'A lot. I've been busy. It's not only you doctors who work long and unsocial hours. Political journalists do too – sometimes. We don't just occupy intervals between bouts of heavy drinking by filling in highly inflated expense claim forms.'

'Okay, so what's going on?'

'It's been very lively since the fall of the Wall. Kohl has laid out a plan which could lead to unification. Bush and Gorbachev are meeting on a Soviet cruiser moored off Malta.' He laughed. 'They're certainly not sunning themselves. The weather's atrocious. They're calling it the seasick summit. They've effectively said the Cold War is over – well we'll see. Other leaders are generally positive.'

'Why only generally? Surely, this is good news.'

'Our glorious prime minister, the dominatrix Maggie, has welcomed the unfreezing of relations but she's equivocal about German reunification. It's said she muttered that we'd beaten them twice and now they were back again. I'm told she carries a map of Germany showing the 1937 borders in her handbag. She brandishes it in the face of other European leaders to emphasise the scale of the Germany problem as she sees it. I think she's also miffed she wasn't invited to the summit.'

'I heard that at lunch,' interjected Gisela. 'Sebastian, whatever his name is, said she's worried about the possibility of a fourth Reich. He also said the French are worried and Andreotti apparently commented that he loved Germany so much he preferred it when there were two of them.'

Martina looked quizzically at Gisela. 'Whoever have you been lunching with?'

'Let's not go there. Ellie's been keeping some dodgy company. Less said the better.' Gisela was about to say something but Mark went on quickly. 'This has been a source of tension between me and my editor. He follows Maggie slavishly, a bit like a spaniel. I've been working over the weekend trying to write a piece which will satisfy him without compromising my integrity.'

'Does that mean you're for reunification?'

'Absolutely, anyhow it's inevitable. It'll happen whatever this prime minster thinks or says.'

'And what about you, Ellie?'

Martina's question was one which had dominated her thinking for the last month. There was no single or simple answer. She paused before answering. 'There'll be some reservations but I'm sure it'll happen whatever your prime minister says or does.'

'Your prime minister too.'

'I'm not sure I want to accept ownership of Maggie.'

'But you always said you've never felt a strong sense of attachment to Germany.'

'That's beginning to change. I think I might need to reconnect.' But it was unclear how she might start to do this or where it might lead.

Martina looked across at her sister-in-law. 'Talking about Germany, has Mark involved you in his obsession about our father's papers?'

Mark butted in. 'I tried to involve Ellie but she doesn't want to know.'

'My memories of that time are very painful. I've tried to leave them behind.'

'But you seem prepared to reminisce with others.'

'Mark, we said we'd put our differences aside for now. We'll talk about it later. Marty doesn't want to hear this.'

Martina looked questioningly at them but said nothing. She turned to Mark. 'I did say you should let me know what was in those papers. You'd better tell me what you've turned up.'

'Not much so far. The journals are revealing but progress has been slow as I've been busy.'

'And?'

'The first bit's quite straightforward. Dad came from Newcastle. He had an older sister called Alice. You probably remember her. She had two boys – our cousins. They're only referred to by their first names, but it's a start. I'm guessing they're about ten years older than us. I'm hoping to find marriage and birth certificates.'

'Yes, I remember going to Newcastle for a holiday. What else?'

'I've only got to 1945 so far. It's intriguing and some of it's a little unsettling.'

'Go on.'

'The diaries are detailed and quite revealing. On the home front, their married life was dominated by Granny and Grandpa.'

'No surprise there.'

'Agreed. It seems Dad wasn't a hundred percent accepted by them. The earliest entries are mainly factual. The later ones are much more personal. I think he saw them as an emotional outlet. One thing's clear, they were both very committed to us.'

'That figures. Even if Mum was a little controlling.'

'The diary entries are backed up by some letters but there's only one side of the correspondence – from Dad to Mum. There may've been others. I can only draw inferences from his side but it's obvious the relationship became more distant as time went on.'

'Are they very impersonal?'

'No. They're affectionate but not passionate. I don't think romantic love letters were his thing. They tend to be emollient and defensive.' He fetched a few and handed one over. 'This one from early January 1942 throws a lot of light on the marriage.' Martina read it and put it aside.

'You're right – definitely affectionate. Had it occurred to you that you're probably the product of those "creature comforts" he refers to so delicately?'

'No, but you're probably right.'

'It sounds as if they might have been in short supply.'

'It didn't really surprise me. Mum was never much of a one for physical contact or hugs.'

'Sex is more of an occasional duty than a pleasure for some women – essential if you want kids although it doesn't necessarily work out,' she said shaking her head sadly.

Gisela looked at Mark. 'There you are. You're the result of, how do you say in this country, a bit of "how's your father". Well, if you're right then he was alright on the night.' Marty and Mark looked at her and burst out laughing.

'I love the way you still mangle some of our idioms.'

'I'm still not sure why you want to spend time obsessing about the past although it's beginning to sound a bit more interesting. What else have you dug up?'

'I've still not been able to trace a death certificate. The name doesn't help. There were far too many George Browns. I need to do some more digging. The rest so far is simply a record of the marriage and his military career. I'll summarise it and send it on to you.'

'That would be good, but don't forget you promised to destroy personal documents unread.'

'Absolutely,' he grinned, 'but I need to look first to see what's personal and what's not.'

'That's pure casuistry and you know it. You always were bloody devious.'

9

3 September 1945

George

Ten days' home leave – a day lost at either end travelling. Great to see the kids. First time for more than a year. God knows how long the army is going to hang onto me. Should I have volunteered for mine clearance? Too bloody late now. Caught up with Mo.

George walked up the hill from the station. The children were playing in the garden. Marty saw him first. She ran over and hugged his legs. He dropped his kitbag, picked her up and kissed her. 'You must kiss Polly too,' she said holding up the rag doll in her hand. 'She likes to be hugged and kissed. We like lots of hugs.' Mark looked on uncertainly. Marty smiled at her brother, 'It's Daddy, he's come home to play with us.'

Mark went over to George cautiously. He put Marty down and crouched beside his son, placing a hand gently on his shoulder. He sized George up for a few seconds and then took a step closer. It was not the time to push it. They had eight days to re-acquaint themselves. 'So, what have you been doing this summer while I've been away?'

Unsurprisingly, Marty took command. 'We went on holiday with Granny and Grandpa. We wanted to go to the seaside but they said it wasn't safe. So we went to a farm and we helped with the chickens and the ducks and collected the eggs and had rides on a tractor. Mark specially liked the tractor.'

'Sounds good. Do you want to live on a farm when you're grown up and be a farmer?'

'Don't be silly, Daddy. Farmers are men. Girls can't be farmers. They can only be farmers' wives.'

'There are lots of farm girls now.'

'Mummy said that was because there was a war. Anyway, I don't want to be a farmer. Farms are very poohy. Have you been on holiday? Mummy said you were in another country.'

'She's right, but it wasn't a holiday.'

'Have you been fighting? Did you kill people?'

'No, I've been helping the soldiers who had to fight.' Perhaps what he had been and would be doing was better than being in the firing line. He had never felt entirely at ease with the possibility that he might have to discharge a weapon in anger.

'Mummy said all the fighting was over and the bad people had been beaten. Granny and Grandpa took us to London to see the flags. There were lots and lots of people and everyone was laughing and walking all over the road and calling for the King and the Queen to come out and wave. Then they did and we waved back. Will you come and live with us now there's no more fighting?'

The words continued to fall out at a rate of knots. George was acutely aware of how little he had seen of his children and saddened by the extent to which he was not part of their lives – merely an occasional visitor. 'I'll be home as soon as I can but fighting makes a big mess and people have to clear it up.'

'You should make the bad people who made the mess do it.'

'We will, but we need to make sure they do it properly. Where's Mummy?'

'In the kitchen.'

He took both their hands and headed for the kitchen. Joan was bending over the table preparing the kids' tea. He went up behind her, put his arms round her waist and kissed her gently on the back of her neck. She jumped. 'I'm sorry – I didn't mean to make you jump. Turn round so I can kiss you properly and give you a hug.'

'Oh, not just now, George. I'm getting tea ready and there's flour on my apron.'

Marty piped up. 'Daddy gave me a big hug and a kiss. Don't you want one as well?'

Joan turned to face him. 'I'm sorry.' She wiped her hands on her apron, took it off, put her arms around him briefly and then stood back. 'Is that better?'

'Yes, and I'll want to do that again.' It was a rather cool reception and far from the welcome he had longed for through the tedium of the dreary journey home by rail and ferry. George raised his hand and caressed Joan's cheek. 'It's wonderful to be back.' He had been haunted by the thought that their prolonged periods of separation might have led to the uncoupling of his marriage. He yearned to be home permanently and have the opportunity to create the warmth and family closeness which had shaped his own childhood. If only he could be demobbed soon – if only.

Marty tugged at the hem of her mother's cardigan. 'I had to tell Mark this was our Daddy,' she said in a superior manner. 'He didn't give him a kiss but boys don't kiss other boys.' She took George's hand. 'Come out again and play and can we go to our bridge again? We haven't been for ages.'

He smiled. 'We can play after I've put my things upstairs and changed out of this uniform. I'll be in big trouble if I make my uniform messy.'

'And you two will be in trouble as well if you make your clothes messy. Playing will have to be after tea now.'

He spent an hour in the garden with the kids later. Mark had a lightweight multi-coloured football and they kicked it around for a time. Marty soon got bored and took him off to a shrubby area at the rear of the garden to see her private den. 'You must take us and dolly Polly to our bridge tomorrow,' she said.

***

Joan announced that William and Helen had handed over their meat coupons for the week and were coming round for supper. She had taken advantage of the additional meat and had added beans and some root vegetables to make a large shepherd's pie. 'It's a welcome home meal. It won't be a feast. There seems to be no end to this rationing. Mum and Dad are keen to see you too.' George was a little disappointed. He had hoped for a quiet evening with Joan but perhaps this was a positive step towards rebuilding his family. Joan's parents arrived with a bottle of claret, already decanted. They raised their glasses. 'Here's to your return home – permanently.'

William turned to George a few minutes later. 'The war in Europe's been over for four months. When will you be demobbed and back home?'

'I wish I knew. More than three million of us have been in uniform. It's taking time.'

'But you were a volunteer. Surely you can just resign your commission?'

'Sadly it's not as simple as that. The Emergency Regulations are still in place and most of us were volunteers.'

'How about release on compassionate grounds?'

'I could ask but it'd be turned down. There are thousands of us with families. We all desperately want to get home. Compassionate discharge is for things like a seriously ill wife or parent.'

'Maybe, but have you tried?' George shook his head.

'Your family needs you. Mark and Martina need a father at home,' said Helen.

George nodded. Was there a subtext, a coded message, behind that remark? Was her hope that his presence would reduce the influence Edna had on Joan and her involvement with the kids? 'Whatever are you doing in Germany now?'

George wasn't prepared to confess what his task would be. 'A lot of repair work. The damage is unbelievable. Far worse than here. Engineers are badly needed.'

'But why should we do it? Let them clear up their own mess.'

'They will. But there are huge shortages of men and equipment and millions and millions of refugees, all over Germany.'

'But that's for their government to sort out.'

George was beginning to tire of this inquisition and the increasingly acerbic tones in which the questions were being posed. 'They don't have a government,' he said sharply. 'We're an occupying force. We are the government. It's not like after the first war. They still had a government then even if it wasn't up to much.'

'Well, I think they should be left to stew in their own juice. It must be costing us a pretty penny. There's a lot of things our money should be spent on here. Everything's getting more and more difficult.'

'I know, but it is awful there. People are living in ruined buildings, orphaned children are living on the streets, lots are wounded and starving.' He shook his head. 'You've no idea how normal things are here by comparison.'

'But they're responsible. They should have known they'd be beaten if they took us on.'

George laughed. 'I don't think any country starts a war expecting to lose. We didn't actually encourage Hitler but we let him take over the Rhineland and Austria and Czechoslovakia. We just protested politely. People who warned us, like Churchill, were criticised as warmongers.'

'Well, one thing's for sure. We'll never trust them again. That's twice in our lifetime. Well, I hope you'll be home soon with your family – where you belong.'

He could assent to that wholeheartedly. The afternoon had brought home to him how much he was missing Marty and Mark as they grew and developed. He was grateful to his in-laws for their support and the time they devoted to Joan and the children. They were privileged by comparison with many kids in England and had incomparably better lives and probably more optimistic futures than those in Aachen. Finally, pleading tiredness he headed for bed. Joan followed a few minutes later after saying goodbye to her parents. She looked tense. She turned to him as he was preparing for bed. 'Why did you have to keep arguing with Mum and Dad like that?'

'I wasn't. I was trying to explain. We can't just leave the Germans to fester. The way they were treated last time meant we've had to fight again.' He thought Joan was about to say more but forestalled her by saying, 'Look, I'm tired. Can't we just go to bed?'

She looked at him. 'Why don't you sleep in the spare room tonight if you're so tired? Then there's no risk I'll disturb you if I'm restless.'

George said nothing. Was this consideration or manipulation? After the tensions of the day, he accepted the suggestion in the hope of a more relaxed few days. 'Alright,' he said emolliently. 'Why don't we go for a picnic tomorrow if it's fine? Just you, me and the kids?'

She relaxed visibly. 'Yes, we should do that.'

George had a rude awakening the following morning

as the kids ran into the room a little after six-thirty and bounced on him. 'What are you going to do with us today, Daddy?'

'Mummy and I thought we might go for a picnic and then we can play some games.'

'When can we go?'

'Well, you'll have to get dressed and have breakfast and we'll have to give Mummy time to get the picnic ready. And we need to find out what else she has to do today.'

Joan came through in a dressing gown and chased the children back to their bedrooms. 'You shouldn't encourage them to burst in like that. They know it's not allowed.'

'I really don't mind. I'm just happy to see them.'

'Well, if you're coming back to our bedroom, they'll know they can't burst in like that. I don't want them to think they can get away with things just because you're home.'

'Okay, but it's so good to see them.'

She grunted. 'Alright, but remember it's me who has to look after them nearly all the time.'

The picnic was a success. George took the children for a walk after they had eaten and they collected large bunches of wildflowers. The day in the sun had reset the mood for the remainder of his leave. The weather was good, they spent much of the time outside in the garden and Joan relaxed. Twice after tea George persuaded Joan to play the piano and they sang nursery rhymes with the children.

Two days before the end of his leave, George suggested he should go to London and see his old boss to make sure his job would be available when he was demobbed. Joan welcomed the suggestion and the implication that he was thinking actively about the future. She then surprised him by asking if he might think of a career change. He responded cautiously saying he was always happy to consider it. He was taken aback when she followed this up by suggesting he might become a regular officer. The thought had not crossed his mind, despite the slightly jocular comment made by his commanding officer. He had said nothing about that discussion to Joan.

***

George's meeting with the head of his section at Southern was brief and to the point. 'George, your job's here. We need guys like you. Engineers are essential to put the country together again. What have you been doing and when will you be back in civvy street?' George had to confess that the date of his release was uncertain and would probably not be for some months in the light of the job he had been given.

'Well, good luck and come back safely. There's certainly a job for you here, though there may be some big changes in the way the railways are run by then.'

The discussion was over in fifteen minutes. There was still half an hour before the pubs opened. He decided to go to Clapham and see Mo. He'd written a couple of times and she had replied saying she was managing and getting on with life. He went to the flat but she was out. He decided to stay in the area and have a beer in the hope that she might be back by lunchtime. He bought a newspaper and went to the pub at the end of the road he and Bob used to frequent. The road had not escaped damage. Two houses had been taken out and three more were severely damaged and boarded up. It resembled the dentition of a down-and-out, gaps and crumbling teeth. The landlord looked hard at him as he went to the bar to order his drink. 'I know you,' he said. 'You're Bob and Mo's friend. Haven't seen you for a bit.'

He nodded. 'You must blame His Majesty for that.' The landlord raised his eyebrows. It suddenly occurred to George that he might have been misunderstood. He laughed. 'No, I've not been in jug. I'm in the army and I've not been discharged yet.'

'Where have you been?'

'Germany, but home for a few days' leave. First time for a year.'

'Must be tough out there.'

'It is. I thought I'd look Mo up to see how she's getting on. I last saw her just after Bob died. She was out so I thought I'd hang around for a bit and try again. You may remember we had a bit of a do here before we went off to do our bit. Do you see Mo at all now?'

'Sure do. Wait a moment.' He went around to the back of the bar and called out, 'Mo, there's a guy here who wants to see you.'

A voice called back. 'Is he good-looking? If he's ugly, tell him to go away.'

He turned back to George. 'Are you ugly?'

'Tell her, no more than any other Geordie.'

This was repeated and a second later she appeared. 'It had to be you. It's wonderful to see you but what are you doing here? Have you been demobbed? Wait a moment.'

She lifted the flap on the bar counter and came out and put her arms around him. 'God, you're a sight for sore eyes.' She looked back to the landlord. 'Jim, can I take five minutes to talk to this guy?'

'Take ten – we're not busy.'

George bought drinks and they sat in a corner. 'This is amazing. It must be a year since I saw you. Thank you so much for writing and not forgetting. It's so good to see you. Tell me what you've been doing. Are you home for good?'

'Afraid not. Clearing all the mines is going to take an age. I won't be out any time soon. The conditions are awful. Far worse than here – and that's bad enough. I'm on leave.'

'So what are you doing here today?'

'I came up to see the boss to make sure my old job would still be there for me. That didn't take long, so I decided not to hurry home and to come and see how you were getting on.'

'Thank you, that was kind.'

'And how are you getting on?'

'Not wonderfully, but okay. I'm adapting. But tell me about Joan and the kids.'

'They're fine; the kids are great.'

She looked at him quizzically. The bar was filling up with lunchtime drinkers. 'George, I'll have to go and lend a hand. Look, what time do you have to get home? I finish at two. Why don't you have your drink and, if I know you, do the crossword and then come back to the flat with me? We can have a sandwich and talk some more if you have time.'

'Sounds good. I'm in no rush. I'll call and let Joan know I'll be a little late.'

'Good. That's settled. If it quietens down, Jim may let me go early. He's a good guy.'

Mo was free earlier than expected. George settled in the lounge of the flat which he had come to know so well in the past. It was as if nothing had changed – yet everything had changed. George looked across at Bob's favourite armchair – his personal domain. It was as if he had simply popped out for some fags or a couple of bottles of stout and would be back any moment recounting some joke he'd just heard in the off licence. The sense of a presence was overwhelming and disconcerting. He looked at Mo. 'This is like a second home to me.'

'Tell me about your first one – the posh one in Surrey.'

He smiled. 'I'd like to hear about you first. I've thought so much about you over the last year.'

'I'm alright. I'm managing.' She paused. 'No, that's not entirely true. I feel I have to say that to most people. They really don't want to hear anything else. They get embarrassed and shy away if I let them see how down I am at times. It's so good to see you. I don't have to pretend with you.'

He nodded. 'Go on.'

'The truth is, I manage some of the time. It's hard. Like you, Bob was around so little after you'd both signed up. I wake up some mornings alone and it can take some time to remember he'll not be coming back on leave and he'll not be coming back ever. Does that seem strange?' George shook his head. 'People keep saying time's a great healer. I'm not sure I believe that. They say I'll get over "it" but that's wrong. Bob wasn't "it". I can't stop thinking about what we might have been doing now – the wonderful holiday we were going to have when the war was over and all the others we might have had. We could still have done all that even if Bob only had one leg. Then I think of our plans to start a family. Even short of a leg we could have managed that.' She paused. 'That's what makes me most tearful. If he was not going to come back, a child would have been the best thing that he could have left for me. I'm not blaming him. We decided together it would be best to wait until the war was over. We just didn't think it through properly. Now it's too bloody late.'

George walked over and sat on the arm of Mo's chair. He put an arm round her shoulders. There was nothing he could say that would make things better.

She looked up at him and held his hand. 'Some things have helped. Jim and Peggy asked me to help out in the pub. They insisted they needed help but they were just being kind. I had no experience as a barmaid. I made some appalling cock-ups at the start.'

'But it got you out.'

'Yes, it did. I already knew some of the regulars, and I've developed a line in easy banter which keeps the punters happy.'

'And new friends?'

'No. Some guys think barmaids are easy game, especially if they know you're on your own.' She laughed. 'The ones who try it on are the ones I wouldn't be seen dead with and the ones I might like to get to know a bit better are always polite and respectful – and married. I won't stay there long. I'll get out and find a job. But it's helped me through some of the worst patches.'

'What about Sarah? Has Tommy come back?'

She shook her head. 'No. He must have died when his plane went down. She's still in a mess. She can't accept it. She fantasises that he's lost his memory and is wandering around somewhere. I try to keep her spirits up but it's impossible without seeming to share her fantasies. I'd like to steer her back to reality but I'm not sure I can do it. I'm not sure anyone can. I can't say, "He's gone, get over it" to her, any more than I want to hear people say it to me.'

Eventually she said slowly, 'There's a sort of emptiness in my life, a Bob-shaped hole – a very large hole. There are reminders of him everywhere: photos, little things he bought for me, some I bought for him, mementoes of his life on the railways, some of his clothes and everyday things like his tea mug. I just so miss his cheerful, noisy, messy presence. Only Bob could fill that hole. I'd like to think I might find someone sometime in the future but I'm in no rush and hints from some of the more obnoxious customers that I might be up for anything are hurtful.' She grinned. 'I haven't given anyone a slap yet but I might just do that one day.' She smiled again. 'That would bring my career as a barmaid to an abrupt end.' She looked up at him again. 'Thank you so much for coming. Now you can cheer me up by telling me all about your kids and family and life in Farnham.'

'The kids are great. Marty's five – very talkative, very bossy. I think she's probably pretty bright. Mark's not quite three and much quieter. Maybe because his sister never gives him a chance to talk. I sense he's an observer and thinks about what he sees. We've had some great times together over the last few days.' He pulled a photo out of his wallet. 'This was taken on my last leave.'

'They look fantastic and so smiley. It's wonderful to hear you talk about them. It underlines how bloody stupid we were.'

'Would you rather I didn't?'

'No, it makes me a little tearful but it's good to know about your family. I'd love to see them all sometime.'

'I'll fix it when I'm back for good.'

'You haven't said anything about Joan. How's she?'

'She's good, very organised and caring. She and the kids get lots of support from her parents.'

She looked at him questioningly. 'There seems to be something you aren't saying. Is all well between you?'

'I think so. But there are times when I feel they're a complete family without me. I guess it's understandable. It's what they've had to be. We've not been together full-time for five years. I'm the father who appears occasionally and disrupts their well-ordered life. The kids love it. I'm not so sure Joan does. But it's been a good leave.'

"Do you know when you'll be demobbed?'

'No. Joan keeps asking – as do her parents. They seemed to think we should all have been demobbed the instant the war was over. With my job there's no chance of early release.'

'What's it like out there?'

'Like nothing I've ever seen before and, hope to God, never see again. There's rubble everywhere. It will take months, years, to shift it all. And huge shortages – fuel, electricity, food and water. Kids are scavenging for food. Most are unbelievably skinny and some have awful injuries.'

'But what about you?'

'My clearance area has a huge number of mines. I'll be overseeing Germans to do this. Luckily, my sergeant speaks German, but I'm going to learn some as well. My German doesn't go much beyond "Zwei grosse Bier, bitte". Not a lot of use for mine clearance.'

'How long will it take?'

'God knows. We don't even know how many mines there are.'

'For God's sake, take care. I couldn't bear it if I were to lose you as well. What does Joan think about it?'

'She doesn't. I didn't tell her I'd been on that course.'

'Shouldn't you have done?'

'Probably, but it's too late now. She said something odd a day or two ago. She asked if I'd thought of signing up as a regular. It was strange after all she'd said about my trying to get early release. It puzzled me. Two thoughts occurred to me. First, if I were to become a regular, their lives would continue in their private little world and would only be disrupted occasionally by fun daddy coming home and stirring the kids up.'

'And are you a fun daddy?'

'I think so. I'm not there to do the messy stuff or the discipline stuff.'

'And your second thought?'

'Joan might think an army officer was higher up the social pecking order than a train driver. Yes, I know I'm not that. But I suspect she and her parents imagine me at work in a peaked cap, dirty fingernails and smears of coal dust on my face. I've been promoted. I'm now a captain.'

Mo laughed. 'You might end up as a general and then they'd have to salute you.'

'Little hope of that. Whoever heard of a general with a Geordie accent? Anyhow, it doesn't appeal.'

It was time to go. Mo hugged him. 'Thank you so much for coming. It's so wonderful to see you. You've made me feel happier than I've done since, well, you know when. Do keep in touch and, for God's sake, don't get yourself blasted into space. I couldn't bear that.'

***

15 September 1945

Wonderful leave. Slightly rocky start but I think we're beginning to get back to where we were before this bloody war started. No sign of Edna.

10

17 MARCH 1990

Mark was scanning the Europe section of The Economist while enjoying a leisurely Saturday morning breakfast. Gisela had not surfaced. His second cup of coffee was interrupted by the telephone. It was Sandy Scott. He was curious. It was usually he who initiated contact. Was Sandy about to offer him the inside track on some developing and potentially high profile political event or scandal? Perhaps there was an upside to Gisela's friendship with Sandy. 'How did you get my home number?'

'Ellie gave it to me.'

'So what can I do for you so early on a Saturday?'

'Hope I haven't caught you at a bad moment but I'd like a word with Ellie. Is she around?'

So that was it. 'No, she isn't just now,' he said brusquely. 'And I'm not sure when she will be. What's this about?'

'I was wondering if she might be free to join Bill Gilbert and me for lunch today.'

'Who the hell's he?'

'My historian friend – modern European history. She met him at lunch at my house. Didn't she tell you?'

Mark grunted. 'She said something about it but I don't remember a name being mentioned.'

'He wants to pick her brains. He's collecting personal accounts of life in Germany after the end of the war, particularly in the British Sector. He believes our pragmatic approach made an important contribution to winning the peace. Particularly relevant now with free elections in the East tomorrow and reunification on the horizon.'

'I'm not sure she's free.'

'Well, would you get her to call me? If she's free we could meet at the usual place. You might also be interested in joining us in the light of what's happening.'

Gisela appeared a moment later in gown and slippers. She poured a cup of coffee and sat at the table. 'Quiet day, I think.' She looked at Mark. 'You're looking a bit grumpy. Who was that on the phone? You sounded rather curt.'

'Your friend Sandy Scott. He asked if you could meet him today for lunch at your "usual place" to meet some guy called Bill Gilbert. You'd better call him.'

'We've nothing particular on today, have we? You said you wanted to work at home with so much happening in Europe.' Mark shook his head. 'Probably wants to follow-up our talk about Germany. You don't mind, do you? It'll leave you in peace and quiet.'

'What's this about your usual place? How often have you been seeing him? It all sounds very intimate.' Mark was tapping the table with his fingers, emphasising each word.

Gisela laughed. 'Don't look like that. There's nothing intimate about it.'

'It suggests you've been seeing a lot of him.'

'Absolutely not. We've met twice since Christmas – both times to get my opinion on a bronze. We met first for lunch in a restaurant in Dover Street, close to some of the galleries. But I've been trying to steer him away from the West End. I've introduced him to one or two sculptors so he can approach them directly and avoid paying Mayfair prices.'

'Why worry, he can afford it.'

'That's not much of a reason for paying over the odds.'

'Why haven't you told me about these assignations?'

'Mark, don't be so bloody silly. They're not assignations. I didn't say anything as you've become so stroppy about what is no more than a professional friendship.'

'Sounds like a lot more to me. I've warned you about him.'

Gisela pushed her chair back. 'As I've told you repeatedly, I don't need warning.'

'He gets into the gossip columns pictured cavorting around with glamourous women.'

'I see the papers too. And yes, he's seen from time to time with two women who are attractive but cavorting, as you call it, doesn't come into it. I've met them. They're just longstanding friends. He's quite open about it.'

'I'd have thought you were a bit on the old side by his usual standards.'

Gisela flushed. 'You really can be an absolute shit sometimes.' She was about to say something further but had second thoughts before saying, 'Mark, I've had enough of this. It is an entirely innocent and, for me, financially advantageous friendship. How about a bit of trust?'

'I don't know that I can trust Sandy.'

'Mark, this can't go on,' she said emphatically. 'You can trust me and you can trust Sandy.'

'How can you be so sure about that?'

'For a very good reason though I can't tell you what it is.'

'Well, I'm still not sure I trust him.'

'Well, you must. I'm going to ring and say I'll meet them for lunch.'

***

Mark mooched aimlessly around the empty house after Gisela had left. Her growing friendship with Sandy, despite her reassurances, had made him profoundly uneasy. He picked up The Economist again but found it difficult to concentrate. He switched on his computer and sat for a long time gazing vacantly at the screen before making a desultory effort to draft a background piece on the East German elections. These would probably be the only free elections in the East as momentum was gathering pace towards reunification. He re-read his efforts and dismissed them as vapid and banal. It would be better to abandon the attempt until the results were available. He highlighted "all" and hit the delete key. After a few minutes, he walked to the newsagents, gathered a handful of competitor newspapers and headed for The Greyhound on the Green. He settled in a quiet corner with a pint, followed by a second one, and browsed through the papers. It was the ultimate displacement activity for a journalist.

After a while, he wandered home for a late lunch. He had some cheese and biscuits with a glass of wine and then fell asleep in a chair. It was quite dark when he awoke. Gisela had still not returned. He collected the file with his father's diaries and started thumbing through them. He had had little time to do so over the previous few months. The questions they had raised were still unanswered. There was absolutely no clue as to the nature of the accident which had caused his father's death but most puzzling was the absence of any record of his demise. Perhaps he had died abroad, but that raised further questions as to why he might have been overseas after leaving the army. Could he have joined up again? It had been suggested. Might it have been a refuge from tensions at home?

Mark's musings were brought to an abrupt end by Gisela's return. 'It's after six,' he said when she came into his study. 'What have you been doing? Not even you can have been lunching all this time.'

'No, we went back to Sandy's flat in the Albany where it was quiet as Bill wanted to record what I'd said.'

'So, how long did that take?'

'Two or three hours.'

'And did you stay on after this Bill guy had gone?'

'I'm not answering that. This is getting ridiculous. I'm not going to be interrogated like this. You're sounding like the fucking Stasi.'

'It wouldn't be a problem if your liaison was as innocent as you claim.'

'Stop right there, Mark. There is no liaison. I'm going to hang up my coat and get myself a drink – and I don't want to hear any more about it.' She looked at Mark as he picked up the telephone. 'Who are you calling?'

'Sandy. I'm going to have it out with him.'

Gisela walked over and took the receiver from him. 'You'll do no such thing. And if you do, it'll just make you look bloody foolish.'

'You've already managed to do that. I'm going to warn him off.' He made a futile grab for the handset. 'I'm not having him trying to get his end away with you.'

'How dare you?' Gisela shouted. 'I'm tempted to let you call him and then you'll see how fucking stupid you are and you'll have to live with the consequences.' She paused before saying more quietly. 'I can't let this go on.'

'Then you should never have started it.'

'That's not what I meant. For God's sake, just try and listen. I'm going to tell you something in confidence but only on condition that it goes no further. And I'm saying it more to maintain my friendship with Sandy than to reassure you.'

'So you're saying your liaison is more important than our marriage?'

'Shut up, Mark. I have had enough of you twisting everything I say. There is no fucking liaison. Just try listening but you must promise this goes no further than these four walls.' Mark nodded reluctantly. 'Sandy is gay. He no more fancies me than he does the other women who join him occasionally for political and social events.'

'Gay?' said Mark incredulously.

'Yes. And he believes very strongly that his sexuality is an entirely private matter. He doesn't want to come out and he doesn't want to shack up with a male partner.'

'I don't believe it.'

'Whether you do or not, it's true. Just because he doesn't behave in a camp manner doesn't mean he's not gay. The other two women know the score as well and they're happy to help him keep his private life private. You mustn't say a word about this. I'll never forgive you if you do.'

'I'm stunned. I'd never have thought it.'

'That's exactly the way he wants it and it should be respected.'

Mark paused and then tentatively went over to Gisela. 'Ellie, I'm sorry. I've been a fool. Thank God you stopped me making that call. Of course I won't say anything. I'm just amazed.' He paused. 'Life has not been so good for me these last few months – though it obviously has for you.'

'It would have been better still without the tensions at home. Surely you don't begrudge me my small successes?'

'No, but perhaps a little envious. I'm sorry. I've been a sod.' She nodded. 'I've been so focused on work and dealing with that bastard of an editor and it's got worse over what's been happening in your country.'

'Not mine now. I know it's difficult but surely even your editor must realise that Germany is going to reunify now.'

'It makes things a bit easier. I can be more open and use fewer weasel words. But the fact that I've been right and he's been wrong hasn't exactly made me a blue-eyed boy. If anything it's made things worse. He's still trying to peddle Maggie's sceptical line in coded form. And he's vindictive.

When I was nominated for that political journalist of the year award, I suggested he might put in a word of support.'

'That must be the least he could do. It will be a plus for the paper if you win.'

'He said it would be inappropriate and would undermine his reputation for independence and integrity. He's living in a fool's paradise if he really believes he has that sort of a reputation. He's a grade A arsehole. What's most galling is that if I do win, he'll trumpet it in the paper.' He paused for a few moments. 'I was also a bit resentful that you were talking with others about Germany when you wouldn't do so with me.'

'I know, but I didn't want to relive my past. It was miserable and it was scary. I wanted to bury it. But things are changing. I'm a bit more positive now and more open to talking about it. That's why I agreed to talk to Bill – and I will share it with you and Michael. Bill will send me a transcript of my recording. He said he might also be interested to see your dad's diaries.'

11

My dearest Michael,

This is the transcript of the recording of my memories of my life in Germany just after the war, which I provided for Bill Gilbert. I am sure he would help if you want more material for your dissertation (he owes me). He has edited it. His English is much more elegant than mine!

But it's not just my memories. I've added some things I've learned since and Oma has added some more. I have also been reading your grandfather's diaries. His vivid and sympathetic descriptions prompted further memories. It's so sad we never knew him. My viewpoint is somewhat different. I hope both will help with your dissertation. Both are part of your family history.

I could not have done this a year ago but, somehow, it seems important to do it now. The suffering didn't end when the war ended. This is our story from the point at which Oma left it. Remember two things as you read. First, we were luckier than many though it often didn't seem so at the time – or later. Second, I was not quite six when the war ended. I have rarely talked about those times. It wasn't all bad but a lot of it was. I've tried to suppress my memories over the years. That's not been easy and I haven't succeeded. Memories often force their way to the front of my mind and I remember what happened – especially when I think about Papa. Will this achieve closure? I doubt it. Painful though it is – I'm not sure I really want it to.

All my love, Mum

BURGSTEINFURT AND KÖLN 1945/1946

We stayed on the farm for four months. I was six when we left. It was a sanctuary, a refuge. Later we realised how lucky we had been. It was an oasis of calm by comparison with the chaos around us.

Mutti and Aunt Ulla looked round the farm after they had finished milking that first day. There were signs of neglect everywhere. Areas had been left uncultivated and were overrun with weeds. Some of the barns were in need of repair. Equipment was rusting. It was as safe a place as any to stay. They knew they had to prove we could make a real contribution, and quickly. Berthe Hoffmann reacted very cautiously to a suggestion that we might all help and that we might all benefit. She remained wary for some weeks.

There were two horses left on the farm. Most had been

stolen by refugees and sold or killed for food. The next day Aunt Ulla and Mutti found a supply of seed in one of the barns. They harnessed the horses and set out to plough one of the fields in readiness for sowing some wheat. It was tough. The ground was very hard after a terrible winter, though nothing like as severe as those in Braunsberg. Friedrich and Ferdinand did some heavy work around the farm and Uncle Hans and Aunt Marthe pitched in. They had become an honorary aunt and uncle. They prepared a large plot for vegetables close to the farmhouse. This was a new experience for them. They had employed gardeners in Danzig. There was not much I could do but I helped in small ways. There were about twenty chickens and I would get them into their enclosure in the evenings. In the daytime they would run around the yard. They would lay in the most unlikely places. I became very good at finding the eggs. When I found them I would hide them again. I was the guardian of the eggs.

The farm was not close to any major routes. The retreating Wehrmacht and the advancing British and Americans generally by-passed us. But there were deserters who were running eastwards. They would avoid the major routes and come scavenging. Most were none too gentle but they didn't hang around long. They were scared. They knew they would be shot if they were caught. Some of the forced labourers, especially the Poles, were more of a problem. Many had been treated very brutally by officials, farmers and factory supervisors. They weren't just looking for food. They wanted revenge as well. Aunt Berthe saw some of them off with her shotgun. She too became an honorary aunt. Uncle Hans no longer had his hunting rifle. It had been stolen by a deserter during our journey. Some came in larger numbers or at night. We couldn't always resist their demands for food because of the risk of violence. Several times I or one of the boys was grabbed and held as a hostage. Luckily, we came to no harm. We learned to store and hide all food in small stockpiles around the farm, as I had done with the eggs, to limit losses. Aunt Berthe warmed to her "own refugees" as she called us. As spring turned to summer we all shared the produce resulting from our efforts.

We only saw British troops once. In April, a tank troop passed about half a mile away. An armoured car detached itself and drove up to the farm. Uncle Hans spoke to the officer. He said we were a family and there were no combatants present. We were made to stand in line but when the officer saw we were only women and children with one older man, he drove off. Uncle Hans reckoned they were eager to push eastwards as fast as possible.

Life on the farm was far from a rural idyll but it was safe and secure. We were a small self-sufficient community. Our days were filled working on the farm. We were spared the soul-destroying emptiness of many refugees bereft of hope, employment and distraction. I probably had the easiest time. I was too young for the heavier tasks and was indulged on account of my age.

We were very isolated on the farm. Those in the towns were not much better off. There was no post, no telephones, no newspapers – only gossip and rumour. As each day and week passed, a little information filtered through. It was impossible to know what was true and what was false. Mutti and Aunt Ulla hoped to hear something of Papa and Uncle

Konrad. But there was no news. I missed Papa so much. I often cried myself to sleep thinking of him. Sometimes I would hear Mutti crying quietly. We were very close in the barn. I would creep over and she would hold me tightly. She and Aunt Ulla went into Münster several times to see if they could find out what might have happened to Papa and Uncle Konrad. There were thousands of sad notices pinned up everywhere – on boards, on trees, in shops and outside churches. Thousands, millions were trying to locate and reconnect in the chaos. There were no records of those forced into the Volkssturm in the east. It had been a ragged militia without uniforms or proper weapons and little organisation or leadership. Mutti would always come back looking very despondent. It was just a matter of chance if anyone got any news.

Mutti and Aunt Ulla felt rudderless. At first they had been driven by the need to seek safety for me and the boys. Then they were fully occupied by the physical demands of the work on the farm. Beyond that, there was a void – an emptiness. The total disruption and destruction of our lives had taken only a few hours. We had left with scarcely a goodbye. The sense of absence and loss of Papa and Uncle Konrad was confusing and baffling. It was a loss without closure. The uncertainty as to their fate had paralysed Mutti's and Aunt Ulla's minds. Their inability to control events had made it impossible for them to think or plan for a future, any future.

Uncle Hans and Aunt Marthe were rocks. They had lost their sons. We had become their adopted family and given them a sense of purpose. They were determined to protect and help us. In August, they suggested we would all have more chances if we went to Köln. Uncle Hans hoped his sister might be able to help. Mutti and Aunt Ulla passively accepted the suggestion.

Berthe Hoffman said she was sorry to see us go and not only because she was losing a number of unpaid farmhands. Her husband would be returning from a POW camp two weeks later. She was happy she could welcome him back with their farm in reasonable shape and with sufficient stocks of food. She provided us with some and a handcart for the journey to Köln, a hundred and fifty kilometres away. When we reached the city, we realised just how fortunate we had been. It had not been easy but, in comparison with what came next, and what we had experienced earlier, it was almost idyllic.

We passed other farms closer to the principal roads as we walked. Many had been laid waste. Barns had been flattened or burned and the metal skeletons of wrecked machinery lay in the fields. The destruction of Köln was as devastating as anything we had seen on our long trek across Germany. It had been hit by a thousand-bomber raid in the spring of 1942 and bombed repeatedly thereafter. The central area close to the Rhine had been almost totally destroyed. There were no untouched buildings; houses had been reduced to ruins, churches gutted and commercial premises were no more than shells. There was rubble everywhere. In the square in front of the remains of the opera house there was an ironic sign, a quotation, in German and English: "Give me five years and you will not recognise Germany, Adolf Hitler, 1940". In this scene of devastation the twin spires of the cathedral stood out miraculously and defiantly against the bright summer sky. Below, the twisted steelwork of the wrecked Hohenzollern Bridge projected from the Rhine like some bizarre abstract metal sculpture. A mass of debris had collected against the ribs on the upstream side. Rotting semi-submerged barges hung on their lines close to the bank. There was little traffic – only British military vehicles and some German army trucks, requisitioned to assist in clearing the wreckage. We couldn't believe anyone could have survived. But many who had fled had now returned. People were living in the remnants of houses, in cellars, in the ruins of commercial and public buildings and makeshift shelters constructed with materials recovered from the rubble. Many undamaged houses had been taken over by the British. We all knew who were the conquerors and who were the vanquished. Lives were spent queueing for what food there was or picking through the rubble for anything which might have a use or a value. There was a sense of despair and apathy everywhere and there was an undercurrent of hate. We hated the Nazis for what they had done to our country, we hated the Russians who had stolen our home and destroyed our family and we hated the British for the destruction they had caused and their superior attitudes. We would have hated the Americans too if we had been in their sector. I know this sounds extreme but that was the way it was. We did slowly come to terms with it. We had to in order to survive. But the shame we felt for all that the Nazis did has never left us.

Uncle Hans had been born in Köln and had known it well. His sister, Karolina, had lived close to the Rhine, near the botanical gardens. We set off from the cathedral using the river as our guide. The gardens were easily identifiable with their ruined glasshouses. There were few other landmarks. There had been little rubble clearance in the residential areas. We walked around the area for over an hour – back and forth, round and round. Eventually, Uncle Hans confessed that he was lost. Finally, as we passed by one of the few habitable houses for the third time, someone came out and asked suspiciously what we were doing. It turned out she had known Uncle Hans' sister. He learned that she had died in a raid a year earlier. She directed us to a house in an adjoining street which had been totally destroyed. Hans was very thoughtful. His sister had never married, one of many who had lost a fiancé in the first war. He suggested we should make a home for ourselves in the cellars. 'I guess I'm as entitled to ownership as anyone,' he said 'and Marthe and I are now used to living in a cellar'. He smiled, 'But there were some differences between us. Karolina didn't drink. We won't find any brandy in her cellars.' It took us a day to shift enough rubble by hand to clear the entrance and another to remove the debris from the cellars.

We walked into the city the next day. Hundreds of people were milling around the assembly centre. We all had to register and were told to attend for fumigation. We protested that we had been living in the countryside and were free of lice. It made no difference. Some food was available but not much. The permanent feeling of hunger we had known during our flight started to come back. For the next two years it was an inescapable part of our lives. There had been a poor harvest that year. The ceding of the fertile farmlands in the east to Poland and the appropriation of livestock for slaughter by the Wehrmacht in the final months of the war had added to the shortages. The pressures were aggravated by the massive number of refugees, like us, from the east. There was some hostility from local people as competition for food increased. And we all harboured a simmering sense of resentment when we saw how much better the British were fed and housed.

That was just the start of months of humiliation which we had to accept without question. Adults were required to fill out a "Fragebogen", a personnel questionnaire, if they wanted to fill an official or responsible position. It was an horrendous document with over a hundred questions but essential to obtain a "Persilschein", a clean bill or denazification certificate. It was even more rigorously applied in the American zone, so many ex-Nazis fled to the British Sector. They would pay others to swear they had not been members of the party and had not been responsible for war crimes. The British often turned a blind eye to dodgy paperwork in the case of middle-grade officials. They were needed to support the administration. People complained we were under colonial rule. Some of the British referred to us as "Kolonialvolk". Our lives were dominated by queueing. We were told queueing was just as bad in Britain. Of course, we didn't believe it.

There was little any of us could do at first. Eventually, we created roles for ourselves. Uncle Hans got a minor administrative post with the city government which was overseen by the British. They desperately needed translators. Then he worked for Konrad Adenauer for a short time. He had been the mayor of Köln between the wars. He was reinstated by the British in May but then dismissed some months later. The British military had absolute power.

Mutti and Aunt Ulla became "Trümmerfrauen", or rubble women, clearing the streets and buildings by hand. They were organised into working columns of ten to twenty people. As a result, they received ration cards which allowed a few more calories which they shared with all of us. It was still not enough. We all lost weight. They only had hand tools, hammers, picks and occasionally a hand winch. Everything had to be lifted by hand. Masonry had to be broken up to make it possible to lift. It was dangerous work and all too easy to trigger a major fall of rubble. People lost fingers or limbs. Some were killed by collapsing walls. And there were unexploded bombs in some buildings. One of their friends lost a leg when she disturbed one. Bricks and timbers were recovered and cleaned and other items such as fireplaces, toilets and plumbing materials were saved for re-use when possible. But much could not be re-used. This was piled up to create a "Trümmerberg".

The boys and I followed Mutti and Aunt Ulla into town at first. There were no schools until the following year. Ferdy and Friedrich grumbled as they were expected to work alongside the women. I was too small to do much and was told to sit out of the way to avoid injury. I would often get bored and wander off. The boys saw this as a chance to skive, saying they should look after me and prevent me from getting lost. We hooked up with a gang of other kids. They were wary of accepting a small girl at first but they quickly discovered I had my uses. We foraged widely in the wreckage. The best pickings were in the areas where clearance had not started. We would collect materials to improve our cellars. Sometimes we would find cans of food. This was where I was most useful. I was small and agile and could get into the smallest nooks and crannies of badly damaged houses. It wasn't good. There was rotting food and rats everywhere. I would sometimes come across bodies or body parts. But I was accepted because I was willing to go where the bigger kids couldn't. They called me "little monkey". We became very successful scavengers. We quickly learned what we could sell or use for barter. The boys became very skilful at wheedling to obtain the best price for anything saleable. This sometimes led to fights with other groups and dealings with some shady people. But the gang stuck together and was almost always able to see off violent attempts to relieve us of stuff we had found. We decided later we could have become successful entrepreneurs and traders.

Ferdinand and Friedrich were my protectors. Spoils I had extracted from the ruins would often be eyed enviously by others. I was sometimes roughed up and items were taken from me forcibly if my cousins were not nearby. There was little I could do to resist. The struggle for survival was violent at times. But my cousins were effective bodyguards and, working with other kids in the gang, they were able to overwhelm most muggers by sheer weight of numbers.

The British occupiers were sometimes sources of bounty. We pestered them endlessly for food and money. Some were very generous, particularly to me as a small girl. But generally they treated us with disdain and occasionally with violence. I became separated from my cousins one day and was physically picked up by a soldier and hustled into the remains of a ruined building. He placed a hand over my mouth and with the other lifted my skirt and pulled my underwear down. He put me on his knee and started to finger me. Then he pushed a finger right into me. It hurt like hell. I wriggled helplessly in his grip. He removed that hand for a moment and stood. He unbuttoned his trousers and, still keeping a hand over my mouth, allowed them to fall to his ankles. I writhed and bit one of his fingers as hard as I could. I tasted the blood. He pulled it away and hissed, 'You little bitch – you'll pay for that.' But I was able to scream and I screamed like crazy. There was a noise from behind. He looked round to see Ferdinand and Friedrich and two others from the gang scrambling over the rubble. He let me go and turned to face the boys.

He raised his fists. 'Alright, let's be having you,' he bellowed. 'I'll show you kids what it's like to be a man.'

Ferdinand shouted, 'Run, Gisela.' I was already scrambling away over the debris. All four approached, each with a lump of concrete in their hands. Friedrich took one look and laughed as the soldier bent and tried to pull up his trousers. As he did so, Ferdy darted forward and hit the now flaccid penis hard with the concrete, pushing him at the same time. With his trousers around his ankles, he lost his balance and fell heavily onto the rubble. The boys stood over him for a moment laughing. Then they raised their hands high above their heads and dropped the lumps of concrete, bombing his willy and balls before making off, roaring with laughter. I never strayed far from my cousins again.

It was a long time before I accepted that I would never see Papa again. Mutti never did fully come to terms with the reality. The loss of our home and family, torn away from us so abruptly, was bewildering and disorienting. Mutti was angry too. They had never been members of the party or involved in politics. She felt we had all been cruelly punished for the appalling sins of others. She would agonise, asking herself if there was anything they could have done to influence events. It was difficult to imagine what. All dissent had been brutally suppressed. Worst of all was not knowing what had happened to Papa. He had been the centre of our lives. There were many others in the same position but knowing that did nothing to ease the pain or relieve the emotional turmoil resulting from the loss. Theirs had been an equal marriage. Mutti felt a major part of her being had been amputated.

***

That was forty-five years ago. I sometimes wonder what our lives would have been like if there had been no war, or if Hitler had sued for peace when it first became clear the war was lost, or if there had been a war and Braunsberg had been liberated by the British or the Americans or if it was still part of Germany today. There are so many, too many, "what ifs". Uncle Hans and Aunt Marthe died nearly thirty years ago. Some flats were built on the site of his sister's house and they lived quietly in one of them. They were very good to us. They were not only an honorary aunt and uncle, they were honorary grandparents too. As you know, Aunt Ulla moved to East Berlin with the boys to be near her mother. She developed cancer soon after the wall went up and died in 1963. She was only in her mid-fifties. The boys were in their early thirties by then. Friedrich was fortunate in a way. He was with his girlfriend in West Berlin the weekend the wall went up. He decided to stay. But they split up and he went to the States. We heard he had difficulty in adapting to life there. Aunt Ulla believed he was involved with drugs. We have lost touch. Ferdy made a life for himself in the east. He now lives in Dresden and I am hoping to visit him next year.

As for me, I am here, living a life I could never have envisaged when I was a kid. The hatred has gone but the sadness and the shame at what my country did and the sense of loss will never leave me.

12

18 September 1945

George

Back to the chaos. Redpath and Thwaites looking a bit more chipper than when I left.

George stopped as he walked into the compound. He looked around the previously empty schoolyard. Thwaites had been busy. More than twenty British and commandeered German vehicles were parked up in line against the boundary wall. He dumped his bag by the entrance and walked round to inspect them. Three Bedford three tonners, six Mercedes L3000 trucks, four Standard twelve light utility vehicles ("tillies") and eight VW Kübelwagens. In the corner by the entrance to the old school hall there were thirty motorcycles: three BSA M20s, a Matchless, four flying fleas, seven BMW R75 with sidecars, fifteen Zundapps and a Hillman Minx. A mechanic was busy with the bonnet up on one of the trucks. Thwaites spotted George from one of the windows and joined him.

'Good to see you back, Sir. We've done what we can so far. Many German vehicles as you can see.' He waved his arm around the yard. 'I've a few more on the way – including a Centaur bulldozer. Still hoping to get hold of a crab but no luck yet. The bikes will be useful for keeping tabs on the groups. Afraid I could only get a Hillman for you. Tried to get my hands on a Humber but was told they were reserved for field officers.'

'No problem. I'll probably use one of the bikes. How about mine-detecting equipment?'

'Thirty Polish detectors so far. Max of five for each group. Not much between a hundred guys. We're testing all of them. There's a lot of duff gear out there. I'm trying to get more.'

'Any idea how long that might take?'

'None at all.'

Redpath had come out and joined them. He looked at George. 'Thwaites and I have been mates for a long time, Sir. If anyone can get anything, it'll be him.'

'Jimmy's right. I do have a reputation to maintain.' He hesitated. 'But I'd just ask you not to look too closely at my methods.' George raised his eyebrows and said nothing. 'Everything's so bloody chaotic here. I'd get nowhere if I did everything according to King's Regulations and Standing Orders.'

George laughed. 'I was briefed by a staffer at Divisional HQ. He said Control Commission Germany, or CCG, was responsible for all the admin. They reckon it stands for Complete Chaos Guaranteed. Keep me up to date and I'll trust you not to overstep the boundaries.' He paused. 'Or if you do, cover your tracks and my back. If you don't, we'll all be up shit creek without a paddle.'

'Message received and understood, Sir.'

'Progress will be hellish slow if we have to rely on prodding with bayonets like the infantry – and we're not going to give this lot bayonets.'

'I'm having several hundred prodders made with very long handles.'

George turned to Redpath. 'How are we getting on assembling the groups?'

'The men are coming through, Sir. Best if I show you inside.'

They walked into the old schoolroom. Redpath had made good use of the school noticeboards. Detailed maps of the area, minefield charts, planners and diagrams of a range of devices and fuses adorned the walls. A corporal was sitting at a large table under the window, collar loosened, a cigarette hanging loosely from his lower lip. He was sorting papers from a box and entering names and personal details into a ledger. Redpath gestured towards him. 'Milstein joined us while you were on leave, Sir.' He started to rise to his feet but George motioned for him to remain sitting. 'His family own an ironmonger's in Shoreditch. Told me he used to help out with the bookkeeping. Seemed the right guy for the record-keeping here.'

'Okay, so how many men have we got now?'

'Close to three hundred. They're coming through in dribs and drabs with their service record books after they've been cleared.' He pointed to the piles of documents on the table. 'I'm making sure each group is led by an ex-Pioneer officer. One even turned up wearing the ribbon of his Knight's Cross. I expected trouble from him but none so far. I'm making sure there's at least one English speaker in each group – ideally the leader. They're being issued with dark brown uniforms with flashes on their arms – "Mine C GR".'

'Any other problems, in addition to limited equipment and the slowish release of volunteers? I use the word loosely.'

'You're right, Sir. These guys have been drafted. Who the hell would volunteer for this? I've been talking to some. Their main questions are: when are we going home and when will the war be over for us? They just want to get back to civvy street.'

'Don't we all?'

'And there's another issue. They're being got at by some of the locals. They think this lot were party members or SS and have been made to do this as a punishment. That's tough. Not only have they been cleared, but they'll be doing a bloody dangerous job for everyone's benefit. Most were simply soldiers like us. We need to look after them. We'll get a lot more out of them if we do.'

'Agreed, go on.'

'They're under military discipline, of course, and will be treated as deserters if they bugger off. But everything's so chaotic they probably wouldn't be caught and brought back. The only real hold we have is that we have their service record books and their "Persilscheins". But I doubt that would hold them back if they were determined to clear off. On the plus side, they'll get leave every six months, a reasonable food ration and a salary based on their old service pay – between 100 and 200 marks, depending on family circs. Not much, as dependents won't get any compensation if they're blasted to hell or a pension if they're crippled.'

'So, you're saying goodwill is everything.'

'Reluctantly, yes, even though we've been fighting the buggers for the last six years. It's essential.'

'Get a couple of English speakers from each group up here, 0800 tomorrow, so I can start meeting them. I reckon I really should try and learn some German. I'll take it up again with the CO.'

'I'll fix it. If you can learn some German, Sir, I think that'd be helpful.' He clicked his fingers and gestured to the corporal to make some tea.

'Is that all the bad news?'

'Fraid not, Sir. I've been talking to some of them. They're as keen as we are to find minefield charts for bloody obvious reasons, but there aren't any for many areas. I've pinned up the ones we've got.' He pointed to the wall. 'There seem to be four types of mines: two anti-tank, the Teller and the Riegel. The second one's a real bugger – up to three anti-handling devices and fuse wires that corrode easily. They'll need to be destroyed in situ where possible. And there are two anti-personnel mines. The S leaps into the air when triggered and sprays shrapnel everywhere, mainly at the level of their balls. Our guys call them Bouncing Bettys – though they won't have much fun with any Bettys if they come across one of these. The other is the Schu which is small and in a wooden box. Almost no metal in it, so it's not picked up by the Polish detectors.'

George grinned. 'You've really made my day. Get

hold of Thwaites and let's go and have a pint. Tomorrow we'll go over the territory again and start to work up a detailed clearance strategy. We'll need to set up field communications, identify exploding grounds, agree priority areas for clearance, and ensure safety for the guys as far as we can.' He hesitated, 'And make sure we have a system for dealing with those injured – or worse.'

'Right, Sir. I've started talking to the powers that be about how we deal with bodies,' he smiled grimly, 'and body parts.'

***

George tasked the first groups with clearing the Hürtgen Forest. He stood at the forest margin with Redpath and lit a cigarette. The difficulties were all too apparent. It was an apocalyptic scene – a Great War Western Front landscape. Trees destroyed in the firestorm of battle remained, a forest of charred stumps silhouetted against an overcast sky. There were derelict trenches, decayed dugouts and countless rotting tools of war – another Passchendaele but with more hills and less mud. The desolate scene was relieved only by isolated blooms of violet-speckled fast-growing weeds. The thought crossed George's mind that Joan could have identified these for him.

They walked a short way in, probing cautiously as they went. There were remains of decomposed bodies and bleached skeletons picked clean by predators standing out in stark contrast to the blackened fire-scorched earth. Parts of uniforms, steel helmets and gas masks showed at a glance which had been a German and which an American Toothbrushes, tin mugs, cigarette packets and shredded backpacks were scattered everywhere, the sad relics of lives ended abruptly and violently. In some places the dead lay in groups where they had been struck by a single shell or mine; human remains united inextricably in death. George picked up a small book by one track. The moist distorted pages were difficult to separate. It was a New Testament in English. The bodies would have to be recovered, mostly unidentified, and taken to military cemeteries. But first, countless mines had to be located, defused, removed and exploded. Only then would it be possible to recover the bodies. They backtracked carefully following the route they had taken into the forest.

They drove slowly back to Aachen in silence. After a solitary drink in the mess, George felt the need to take a walk to clear his mind. Those scenes would stay with him for a long time. The physical damage to the city and the parlous state of the inhabitants had been shocking enough but that day had brought home to him the appalling human cost of the conflict and the total futility of Germany's last stand. He was lost in thought as he rounded a corner and saw a group of men about fifty metres ahead in the dusk. There was a woman in the centre shouting loudly, 'Nein, nein' and 'Hände weg.' He walked over. She was surrounded by a group of five Tommies who were grabbing at and lifting her skirt. Each time she turned to escape from one pair of hands another of her tormentors would lift her skirt from behind saying, 'Come on – show us your knickers. Let's see your pussy.'

They looked up as George approached. 'That's enough,'

he said loudly. 'You lot can just fuck off. You're clearly not wanted and looking at you I'm not surprised.' They backed off slowly. 'I've seen your badges, I know where you're billeted and, if you're not gone in seconds, I'll be having a word with your CO.' He didn't have a clue where they were billeted but they weren't to know that. He could find out easily enough. They started to back away looking a little sheepish. He heard one mutter, 'Bloody officer, probably wants to screw her himself.' He turned sharply. 'Another word and I'll drop you into the deepest shit you've ever known.' They slunk away silently.

George looked at the woman. She was in her mid-twenties, tall and slim with short cropped hair. 'Ich spreche sehr wenig Deutsch,' he said hesitatingly. That was about the limit of his German. He had to resort to English. 'I hope you can understand. I'm very sorry, that shouldn't have happened.' He turned to walk away once the men were out of sight but stopped as she said, 'Thank you, Sir. That was very kind,' in almost accentless English. 'I'm really very grateful.'

He turned to face her. He was irritated. 'Why the hell didn't you just tell them to clear off in English?'

'I'm not sure. I was a bit scared. I thought they might feel they were being encouraged if they found out I spoke English.'

'Well, I'm sorry it happened. They shouldn't behave like that.'

She shrugged. 'It's not the first time and probably won't be the last.'

He paused. He was curious. Her English was excellent. 'Tell me, how is it you speak English so well?'

'I was taught by my mother. She was an English teacher and was keen that I and my brother should speak the language. She lived for two years in your country. She has happy memories of that time.' She hesitated. 'She's hoping to get a job with the British.'

It was clear to George that there might be some convergence of interests here. The administration was short of translators and, if this woman's mother was a qualified teacher, she might well be offered a job. Possibly, he could also get her to teach him for an hour or so in the evenings. 'What's your mother's teaching experience?' he asked cautiously.

'She taught at High School to the level required for the Abitur.'

'What's that?'

'The school leaving exam – a qualification for university.' She shrugged. 'Not that we have any universities now – nor any schools come to that.'

He took a deep breath. 'Will you ask your mother to come and see me at six tomorrow evening? I'll give you my name and the address of our HQ.' George was aware he had no authority for what he was proposing – but what the hell. Others were operating off-piste. There was no good reason not to join them. In his short time in Aachen he had discovered that some amongst the occupying forces were operating independently – running scams and developing private markets in tradeable goods. They were no different from the skivers and profiteers who had made a good living out of the war back home. At least this, if it worked out, would be for positive reasons.

She nodded and looked at the scrap of paper he had given her. She smiled. 'She'll have no difficulty finding it. This is the school where she taught and where I was a pupil.'

'I can't promise anything,' he said hurriedly. He hoped this would cover his back sufficiently if necessary. 'What's your mother's name? I shall have to alert the guard.'

'Irmgard Becker.' She paused. 'My name's Hannelore. I must get home. Mutti worries. Thank you for your help.'

He walked with her to the street corner to make sure she was in the clear. She kept glancing at him apprehensively as they walked. The penny dropped. She must have heard and, with her command of English, understood the last comment made by the squaddie and assumed he might be right. George stopped when they reached the corner. 'You should be alright now. I'll leave you to get on your way.'

'Thank you.' She turned and was gone.

George saw the officer heading the local administration the next day. He was reminded sharply that fraternising was not permitted. His attitude softened as George explained the circumstances. 'Alright, we do need translators and, if she's lived in England, I guess her English will be good. But she'll have to go through clearance. Let me know when you've seen her. If she looks okay, I'll see her with a view to taking her on. I'll have a word with the CO of the men who were pestering the girl. It won't stop these things happening, but it might just make that lot think twice before trying it on again.' He gave a resigned sigh, 'Or maybe not. Some feel they're entitled to some spoils. At least it will cover our backs if questions are raised about how this woman was recruited.'

***

George met Irmgard Becker the following evening. She was in her late fifties, cleanly and tidily, if shabbily, dressed. Her English was excellent. She confirmed she had taught in the High School and also tutored students at the Technische Hochschule but had resigned, as a protest, against the Enabling Acts which had suspended civil rights and progressively discriminated against Jews and communists. George explained she would require official clearance and a "Persilschein". She produced the certificate with a flourish.

George warmed to her. He sensed that his impulse to get this particular ball rolling might work out well. She had been in England before the first war, living with a family near Alnwick. They spent twenty minutes chatting as she recalled fond memories of the town, the friends she had made, the beaches north of Alnmouth and the Northumbrian countryside. She had been sad when forced to return home early as war was threatening. She said she would be happy to spend an hour teaching George three evenings a week and insisted she would do so without payment for services rendered to her daughter.

She hesitated for a moment as she was preparing to leave. 'I wonder if I might take up a little more of your time.'

'Alright. I've nowhere much to go.'

'I have not had a chance to say this to a British officer before.'

George shifted uncomfortably in his chair. 'Go ahead,' he said cautiously. 'I can listen. But remember, I'm not a senior officer and I can't do much to change things.'

'But you said you'll be working with Germans. What I'm about to say might be helpful.'

'Okay, go on.'

'We're all very down just now but people are resentful too. They're resentful of the profiteers and having to share with refugees what little there is. Unfair I know, but it's how people feel. But people are angry with you too – for the bombing and then taking over many intact buildings. We're short of everything. People are selling anything and everything: food, cigarettes, sex, whatever they have. There is even a new occupation here: "Kippensammler".'

George had been about to react strongly, pointing out that they had been the principal architects of their own downfall but was distracted by that last word. 'What the hell's a Kippensammler?'

'A guy who collects cigarette butts full-time to make and sell smokeable cigarettes. People are that desperate.' George said nothing. She paused. 'Perhaps I shouldn't have said all that. I guess you'll not want me now. I'll go.'

George was taken aback but simply said, 'The decision to employ you or not is not mine. It's down to the head of administration. I'll recommend that he does but it might be a good idea if you were a little less outspoken, at least until you're on the payroll.'

She laughed. 'That reminds me of something I loved about the English. The way you wrap things up in diplomatic language without losing the message.'

'I hope it works out for you.'

'I too. You told me what you'll be doing. It really wasn't fair of me to dump all that on you. I'm sorry.'

'Let's see. Even if you're not employed it would be good if you could teach me some German. But I should warn you, I wasn't much cop at languages at school.'

***

28 SEPTEMBER 1945

Worrying letter from Joan. Marty has some bug. High temperature, sore throat, stiffness, pains in her arms and legs. Had it for ten days. Worried sick. Spoke to the MO. Said it could be polio. Hope to God he's wrong. He says most people don't become paralysed. Not much reassured. Will apply for compassionate leave if it gets worse. She's been isolated from Mark. He's alright – so far. If only I could be at home. Must focus but my mind keeps going back to Farnham and Marty.

Mine clearance under way. It's a bloody slow process. There's no way we can clear the area by the planned date. Getting the men together has taken time. Many were in POW camps, others from elsewhere. First lot now trained. I now have over 500 men in the groups. Discipline sometimes difficult. There's an underlying current of resentment. Most want nothing more than to escape from military discipline and get back to their families – as their Wehrmacht contemporaries are doing. Who can blame them? It's an aspiration beyond the reach of many far from home and particularly those from the east who no longer have a home and, often, no longer a family. Redpath is an excellent link with his fluent German and "no nonsense" approach. He has managed to imbue a fair number with a sense of purpose and commitment. Enthusiasm would have been too much to hope for.

***

25 OCTOBER 1945

Regular updates from Joan. It is polio. Marty rather better. Some weakness in her legs tho' not too severe. Now out of isolation. MO says very unlikely to get worse now and could improve. Doc at home says the same. Marty can walk and being encouraged to keep moving. Determined to be involved in everything again – a good sign. Joan's dad has made a small stick for her. Joan says she uses it very conspicuously. Apparently Edna very supportive! Mark is fine. I need to focus here. Getting close to full strength. Must make sure I get home in one piece.

***

There were about 1200 minefields in the sector, only two-thirds with charts. George was submitting his monthly progress report to the CO. 'It's difficult to calculate the total number of devices with any certainty. We know eight thousand were laid in the Hürtgen and, calculating from this, and the density in other areas where we've made a start, the total's probably close to 80,000.'

'And at what rate are you clearing them?'

'It varies. At best a team can clear a hundred in about twenty hours, but it can take up to four times as long. The average is nearer the latter figure.'

'Why such variation? Surely all groups should be achieving rates that match or are close to the best.'

'Not possible, Sir. There are bound to be wide variations with the differences in mine types, limited charts and the difficulty of some of the terrain. And there's another problem in wooded areas. We're having to divert men to keep civilians out. They're looking for wood for fuel now winter's coming. That makes everything even more hazardous. We've trained teams in safe disposal but "safe" is a relative term. There've already been nine deaths and thirteen serious injuries and that's after only six weeks. I know we need to get on as fast as possible, but I cannot and will not pressurise these guys into working at a level that'll lead to even more casualties.'

The CO grunted. George leant forward and thumped his fist into the palm of his other hand. 'Sir, these men aren't volunteers. None of them chose to do this. They just want to survive and get free of the military – permanently. If I push too hard, casualties will rise and there'll be desertions. And if that starts, it'll snowball. We need to look after these guys and, as far as possible, retain their goodwill.'

'And what are the implications of this?'

'If our estimates are anywhere near correct, this area will not be cleared by the target date. It's only just over eighteen months away. At the current rate, it'll be at least another year after that. If I may say so, Sir, this is typical of bloody politicians. They set targets when they have no idea of the size of the task, the practicalities involved or the level of manpower required.'

'Alright, Brown, 'twas always thus. You've made your point. Do the best you can.'

***

7 NOVEMBER 1945

Major worries about Marty mainly over. Back to school next week.

***

18 NOVEMBER 1945

Updates weekly now. Marty feels well. Weakness improved a bit more tho' she walks with a slight limp. Joan says this becomes more pronounced when she doesn't get her own way. I'm sure Joan doesn't fall for that. The doctor says it's unlikely the limp will improve much more now. Not wonderful, but much better than it might have been. It's unlikely to hold her back to any major extent. Applied for leave over Christmas but refused. It's ironic. I think it would have been granted if Marty had been getting worse. Guess I need to look at this positively.

***

26 November 1945

Letter from Alice. She's been to visit – a little worried.
Even more so after one from Joan today.

Alice's letter to George had arrived a week earlier. She
had been in London staying with a cousin and had gone
to Farnham to see Joan and the kids. She wrote to say the
children were fine and Marty was managing well but one
part particularly worried George. Edna had been there for
lunch. It had been clear that she was spending a lot of time at
the house and Alice felt her presence was neither benign nor
in the best interests of the family, particularly the children.
She was worried by Edna's tendency to discipline them and
regulate their behaviour. She was particularly severe with
Mark, who would get very upset by her strictures. She was
apparently less forceful with Marty who was more likely to
shrug it off or confront her. She had left during the afternoon
and William and Helen had joined them for tea. Alice had
wondered if she should raise her anxieties with them but had
held back, concerned that to do so might add to tensions.
She was relieved when Helen said privately that they had
delayed their arrival until Edna had gone. Alice accepted
this comment as an opportunity to express her concerns.
These were shared by George's in-laws. Helen said they had
remonstrated with Joan but been rebuffed on the grounds
that Edna provided invaluable support while George was
abroad and had been good with Marty when she was ill.
George was upset by the implication that, as an absentee, he
was failing as a husband and father. He could not see that

it was in the kids' interests for Edna to assume the role of a second parent.

A letter from Joan arrived a few days later. It was evident that concerns about Edna's role had directly or indirectly been relayed back to her. The letter was extremely brusque. Joan complained that George had sent Alice to spy on her and said that he shouldn't think it would be part of his role to rearrange the way the family was organised when he was demobbed. She added that he had been away so long he was now largely a stranger. True, but it hurt like hell.

13

12 APRIL 1990

It was early evening when Mark got home. He let himself into the house and called out to say he was back. There was no answer. He dropped his bag in the hallway, went through to the kitchen, poured himself a beer and headed for his study. It was beginning to get dark. He switched on the small desk light and spread the contents of his mother's leather writing case over the desk. He had first read the letters late the previous evening. The emotions they revealed were confusing and unsettling. The desires and yearnings expressed had been bugging him all day. He re-read two or three letters and then pushed them to one side. He leaned forward, arms on his desk, lost in thought. The essence and force of the words were all too clear. But was this really about his mother? Could it possibly be right? It was getting darker but he made no move to switch other lights on. He was suddenly aware of a soft noise behind him. He turned, startled as the central light was switched on. It was Gisela.

He looked up. 'God, you made me jump.'

'Sorry. I heard you come in. I just didn't feel like talking.'

Mark looked at her more closely. She was in tears. 'What on earth's wrong? What's happened?'

'It's these,' she said haltingly holding out some of his father's diaries. 'I've read a few. Your dad really did tell it like it was. It hit a nerve. It's why I didn't want to be involved at first. I'm sorry about what I said back then. Your dad was one of the good guys.'

Mark went over and put his arms round her. 'I need a refill. I'll get you a glass.'

Gisela nodded. 'I need a minute or two to dry my eyes and straighten my face.' She sat in the leather armchair facing the desk. External events and family pressures were progressively dismantling her defences and reviving memories of the past. Each act of recall was forcing her to confront her gremlins. Would she be able to banish or tame them? Only time would tell. She was more composed when Mark came back. He retreated behind his desk. They sat in silence for several minutes.

'You alright, Mark?' He nodded imperceptibly. 'Is something wrong?'

'I'm not sure. No, there is.'

'What is it?'

'It's these.' He pointed to the desk.

'What are they?'

'Mum's papers. I've only just opened her writing case.' He looked up. 'I didn't think there would be much of interest in it, but there are things there which have thrown me. I'd like to know what you make of them.'

'What have you found?'

'A lot of letters, poems. They're quite disturbing.'

'Do you really want me to read them?'

'Yes, if you wouldn't mind, but it might be best if you read two from my Dad from late November and early December 1945 first. There were a lot of earlier ones that autumn mainly about Marty and her polio. These ones shed much more light on the marriage.' He walked round his desk, perched on the arm of the chair and handed two letters to her.

Dearest Joan

I hope you will be able to get something suitable for the kids for Christmas.

I was quite upset by your letter and some of the things you said. I'm sad I can't be with you and more involved with Marty and Mark. I have tried to obtain my release more than once but my requests have all been turned down. I've been told time and again that my skills are in short supply and there is no likelihood of my release until sometime next year at the earliest. I'm as sorry about that as you must be. I do understand that bringing up the kids on your own is difficult – especially as Marty has been ill. Thank God it was not worse. I know you've done an amazing job looking after her. Nevertheless I still worry about you all. My absence does not for one moment diminish my responsibilities as a father.

You are quite wrong to suggest that I asked Alice to spy on you. I didn't know she was planning to visit. It was her own idea as she was in the south. I am also unhappy that you suggest she should not comment on family matters. Alice is family. She's not one to "stir up trouble" as you put it. She was just concerned by what she saw of the way Edna dealt with the kids. You know I worry about it as well. I don't think she's good for them despite her support when Marty was ill. Your parents worry about it too – and please, don't think I have been writing to ask them to put pressure on you. All three of us have the best interests of the family at heart. You and I will have a big job to do when I get home to make sure that we are the best possible parents we can be.

Love and hugs to Marty and Mark and to you.

'Well, there's certainly tension there but it's quite affectionate and diplomatic. A lot of thought must have gone into it.'

'The other was written a fortnight later. When you've read it, I'll tell you about the ones that have so upset me.'

Dearest Joan

I really am sorry we don't seem to be able to agree about matters at home. I know you're doing a great job carrying the load of caring for the kids with help from your parents. I don't want to disrupt your friendship, but Edna cannot and should not be thought of as a substitute father. We shall have a lot of sorting out to do when I get home. I have applied again for early release but again it has been denied.

I know it's taking time for England to get back

on its feet. It must be very galling that rationing has become more severe, particularly as it's necessary to ensure that Germans don't starve. I understand that doesn't arouse much sympathy. But I think you would feel differently if you were to see the condition of people here, especially the kids. We really have to do this. We can't let people starve and we must avoid creating a situation where all Germany's ills are placed at our door. None of us wants another war.

My love to Marty and Mark and to you.

'I don't have the other half of the correspondence but it seems George, Dad, got the brush-off. I guess Mum's letter was pretty blunt. The diary suggests that.'

'Yes, it looks as if a long-distance froideur had set in – even an ice age. It must have been difficult. Your dad was obviously desperately worried. But you already knew your parents weren't close.' Gisela sipped her wine. 'But there's something more, isn't there?'

'It's all these.' Mark gestured with those in his hand and pointed to the letters on the desk. 'They're mainly from Edna to Mum; one or two from Mum to her. They were written during the war and afterwards, before Dad was demobbed. There are thirty or forty of them – and poems.'

'So?'

'They're love letters. There's no other word for them. Some are quite explicit and they're creepy.'

'Are you sure?'

'Yes. Edna was brusque, prickly. It's difficult to think of her as romantic and that's why they're so extraordinary.'

Mark unfolded one letter. 'Listen to this. "Thank you for a beautiful day yesterday. After you had gone, all the glory seemed to have departed. I look upon my home as a place to be kept for you – a refuge when things oppress and trouble you. A sanctuary where we can be alone, a refuge of loving arms, the sanctuary of a loving heart, and a place where you can lay your dear head. I want so much to remove any doubts you have about us. We must build this up together, my darling. Do not listen to the voices of others. They do not know the strength of the bond between us and probably would not understand." Others are much the same.'

Gisela looked at him. 'I don't know what to say. It's difficult to get my head around it. What do you remember about her – them?'

'Not much. All I can really remember is that I hated it when she was around.'

'It's hard to think of your Mum in this way.'

'Yes, she was very non-tactile with us as kids – apparently with Dad too.'

'How far do you think it went physically?'

'I don't know. Some phrases suggest it was quite intimate.' He picked up several letters. 'I've highlighted some: "my ears are still ringing with the sweet words of love you spoke to me" and "I still feel the glory of your presence", pretty flowery language. Here's another: "I feel thrilled by the closeness of you, you are very desirable". I've only found one note of friction, when Edna apologises for "forcing herself" on Mum. I don't know if this was a temporary glitch in an intimate relationship or whether Mum's reserve and conventionality held her back. There's also a poem from Edna entitled "Self-Denial" which suggests there were boundaries which were not crossed.'

'Or crossed and then retreated from?'

'Perhaps. We'll never know. I'm not sure I want to.'

'You mentioned poems. How many?'

'There are about twenty, and they're love poems.' He picked one out. 'Like this:

"If you're feeling tired and worried by uneasy vague alarms
Remember here awaits you a loving pair of arms,
And ever they are waiting to fondle and caress
To give you peace and courage in days of storm and stress."

'Not exactly poet laureate material but quite explicit.'

'Anything from your mother?'

'Very little – a poem expressing similar sentiments but less explicit and a letter which she signs off "All my love, darling heart". There's also an odd letter from Edna written just after Dad's death. She says, "Now George has gone, you must not grieve too much. You must enjoy your freedom". That sounds calculating and callous.'

'I guess your mum was bisexual or, more likely, a lesbian who hid her sexuality to conform.'

Gisela was right. 'I'm not sure how I feel about this. Maybe we should have destroyed everything or at least what was in her box. It's obvious now why Mum attached that note.'

'But why didn't she do it herself?'

He shook his head. 'I don't know. It's odd.'

'Perhaps she meant to and then forgot about them or

maybe it was difficult to relinquish memories of a lost love. Do you really want to share this with your sister?'

'I feel I should.'

'Why?'

'I can't explain it but I just think she should know. I'll have to tell her if she asks. She may want to see the letters and poems.'

'Why not tell her she was right and you've burnt the contents of that box.'

'I wouldn't get away with it. She'd smell a rat. Perhaps she already had and that's why she wanted them destroyed.'

'Perhaps you're right.'

'But it explains some things. I remember complaining once to Mum that Edna treated me more harshly than Marty. I always seemed to be being picked on.'

'Perhaps she worried that your hormones were on the warpath, even at the age of six.'

'If they were surging, they certainly wouldn't have surged in her direction. But it explains why Mum never really had any other relationship after Dad's death.'

'And you say she disappeared about a year after your dad died?'

'Yes, I don't know what happened to her. Probably I never asked. I was just pleased she was no longer around.'

'Perhaps there was a rift or possibly she was seen off the premises by your Gran.'

'Possibly.'

She looked at Mark. 'Do you want to go on with this?'

'I can't stop now. Dad's concerns about this were obvious from very early in the marriage, even if he wasn't sure of its extent. I was beginning to wonder if this might have had something to do with his accident.'

'Perhaps. This is taking both of us back to uncomfortable and painful parts of out pasts.'

'I need to read more of those diaries.'

'Are you really sure you want to go on?'

'I can't stop now.' He laughed. 'Perhaps there are other skeletons in the cupboard. There may even be storerooms full of them.'

14

6 December 1945

George

St Nicholas Day. Another Christmas far from home. Missing the kids so much. Still a bit worried about Marty – tho' obviously much better. Can the docs really be sure it won't get worse again? MO is reassuring. Hope he's right. If only I could be there. Still worried about Edna. Will I be home by next Christmas? Might have to stay until the deadline (which we're not going to meet) for completing the clearance. Might have to stay until it's all done. Could be two more years. What a bloody depressing thought.

As the days of December passed George's thoughts turned repeatedly to home. If only he could share the children's growing excitement as Christmas approached. Marty was heading towards her sixth birthday and Mark was three. Two years earlier he had been no more than a happy spectator.

George could envisage Marty, overactive, involved and voluble, busy organising everything, including her brother. She would be first down each morning to open the next window on the advent calendar before heading off to school. The two of them would pick up the post, morning and afternoon, as soon as they heard it drop onto the mat and take it to Joan. He was sure Marty would insist the cards were opened immediately, looking over Joan's shoulder as she did so, and then help arrange them on the mantelpiece. They would both be entranced by the paper chains and the tinsel-covered Christmas tree in the bay window of the lounge and would be looking longingly at the brightly wrapped presents, inspecting the labels, feeling and shaking them speculatively as they tried to guess their contents. George longed to be with them, sharing their fun.

The men and local people all tried to make something of an event of St Nicholas and Christmas despite the bleak weather. The padre led a carol service and the mess cook promised something special. It wasn't bad. Everyone was buoyed up by food parcels from home. They were well supplied with drink and cigarettes. George's evening sessions with Irmgard had developed into something of a social occasion and she would occasionally linger for a drink with him. One evening George mentioned his regret that he wouldn't see his children at Christmas. The following week she suggested he should join her family at home on Christmas Eve, saying this was the day they had their major celebration. It was tempting but he was cautious about accepting. He discussed the invitation with the local military administrator. He said, in his view, that it made no sense to isolate themselves entirely from local people although he made it clear that he was not formally approving acceptance of the invitation. George took the earlier comment to imply that he was not barred from doing so.

George joined Irmgard and her family outside the shell of one of the protestant churches early in the evening. A large crowd had gathered. On the stroke of five, the priest and the choir assembled in front of the ruin. A young chorister stepped forward and the crowd fell silent. He started to sing "Stille Nacht, heilige Nacht" in his pure treble voice. His breath hung in the still cold air, highlighted by the spotlights trained on the church. He sang the first verse solo. The other voice parts joined him for the second verse and then all raised their voices to sing the final verse:

Stille Nacht, heilige Nacht,
Gottes Sohn, o wie lacht
Lieb' aus deinem göttlichen Mund,
Da uns schlägt die rettende Stund'.
Christ, in deiner Geburt!
Christ, in deiner Geburt!

They then processed into the roofless church for further carols. It was lit only by a pale moon and candles guttering in the wind. It was moving even for a non-believer. It brought a lump to George's throat as he thought back to the carols he and Joan had sung together at the old people's home seven years earlier.

He walked back to the flat with Irmgard, her husband Rudolf, son Berthold and Hannelore. 'Sadly this will be a poor meal compared with those before the war,' Irmgard said. A carp and potato salad was followed by rabbit with red cabbage and potato dumplings. 'Ten years ago we might have had a goose or a roast suckling pig but these are luxuries now – only available on the black market at crazy prices. But thank you for adding the wine.'

'It was nothing. It is kind of you to offer me a taste of home life.'

'It's a thank you too. You rescued Hannelore and it led me to a job.'

'I've not seen you since and never thanked you properly. I was scared that evening.' Hannelore smiled. 'And again when you started to walk with me. I'd heard what those guys said.'

'I'd guessed, but my motives were entirely proper.'

'I know that now.'

'We've been lucky. Rudolf's services as a dentist are always needed and Bertie has come through it all unharmed. People are now calling this "die Stunde Null", zero hour. Everything will have to change. Let's hope it's for the better.'

'I hope so,' said George non-committally. He had no wish to get involved in a political discussion.

'It's difficult to explain how we feel. We've been beaten but we're scared our zero hour might become zero months or even zero years. It's difficult to see how we can ever pull our country together again – if it ever was truly together. You can help but we need to mend ourselves.'

Hannelore put her arm round her mother. 'Mutti, it's Christmas. It'll take time but we'll get there. We mustn't load our anxieties onto George.'

'You're right. He has enough of his own.' Hannelore looked at her mother enquiringly. 'He told me before Christmas that his little girl has polio.'

She put a hand gently on his arm. 'George, I'm so sorry. You must be worried sick.'

He nodded. 'My wife keeps me up to date with progress. It's turning out not too badly. She's been left with a bit of a limp but she gets around well. The doctor says she's through the worst.' He was anxious to change the subject. He walked over to the corner of the room where a chess board and pieces were set out on a table. 'Are you a chess player, Rudolf?'

'I am. Do you play?'

George nodded. He had picked up some of the pieces and was examining them. They were very finely crafted. 'This is a beautiful set. What are the woods?'

'Rosewood and box. I made it myself.' George turned the pieces over in his hands, admiring the delicacy of the detail. Rudolf smiled. 'I'm a dentist. I'm used to working on a small scale and one or two items of dental equipment can be used for other purposes. Would you like to play sometime?' George nodded.

'You should join us one weekend and then you and Rudolf can play. I'll fix it when I come for your next lesson.'

***

18 APRIL 1946

Fewer letters from home now. Little detail, just a record of Marty's progress at school and Mark's at nursery.

I've been sent extracts from Marty's first two school reports. Progress good academically but comments that she tends to boss other kids around – no surprise there.

***

17 MAY 1946

Life here is acquiring a rhythm. Satisfying in some ways. The job is essential. And I now have something of a social life – regular events in the mess and one or two Mine Clearance Groups have invited me to join them for their own social events. Some, but not all, have developed a real sense of teamwork. Several visits to the Beckers.

Early in the year George had been invited to lunch with the Becker family to be followed by chess with Rudolf. He proved to be an excellent player, considerably better than George's father-in-law. It was a close game and a good day. The invitation was repeated several times. One day, when George arrived, Irmgard said Rudolf had a heavy cold and would prefer not to play. He was about to leave but she insisted he should stay for lunch, saying Hannelore would like a game. She added that her daughter was quite a good player too. It didn't take long to discover that Irmgard was wrong. Hannelore was an excellent player – even better than her father. She quickly sorted him out.

He saw Rudolf two weeks later. 'I hear you had a good game with Hanny.'

He smiled. 'Other way round. She had a good game with me. I'm not in her class. Where did she learn?'

'She used to watch me playing with a friend – sadly no longer with us. His days ended in a camp in Poland, Treblinka, we think. The whole family too. When Hanny was about nine, she asked me to teach her. She really didn't need much teaching. She was a natural. She was beating me regularly when she was in her teens.'

George turned to her. 'What are you going to do with your formidable brain?' he asked.

'Oh, it's only good at a few things. I used to teach maths and physics at the Hochschule on the other side of the city. I had an apartment there.' She looked at him sadly. 'The apartment is no more.' She hesitated. 'Nor is my fiancé. He was there when it was bombed on the first of October eighteen months ago, just before the Americans took the city. He had survived three years in the Wehrmacht and was home for a few days leave.'

'I'm so sorry.'

'It was terrible, but we've been lucky in other ways. We can't and won't forget, though it's not easy to talk about it. But we try to think positively.'

Her eyes were beginning to fill with tears. On an instinct, George went over and put his arms around her. She hugged him tightly before standing back. 'I'm sorry,' he said. 'I shouldn't have done that.'

There was a slight smile on her face as she came closer. She put her hands on his shoulders and whispered in his ear, 'Perhaps not, but thank you. I'm happy you did.'

***

10 July 1946

Methodically clearing the mines – square kilometre by square kilometre. I've been lucky. I've been able to keep Redpath and Thwaites. Couldn't have asked for two better NCOs. Their organisational skills and management of the guys have been outstanding. The German Pioneer Leaders have generally done well, though I've had to replace two. We've managed to build a level of trust. Redpath's fluent German and my efforts to speak the language have helped (though it has sometimes caused some amusement). One hairy episode contributed greatly to morale. I still shudder when I think of it.

It was a blisteringly hot day. George and Thwaites were inspecting one of the groups in the Forest. George leaned back on the bonnet of one of the trucks taking frequent mouthfuls of water from his canteen as he was briefed by the group leader. The clearers, stripped to the waist, were deployed in a line probing methodically as they edged forward. There were frequent pauses as devices were found and defused. The line had come to a halt once more as two men had located an S mine with a long-handled prodder. There were still all too few metal detectors. The men were on their knees exposing the pressure pad. They had disarmed it by inserting a pin into the sensor but it was proving difficult to lift as it was held firmly by the impacted earth. It suddenly came free. The man who had been easing it out momentarily lost his balance. He took a step back to recover but as he did so he triggered another. The blast threw him against his colleague who was standing close by. Both went down, triggering a third mine. The two devices launched themselves into the air spraying shrapnel all around. George told Thwaites to stay back. He took a metal detector from the car and crossed the cleared area to where the two men were lying. There were two other mines very close by. He defused these and then, with Thwaites and the Group leader, carried the two men back to a safe area. One was badly injured. He had severe wounds in the genital region and would certainly lose a leg. The other had been more fortunate. He only had superficial injuries as he had been lying face down following the first explosion and had been shielded by his colleague's body. Thwaites took the badly injured man to the hospital after commandeering one of the Group's trucks as a makeshift ambulance – not the first time it had been used for that purpose. The guy made it, but his mine clearance days were over. George wondered if he would think the loss of a leg was an acceptable exchange for a certainty that he would not have to return to such a hazardous occupation.

George stayed until Thwaites got back. He was warmly thanked by the Group. Such events were far from unique. There had now been nineteen deaths and nearly thirty serious injuries. His active involvement had added to the degree of trust they had created in a way which could not have been achieved by verbal exhortation.

This episode strengthened George's arm when he went to the CO and argued for more metal detectors. It was short-sighted, he pointed out forcefully, not to equip the groups properly and unacceptable that German mine lifters should be regarded as dispensable. More metal detectors would make it possible to proceed more quickly and more safely. If losses and injuries were to become more frequent it would simply not be possible to get the ground cleared and some would desert. There would be little chance of finding them if they did. Threats of discipline were largely meaningless. Additional equipment was delivered within six weeks.

***

28 July 1946

72-hour leave. Not enough time to get home – but what the hell is there to do here? Just R and R. CO agrees I'm overdue a lot of leave. Granted ten days over Christmas. It's an age away. Written to Joan. Doubt she's got round to thinking about Christmas yet. Suggested it would be good for us to go away as a family for a few days. Need to mend (? build) fences. Would be good to start doing so before I'm demobbed. Obviously won't be this year as I've been granted Christmas leave. Fingers crossed for 1947.

George took his leave over the last weekend in July. There wasn't time to get home. To do so would require two full days' travelling and only one at home. He wrote to Joan to let her know. She replied saying she understood adding, unnecessarily in George's view, that it would be disruptive for the children if he were only home for a day. He was upset although he knew it was somewhat unjust to react negatively to her acceptance of his suggestion. He had hoped to be challenged and urged to come back even if only for a short time. He scarcely knew the kids. It was going to be hard to get to know them over the winter and when he was eventually demobbed. Only then would he be able to play a meaningful part in their lives – and they in his.

George was unsure how to take advantage of the break. He wandered aimlessly between his billet and the mess on the first two days – drinking a little too much. Leave in Germany seemed pointless. His final day was warm and almost cloudless. He had been invited to join the Beckers for lunch. He was greeted by Hanny saying she and Bertie had decided it was a good day for a picnic, adding, 'You'll know where we can sit without being blasted into space.' They found a spot on the fringes of a small copse and close to the border. After their lunch they lay back enjoying the sun filtering through the branches of the trees. A few gossamer-like wisps of cirrus drifted unhurriedly across the sky. George's thoughts oscillated haphazardly between home and his life in Germany. He had been in Aachen for a year.

It was still difficult to think of Farnham as home. He was uncertain about where he stood with Joan, or where she stood with Edna. It was no longer possible to suppress the realisation that Joan had struck up an unusually close relationship with her. He didn't want to imagine what it might mean and it was difficult to conceive how things might play out when he was home again.

George's reverie was interrupted by a loud snore. He raised his head and saw that Bertie had fallen asleep. Hanny was lying propped up on one elbow looking across at them with an amused smile on her face. She got to her feet and stood over him. 'Let's take a walk. This is too nice a day to waste by sleeping. We can leave Bertie for a bit.' She took his hand and pulled him to his feet. They walked a short distance along the fringes of the wood until they reached a fallen tree. She suggested they should sit for a time in the shade. They did so in silence for some minutes, looking out over the sunlit valley stretching away towards the border. She looked at him. 'It was kind of you to comfort me when I told you about my fiancé. I miss him badly. We had decided to wait until after the war to get married. If we hadn't it would have been a short marriage. I'm sorry about that.'

He took her hand. 'I had a very close friend who was wounded during the invasion and then died. I saw his widow when I was last home. They'd decided to put off starting a family until after the war. She regrets that decision so much. She feels it would have left her with some part of him.'

'I guess we all make terrible decisions at times.' George nodded. 'I try to think positively. But it's difficult. I miss Georg. He had the same name as you. He was an engineer too, in the Pioneer Corps. He might have been working for you if it hadn't been for that bomb.' She smiled. 'You were looking very thoughtful and a little sad when I was watching you.' It was clear that there was a question implicit in the comment. 'You don't have to share your thoughts but I'd like to hear about your family.'

'I was thinking about home,' he admitted hesitantly, 'though I'm not so sure where home is now. I've been there so little since I've been abroad and very little earlier in the war too. I hardly know my children. I couldn't even be there when Marty was ill. My wife sends details of things they've done and keeps me in touch, but it's not the same as being there. I have their photographs.' He took two small dog-eared snapshots from his wallet and handed them to Hanny.

'They look great. How are they doing at school? I know kids start younger in your country.'

'They're doing well, but I don't have a rounded picture of them in my mind. I feel I'm losing my family, though I know that's not true. They'll be there when I get back. But I'm not sure how well I'll be able to get to know them. Sometimes I feel superfluous,' he hesitated, 'or that I've been displaced.'

'How's that?' She paused before adding tentatively, 'Has your wife become close to another man?'

'No, it's a woman I'm worrying about.'

Hanny raised her eyebrows.

He paused before continuing. 'I'm just not sure how it'll be when I get home. They seem to manage well without me. I'm glad they do, but it worries me that I'll just be an appendage. There must be a lot of us in the same position, well maybe not quite the same position. There'll be a load to sort out and it won't be easy. It may not even be possible.' He stopped. This was the first time he had shared his anxieties and worries quite so openly. He had been more circumspect with Mo.

They sat silently for many minutes before Hanny said quietly, 'I guess I'm sad because of what might have been and never can be, and you're sad about what might or might not be. Do you know when you'll be free to go home?'

'No idea. We have a huge job here. It's not even half done. I've been lucky. I have good colleagues and I'm grateful to your mum for teaching me German – successfully. And the Becker family has helped to keep me grounded and,' he grinned, 'a certain member has helped me improve my chess.'

'It's not all been one way.' She quickly kissed him on the cheek. 'We should get back to Bertie. He may be feeling abandoned – if he's awake.'

***

2 December 1946

CO's office to confirm dates of home leave for Christmas. Raised the question of my discharge yet again. He raised the possibility of my signing on as a regular once more.

'Can you give me any hint as to when I might be demobbed? I've a young family. I'm keen to be back to civilian life.'

'You're not alone in that, Brown, but I've absolutely no idea. These decisions are not in my hands. As you know, you're one of the designated "key men" in the sector. Inevitably many of us are sappers. We have much needed skills.' He gestured to a chair. 'Have a seat.' He buzzed through to the outer office to organise some coffee.

'Any further thoughts about signing on as a regular?' he asked as they waited for the coffee.

George hesitated. 'Yes. In many ways army life has been good despite some frustrations. Also my wife rather surprised me by being enthusiastic about the idea but I don't think it's for me.'

'Men like you are needed. It's your decision but if you're interested, come and talk to me. I can't make commitments but I think you have the potential to go reasonably high in the service. Your competence and leadership are obvious. Not all my peers, and no names, no pack drill, have those abilities at a level to match yours. Think about it.' George nodded. It was not the time to make decisions about his future. He agreed to think it through. It was tempting but it would need a detailed discussion to see if it would work and be compatible with a reasonable family life.

'One bit of good news,' the CO continued. 'The powers that be are beginning to realise that mine lifting in your area will not be completed by next summer. At long last, there's some planning in the pipeline to accelerate the process. That's all I can say just now, simply because that's all I've been told. It's being looked at in detail by the brigadier as Chief Engineer of 1 Corps.'

'We're clearing as fast as possible. We were very short of equipment at first – and the nature of the terrain and safety issues have limited progress. You'll remember, Sir, I flagged up the impossibility of getting through by next summer as soon as we'd completed our initial survey and discovered the limit of the resources available.'

'Brown, there was no implicit criticism in what I said. I know you've never had the number of men or the gear specified in the initial mine clearance plan. That's true of other areas too. Your area is amongst the most heavily seeded in the sector. I repeat, the quality of your leadership and efficiency have not gone unnoticed. Now go off and enjoy your leave.' There was a knock and the CO's batman handed them their coffees. 'Let me just ask you something informally, Brown. I hear you've got close to some local Jerries. Gossip has reached my ears that you have a Fraulein as a mistress.'

George was about to react strongly but caution moderated his response. 'Not true, Sir. At least the last part's not true, but I have become friendly with the family of the woman who's been teaching me German. With your approval,' he added emphatically.

'Think back, Brown. I gave my consent, not quite the same as approval.'

'No, Sir. But I've got to know this family. They could not have been further away from the Nazis. It's true I have seen quite a lot of them and socialised with them. Their daughter is a great girl and we've spent some time together. She lost her fiancé in the bombing of the city. They're good friends but I'm a committed family man.' He stopped and looked up. The CO was smiling.

'You don't need to be so defensive. I was not being censorious and you wouldn't be the first man on this planet nor the first member of the occupying forces to play away from home. But I would say, as I've done before, you should tread warily. Some senior to me take a less relaxed view of contacts with locals. Fraternisation is still officially frowned on. Enjoy your leave and I'll see you back here at Area HQ in January.'

The discussion with the CO gave George cause for thought. His time in the army had been satisfying in many ways. He was enjoying the challenges of his task, the camaraderie of his colleagues and the sense that he was respected and trusted by the men. He was on the fringes of "the establishment" in the British Sector. He'd been invited to some official functions, including the opening of the Patton Bridge, built to replace a Bailey bridge, over the Rhine at Cologne with spans sufficiently high to enable commercial traffic to flow once more. He had also been invited to social events organised by Mine Clearance Groups. Although under military supervision, they had more freedom off duty than the British troops. One lot named itself the "Rabauken". George had difficulty with this. His dictionary translated the word as "bullies", but that didn't seem right. He discussed it with Irmgard who said it had a more positive connotation than that. They agreed that "ruffians, "hellraisers" or "rowdies" might be a better translation. They certainly lived up to that off duty.

The comment about Hannelore had touched a sensitive nerve. His first instinct had been to deny the charge forcefully. She was not his lover, but he was spending increasing amounts of time with her. He could not recall ever having been so happy and relaxed and open with a woman friend before. Perhaps that wasn't entirely right. He'd always felt close to Mo, but he regarded her more as an honorary sister. He and Hanny had talked endlessly since the picnic in the summer, exchanging confidences and sharing aspirations and fears for the future. They had laughed together and commiserated with one another, but they had always maintained a degree of emotional reserve although, at times, that had become vanishingly small. George knew he would leave Germany and Hanny with mixed emotions. It would neither be possible nor right to maintain contact after he was demobbed but he knew he would part from her with a great deal of sadness.

***

CHRISTMAS 1946

Joan had taken up George's suggestion that the family go away for a few days over Christmas. It was not clear why she had chosen Broadstairs on the Kent coast. Many of the coastal defence installations were still in place. Large concrete cubes lined the promenade above Viking Bay and along parts of the cliff. It was cold, cloudy and wet. The kids were excited at the thought of seeing the sea for the first time and making their first journey of any distance by train. They sat with George looking out of the window watching the smoke streaming past the carriage and dispersing over the fields. They were mesmerised by the rhythmic clatter of the wheels, the rattle as they went over points, the rush of the wind as they passed through stations without stopping and the changing pitch of the whistle from passing trains. It was early afternoon when they arrived. They walked from the station to a guest house a few streets back from Victoria Parade. George and the kids walked to the beach while Joan unpacked. Marty and Mark ran excitedly along the tideline, challenging the incoming waves and being struck by flurries of spray whipped off the crests by an easterly wind. George got some stick from Joan when they got back as there was salt on their sou'westers. She insisted they should have a bath straightaway in case they caught a cold, despite protests that they were not at all cold and didn't need a bath. Their wish was granted. The bathroom along the corridor was locked. A notice pinned to the door stated that hot water for baths was only available for children between six and seven each evening and for adults between nine and ten-thirty. The guest house was a temperance establishment and George established with Joan that he would take advantage of the children's bath hour each evening and go to the pub. The rest of the time he spent with Marty and Mark.

The boarding house was almost as depressing as the weather. It was cold. The landlady appeared to have an unwarranted belief that the thermal properties of the Gulf Stream and two lumps of coalite were sufficient provision for heating. And it was gloomy. The corridors were covered in dark brown linoleum and the walls were a drab beige. The rooms were illuminated by low wattage bulbs and there were reminders everywhere urging people to switch off lights. They were the only family there and Marty and Mark were the only kids. Most of the guests were long-term residents, mainly elderly women in thick cardigans who glared at the kids and shushed them whenever their voices were raised much above a whisper.

George took the kids out each day despite the showers and a keen wind. He bought them small spades and a bucket and they built ever more elaborate sandcastles which they would then watch being washed away by the incoming tide despite the protective moats they had built. One afternoon he sat with them in the lounge playing snap but this was quickly stopped by one of the residents who protested that it was disturbing her afternoon nap. He gently suggested she might snooze in her room. This was firmly rejected on the grounds that the bedrooms were cold and she always slept in the lounge in the afternoon. She was emphatic that her routine should not be changed to satisfy the entertainment needs of young children who would only be there for a few days. This was reinforced by the owner, who said that it was essential for her business to keep the residents happy. It had suffered during the war as older people in Thanet had been evacuated for fear of invasion or coastal attacks.

George took the kids to see "Bambi" on Christmas Eve, their first visit to a cinema. They were enchanted by the animation and the tale of the young fawn, although they covered their eyes when the hunters shot his mother. George promised to take them to the cinema again as soon as he was home. They asked repeatedly when that would be and he had to admit he didn't know. They looked a little downcast but were partially mollified when Joan said she would take them the next time there was a suitable film.

The Christmas lunch was meagre as many items were still rationed. This was followed by charades and little competitions. The elderly residents thawed in the atmosphere of enforced jollity and made a fuss of the children, reminiscing about the Victorian Christmases of their childhood. Their tales of carol singing, roaring fires, goose and plum pudding contrasted strikingly with the modest fare provided. George said nothing. He was acutely aware that his colleagues in the mess would be having a better meal and a more cheerful and bibulous time. Joan helped to enliven the day by playing the piano for the residents and encouraging them to sing carols with George and the children.

They were relieved to get back to Farnham. The kids were able to play with their familiar toys and run around freely and Joan was more relaxed in her home surroundings. It remained difficult for George to overcome the feeling that he was not much more than a visitor. It was reassuring that family life ran smoothly in his absence, but he would have been happier if his occasional appearances were greeted with greater warmth by Joan. But that was how it was. He had pursued her and won her. Joan asked once more if he would consider taking up a regular commission but she made it clear she would not be prepared to give up the family home to make frequent moves and live in army married quarters. George's time with his children had reinforced his decision that a life in the army was not for him. Not to be involved in their development and futures did not bear thinking about.

The instinct that his presence was regarded as superfluous was emphasised on the final day of his leave. Edna came to the door and was greeted with a hug from Joan. She looked over her shoulder and saw George in the background. 'Sorry, I thought you'd already gone.' She turned to Joan and beat a retreat saying, 'I'll be back after George has left.' This episode, trivial though it was, reinforced George's disquiet about Edna. It was difficult not to contrast the warmth of her reception with the cooler greeting he had received a week earlier. He was not sure how much to make of it. Perhaps he was being unduly suspicious about someone who meant well but had an unfortunate manner. However, it was not the time to raise the matter as he was leaving an hour later. This was unfinished business. It would have to be faced when he was finally discharged.

15

21 April 1990

Mark and Gisela were sitting on the patio enjoying a coffee after lunch. The Saturday papers and colour supplements were strewn over the table. Mark was struggling with the cryptic crossword. Ellie was browsing through the travel section. She was about to put it to one side and energise herself sufficiently to cut the grass when the phone rang.

She went inside and picked up the receiver. 'Ellie, I need to come to London. Can I stay for a couple of nights?' Martina sounded very tense.

'No problem. When do you want to come?'

'Today, later this afternoon. Is that okay?'

'Yes, we're here. Something special going on?'

'I'll explain when I get to you,' she said abruptly and rang off without a further word. Ellie walked outside.

Mark looked at her enquiringly. 'Who was that?'

'Your sister. Says she needs to stay – arriving later this afternoon. She wouldn't say why or what was so urgent.'

Martina arrived about six. 'Sorry to land on you like this.'

Gisela had just finished gardening. 'No problem. We weren't going anywhere. Go and sit in the kitchen and I'll make some tea.' She put the tools and lawnmower away and followed Martina inside. She was standing by the sink looking out over the garden and the, now fading, display of tulips and hyacinths. She stood aside as Gisela filled the kettle and placed mugs on the counter.

'If you don't mind I'd rather have a drink.'

'Of course, what will you have?'

'A glass of wine.'

'Okay. So what do you have on in London at such short notice?'

Martina shifted her feet uncomfortably. 'Nothing really, I just needed to get away. I'm not on call and I couldn't stand the thought of a hotel on my own.'

Ellie walked over and put her arms around Martina, then stood back, placing her hands on her shoulders. Her sister-in-law was looking very edgy. 'Why don't you take your bag upstairs? Come down when you're ready and we'll have that drink. Mark will be back in a minute. He's just gone down the road to get one or two things for our meal.'

It was half an hour before Martina came down and joined them in the kitchen. 'Have a seat. Mark will get you that glass of wine. We can talk while I'm cooking. Boeuf bourguignon alright for you?' Martina nodded. 'Australian shiraz?' She nodded again. 'By the way, Michael will be back this evening. That's a first for a Saturday night for some time. His girlfriend has gone home to her parents.'

'Good, I haven't seen him for ages.'

Mark handed her a glass of wine. 'So what's going on? Is Paul at home?'

'Mark, I think we should let Marty talk in her own time – if she wants to.'

'It's alright, Ellie. Yes, he is at home. He has nowhere else to go. Half the house is his. I can't turn him out. He's got almost no money and his credit cards are maxed out.'

'Awkward. How are you managing?'

'It's difficult. Not so bad in the week – I get into work early and am generally home fairly late. I can hang around the hospital at weekends when I'm not on call but that's not a lot of fun. Frankly, nothing's much fun at the moment. I'm not sure it ever was.' She stopped and leant forward with her elbows on the kitchen table and her head in her hands.

Ellie handed her a knife and a chopping board. 'Here, you can slice the mushrooms and onions, dice the bacon and crush the garlic while we talk.'

'Okay, but I might give the onions a miss.'

Ellie smiled. 'Fair enough. Mark can get us a couple of fresh bay leaves from outside?'

Martina sat shaking her head. 'I just need to get through this. We've put the house on the market and we'll split the proceeds.'

'What'll happen next?'

'Everyone reckons he'll get a suspended sentence. His firm are making good the losses. They tried to argue that the sums he'd filched from Mum's estate were his and they shouldn't be liable. I went to another firm. They pointed out, as I had done, that the money was not his but Mark's and mine, so that'll be settled.'

'I guess that's one bit of good news.'

Martina smiled wryly. 'Yes, but my share will now be taken into account when putting together the financial statements for the divorce. So he'll get his hands on some of it – legally this time. But it's a price worth paying to be shot of him.'

'What'll he do?'

'I don't know. It might not be much more than stacking shelves. I've tried to get him to think constructively but he's full of self-pity. I give him a bit of money each day, just enough for him to do something to fill his time – like going to the cinema. It's a bit like dealing with a kid in the school holidays. If I give him more, I worry he'll simply spend it on slot machines or booze. Perhaps he does anyway. Weekends are worst. This morning I'd had it up to here so I gave him some money and told him to get lost for the day. I left while he was out.'

'Did you leave a note?'

'Reluctantly, yes and a bit more cash for the weekend. For God's sake, give me another drink and let's change the subject.'

Mark had come back in. He looked at his sister and said tentatively, 'Well, there is something else. I know you weren't keen to look into our family history but perhaps we might talk about it a bit.'

'Mark, are you sure that's a good idea? Marty's not in a good place just now.'

'That's for her to say,' he said sharply.

Ellie was about to respond but changed her mind. She shrugged, 'Alright, top up your glasses and go through to the lounge. I'll carry on here.'

When they were seated Martina looked at him. 'What's Ellie worried about?'

Mark hesitated. Perhaps she was right and he should tread carefully. 'She's been reading some of the diaries. They've brought back memories,' he said cautiously. 'That time was tough for her.'

'Just that? It didn't sound as if it was the only reason. You'd better tell me.'

Mark paused for a moment. He was thinking how much he should reveal when the lounge door was pushed open.

'Hi, Dad, I'm home. Hi, Aunt Marty. I didn't know you were going to be here. How's my favourite aunt?'

'Last minute decision. And favourite aunt? I'm the only one you've got so there's not a lot of competition for the title.'

'You'd still be my favourite aunt even if I had dozens.'

Martina laughed. 'Alright, favourite nephew. Come and give your favourite aunt a hug.' Michael went over and embraced Martina. 'I think your dad was about to let the family skeletons out of the cupboard.'

'I've been reading those diaries. They're fascinating. And they'll be useful for my dissertation.'

'How come?'

'It's on the occupation of Germany after the war. My granddad, your dad, was quite a hero. There's a lot in those diaries. I'm just going to say hi to Mum. I'll see you a bit later.'

Martina turned to Mark and sighed. 'You'd better let me have it.'

'There's a lot there but Michael's right. Our dad did an incredible job. I'll show you later.' He paused again. He was surrounded by thin ice. Eventually he said, 'There's a lot about our early childhood. I've been wondering how much you remember?'

'Some, but I was only five at the end of the war. My memories are fairly hazy.'

'And afterwards?'

'Mostly talking about the war and how things had been so much better before. If people were to be believed, things were cheaper, no rationing, everyone was more polite, even the weather was better. The words "before the war" were repeated like a mantra over and over as if it had been a golden age.'

'For the few perhaps, but not for most.'

'And everyone grumbled about shortages: food, coal and rationing. There were coupons for everything – meat, butter, eggs, sugar, sweets.'

'You make it sound pretty grim.'

'I guess it was. But we were quite protected. And there were good times, like going to Newcastle with Dad. And Granny and Grandpa were around a lot. That was good. They had a television long before we did. We would have tea there and watch children's hour at weekends – Muffin the Mule and Oswald the Ostrich. It made a change from children's hour on the wireless with Uncle Mac.'

Mark laughed. 'Wireless? I haven't heard that word for years.'

'Have you been through all the diaries now?'

'No, there's a lot more. I've got to the end of 1946. I'll get to the others soon.' He hesitated, uncertain about saying more.

The decision was taken from him as Michael came back into the room carrying a beer. 'Has Dad brought you up to date? Has he told you about your dad's bit on the side?'

'What do you mean?'

'Hold it,' Mark interjected hurriedly. 'I'll explain. It seems our dad became friendly with a family in Germany. The mother taught him German and he got to know her family.'

Michael could not resist adding, 'Especially the daughter.'

'There's nothing there to suggest it was anything other than a friendship.'

Michael had been about to say, 'Watch this space' but decided against it after a warning glance from his father.

'And is that all Ellie was worried about?'

Mark hesitated. He was conscious of the need to pick his words carefully. 'There's also a lot suggesting Mum and Dad weren't that close.'

'Not surprising. He was away so much.'

'I think there may have been more to it than that.'

'What are you saying? Is this what Ellie was hinting at?'

'There are a lot of references to Edna in his letters. She seems to have come between them in a big way.'

'What are you saying?' She paused for a moment. 'No, absolutely not. She was just a good friend,' she said very emphatically.

'Maybe, but I'm not so sure.'

Martina got to her feet and started pacing up and down. She stopped by Mark and looked down at him. 'You're holding something else back, aren't you?'

225

'No, just putting two and two together.'

'And making seven or more.'

'No, only four. I think it was quite an intimate friendship.'

'What the hell's that word supposed to mean?'

'I can show you some letters.'

'Are you saying there are letters between Mum and Edna?'

Mark nodded. 'Yes, a lot. I've only just found them. I can show you.'

Martina was getting very agitated. 'I don't want to see them – and, if you had had any decency, you would have burnt them as Mum asked.'

There was an uncomfortable silence which was only broken when Ellie came back into the room. 'Come and eat. It's all ready.'

The silence continued throughout the meal despite Ellie's attempts to lighten the atmosphere. Martina turned down the offer of coffee as soon as the meal was over and, pleading tiredness, headed for bed.

***

Michael followed his parents into the lounge. Ellie poured coffee for them. 'So what exactly went on between you before dinner? I didn't like to ask while Marty was there as the atmosphere was so tense.'

Michael looked up. 'I'm afraid I rather put my foot in it.'

'What did you say?'

'I hinted that my grandad might have had an affair in Germany.'

'It was more than a hint. It was a fairly prattish thing to say.'

'Hang on, Dad. This was over forty years ago. The poor bugger's dead and Gran's dead. It shouldn't be a big deal.'

'That's not the way your aunt would see it.'

'Come on, be fair. She was much more on edge over your comments about Gran and this woman. What are these letters you were talking about?'

'They're very intimate.'

'You keep using that word. Are you saying what I think you're saying?' Mark nodded. 'So what, if Gran had lezzy tendencies?'

Ellie shook her head. 'God, you were each as bad as the other, putting one foot after another right into it.'

Mark paused. Both Ellie and his sister had tried to discourage him from embarking on this search, albeit for very different reasons. Martina's reluctance suggested that she might have already sensed there could be revelations about their mother's sexuality and didn't want to confront the reality. It would have become unavoidable and even more uncomfortable if she were to see the letters and poems.

'I'm sorry. I'll talk to her in the morning and try to rebuild some bridges.'

'Has it not occurred to you that this revelation about your mum might hit her particularly hard?'

'Why do you say that?'

'For God's sake, just think about it. Her marriage

is falling apart and whatever led to that, it is overlain by her sadness that she and Paul failed to conceive. It must be painful for her to think that her own mother had had no difficulty in conceiving despite her evident lack of enthusiasm for sex. And it must be even more difficult being surrounded by kids all day.'

'I guess Mum's right. Aunt Marty was always fantastic with me when I was a kid. She would get down on the floor with me and play. And she never talked down to me.'

'I imagine she's amazing with the kids at work too.'

There followed a silence which was broken by the doorbell. Mark looked at his watch. 'Who the hell? It's after ten.' He went and opened the door. Paul was leaning against one of the pillars of the porch, clutching it in a firm embrace. As Mark studied him in the dim light from the street lamp, he saw a car drawing away down the road. His clothes were dishevelled, his coat was torn and there was a long muddy stain down one side. He looked more closely. There was a substantial bruise on his left cheek. 'You look bloody terrible. What's happened?'

'Knew I'd get a warm welcome from my brother-in-law,' he mumbled incoherently. 'Been mugged – everything taken – wasn't much – didn't have much – the bitch doesn't let me have much. Been with the police. They didn't seem interested. Said I was pissed. But gave me a lift here – so here I am.' He gave an exaggerated flourish with one arm but quickly wrapped it back round the pillar for support.

'You'd better come in.'

'Knew I could rely on you – good old Mark. Is that fucking woman of mine here?'

Mark helped him in and sat him on a chair in the hall. 'Stay there.'

'Don't worry. Not going anywhere, old boy. No money. Will fall over if I try. Just want to see my darling wife.'

Mark went back into the lounge. He beckoned to Ellie who came out and looked at Paul. 'What's happened?'

'He's been mugged.'

'Is he alright?'

'Think so. Just a bit battered.'

Paul looked up. 'I'm seriously hurt. It was grievous bodily harm. Need my doctor wife.'

'She's in bed. You're just a bit bruised and you won't get much sympathy from her.'

He shook his head. 'Been the problem all along.'

Mark turned back to Ellie. 'I guess he decided to follow Marty and got pissed somewhere along the line. Must have been an easy target for a yob. He'll have to sleep here. Michael can help me get him upstairs and cleaned up. We'll get his outer clothes off and put him on top of the bed. We can sort things out in the morning. There's no point in waking Marty and her giving him a bollocking just now.'

***

Martina was up early the next morning. 'I don't want to see him,' she said emphatically. 'I'm going home. I'll give you the money for his fare back to Birmingham. Will you put him on a train, a late train, and let me know what time it gets in? I'll pick him up from the station.'

She was about to go when Paul came down looking very shaky. 'I need coffee and paracetamol – lots of both.' He walked into the kitchen and saw Martina.

'I'm just leaving to go home.'

'But I've come all this way to see you. I've been mugged and I don't have a sou. You can't just bugger off. What's going to happen to me?'

'I've given Mark money for your fare. He'll put you on a train later. I'll collect you from New Street. I don't want you around any more than necessary.'

'Marty, I've been mugged. How about a little sympathy?'

'You don't deserve any bloody sympathy. Your problems are all of your own making.' She glanced at Mark. 'Sorry to lumber you and Ellie with this but I'm going.' She turned abruptly, collected her bag and stick and walked out, slamming the door behind her.

Mark shouted out as she was leaving. 'Hang on, Marty, you can't just sod off like that and dump your marital problems on us.' It was too late. She'd gone. He went back into the kitchen. 'She can move fast enough if she wants to. I don't know how much sympathy that fucking stick gets her, but her behaviour doesn't earn her any.'

Paul sat down heavily on a chair. Ellie handed him a cup of black coffee.

'What am I going to do now?'

'The rest of your day's been mapped out for you. We'll take a walk in the gardens for you to clear your head and we'll get you on a late train. Then it's up to you. You need to sort things out with Marty.'

'Bloody impossible, she doesn't do sorting out. Takes

no prisoners. You'd drink if you were married to a woman like that. I know she's your fucking sister but it's true.'

'Hang on, you can't lay all the blame for your problems at her door.'

'Perhaps not. But she's too bloody rigid and uptight. Should never have married her.'

The rest of the day passed without incident. Mark and Ellie retreated to The Greyhound after seeing Paul onto the train back to Birmingham. 'That was quite a weekend,' said Ellie. 'I'm not sure I want many more like that.'

16

10 January 1947

George

At last! It's going to happen. I'm to be demobbed.

George was summoned to see the CO on his return. He gestured to him to sit. 'How was your leave?'

'Fine, Sir.' He hesitated, 'Though there are one or two issues I need to sort out back home.'

'Nothing too serious, I hope.'

'I think not, Sir.' He was far from confident this was the case, but he didn't want to get involved in a discussion about his home life with the CO.

'I'll come straight to the point, Brown. Your wish has been granted. You'll be demobbed at the end of February. I know that's late by comparison with most of the "for the duration only" guys but it's early for someone playing a key role like you. The adjutant tells me you still have some accumulated leave due. That means you'll remain on the strength and be paid for your first few weeks back home.'

'Thank you, Sir.' George's heart lifted. An intricate patchwork of thoughts instantly colonised his mind – Joan, his children and his marriage at the forefront. He had not lived with Joan full-time since the move to Farnham more than six years earlier. It would be the start of a new chapter in his life.

George's musings were brought to an abrupt end by the CO. 'Get your brain back in gear, Brown. We need to discuss plans for the here and now and the clearance of the remainder of your area.'

'Sorry, Sir. What are the arrangements for a handover?'

'I told you before Christmas that plans were being prepared to strengthen the operation. These have now been worked through with Brigadier Pike's staff. There's to be a fresh operation called Operation Tappet.' George raised his eyebrows. 'I know, there's probably a department in the War Office headed by a highly paid civil servant devising names for military operations. I doubt if they know the difference between a tappet and a camshaft. Anyhow, additional groups are to be recruited. The number of personnel will be almost doubled to over two thousand in your area and another two hundred and fifty vehicles will be provided. The push is on to clear the rest by the summer, as originally agreed. I stress it's clearly understood that you were under-resourced and undermanned. The decision to provide these additional resources underlines that.'

'Will Redpath and Thwaites stay with the officer who'll take over? They're essential.'

'Yes. They'll remain until the job's done. Your

replacement will be here at the end of this month and a second officer will be drafted in to assist him.'

'Sounds impressive – I'm almost regretting I shan't be around to see the job through.'

'For God's sake, don't say that after all I've done to get you released as early as possible.'

'No, Sir – thank you.'

'I've also strongly recommended you for an award through the brig's office. I don't know if anyone will take any notice – but I'm telling you in case nothing comes through. I wanted you to know how much I've valued your efforts.'

'Thank you, Sir.'

He grinned. 'One other thing. I'm sure there'll be a send-off in the mess. Don't forget to invite me.'

That was it. George's war was coming to an end. His groups had cleared over half the devices in their area despite the slow start. But it had been achieved at a cost. There had been seventy-one deaths and as many serious injuries.

***

27 FEBRUARY 1947

Great send-off in the mess after one in the sergeants'
mess yesterday. I shall miss Jimmy Redpath and Reg
Thwaites. We were a good team. Farewell drinks
with some of the groups. Very touched – three of them
presented me with a booklet and a photographic record,
thanking me for my work and efforts. Off home in two
days. Icy cold here and in England.

***

1 March 1947

Yesterday was my last full day in Germany. Spent the day with the Beckers. Knew I should be leaving with mixed feelings. It was a day I shall never forget. Life will never be quite the same again. Now on the journey home by ferry and rail.

Irmgard had invited George to join the family for lunch on his last day. It was an emotional occasion. She had taught him German and he could now speak it fairly fluently. Even Redpath had complimented him on his command of the language. The Beckers had been his family in Germany. It was a long lunch and they made plans to keep in touch. Late in the afternoon, as George was about to leave, Hanny suggested they go for a farewell drink together in the centre of the city.

They sat comfortably in a bar near the cathedral with their drinks, sharing a companionable silence. She turned to him after some minutes. 'We were all happy you came to see us today.'

'You've all been wonderful, a home from home. Brought back thoughts of Newcastle.'

'Mutti would say that's quite a compliment.'

'It is. I'm just sorry you can't all meet my northern family. Perhaps I can arrange a visit. Your mum would enjoy it. Your family's friendship has meant so much to me. I'm not sure I have the right words to say how important it has been.'

Hanny took his hand in both hers. 'George, I know you have to go. Your place is with your family. You've told me so much about them, especially Marty and Mark. I'm just sad I'll never get to meet them. But it'll be wonderful for them to have you back.' They sat silently for a long time, oblivious to the chatter around them. Hanny gently stroked his hand. Eventually she leaned towards him. 'I just wanted to have time alone with you to say you'll always have a very special place in our hearts,' she paused and added very softly, 'particularly in mine.'

'Hanny, I don't know what to say. I'll miss you. I'll write.'

'That would be wonderful but I'm not sure it's such a good idea. It might make it difficult, more difficult than I think it is already.' She hesitated before continuing, 'I think this is painful for both of us. It certainly is for me.' She leant forward, put an arm around him and drew him closer, whispering into his ear. 'George, you may not have the right words. I may not either but I know what I need to say. You've become everything to me. I love you so much. It just happened. I didn't expect it but I'm so happy it did.' She moved away a little and he saw that her eyes were moist. 'It seems it's my fate to love men called George and then lose them,' she said with a rueful smile.

George put his hand up and caressed her cheek gently, looking directly into her eyes. 'Hanny, I was wrong. I do know the words. I just wasn't sure I should say them. I love you too. I've never known or wanted to be with a woman as much as I have with you. These feelings have just grown and grown.' He felt a twinge of guilt as he said it, but it was true. 'I'm just sad it cannot be.'

'For both of us.'

They sat for a long time, their drinks untouched. George took Hanny's hand and stroked it gently as she caressed his thigh. He knew he should leave but any resolve he might have summoned up to do so deserted him. Was there any way they could keep in touch? It was hard to think of one, yet the thought of separation was unbearable. But Hanny was right; maintaining contact remotely would not be any easier. The thought of the loss of what might have been, had circumstances been different, would be heart-rendingly painful. Would it ease over time? How could he tell? The pain might be alleviated by the pleasures of family life, particularly if he and Joan could establish a warmer and closer relationship, but was that possible – or even likely? George was not sure. It was difficult to envisage – maybe even more so now.

Hanny eventually broke the silence. 'George, I want to retain as many memories of you as possible.' He looked at her. She paused before continuing very tentatively. 'I have a friend who has an apartment nearby. She's away this weekend and has lent me the key. I should like to go there just to be alone with you for a time. May I take you there?'

It was no more than a hundred metres away. Hanny let them in. They walked up to the first floor apartment. 'Have a seat, I'll make some coffee.' She was back within minutes and set the cups down in front of them. 'I've also raided Inge's stock of schnapps,' she said as she placed glasses on the coffee table. Nothing was said for a long time, both were lost in their own thoughts.

George put his arm around Hanny and drew her

towards him. She rested her head on his shoulder. 'I don't know what to say.'

She whispered in his ear, 'Then say nothing, just hold me. I simply want to feel the warmth of your love close to me – as close as possible.' She lay across his lap and pulled his head down so that his lips met hers. After a few minutes she pulled him gently to his feet and led him into the bedroom. She put her arms around him and held him tightly, swaying gently from side to side. He made no attempt to conceal the extent of his arousal. She leant back very slightly and whispered, 'George, mein liebster Schatz, I know we must part but I want to store wonderful memories of you to treasure for now and for always. I want to carry the memory of you deep inside me. I should like you to take off my clothes one by one and to kiss and touch every part of me as you do so. Will you do that?'

There was no way George would or could refuse – there was no way he could hold back and no way that he wanted to hold back. She stood and raised her arms above her head as he slowly removed her top clothes. He ran his hands gently down over her body, caressing her breasts and then slowly started to kiss her – her lips, her neck and her nipples. He slipped his hands into the waist of her skirt and slowly loosened it. It slipped to the floor followed by her underwear. As he undressed her, she put out her hand, slipped it between his legs and gently fondled him. She stepped back out of the garments around her ankles. 'My God, you're so beautiful, Hanny. I love you so much.'

She pulled him close again and whispered, 'Now it's my turn.' She gradually removed his clothes one by one, kissing him slowly and languorously as she did so. She nuzzled up to him again and they held each other tightly. She led him to the bed and lay back – her arms above her head, her legs slightly parted. 'Kiss me again and again all over and then come inside me.' This was different. This was not just sex. It was love as George had never known it before, warm, passionate, fulfilling – and shared. They gave everything they had to one another. Finally, sated, they lay back, gently caressing each other and drifted off to sleep in each other's arms. He awakened as it was starting to get light to find Hanny's gentle touch arousing him once more. She climbed on top of him and they made love once more, slowly and luxuriantly, their sensations heightened by the emotional high of the previous evening.

We parted tearfully. There can be no way back. It was a love like no other in my life. It will never be possible to erase those memories – not that I want to. They will endure. It was a love, affectionate and light-hearted at first, which became deeper than anything I've ever known. We had shared so much – pleasures, hopes and fears. The enjoyment of each other's bodies seemed the most natural conclusion. I know I cannot allow this extraordinary love to affect my behaviour at home. But it will be hard. One of many challenges ahead.

Pulling into Charing Cross. Long difficult journey home. Many delays. Two full days. Country covered in snow and ice.

***

12 March 1947

Home, adapting slowly – about to write re-adapting but this is all new. Can't get images of Hanny out of my mind – I don't want to, but I must. Have survived the first ten days.

George struggled to make his way up the hill from the station along unlit streets through snow inches deep. He turned and looked back at the town spread out below and the castle on the hill beyond. The moon was shining faintly through the light cloud creating a scene with a strange numinous quality. The house was in total darkness. He looked around – there was not a light to be seen in any of the buildings in the street. He knocked. A moment later Joan opened the door. She took his arm and pulled him inside. 'Come in quickly. Let's keep the heat in.' She kissed him briefly on the cheek. 'Thank God you're home. I really could do with some help. You've no idea how bad it is here.' It was cold in the hallway. 'Let's get into the only warm room.' She led George into the lounge. There were two flickering candles on the mantelpiece and another pair on a side table. Martina and Mark were sitting on the hearth rug close to the open fire playing cards, the glow from the coals lighting up their faces. Marty got up and ran to George. He bent down and kissed her and then walked over and gave Mark's shoulder a squeeze. 'Hi, big boy.'

'How long are you home for Daddy?'

'For ever and ever.'

'Will you play with us in the snow?' There was no way

he could stem the flow of words. 'We don't go to school every day. Sometimes the snow's too deep and the teachers can't get there and sometimes there's no electricity.'

George grinned. 'I'm sure we'll have some fun now I'm back.'

The appalling weather had kicked in during the last week in January and had not relented since. The cold had been extreme with a biting easterly wind and snow on most days. Power had been cut to all houses for five hours each day for the previous three weeks to conserve coal. There appeared to be no end in sight. Most goods were rationed and for some items the rationing had become more severe. Joan's grumbles in her letters had been justified.

George sat with Joan after the children had gone to bed. He had been cajoled into taking them upstairs and then carrying them across the cold linoleum floors of their bedrooms to deposit them in their beds. He kissed them goodnight and joined Joan for their evening meal, Woolton pie which they ate off trays in front of the fire in the lounge. Power had been restored. 'It's been like this for weeks and even when we don't have a power cut, we can't always listen to the wireless as it's not on the air a lot of the time.'

George put his arm around her shoulders. 'I'm on leave. What do you want me to do while I'm here?'

She pulled away from him. 'What do you mean "on leave"? You've been demobbed, haven't you?'

'I have. But I had some untaken leave. So I don't need to go back to work immediately. You give the orders.' He laughed. 'I'm used to obeying orders now.'

Joan relaxed. 'Well, the forecast says there'll be more

heavy snow the day after tomorrow. There are things I've lined up for you to do.'

George's first task the following day was to clear a track across the yard to the coal store. He filled the coal scuttles, emptied the ash pan and banked up the boiler to provide hot water while Joan was giving the children their breakfast. He said he would walk the children to school. There had been a hard frost. The snow crackled under their feet as they broke through the icy crust. The easterly wind had piled the snow up in places, blocking the pavement. George swung Mark by his hands over the deepest drifts to prevent snow getting into his wellingtons. 'Swing me, swing me', he shouted each time they came to a deeper patch. George left them at school and made his way back to the house. An idea occurred to him. He went into the garage where there was some wood left over from shelving Joan had had installed. It was not ideal but would be adequate to make a sledge for the kids. He could buy anything else that was needed from the ironmongers.

He volunteered to go into the town to stock up with food. Joan laughed, saying stocking up was out of the question. Even modest quantities of essentials were in short supply. The weather had limited deliveries and much was simply unobtainable. Vegetables had frozen in the ground. George picked up their ration books and Joan gave him a list. She suggested he should look for unrationed items which might add some variety to their meals. He was just leaving when Joan called after him, 'Get some spam if you can but for God's sake not brains or snoek.'

George's second week as a civilian was taken up with the

practicalities of demobilisation. He handed his uniform in at the local centre and was given an ill-fitting double-breasted pinstripe demob suit, a felt hat, two shirts with matching collars, a tie, shoes and a raincoat. Joan took one look at him in the suit and hat and declared that he looked like a Chicago mobster. He played along with it. He picked up Joan's violin case, tilting the brim of the hat down at the front and muttered in a faux Chicago accent, 'Babe, I'm gonna make you an offer you can't refuse.' It was difficult not to agree with her. He was forbidden to wear the suit again.

***

17 MARCH 1947

Weather a little better but wet. Developed a routine. Lot of time with the kids – indoors and out. Great having this time with them before I go back to work.

George took Martina and Mark to school each day. He would walk home with them in the afternoon and join them at the kitchen table as they had their tea before listening to children's hour with them on the radio. The sledge was a great success. George pulled Marty and Mark to and from school on it for several days after the heavy snowfall. He took them up the hill at the weekend and they slid down shrieking loudly, steering erratically and falling off into the snow amongst gales of laughter.

***

20 March 1947

London to fix details for return to work – April 14.
Chance to see Mo. Government plans to nationalise rail
companies next year. Unlikely to make much difference
to the job. Marty asked why I was going to work – said
it was more fun if I was at home!

George received an enthusiastic welcome from Mo. 'Life's a
bit better. I've stopped working at the pub. It was helpful for
a time, but I'm thirty-three now. Jim and Peggy were very
good to me. I still help out sometimes when they're short-
staffed.' Mo made some tea and led George into the lounge.
He looked around. This had been his second home. A photo
of Bob was on a side-table with another of the three of them
together in the pub just before they joined up. She paused
for a moment before gesturing, 'Why don't you sit there?'
She pointed at Bob's regular chair.

George hesitated. 'Are you sure?'

'Yes, I can't keep this place as a shrine. I have to move
on. It's what Bob would have wanted. And I can't think of
anyone I would rather see sitting there.' She handed him a
cup.

'So what are you doing now?'

'I've started work in the library of one of the University
of London colleges and I'm aiming to get a qualification in
librarianship.'

'Which one?'

'Goldsmiths. It's quite exciting. The buildings were badly
damaged and the college was evacuated to Nottingham.

Repairs are nearly done now. There's a buzz around the place – a new beginning. For the college – and for me.'

'Sounds good.'

'It is. I have good colleagues. There are the old hands who think they know everything and some newer recruits. And the students are great. A lot are quite mature having been in the forces. Their positivity's fantastic for banishing the blues.'

'And otherwise?'

'Still difficult sometimes, but much better. I feel I've got my life in some sort of order and it has a purpose again.'

'And away from work?'

'I still miss Bob desperately. I'm not quite sure how to say this. I still feel the loss. I always will. You know how it was. He wasn't just my lover; he was an amazing friend. But the feeling of loss doesn't dominate my life as it did. It'll be three years in June.'

'And a social life?' George asked tentatively.

She laughed. 'George, you are wonderful. You're really asking if I have a man.'

He laughed at her directness. 'Not entirely. You could have a social life without it involving a man – or men.'

'In a way, I've lots of men. I've joined a choir.'

'I sang in one with Joan before the war. It was something we shared. It was good.'

'It's been good for me too. We rehearse once a week. Sometimes we go to the pub afterwards. But no, I don't have a man. Now tell me about you. How are you adapting to civvy street and have you gone back to the railways?'

'I'm going back to my old job in April. But it'll not be the same without Bob.'

'And life in your posh house?'

'It's alright. I'm adapting.'

'And the kids and Joan?'

'The kids are great. I'm getting a lot closer to them. We have a lot of fun. I'm taking them to Newcastle for Easter so they can get to know their Geordie relatives.'

'And Joan?'

'Much the same as ever.'

'That's very non-committal.'

'Joan's a very private person. It's all become rather formal – it always was to an extent. I think being away so long has sort of frozen the marriage. We rub along alright and we managed well during the terrible weather. There are some tensions but that's true of many, probably most, marriages. Nothing too serious. Yours and Bob's was an exception.'

'George, you look troubled as you say that. Do you want to say more?'

Did he? His diary had become his familiar, his alter ego and his confessional. The opportunity to share some of his thoughts with a human confidante was appealing. He knew he could trust Mo as he trusted Alice. But should he? Would it be disloyal to Joan if he did? And if he did, how far should he go? Images of Hanny were rarely far from his mind. Finally, he said hesitantly, 'Joan's a very good mum, very organised, though sometimes a bit controlling which can limit the children's fun. I also worry about her friendship with this woman, Edna. I'd have said something to her face but she avoids the house when I'm around. My in-laws agree. Alice has seen it too. She wrote to me in Germany saying her personality was poisonous. That's unusually strong for my sister. I've talked to Joan about it but she'll not hear a word against the woman. I think she's there a lot when I'm not home.'

Mo looked at him quizzically and then said quietly, 'George, I don't want to probe. I'm here and if it helps to talk to someone, you can unload on me. I've done so on you – more than once.'

He looked up. 'I know. I'm just not much good at showing my feelings.'

Mo went over and put her arms around him. 'None the worse for that. Do keep dropping in. You have no idea how good you are for my morale.'

**

8 APRIL 1947

Had suggested to Joan we should take the kids to Newcastle to see Alice, Joe and the boys. Joan not keen. Not seen them for nearly four years. Her face lightened when I said I'd take the kids on my own. They were excited by the thought of a long train journey. Warm welcome. Wonderful weekend.

Martina and Mark remembered Alice from her visit more than a year earlier. She had been a hit in the short time she had been in Farnham. Ian had left school and was now an apprentice joiner although he would have to take a break to start his National Service the following year. Aidan was planning to leave school in the summer and return to work at the farm where he had spent some of the war years.

The boys were wonderful with the small ones. Endlessly patient, they played with them non-stop over the weekend. Easter Day was good. They walked along the Quayside and explored the market. Mark was fascinated by the High Level Bridge and stood open-mouthed for a long time watching the trains crossing on the upper level with the cars on the deck below. In the afternoon, they visited the farm near Corbridge with Aidan. The children tried milking a cow and were given a ride on a tractor before being treated to tea by the Robson family. They got gloriously dirty and Alice, uncomplainingly, washed their clothes. George heard Marty whisper to Mark that they shouldn't tell Mummy they had got so dirty. It had to be their secret. It was difficult not to draw comparisons. Joan was very close to her parents and George was sure the bonds of kinship were just as strong as those between him and his family. The difference was the openness and warmth, which were such an integral part of his family – and that of the Beckers.

Marty and Mark were full of their trip when they got back to Farnham. They regaled Joan with details and asked insistently if they could go back in the summer. Joan was rather non-committal but finally agreed. Marty added, 'You don't need to come Mummy. Daddy can take us.' George was not sure what Joan made of this apparent slight. 'Very well,' she said. 'Your Daddy knows I don't like Newcastle very much.' He tried to encourage Joan to consider the whole family making the trip and reminded her of the beaches in Northumberland, but she was adamant, saying it would be good for him to have time on his own with the kids. Privately, George was pleased. It seemed this was likely to be a regular feature of his semi-detached marriage. Probably it would be easier that way.

***

1 May 1947

Weather better. Getting outside more. Mainly the three of us. Joan often says she needs to see her parents – or Edna, who has kept away. Sometimes she joins us for a walk. Marty has a bicycle. Fitted stabilising wheels to her old bike for Mark. I've bought a second-hand bike for myself and off we go together. The lanes are quiet as petrol still rationed. The kids are quite competitive though Marty always wins. She has a larger machine and her balance is better despite some weakness in one leg. Mark gets very frustrated. Amazing letter saying I was to be awarded an OBE. Joan over the moon. Went straight out and bought a hat that afternoon for a visit to the palace.

***

12 August 1947

July was an amazing month. Investiture at Buckingham Palace. All togged up in hired morning dress, Joan in her hat. Mum and Dad came down. Joan's parents organised a celebration lunch. Ten days in the north-east this month.

George tried to persuade Joan once more to join them in Newcastle. She reiterated that it was good for him to have time with Marty and Mark on his own. Aidan had left school and was working on the farm and they took the bus to Corbridge to see him. The following day Joe drove them to Beadnell. They parked near the old lime kilns by the sheltered harbour. They walked out onto the harbour wall and looked towards the south over the expanse of golden sand backed by dunes with the upraised craggy fingers of the ruins of Dunstanburgh Castle in the distance. Sailing dinghies were criss-crossing the bay. Others were beached on the sand, together with small rowing boats, tenders for yachts moored offshore and bilge-keel sailing boats standing erect on their twin keels. Children were playing beach games or running in and out of the water. Others were sliding down the dunes or hiding behind them. Gulls wheeled overhead shrieking stridently. They walked along the beach and, finding a quiet area, laid out their picnic. George took the children down to the sea and they plodged happily in the waves until Alice called them back for their lunch.

George stretched himself out on a rug in the sun after they had eaten. He watched the clouds scudding across the sky. Memories of the picnic in Aachen a year earlier and all that had followed flooded back. He suddenly felt the need to be on his own. Marty and Mark were playing hide and seek in the dunes. He asked Alice and Joe to keep an eye on them saying he needed to take a walk. Recalling holidays from his childhood, he set off to the southernmost extremity of the beach and sat on a tussock of grass on a small rise. He looked down to the Long Nanny where arctic and little terns and a few ringed plovers were congregating at the point where the burn entered the sea. It was more than five months since he had left Germany. He was forging strong links with Marty and Mark, and the marriage was underpinned by his and Joan's shared commitment to their children. A modus vivendi had evolved. But aside from this, George worried that there had been a tacit acceptance that this was a marriage which had become a partnership of convenience. Was this an ineluctable consequence of his prolonged absences or was this the relationship Joan had always envisaged? It was impossible to know. Might it be possible to re-create some of the bonds they had shared early in the marriage? Joan had been teaching the piano to both children, and once or twice they had all sung together. George had suggested that they should join a local choir and Joan had agreed to consider it. That could be a first step towards establishing a closer and a warmer relationship.

Times in the bedroom had been most difficult. George had rarely seen Joan fully unclothed. She had always been extremely reluctant to be seen naked and was quite prudish when any topic related to sex was raised. It was rarely on the menu. On the few occasions when George's advances were accepted, images and memories of Hanny would force themselves to the fore. It did nothing for his libido. Memories of that unforgettable night would also arise unbidden at other times with an erotic urgency. It was impossible to avoid comparisons. But that was the past – he must not allow such thoughts to jeopardise his marriage.

His musings were brought to an abrupt end as a shadow fell across him. Alice looked down. 'Marty and Mark are clamouring for their dad. They reckon you're not doing your duty sitting here reminiscing about our childhood when you should be playing with them.' He rose to his feet. He had to put the past behind him. He was home.

17

29 JULY 1990

'You got back late last night.' Michael had just appeared for breakfast. It was after ten.

'Sorry, Dad. Hope I didn't disturb you.' Mark grunted. Michael placed a brightly wrapped package and an envelope on the table in front of Gisela. 'Happy birthday, Mum.' He leant over and kissed her.

'Thanks, sweetheart.'

He touched the side of the coffee pot. 'It's cold.'

'What do you expect if you come down at this time?'

'I'll make some more.' He looked at his parents. 'You up for another mug?'

Gisela looked at the clock on the oven. 'Alright, a quick one and then I must get on with lunch.'

Michael put the kettle on and dropped a slice of bread into the toaster.

Gisela opened the card and unwrapped the present, pulling out a copy of Herbert Read's "Modern Sculpture". 'This is fantastic, Michael. Where did you get it? I've tried again and again to find a copy. It's been out of print for ages. Thank you so much.' She went over and hugged him.

'Found it in a second-hand bookshop. What did Dad give you?'

'You'll see when you go into the garden.'

'Not just a plant? How boring.'

'Wait and see. Now get on with your breakfast. I might need a hand later.'

Michael poured more coffee for Mark and Gisela, then settled at the table and spread marmalade liberally on his toast. 'So what's on today?'

Gisela had called Martina the previous day and invited her to lunch. She felt it was incumbent on her to extend an olive branch. Mark claimed he had had little time to make the effort to reconnect with his sister over recent months. Gisela had to concede that the claim had some substance, but she knew this was also a cover for his failure to take steps to rebuild bridges. But it was true that he had been exceptionally busy. The moves towards German reunification had gathered momentum during the previous month, although German politicians were being careful not to use the word "reunification" to mitigate the anxieties of those who had fears of a resurgent Germany. They were referring to the process delicately as "die Wende' – the turning point. The wall was being "officially" dismantled and the Treaty agreeing to merge the economic systems had come into effect at the beginning of the month. Everything was changing in continental Europe. The Cold War did really seem to be coming to an end. The Singing Revolution in the Baltic states and early steps towards democracy in

Bulgaria and Romania were marking a further lifting of the Iron Curtain.

'Your aunt's coming for lunch. It's a joint celebration – my birthday and your dad's award as political commentator of the year.'

'Sounds good.'

Mark got up from the table. He raised his eyebrows. 'The editor's cock-a-hoop about it. I might even be his blue-eyed boy for a month or two,' he shrugged, 'more likely only a day or two. I'm off to get the Sunday papers.'

'Dad seems a bit grumpy this morning.'

'I'm not sure he's that keen on seeing your aunt.'

Michael nodded. He was aware that his father had always been a little in awe of Martina and, possibly, a little scared of her. 'Does this mean diplomatic relations are being re-established?'

'I hope so – we don't want a repeat of that evening in April.'

'No, I'm sorry about that.' Michael sat back and shifted his chair as the sun which was streaming through the window was directly in his eyes. 'Do you think she'll ask any more about my granddad's journals?'

'Wouldn't have thought so. She made it very clear that she wants no part in your dad's quest.'

'But if she does?'

'Well, we've got no further with them. I don't see a problem.'

'Not entirely true. I read another batch yesterday. I'm ahead of you and Dad. There's still a final section I haven't read yet.'

'And?'

'Well, you remember he was growing rather close to this girl he'd rescued?' Gisela nodded. 'It seems he'd found a soulmate. He did have an affair.'

'Are you sure it wasn't just a friendship?'

'Absolutely sure, that bit's quite explicit. Much more so than I would have expected. There's no question about it. It reads like romantic fiction, almost erotica.'

'Are you sure your dad hasn't read it?'

'Absolutely. I've had it up in my room during the vac and it's still there.'

Gisela drew her finger across her closed lips. 'Okay, if she asks, let Dad answer. He can say quite truthfully that he's found nothing new. We'll tell him after Marty has gone.'

'It says a lot about the two of them.'

They could hear Mark coming back. He dumped the papers on the table. 'These things are getting too bloody bulky. I'll never have time to read all this.' He looked at them. 'You're looking a bit shifty. What have you been talking about?'

'Nothing much. Just saying we hope Marty won't raise questions about your dad – or your mum if it comes to that.'

'I hope so too. I want a peaceful Sunday.'

Gisela started to clear the breakfast things away. Michael got up and helped her stack the dishwasher. 'We should have lunch outside – it's such a great day.' She took his hand. 'Come on, I'll show you what your dad's given me.' They walked out through the French windows onto the terrace. She pointed to an abstract sculpture on a plinth. The sun shining through it created an elaborate tracery shadow on the patio.

Michael walked over and caressed the smooth, sinuous, mottled olive-green curves. 'What's the stone? I've never seen anything quite like it before.'

'Serpentine – it's a silicate, with a lot of iron and magnesium in it.'

'Where's it from?'

'Zimbabwe. They describe it as an earthing stone. They believe it has a special energy and it's an aid to meditation. I don't go along with all the ethereal stuff – but I love the shape and the texture. The sculptor has called it "Spirit of Hope".'

'It's great – the start of a collection?'

'Maybe. I'll leave you out here to set everything up for drinks and lunch.'

Michael wiped the garden table and chairs down, opened the parasol, collected cushions from the store and set up four garden loungers at one end of the patio around a small table. This had to be a champagne day. He collected four flutes and a bottle cooler from the house. If his father hadn't planned some bubbly he could scarcely fail to take the hint.

***

Martina arrived a little after twelve. She walked over to Gisela and put her arms around her. 'Happy birthday. Thank you so much for asking me. And before you say anything, I owe you an apology. It wasn't fair to walk out and leave Paul with you the last time I was here.'

Mark was standing close by. He gulped. It was difficult to recall any occasion when his sister had made such an unequivocal apology for anything. 'That's alright,' he stammered.

'It had just been a very bad week. Paul's appearance that evening was the last straw.' She kissed Mark briefly on the cheek and hugged Michael.

'Come and admire Mark's present to me.'

Gisela and Mark walked into the garden with Marty. They led her over to the "Spirit of Hope". 'I love the name. It just fits with my feelings about all that's happening in Germany.'

'With my life too.' Gisela looked at her enquiringly. 'Things are better, much better. We have a buyer for the house and have exchanged contracts – and I've found a nice flat in Edgbaston, close to the cricket.'

'And Paul?'

'He's also found somewhere. He's been given a suspended sentence.'

'That's a relief. But what next for him?'

'I've got him fixed up with a local charity which will help him find a job. In the meantime he's doing voluntary work with the Citizen's Advice Bureau. I think he's genuinely turned a corner. That awful weekend was the pits. But it really had an impact on him. He rarely drinks now and he's getting himself together again. He's much more like the Paul I married. He's even picked up doing things he hasn't done for years – like playing the piano. I'd forgotten how good he was.'

'Might you get together again?'

She hesitated. 'I can't see it.' She put her sunglasses on. 'But I feel much more ready to help him now. I think we might be able to be friends and occasionally do things together.' She dropped a small package on the garden table. 'Happy birthday, Ellie.'

'Then we all have things to celebrate. Perhaps we should start straightaway. Michael is the sommelier today.' They settled on the loungers.

On cue, Michael walked out with a bottle of champagne and small bowls of nuts and cheese footballs. They watched as he released the wire cage and eased the cork out, holding it aloft with a flourish. 'One of my posher mates says that the noise should be no greater than that of a maiden's sigh.'

Mark laughed. 'Just get on with it, Michael.'

'We simple London students have to be instructed in these things. It's different for you Oxbridge lot. You probably had tutorials on pulling champagne corks.'

'He's right to take care,' said Martina laughing. 'There was a thing in the Christmas issue of one of the journals saying corks can leave the bottle at over 30 miles an hour and cause eye injuries.'

'Come on, Marty, you're off duty – and I'm quite sure your young patients don't spend their days opening champagne.'

'Alright, but here's another topic that should be off limits: our father's diaries and Mum's correspondence. I'm assuming you've not found anything else of note.'

'Not a thing.' Gisela glanced at Michael and winked.

'I still don't think you should be doing this but you're

obviously not going to stop now. I guess I must put up with it – but I don't want to hear any more about it.'

Mark nodded in acquiescence.

***

Martina left late that afternoon to drive back to Birmingham. It had been a relaxed, low-key day. Mark retreated into the house to read the papers. Michael cleared the remaining plates and glasses and carried them through to the kitchen. He collected the files with his grandfather's diaries from his bedroom and went back to the patio. He stretched out on one of the loungers in the late afternoon sun, reflecting on the most recent section he had read. The contents had been profoundly discomfiting. The diaries had given him the insights of a voyeur or a psychoanalyst progressively probing and uncovering his grandfather's most intense emotions and mental turmoil. But the narrative had also become intensely compelling. Like his father he felt impelled to read on. The affair had come as no surprise to him. It was the emotional release and the depth of the feelings expressed that had astonished him – his passion for Hannelore and his unconditional love for Martina and his father. Conflicted came nowhere near describing his mental anguish as he sought to reconcile the irreconcilable and meet the commitments he had made to his wife and family.

And the diaries had raised another unsettling question. When they had first found them, Michael had asked Mark how much he had missed having a father. He had been surprised by the very neutral response that that was simply the way it was. It contrasted oddly with his grandfather's absolute commitment to and love for his own father and aunt, despite the tensions in the marriage and the pull of his love for Hannelore. His level of engagement had gone far beyond that of a dutiful father home on leave and he had done so much with them in the short time between his discharge and his death. Could, Michael wondered, the absence of such a committed and involved parent have limited his own father's vision of his role as a father?

Gisela had wandered outside and was standing by the French windows. She stood for a few minutes looking at Michael. He was suddenly aware of her presence and turned. She walked over and sat down, pulling one of the loungers close to him. 'You were looking very thoughtful.'

'I keep thinking about these diaries. There's so much in the latest section I've read. Not just his affair but all the detail about his first months back home and the amount of time he spent doing things with Dad and Aunt Marty. He was an amazingly involved father. Dad must have lost a lot by not having him around – even if he didn't know it.'

'You may well be right.'

'The phrase he used when I asked him about it way back has stuck in my mind – "more a periodic awareness of absence than a feeling of loss". It seems to me to be almost a denial of the significance of a father's role.'

'Are you sure that's what he said?'

'Yes, and then he said that the only times he had thought about what he might be missing were when he saw some of the things his mates' fathers did with them.'

Gisela stretched out and took his hand. 'Don't be too

critical. It wasn't easy for him. Your Gran wasn't the easiest of people.'

Michael nodded. 'You both lost your fathers at much the same age. Did that create a bond between you?'

'I've never thought about it in that way,' she paused, 'but no, I don't think so. I was devoted to my papa. He was a constant in my life every day until the time we had to flee. Thinking of him still makes me sad. Despite what the diaries say, I'm not sure George ever really had enough time to become as close to your dad or to Aunt Marty as he'd obviously wanted to do. The one thing we do have in common is that neither of us knows exactly how our fathers met their ends.'

'Do you think we'll ever find out?'

'For me – I don't think so. For your granddad, I don't know. Your dad's got his tail up. He won't give up easily.'

'You should read this latest section of the diaries.'

Mark had walked out and joined them. 'That seemed to go alright, but what's going on between you two? I saw you wink at Michael when we were discussing my dad's diaries. Are you hiding something?'

Gisela looked directly at him and smiled. 'Yes, we were. Michael has read more than we have – though he hasn't yet got to the end. There are apparently other revelations.' Michael handed over the final sections to Mark. 'We thought it would be better to keep them from you until after Marty had gone. We should make an effort to catch up with Michael and then read the final section.'

18

15 August 1947

George

Two letters from Germany. I don't know what to do.

Joan handed George an envelope when he got home from work three days after the holiday in the north-east. 'This has come from Germany. Who would be writing to you from there?'

He recognised Irmgard's writing on the envelope. His heart sank. Something must have happened to Hanny. He managed to control his anxieties and emotions sufficiently to say, 'Probably just one of my colleagues updating me on progress with our projects. They said they'd let me know how things were going. I'll go and change and have some tea and then I'll read it.' George retreated to the lounge after a hasty cup of tea and tore open the envelope. Two letters fell out. The first was from Irmgard and written in German.

Dear George

Jimmy Redpath gave me your address. He sends his regards. He says you are much missed. I had hoped to write to you earlier but you will understand why I did not from Hanny's letter.

Rudolf and I were very aware how much you and Hanny had come to mean to each other. Perhaps we realised this before either of you did. We believe your love crept up on both of you unknowingly and perhaps the depth of your feelings for each other took you both by surprise. I suspect you only realised how much you loved each other when the time came for you to leave. We have learned painfully how important it is to enjoy opportunities for love when they arise in this world. We know you both agreed there should be a complete break – painful though it might be. That was the right decision.

I am writing now with Hanny's very reluctant consent to tell you she is pregnant and is expecting at the end of November. You will know from this that the pregnancy is well advanced. Hanny was originally very emphatic that you should not be contacted. She was worried it would put you in an impossible position. She is right. But I have persuaded her that it is also right that you should know you have a child on the way.

I want to say we were very happy to welcome you into our family. It may surprise you to know we are also happy to welcome a grandchild into the family knowing you are the father. We desperately need to look forward to the future positively and for us there could be no better way. We had already come to think of you as a member of our family and now we are happy that we have a further link. The boy or girl will be cherished and spend their childhood here, just as we have cherished Bertie and Hanny. I don't know if it will be possible for you to see your son or daughter. I hope it may be but neither we nor Hanny wish to disrupt your marriage or create barriers between you and your children. We know how dear they are to you.

With fondest love
Irmgard

He sat back in his chair shaking his head. He was stunned. Eventually he picked up the letter from Hanny.

My dearest, dearest George

You will have read the letter that Mutti has written. My mind is in turmoil. I missed you so much after you left. I have so much wanted to see you and hold you and feel you close to me again. I was tempted many times to break my promise and contact you and try to find a way of seeing you – but I knew it would be wrong. I know how much your Marty and Mark mean to you. They must be getting to know and love you so well now.

I want you to know that when we made love that night, I had only finished my period two days before and I didn't think for one moment I could become pregnant. I can only apologise. Please don't think I was trying to trap you. That thought never crossed my mind. I knew we had to part and I just wanted to show you how much I had come to love you. I wanted to carry memories of all you had become to me close to my heart forever. I realised I must be pregnant in April. I didn't know what to do for the best. I was so happy when I discovered I was carrying your child and I so much wanted him or her to know their wonderful father, but I knew it could not be. I was determined not to break my promise and contact you, but I was eventually persuaded by Mutti that it was right that you should know.

The child will be much loved and cherished and will be brought up to admire you even if he or she does not have the benefit of you being around as a father throughout his or her childhood. Maybe at some time in the future he or she may come to know you. I hope so. Mutti and Papa have been amazing. They had grown to think of you as one of the family. They knew how happy I was with you. They will be wonderful and caring grandparents. We are all agreed that we are not asking anything of you. I will let you know if you have a son or a daughter in November. I am happy that, if I cannot have you, I shall have a part of you with me forever.

As always with all my love
Your devoted Hanny.

George's mind was a maelstrom of confused and disordered thoughts. He sat forward with his head in his hands. He was to be the father of a third child, one conceived that unforgettable night. But he had a family. His two children, his other two children, were immeasurably important to him – born to a wife to whom he had made a binding commitment. He was getting to know Marty and Mark and to play a role in their lives and they in his, and yet he yearned to see and be with Hanny and to know his new son or daughter. Would it, could it ever be possible to be a father to all three? Would it be possible to bring Hanny to England and lead a life apportioning his time between two disconnected families? Such an arrangement would be fraught with difficulties. It could not happen without Joan's agreement which he was certain would not be forthcoming. He got to his feet and paced up and down the room. There seemed to be no option other than to accept Hanny's insistence that he should do nothing to disrupt his home life. But was that what he wanted? The letters had brought all his longings and passion for Hanny to the fore once more, but it was clear that it would be impossible to play a significant role in the upbringing of all three children. He was impaled on the horns of a dilemma from which there appeared to be no escape. He paused by the French windows and gazed abstractedly over the garden to the fields beyond.

'George, are you alright?' Joan had come quietly into the room.

He turned. What could he say? He hesitated before answering. 'I've had something of a shock. Someone, a colleague, in Germany has had a serious accident.' Equivocation seemed to be the only course.

Joan glanced at the letters on the coffee table. 'But why is this all in German?'

'It's about a German colleague. It's from one of the German group leaders. We had to work alongside local people. That's why I learned the language.'

'Is it serious?'

He had no problem in answering, 'Yes – very.'

'Is it life-threatening?' He nodded. It was, although not in the sense she had meant. 'Well, you know what I think about Germans but I'm sorry to hear that.'

He suddenly felt unable to face further interrogation, however well-meaning and sympathetic. He needed to get out of the house. He needed time to get his thoughts in some sort of order. 'Joan, I need to clear my head. I've been cooped up in meetings all day. I think I'll go for a walk and pop into the Jolly Farmer for a pint.'

'Alright, but don't be more than an hour. Mum and Dad are coming round for a meal this evening.'

George pushed the letters into his pocket and headed for the pub. He ordered a pint and retreated to a quiet corner of the lounge bar. He lit a cigarette and re-read the letters several times. He went through possible future scenarios in his head over and over again. There were no conceivable outcomes which would not leave someone or everyone scarred. The only one which might limit the damage was the one suggested by Hanny. This would not rock the Farnham boat and life would presumably continue much as it was – on the surface. But it would create a distance between him and his unborn child which might be unbridgeable in years to come unless circumstances were to change. It would involve a partial denial of his paternity. This was not a future he wished to contemplate, but nor were any of the other scenarios he could envisage. Thoughts and memories of Hanny flooded back, invading and possessing his mind. He was overcome by a desperate longing to see and be with her.

He put the letters down on the small table in front of him while he took a drink. He suddenly became aware of a figure standing over him, looking down at the table and swaying slightly. 'That looks like German. Can't think why you're reading German – we beat the buggers.'

He reached out for the letters but George grabbed them and held them protectively. 'That's private correspondence. Now just piss off.'

'So, what are you – some sort of fascist?'

'Look, just fuck off.' He had raised his voice. The landlord came over quickly. Looking at George, he said, 'I'm not having that language here.' He then faced the other man, 'As for you, you can finish your drink in that corner and then get out. You've already been barred from this pub once and you are again.' The man retreated. The landlord turned back to George. 'Sorry about that. He can be trouble. I don't know what that was all about and I don't want to, but I don't tolerate bad language here. But if you'll put something in the swear box on the bar that'll be the end of the matter.' George apologised saying that he had had something of a shock. He finished his drink and headed back to the house.

He knew he was being uncommunicative during the meal. William Watts looked across and said, 'Joan tells me you have had news of a serious accident involving a German friend. I thought fraternisation was forbidden.'

'It was at first, but we had to work with Germans on

projects. We needed to have sensible working relationships with them.'

'But that doesn't mean you had to be friends.'

'No, but working closely with them, some friendships developed. Not all Germans were Nazis.'

'Sounds very unprofessional to me.'

'Not at all. Unless you've been there, it's difficult to understand how much needed to be done. Teamwork was essential.'

'They should have been punished.'

'A lot were but it wouldn't have been fair or sensible to punish the whole population. By working constructively we should reduce the chance of further conflict.'

'So what was this serious accident?'

'I don't know the details. All I know is that it's life-threatening.' George was relieved as the talk drifted away into general family matters. He was pleased to get away to bed that night and, pleading tiredness, headed for the spare room. Joan accepted this with equanimity. It was not the first time they had slept apart since he'd been home. He had a restless night as he struggled unsuccessfully to think of a way in which he might have meaningful contact with Hanny.

***

23 AUGUST 1947

Wrote to Hanny to say how pleased I was at news of the pregnancy and that I hoped to be more than a distant father. It was more formal than I'd wanted but I didn't want to say more or make promises I would be unable to keep. Still don't know what the hell to do.

George remained agitated and confused over the next few days. He was unable to see any acceptable way of resolving the morass of uncertainties which would inevitably accompany any decision he made. It affected his ability to focus at work and impacted on his behaviour at home. He was snappy with Marty and Mark and uncommunicative when Joan asked what was troubling him. She seemed unpersuaded that a serious accident to a former colleague was an adequate explanation for his ill-humour. Joan might be remote and aloof at times, but she was also perceptive. George was adrift without an anchor. If only Bob was still around. He needed a confidante. He wrote to Alice to say he would be travelling north the following Saturday after he'd finished work at lunchtime and that he needed to talk before returning home the following day. He told Joan he needed to go as Joe was ill and Alice was worried about him.

He was surprised to see Alice waiting at the barrier at the station as the early evening sun filtered through the glazed panels between the wrought iron ribs of the arched roof. She hugged him and stood back. 'I've never seen you look so worried, George. What's up?'

'It's a long story and not a very happy one.' He hesitated. 'No, in one way it is a happy one but it's a difficult one and whichever way you look at it, I'm more the villain than the hero. Can we go somewhere quiet to talk?'

'I guessed you might want to talk quietly. Home at

weekends is noisy as you know. It's a lovely evening. Why don't we take a bus up to the Moor and walk and talk there? Not a word until we get off the bus.'

They walked out onto Neville Street, caught a bus and alighted in Claremont Road. Alice linked her arm in his as they walked out onto the Moor with the sun on their backs. 'Just start talking when you feel like it. There's no hurry. I'll just listen.'

It was difficult to know where to begin. George had planned to start by talking about home, the atmosphere, his relationship with Joan, his love for his kids, and his concerns over the intermittent but pernicious influence of Edna. But Alice knew all this. To go over it again would be seen as an attempt to justify and exculpate himself. Eventually, he just said, 'Something happened in Germany and it's had consequences.' Slowly, he recounted the sequence of events and experiences which had led to his present quandary: the impact of the destruction, the tensions involved in clearing mines, the injuries and deaths, meeting and becoming close friends with the Beckers, then his love for Hanny which had grown so gradually and, finally, the one wonderful night they had shared when it overwhelmed them. 'It just happened, Alice. I wasn't looking for an affair. It just grew. It crept up on both of us. We knew it could go no further but now everything's changed. I love Hanny in a way far beyond anything I've ever felt for any other woman. But I've responsibilities to Joan and Marty and Mark and I don't want to let them down. You've seen how the kids are with me. They're all important. But I also long to see Hanny and know our child. I can't see any way through this. I'm not even sure there is a way.'

'Let's find a bench and sit.' They sat silently for many minutes basking in the rays of the setting sun. Eventually, Alice said, 'I'm not altogether surprised. Once or twice, when we were on the beach a fortnight ago, I felt you were on the verge of saying rather more than you did. I'm sure you've thought this through endlessly. What do you see as the possibilities?'

'It's difficult. We could go on as we are now – total separation from Hanny. I'm not sure I could live with that. Could I be a part of two families? Joan and her parents wouldn't accept that. They wouldn't understand. It would be the end of the marriage. Could Hanny come to England? She could but she would be isolated from her own family who are close and supportive, and I simply don't have the income to support two families. The only other possibility would be to leave Joan and the kids and move to Germany, but I can't do that.'

Alice was silent for a long time. Finally, she turned to him. 'George, whatever you decide, people are going to be hurt. Even if the present situation continues people will be hurt. And things may change and evolve. Sooner or later Joan will sense there's been a change and that your heart is torn. When that happens a very difficult situation may become an impossible one. I can't advise. I can't think what would be the best or even the least worst thing to do. All I can say is that I will do what I can to support you whatever happens.'

They talked round and round the possibilities but kept

coming back to the same point. There was no ideal or even moderately satisfactory way forward. George could not conceive of the possibility of explaining to Joan what had happened and getting a sympathetic or an understanding hearing – either then or later.

He hadn't expected his stay in Newcastle to resolve the conundrums he was facing but he was relieved to have been able to air and share his concerns and anxieties. Alice's non-judgmental sympathy and assurance of her and Joe's unconditional support offered some comfort.

***

3 September 1947

Eighth anniversary of the outbreak of the war and third of my embarkation for France. I'm not sure why I feel the need to write that, but it seems appropriate. Must prepare for tomorrow.

The need for George to decide on a way forward was taken from him. He arrived home from work that evening. The kids usually ran out to greet him but the house was unusually quiet. He opened the door and walked into the kitchen. Joan was sitting at the table, wearing her coat, with a stony look on her face. 'Where are Marty and Mark?'

'They're spending the night with my parents.'

'I didn't know that was planned.'

'It wasn't.' She held up two sheets of paper. His heart sank. They were the letters from Irmgard and Hanny. 'I found these. I knew you were lying. I took them to someone I know through the school and she translated them.' She turned angrily. 'I have never been so shamed or humiliated in my life. You've betrayed me and our children with some German tart.' He was taken aback by the vitriol with which she delivered those last few words, her face twisted with disgust.

'It wasn't like that. She's anything but a tart.'

'What do you think she is then?'

George sat down at the table. 'Get up,' she shouted. 'Don't think you're going to get round me or even think you'll be staying.'

He stood. He knew he had to remain controlled even though that was the last thing he wanted to do. Referring to Hanny as a tart had infuriated him but he managed to control his voice. 'Joan, I know it will be difficult or even impossible for you to forgive but I hope you might try to understand.'

She thumped her hand on the table. 'I do understand. I understand everything. You felt you could play around with other women just because you were far from home. God knows how many women you've had.'

'Hanny was the only one.'

'I don't believe you. You were always pestering me for sex. Probably you've been with other tarts in England on the nights you've said you were away working.'

'That's totally wrong. I've been entirely faithful to you apart from this one time.'

She looked at him coldly. 'I'm not prepared to discuss it. I went to see Mum and Dad when I discovered what was in those letters and we went together to see their solicitor. He said, in his experience, that it was very rare for any man to have only one mistress.' George tried to protest but she faced him and continued relentlessly. 'We're staying with Mum and Dad tonight. The solicitor has told me what to say.' She unfolded a sheet of notepaper and read from it, 'You can stay in this house tonight – alone. But you must have your clothes and personal things packed by tomorrow morning and leave before ten. You are never to come back to this house and you're to have no further contact with the children.'

He was stunned. 'You can't stop me seeing my kids.'

'I can and I will. You have forfeited any rights you had as a father.'

'You can't do that. I can understand why you want me out but please don't stop me seeing Marty and Mark. I can have them to stay wherever I'm living. I'll promise not to approach you, but please, please I must see the kids.'

'No. We've agreed it's better they shouldn't know they have an unfaithful father. And you've been an absent father. They hardly know you.'

'That was true but it's not now. You've seen how they run out as soon as I get back from work.'

'You will leave this house, my house,' she added pointedly, 'and you will leave this town. If you try to contact the children, I'll raise such hell that you'll wish you'd never even thought of it.'

George could see there was little point in arguing further. 'I should like to see them to say I have to go away. I'll not say anything to upset them or to counteract anything you've said or might be going to say.'

'No.'

'Let me at least write to them and send presents on their birthdays.'

'No.'

'What are you going to tell them? How are you going to explain my disappearance? They're seven and nearly five now.'

'That's up to me and I know very well how old my children are. You've no longer any rights as a parent. Go away and be a father to your bastard son or daughter – if you can be sure it's yours. God knows how many men that tart will have been with.' George was very close to reacting violently in the face of her venom but managed to hold back as she continued. 'Mum and Dad also feel they've been betrayed, particularly after all they have done for you. I'm going now. Make sure you're gone by ten tomorrow.'

There was little more he could say. He simply said, 'I'll send you my address when I know where I'll be living.'

'Don't bother. I'm not interested. Just transfer money regularly for the kids to my account. The solicitor has set down what you should pay in this letter.' She slapped an envelope down on the table. 'Any further communications will be sent to you by way of your sister. I'm keeping these letters and I'll use them if you ever try to come into our lives again. And leave the keys on the table.' A moment later she was gone. George's home, his marriage, his life and his relationship with his children had crumbled to nothing in less than thirty minutes.

***

After Joan had gone, George sat down at the table with his head in his hands. He was shaking with suppressed anger. The only sound breaking the silence was the intrusive ticking of the kitchen clock. What the hell was he to do and where was he to go? Eventually he got up and poured himself a large whisky. He walked slowly up to the bedroom. All his clothes were laid out on the bed and two suitcases had been left open on the floor. He slowly packed, closed the cases, carried them downstairs and placed them by the door. He had no idea what his future might hold.

George placed his keys on the kitchen table. There was nothing more he could do. "Must prepare for tomorrow," he wrote in his dairy. He looked at that last sentence. It was a simple statement bordering on the banal. 'I don't know what I can do to prepare for tomorrow or for all the tomorrows that will follow,' he muttered to himself. He pushed the diary aside and poured himself another whisky and then another. He walked into the lounge and sank into a chair. After a further drink he fell into a fitful sleep.

19

2 August 1990

The final sections of George's diaries and the letters from Irmgard and Hannelore were spread out on the desk. The content of the letters was clear from the diary entries. Mark sat shaking his head from side to side. The discovery that he had a half-brother or sister, presumably somewhere in Germany, had hit him like a thunderbolt. But what was he or she like and did they know of his and Martina's existence or had they been kept equally in ignorance of George's other family? If they did know of them, surely they would have taken steps to make contact? Or perhaps not. It might have depended upon what narrative had been spun to them – if any. And he was still no closer to discovering how his father had met his end. His mother's fury and resentment following that final stormy confrontation went a long way to explaining her desire to eradicate all traces of his father from the home. He sat silently for several minutes and then picked up the final section. He stared at the enigmatic last phrase, "must prepare for tomorrow". But for what sort of tomorrow had he been preparing? Much about his mother, his father and their marriage had become clear. But many unanswered, and possibly unanswerable, questions remained. Why had he left his journal behind? It reflected his most intimate thoughts and it had offered innumerable hostages to fortune. The contents would have damaged irreparably any hopes he might have had of re-establishing relations later when the emotional temperature had dropped. And where did he go? Presumably he still had to go to work – but what then? Did he go to Germany? Did he seek refuge in Newcastle? Or did he go elsewhere, and if so, where? Above all, the central question remained – what was the nature of the accident that led to his death? Perhaps the word accident was simply a euphemism. Could he have committed suicide – perhaps later that night or early the next day? It seemed entirely possible in his state of desolation. That would explain the abandoned journal. But would he not have ended the entries with a suicide note? Possibly – or possibly not. If he had killed himself, this would inevitably have had an impact on Joan. She would undoubtedly have felt a sense of shame and guilt. It would certainly account for her stubborn refusal to discuss his fate.

He carried the diaries and letters through to the lounge where Gisela and Michael were sitting on the sofa watching an episode of "To the Manor Born" on the television. He sat on the arm of the sofa and watched with them until the programme came to an end. 'I need your help. I don't know what to make of all this – it seems I have a half-brother or sister. I don't know what to think or what to do or where to look now.'

'Are you sure?'

'Read the last bit of the diaries. There were also two letters with them.' He handed them over; poured himself a brandy and slumped into one of the chairs and waited.

Gisela looked up when she and Michael had read the last few pages and the letters. 'I don't know what to say or make of it any more than you do – and now you find you have a half-brother or sister. You seem to be no nearer the truth than ever. It's like that old phrase about a riddle wrapped in a mystery inside an enigma.'

'I can now see possible reasons why Mum might have erased all traces of my dad. But a half-brother or sister. I can't take it all in.'

Gisela walked over and sat on the arm of the chair and put her arm around Mark's shoulders. 'I'm as mystified as you. What are you going to do next?'

'I don't know. My efforts to find a death certificate have got me nowhere. And now it seems possible, even probable, that he died in Germany.' He paused. There appeared to be two lines to follow. One would be to find his family in Newcastle. His grandparents would no longer be alive, but his aunt might be. Her married name could probably be found from a marriage certificate. The ages of her children suggested that she had probably married in the late twenties. Even if she was no longer alive, it might be possible to trace his cousins, although that might be difficult if they also had a common surname or had moved out of the area. The other possibility would be to find the Becker family and Hannelore and his half-sibling. It was impossible to know what the chances were of tracing them in Aachen. Even if

Hannelore had eventually married, it might be possible to locate her brother, although he might have moved elsewhere in Germany or even abroad.

Mark had been mulling over these possibilities when Michael turned to his father suddenly, 'I've been thinking this through. Why don't you put yourself in his shoes?'

'What do you mean?'

'Well, look at it. Here's this guy, torn apart trying to reconcile his passion for Hannelore with his responsibilities to you and Gran. He's desperately trying to think of a way of doing it. But as he's juggling all these potentially explosive emotional devices in his mind, everything goes totally pear-shaped. Gran finds out what he's been up to and throws him out. What would you have done?'

'God knows.'

'As you said, it might all have become too much for him and he might have killed himself. That would explain the abandonment of his journal. But if so, there would have been an inquest and, presumably, a death certificate with the other documents.'

Mark nodded. 'Alright,' he said cautiously, 'but that only diminishes the likelihood of one possibility.'

'Yes, but it's not the only explanation as to why the journal was abandoned. That could just have been the result of his mental turmoil. Would you be thinking straight after an evening like that and hungover after necking most of a bottle of scotch?'

'I guess not.'

'So we can't entirely rule out suicide. But, as I said, if that's what happened, there should be a death certificate or some record. Or just possibly not. Could he have committed suicide in a remote spot and his body never been discovered or, if discovered, not identified? Unlikely. Bodies have a habit of being found, often by dog walkers if the papers are to be believed. I guess it's just possible he threw himself off a cliff and was never found or he could have committed suicide in Germany or even some other country. As you said, locating a death certificate might then be difficult or impossible.'

'Okay, that all makes sense. But I don't see where it's getting us.'

'But it doesn't make sense. If it had got to the point where he felt he could no longer go on, why would he go abroad to commit suicide? There'd be no point in that. And we know from those letters, if he'd gone to Germany he'd have received a warm and sympathetic welcome. After what had happened, he might well have wanted to be with Hannelore and, when he or she was born, his other kid. Anyhow, I just don't see him as a potential suicide. He sounds to me like a guy who faced up to things. And the last line in his journal suggests that that was what he planned to do, even if he didn't know exactly what the hell to do next.'

'Okay, but where's this taking us?'

'I'll tell you. I've read all the journals now. I feel I know this guy. He's been thrown out of the house. He knows it's unlikely he'll ever be able to go back again. But he's torn between his love for you and Aunt Marty and his love for Hannelore.'

'Okay.'

'Two other things: your dad sounds as if he was very methodical. He had to be to clear mines, and he was very aware of his obligations. And he had a job. I don't believe he would just walk out on it. He'd have wanted to provide for you and Aunt Marty as well as for his unborn kid. So what do you think he'd have done? What would you have done?'

Mark shook his head.

'Well, I'll tell you what I think. First, he would have to go somewhere. He would need a place to stay until he had sorted himself out. The obvious place would have been Newcastle. His sister knew of his dilemma and they were close but he couldn't simply bugger off to the north-east. He had a job and he couldn't afford to put that at risk. He needed a refuge in or close to London.'

Mark suddenly saw what he was driving at. 'Mo,' he said.

'Exactly. They were also close. She knew there were tensions in the marriage and would probably be sympathetic. There were even times, reading the journal, when I wondered if that friendship would develop into an affair. Perhaps it did.'

'It might be a hell of a job to track her down. We don't have an address. We only know she lived in Clapham and close to a pub. That's not much to go on.'

'No, but we do have a surname. It may have changed if she remarried but it's a start. What might be a better line would be to pick up on another clue – her job at Goldsmiths and her plan to become a librarian.'

***

Mark called the college the next day and asked to speak to their personnel department. They were not helpful, saying that they could not discuss details of present or past members of staff without their permission. He explained that this seemed to be the only way he might be able to trace his father who had disappeared after the end of the war. He was about to ring off when the woman the other end softened a little. 'It was a long time ago and I don't recognise the name,' she said. 'Our files from those days have been archived and are stored off site but you could try visiting the library. Some of the staff have been there for years. Someone might remember this person.'

It offered a glimmer of hope. One of Mark's colleagues was a graduate of Goldsmiths and agreed to go with him. One member of the library staff said she had known an older colleague about twenty years earlier called Mo who was married to a senior member of the academic staff. She assumed it was the same one as she knew she'd been widowed during the war. The librarian said she did have an address as Mo's husband, although retired, still used the library occasionally. She agreed to forward a letter in which he could explain the circumstances. It would then be a matter for her to decide whether to respond or not.

Mark wrote a short note on the spot and handed it to Mo's former colleague to post. Mo must have replied by return as he received a response three days later.

Dear Mark

Yes – I am the Mo who was married to Bob and we were both great friends of your dad. I am so happy you have contacted me. There is much I can tell you and much I can share with you. But there is also a lot I don't know so I won't be able to answer all your questions. I am not sure how much you know of your father's life but, I should warn you, there are parts of George's story you may find upsetting.

I should love to meet you and your family – I heard so much about you and Marty when you were small. You didn't mention her in your note. I hope she is well. It would be really good to meet you, and her, if possible.

Yours

Mo (Newton formerly Burgess).

***

Mo joined them for lunch the following weekend. Mark opened the door. She was a little overweight and casually dressed. She stood back for a moment looking at him. 'My God, you're the spitting image of your dad.' She hugged him tightly. 'I was so happy to get your note. Your dad was such a wonderful friend and I've often wondered what happened to him and to all of you. You must tell me everything about yourselves.' Mo's warmth was all-embracing.

Mark laughed. 'I will but we're hoping you can tell us about my dad.'

'I'll tell you what I know but there'll still be some unanswered questions for you – as there are for me.'

'Come on in.' He introduced Gisela and she was hugged in turn. It was a glorious summer day. They led Mo out onto the terrace and handed her a glass of wine. She looked round the small garden bright with gaillardias, penstemons, aquilegia and windflowers. A cluster of hybrid tea roses were enjoying a second flowering in one corner. The vivid colours of pelargoniums decorated the garden urns which edged the patio.

Mo sat back in the chair and looked around. 'One thing I really regret is that my garden is no more than three window boxes. But I love coming to Kew. I must have walked past your house many times on the way to the gardens from the tube. You're so like George that I would have said something if I'd clapped eyes on you.'

'If only – it might have made things simpler.'

'But tell me – you only said a little in your note. Why are you trying to trace your dad now?'

'It's really quite simple. Mum died just over a year ago. We found a load of papers hidden in her attic. I knew very little of Dad and nothing about his war service. It was the papers and the fact that they were hidden that intrigued me.' He smiled. 'I'm a journalist.'

'And how was it that you worked out George came to me after being turned out of the house?'

'That was our son, Michael. Dad kept a diary. We knew he'd lived with you at one time and had remained in touch after your husband's death. There seemed to be only two people he might have turned to, you and his sister Alice – and you were in London.'

'I knew he kept a diary. I think it was a very personal record. You should congratulate Michael on his sleuthing. If he's here, I'll do so myself.'

'Afraid not just now. He plays cricket for his college and they're away on tour in Devon this week. But you're right about the diary. It's an incredible record of his life and thoughts and feelings. We just don't understand why he didn't take it with him when he left the house.'

'I think I can answer that. Everything happened too quickly for him that day. When he got home from work that evening he was confronted by your mum who'd discovered some letters from Germany. I imagine you know about those and what followed?'

They nodded.

'She told him to go – permanently. He was devastated.'

'That's obvious from the last entries.'

'I think he'd also had a few drinks and could see no other way than to do as Joan demanded.'

'More than a few, I think.'

'He told me he'd been getting ready to leave the next day when a taxi rolled up at the door. His father-in-law came in and told him to leave straightaway. He said he'd paid for the taxi to take him to the station and that was the last thing any of them would ever do for him. He picked up the suitcases and carried them to the taxi. I think George was so shell-shocked and hungover that he didn't argue. He said it was only when he was on the train that he remembered he'd left his diary behind. He had hoped to go back to make some sort of arrangement for keeping in touch with you and to collect the diary, but he knew the chances of that were small. I guess it said something about the difficulties in the marriage and about his love for Hannelore. If Joan had read it, it would only have confirmed in her mind the rightness of her actions. Deep down George knew he could never go back.'

'That fits with what we've read. So, what happened next?'

'He arrived at my door after work that day. He was standing there with two suitcases looking totally forlorn. I've never seen a man look so down. He just said he was in a terrible mess and it was all his own making and he didn't know what to do or where to go. He came in and the whole story poured out of him. I learned about Hannelore and his longing for her and, I hope you don't mind me saying this, how sterile his marriage had become. He was struggling with the conflict between his love for her and the love and commitment he felt towards you and Marty. He needed time. I said he should stay until he had sorted himself out. At first he said he couldn't do that. He said it would be quite wrong for him to stay with a widow as it would damage my good name.' She laughed. 'There was always something a bit old-fashioned about your dad. I think the actual words were that he couldn't possibly "compromise my reputation". I told him not to be such a silly bugger and that he could stay as long as he needed. I always looked on him as the big brother I'd always wanted but never had. And it was a bonus for me. He was a link to Bob.'

They smiled. 'And did it compromise your reputation?'

'Of course it did. This was the forties. I got a lot of disapproving looks from people in the other flats. One or two said they were shocked. One even delivered a homily saying I should either marry your dad or turn him out as his presence would reduce my chance of ever marrying again. I told her she was a suspicious, mean-minded cow and she should fuck off. I said a bit more than that too. My time as a barmaid had enriched my vocabulary no end.'

Mo's openness and obvious generosity of spirit was affecting.

Gisela asked if they could press the pause button for two or three minutes while she laid out the lunch and refilled their glasses.

'How long was he with you?' she asked when she was seated again.

'Nearly six weeks.'

'And then?'

'George wrote to Joan the next day saying how sorry he was he had let her down so badly and he understood she wouldn't want to see him again. He begged her to let him see you and Marty. He pleaded with her to understand his feelings as a father. He showed me the letter that came a few days later. It was very curt. It said he'd betrayed the family and, therefore, had no claims on the children and he was not a suitable person to be a parent. It said two other things: she would never agree to a divorce and the shame it would bring, it was the forties, and she had read his diaries. She had been shocked by the way he had allowed an affair to develop and how appalled she had been by the details of his time with "that German tart". I must say I was surprised that he'd apparently been quite so frank. Your dad didn't generally expose his feelings but deep down he was a very caring and warm man. I think the diary was his emotional outlet. Joan said she was not prepared to return it or the letters and these would be used if he ever made any approaches to the family.'

'That figures.'

'But what did you know at the time of your dad's departure?'

'Very little. I was not quite five and Marty was seven.'

'But didn't you sense your mother's anger?'

'I don't think so. Mum was very controlled, very buttoned up as well as very controlling. She never showed much in the way of emotion. As I remember, she simply said Dad had had to go away for a time. That wasn't unusual. He had been away so much. But what happened then?'

'Your dad told me a lot about what he had been doing in Germany and his friendship with the Becker family. I knew some of it already, particularly his involvement in mine-clearing. Did you know he was awarded an OBE for his efforts?'

'Yes, but only after Mum died. It was hidden away with the diaries and some of her papers.'

'Your dad was quite open about his marriage. I'd known there were tensions. But he always said that he had pursued your mum and it was up to him to allow for differences in personality. He was a bit uncomfortable sometimes at the part your grandparents played in the marriage but much more so by the presence of some other woman whose name I've forgotten. I think he found a soulmate in Hannelore. Knowing she would be having their child, he longed to be with her. On the other hand, he felt there might still be a slim chance of seeing you and being involved in your upbringing. But he knew that chance would vanish entirely if he were to join Hannelore in Germany.'

'So, what did he do?'

'Alice came down from Newcastle and we talked all through one night. She offered to act as a go-between. We agreed it might be best if she made an unannounced trip to see your grandparents first. We knew it was unlikely to change anything but it seemed worth trying. We were right. Alice adopted a very apologetic tone and was invited in. They talked over a cup of tea. I think they were a bit more sympathetic than your mum. They called Joan while Alice was there but she was adamant that she wouldn't see her. She said the marriage was over and the rift could not be repaired. But one good point did come out of it. Alice had raised the issue of this woman – what was her name? Something like Edna? Anyway, Joan's parents said firmly they knew she was a bad influence and they were taking steps to bring the friendship to an end. Did that happen?'

'Yes. After the end of that year we never saw her again. We never knew what happened to her.'

'George knew after Alice's trip to Farnham that he was unlikely to ever see you again – at least while you were still kids. A solicitor said he could try and establish some rights of access, but after a lot of heart-searching he decided against. He didn't want a contest with Joan in court. Needless to say, he was very down but felt that, whether successful or not, it would involve a painful battle in public and that wouldn't be good for you two. The solicitor also said that, even if successful, obstacles might well be put in his way whenever he tried to arrange visits.'

'So, did he decide to go to Hannelore?'

'Yes. He and Alice and I talked again. We knew that there was almost no chance of a reconciliation or contact with you so it seemed that joining Hannelore and their child would offer him a chance of some happiness. So he decided to go to Germany and build a career and home there. As he spoke the language reasonably well, he thought it would be easier to live there rather than here where so many had strong negative feelings about Germans.'

'And so he went?'

'Yes. He handed in his notice and left at the end of October. He went up to Newcastle the next day and then took a boat across to the continent.'

'Did you ever see him again?'

'Sadly, no. He was a lovely friend and he was very good to me. I know I'm prejudiced but I couldn't bring myself to be judgmental. I could see how he'd found love in circumstances which must have been awful and against the background of strained relations at home. Please don't judge him too harshly. That may be difficult, but he was devoted to you two and he did try his utmost to make arrangements to keep in touch. I know he wrote to Joan and her parents several more times. I don't know if he ever got a reply.'

'Did you keep in touch after he'd gone?'

'For a time. I was very low when he left but I knew it was right for him to go.' Mo paused. 'I said earlier I'd always looked on your dad as a big brother. If I'm honest, if circumstances had been different, I might have had designs on him myself.' She smiled. 'He was a lovely man. It makes me sad it was never meant to be. I never saw him again. That made me sad too. I wrote several times. He wrote when his son was born. His name was, is, Horst. The correspondence stopped sometime the following year. I wrote once or twice more but never got a reply. I guess he must have moved – and I had moved too. Whatever it was we lost contact.'

'It was sometime in the next year that Mum got us

together and said she had some very sad news and that Dad had died.'

'Oh God, I am so sorry.' Mo stopped. Tears were welling up in her eyes. 'That explains it. I just hope he found some happiness in the short time he had with Hanny and his son.' Gisela walked over and put her arms around her. 'I'm afraid I can't help anymore.' Gisela handed her a tissue. She dried her eyes. 'I'm so sorry. It's just so sad you never really had a chance to know him.'

'I know that now.'

'Please cheer me up by telling me all about you and your family. I'd so much like to keep in touch now you've found me. It was one of the sadnesses in my life that I never had children. It was too late by the time Freddy and I married.'

'Yes, Dad's journal said how sad you were that you hadn't had a child with Bob.'

She looked up in surprise. 'Did that go into his diary?'

'There's a lot about you and Bob there.'

'Could I see it?'

'I'll send you a copy.'

Mark looked over at Gisela. 'It seems this quest is still not over. I need to go to Germany to try to find a stepmother and a half-brother. I hope he shares our name.'

'Will you let me know what you find?'

'Of course. As it happens, I have an assignment in Germany in a month or so. I'm covering the reunification ceremonies. I'm making an earlier visit in September but I won't have much time then. I'll take some leave after the ceremonies to go looking.' Mark looked at Gisela. 'I've already spoken to the editor and persuaded him it would be helpful if you came with me as a native German speaker. How about it?'

'I'm up for that.'

'And a trip to Aachen afterwards on a Hanny and Horst hunt?'

'Yes, after all, I started it. I found the boxes in the attic.'

***

Gisela turned to Mark after Mo had gone. 'Well, that takes us a little further forward. Have you spoken to Marty since my birthday?' He shook his head. 'You'll have to tell her she has a half-brother.'

'Why?'

'Mark, this is a close relative. She has to be told. And if we trace him and, possibly, a stepmother too it's all bound to come out.'

'No. She's made her feelings perfectly clear. She's been dead against me finding out what happened to my father all along. She doesn't seem to care or even accept that he was her father too.'

'But she has a right to know.'

He raised his hands above his head. 'Alright, I surrender. I'm not sure she has "a right", but perhaps she should be told. But I don't much look forward to telling her. I'll write. Everything we've discovered since March about both our parents has made her uncomfortable. I reckon she'll be highly critical when she learns of Dad's affair and its consequences. That will only add fuel to the fire.'

Mark's apprehensions were well founded. He received

an angry letter in return. Martina was emphatic that she would have preferred to have remained in ignorance of their father's affair. 'It's interesting,' observed Mark, 'that she's so critical of our father's affair but doesn't comment on our mother's. She said she had no wish to know anything of our father's "bastard son".'

He passed the letter to Gisela. 'I think I've created an unbridgeable gap,' he said when she had finished reading it. 'I guess it'll be up to me to try and build bridges. I don't see olive branches being extended from Birmingham.'

20

1 – 3 OCTOBER 1990

Berlin. Everything had moved with amazing speed towards reunification. The East German parliament had passed the Accession Act and the Unification Treaty was signed by both governments on the last day of August. The union of the two Germanys would take place on the third of October. Berlin would be the capital once more. Mark made a short visit early in September to research the background and get a preliminary view of the attitudes and reactions of local people. He and Gisela arrived for the ceremonies on the last day of September. The city was buzzing.

On their first evening they found a weinstube in a side street. They descended to the dimly lit cellar. It was packed with young people. The hubbub enveloped them. The feeling of excitement and sense of anticipation was palpable. Gisela put her hand in Mark's. 'I feel quite emotional. I can't believe this country has got here at all – let alone so quickly.' She pushed him towards a table littered with empty bottles and glasses which was being vacated by a small group. She scanned the menu chalked up on a board as they walked towards it. 'You sit, I'll order.'

Gisela was back from the bar a moment later carrying a couple of beers. 'We're having Königsberger klopse.'

'What the hell's that? Sounds Prussian.'

'You'll find out.'

'I've done a lot of background work for this – but not on the cuisine. I've been trying to get a feel for what it's been like living in a divided country.'

'A lot of the time it didn't feel divided for most of us. It just felt like two entirely different countries,' she paused, 'except, of course, for those here in Berlin.'

'I've looked again at what you wrote. You never told me you'd been assaulted.'

'I didn't tell anyone. I was embarrassed.' She shrugged. 'But back then it didn't seem any worse than a load of other things. Leaving our home and losing Papa was much worse. That's what hurt most. It still does.'

'But you survived.'

There was a long pause. Gisela shook her head. 'I'm only a survivor in the sense that I'm still here. None of us are really survivors. None of us are complete. None of us will ever again be the people we were or even the people we might have become. Just being alive isn't the same as surviving.'

Gisela was looking very introspective. Mark was stunned, uncertain how to respond. He put his hand on hers. Finally, he asked, 'Can I use that thought?' She nodded.

'Does this seem like another "zero hour"?'

'I think so. What happened then was scary and painful,

but Mutti was determined that it shouldn't cloud my life. The past really is another country. Things are different now.'

They paused for a few minutes as the food was served. Mark looked suspiciously at the plate, prodding the food with his fork. 'Looks like a meatball lurking under that sauce.'

'It is – but one with a difference. Try it.'

Mark tasted a mouthful. 'Um, interesting. What's in it?'

'Veal, onions and anchovies cooked with lemon and capers.'

He cautiously tried another mouthful. 'Yes, it's alright.' He paused. 'And named after your homeland.'

They ate in silence for a few minutes before Gisela looked directly at him. 'Right, now tell me what we have to do.'

Mark was relieved by her change of tone. 'Well, you're an accredited member of the press corps.' He handed her a badge. 'This will get you into some places. But mainly it'd be great if you would just keep your eyes and ears open, jot down what you see and hear. Tomorrow we'll go to where the ceremonies will take place. We can then look at the remains of the wall and wander around the old centre in the east.'

***

After a leisurely breakfast they walked to the Tiergarten and across to the Brandenburg Gate. They mingled with the crowd in front of the Reichstag. Stands and viewing platforms had been erected in readiness for the ceremony.

Gisela took his hand. 'I can't really be your guide. I've only been here twice and never to the east. But I've been – how do you say it – "boning up" on the history. The Gate is important. It was built by Frederick William II of Prussia.'

'The Great?'

'No, this was his nephew. His uncle was almost certainly gay – Frederick William II was anything but! He was known as der Vielgeliebte, the "much loved". He did nothing by halves. He was married twice legally and twice bigamously! The arch was meant to be a symbol of peace. It's been the focus of many events, some far from peaceful. Napoleon used it for his entry after the Battle of Jena and he nicked the quadriga from the top. It was returned after his defeat. There were big demonstrations here during the 1848 revolution and the Nazis marched through with torches when Hitler became Chancellor. It was just on the east side after the wall went up. The Reichstag was on the west with the wall right behind it. It's been partly restored but it's not in use. I don't know if it'll be the parliament again.' She paused.

A few people had gathered as she was speaking, assuming she was a guide. She looked up surprised to find she had an audience. She started speaking in German. 'I'm not a guide. I am, or was, a German. I'm married to an English journalist.' She pointed to their press badges. 'We're here for the ceremony.'

Mark whispered in her ear, 'Why don't you carry on?'

She smiled and whispered back, 'Okay, I've always fancied your job.' She turned back to the group. 'We'd love to hear your thoughts on how you see things developing after unification.' She winked at Mark. 'I'll get my junior assistant here to make a note of what you say. Perhaps you could also say where you're from. Speak English or German whichever you wish. Wir können Englisch oder Deutsch sprechen – je nachdem, was Ihnen lieber ist.'

There was silence for a few moments and then a young man said, 'I'm a student. It's good to speak English. I'm from Leipzig. I welcome unification but I'm also a little fearful.'

'Why's that?'

'We're poor relations. We're "Ossis". We're worried we won't be competing on equal terms for jobs. There won't be open discrimination but we're worried there'll be an underlying prejudice.'

'You speak English well.'

'A lot of us do. Our school education was generally good but opportunities after that were limited. Membership of the party was essential for career advancement. I think many of my generation from the east will seek their future abroad.'

'But you've been treated very generously. We've made huge contributions to you,' an older woman interjected. 'I'm from West Berlin.'

'In financial terms that's true but the way you say it implies we're under an obligation to you. It suggests we're recipients of charity and a lesser class of citizen.'

'I'm also from the east,' said another, 'from Jena. We were unlucky. We just lived in the wrong place when the country was carved up. Others were luckier, as I guess this lady journalist was.'

'Yes, some of us were lucky – in some ways but not necessarily others. I had to flee from East Prussia as a kid with my mother. I never saw my father again.'

'Some of us have been luckier. We need to share it.'

This brought a round of applause from the small group which had been growing. Gisela then asked, 'How do you think the outside world views the unification?'

An older man raised his hand. 'I've lived in the soviet sector since before the wall was built. I know some countries, like yours and France, are fearful. They worry that a united Germany will lead to fascism again. I understand that. Sadly, we have to live with our past. But I believe and pray it won't happen. Kohl hasn't been very sensitive about this. Our President has been better.'

'But the young shouldn't be made to feel guilty for the sins of earlier generations.'

'No, but we need to be sensitive to the effect our country's history has had on others.'

'And we do have feelings of guilt,' added a young woman.

'It's all happened so quickly – too quickly. It's less than a year since the wall came down.'

The discussion continued to ebb and flow around the issues amongst the group. Gisela finally called a halt, thanking them and promising to report the various views as fairly as possible.

Mark put his notebook away. 'That was brilliant. It mirrors much of what I'd picked up three weeks ago. Let's go over to the east.' They walked past the gate to the Unter den Linden and strolled a little way before stopping at a cafe. He looked at Gisela as he stirred his coffee. 'There are huge anxieties but people know this is inevitable and there seems to be a determination to make it work. I met a guy from

Munich last month. He told me a parable that I'm going to use. He said it was like a man visiting Nymphenberg Palace on a sunny day after a spell of very cold weather. There was a boy on the ice on the lake and it was beginning to thaw. He wasn't sure how to help. He wanted to protect the boy, but he wouldn't respond to pleas to walk gently to the edge. He worried that if he went onto the ice to help, it might not support his weight and both would fall into the icy water. He saw the DDR as that child and the fable illustrated the goodwill and wish to help by the west. But it also reflected the uncertainty they felt about how to go about it. He said they were scared they would all be dragged down to the standard of living of the east.'

'It's a neat story.'

'It summarises a lot of what we've just heard – paternalism and a worry that it will be impossible to strike a balance between maintaining the quality of life in the west while providing support for the east. They're also worried that the "sanitisation" of party members will be necessary, not to mention the thousands of Stasi informers. That will expose some very raw nerves.'

'Perhaps not so different from denazification forty-five years ago.'

***

After their coffee, Gisela and Mark walked further to Museum Island, Humboldt University and the cathedral. Mark had lined up a series of interviews with senior officials of the former DDR in the afternoon so he suggested Gisela should be a tourist for the rest of the day. They arranged to meet at eight for dinner.

Mark bumped into a former colleague during the afternoon who was covering the ceremony. He insisted they should have dinner together to exchange impressions. Mark called the hotel and left an apologetic message for Gisela, saying he hoped she wouldn't mind dining alone. She was asleep when he got back after midnight and hardly stirred as he slipped into bed beside her.

Gisela was already up the following morning when he awoke. She appeared from the shower wrapped in a towel, looking preternaturally cheerful. 'Good morning, or "grüss Gott" as they would say in the south. I assume from your snores that you had an evening with Bacchus as well as your mate. I had to turn you over twice to reduce the volume.'

He groaned. 'Sorry, I was well marinated by the end of the evening. We didn't talk much about current affairs. It was mainly gossip about mutual acquaintances.'

'Come on, let's have some coffee and breakfast and I'll tell you about my evening.' Mark looked a little surprised. 'Well, you didn't really think I'd spend my evening alone eating in this boring hotel, did you? I'll tell you about it.'

'Ellie, I need a bucketload of coffee before I listen to your adventures. And I hope there's some good copy there. I managed to get press accreditation for you but that mean sod of an editor wouldn't agree to pay you. But I can probably wangle expenses for your evening.'

'So you should. You may have been getting pissed with your mate, but I was working.'

'So what did you get up to?'

'I went back to the Gate. It was awesome. There was quite a crowd there. Everyone was hugging everyone else and sharing wine and schnapps. It was one hell of a party. I linked up with some students and was swept off to a Kneipe in a side street near the Unter den Linden. They were from both sides and some of their lecturers were there too. It was fun, but there was a lot of serious talk as well. I was asked why I was in the crowd when I was wearing a Press badge. I said I was trying to gauge the feelings of people in the street. There was no stopping them after that. Their views were mixed, much like the ones we'd heard earlier. One of the older guys said something interesting. He said the wall dividing the city and the fences dividing the country might be going but it would take more than a generation to remove the fences and barriers in people's minds. He also said it was still difficult to articulate an honest and undistorted view of our history. That chimed with me. Anyway, I got back late and made a lot of notes.'

'Okay, well done.'

She grinned. 'I'm really enjoying this journalism thing. It's a lot of fun wandering around, chatting people up, drinking at the paper's expense and partying like a student. It's a doddle. I think I might take it up.'

'It's not all like that.'

'Seems pretty straightforward to me – don't know why you make such a big deal of it.'

**

Mark and Gisela made their way to the area around the Reichstag and the Brandenburg Gate early in the afternoon. Large crowds had already gathered. Mark had agreed that his local colleague would be in the press enclosure and he and Gisela would mingle with the crowd near the dais set up for Kohl and the other dignitaries. They joined the crowd and stayed close for the rest of the day to ensure they wouldn't lose their chosen vantage point. A young man with a portable radio said a million people would be there. Most were young and of a generation which had spent its entire life in the shadow of the wall. People were draped in flags; firecrackers were exploding and groups were singing. As it grew dark and the hours and minutes passed, there was a growing sense of expectation. The final few minutes were to be triggered by the tolling of the bell of the nearby Schöneberg Town Hall. The dignitaries gathered in front of the Reichstag and a giant German tricolour lay ready to be raised on the stroke of midnight. As the hour approached, the crowd momentarily became quieter. Gisela took Mark's hand and pulled him towards her, holding him tightly. Tears were streaming down her cheeks. Many lit torches, flourished flags and started counting down. Their voices reached a crescendo as they chanted fünf, vier, drei, zwei, ein as the hour approached. Then at midnight the flag was raised and the Liberty Bell, a replica of the original in Philadelphia, started to toll. This was followed by bells all over the city and the country. Germany was one once more. The crowd erupted, cheering and singing the Deutschlandlied as fireworks exploded on both sides of the former border.

Mark had persuaded one of the British diplomatic staff

to smuggle them into the official reception. This enabled them to mingle with the great and the good (or at least the moderately great and, hopefully, good). There was no chance of approaching the leaders but Mark managed to speak to some higher ranking officials and lower ranking politicians.

It was after three before they left to go back to the hotel. Gisela snuggled up to Mark as soon as they were in bed. 'I can't sleep now. We need to celebrate as we did the night the wall came down.'

***

They woke late the next day. Mark asked Gisela to go out and buy some of the German papers, Die Welt, Frankfurther Allgemeine Zeitung, Der Tagesspiegel and Neues Deutschland, to get a spread of political views, as well as early editions of the London papers to gauge their reactions. She was out when the paper's local correspondent called. He said he'd been contacted by the Ministry of the Interior and an official wished to speak to him. Mark said he would deal with it when he got to the local office to prepare his copy later that morning. He was puzzled. He couldn't think of any reason why they should want to speak to him. He waited for Gisela to return. He wanted her with him in case of difficulty with the language.

He was greeted cheerfully by the stringer. 'What have you been up to? It sounded mysterious. Perhaps they've turned up something about you in the Stasi files.'

Mark was intrigued and a little apprehensive. He called

the number and extension he had been given and put the phone on speaker. He introduced himself. There was a pause before a voice the other end said in English, 'I was looking through the list of correspondents in Berlin and saw your name. Your office said they would contact you. Please forgive this unannounced approach but my name is Horst Brown – Brown spelt the English way. I believe we might be related. I know I have a half-brother called Mark Brown, a journalist, in England and wondered if this might be you.' Mark was stunned and unable to respond for several moments. Gisela put her arm around him. 'Are you still there?'

He paused a moment longer before replying. 'Yes, I'm still here. I was just completely taken aback by what you said.'

'I apologise. I knew it was possible that an approach might not be welcome – particularly coming out of the blue. If I have upset you or if I've got the wrong man, I can only say I'm sorry and I won't trouble you again.'

'No, no,' said Mark hurriedly. 'Please don't go away. I was just struck dumb. We might be, must be, related. I've been trying to find out what happened to my father for more than a year. In fact, my wife and I were planning to go to Aachen this weekend to try to find a family called Becker. Is your mother's name Hannelore Becker and was your father George Brown?'

'Yes.'

'This is amazing. Can we meet?'

'I was about to suggest that. I'm so happy we've made this connection.'

'I've got some work to do and a deadline to meet but that'll only take me a couple of hours. Could we meet for dinner, somewhere quiet where we can talk?'

'Come to my home. Come early, say at six so you can meet my wife and children. We shall have so much to talk about. I'll give you the address. From the press list, I see your wife is with you. Do bring her too.'

'She's here. We'd love to come.'

'We're on speakerphone,' said Gisela. 'That sounds wonderful. I have been so excited by what's happening. It's just incredible and then finding you is unbelievable.' She had switched into German part way through the sentence.

'You're German,' said Horst in surprise. 'That's even more wonderful than you might think. My wife is English. We'll have so much to share. Until this evening.'

It was difficult to focus on the work that had to be done but by mid-afternoon Mark had prepared an analytical piece speculating on what the future might hold for a united Germany within Europe, reflecting the ambitions of the political elite and the fears and hopes of the people.

21

3 & 4 OCTOBER 1990

'I can't believe the end is in sight.' Mark and Gisela were on the U-bahn heading towards Horst's apartment. 'This trip's been amazing. Just one high after another. At last I'll find out what happened to my dad.'

'And maybe meet a stepmother?'

Mark nodded. 'I was so thrown by what Horst said that I never thought to ask if she's still alive. It's difficult to think of someone as a stepmother when I never knew I had one. I hope I like her. It would be terrible to get this far and find out she's awful – or, even worse, to discover that Marty's assessment of her was right.'

'Don't be such a pessimist.'

They located the apartment not far from the Kurfürstendamm and rang the bell. The door was opened by a small girl. She eyed them gravely for a few moments before asking in English, 'Are you Daddy's English brother and sister?'

'I think we must be. What's your name?'

'I'm Anna. I'm ten and this,' she pointed behind her, 'is Emilia. She's eight. Papa,' she called out, 'it's your brother and sister.'

Horst came through, looked at Mark and laughed. 'You look just like our father from the photos I've seen of him when he was younger.' He walked over and put his arms round Mark. 'This isn't just a great day for Germany. It's a great day for me too.'

'This is Gisela, Ellie.' She went over and hugged him and whispered something in his ear in German. She laughed. 'It was no secret. I simply said I'd not felt part of Germany for years but, after today, I'm starting to think I have two homelands. It feels good.'

Horst's wife had come through quietly from the back of the flat. 'Hi, I'm Clare, but everyone here calls me Clara.' There was a trace of a Geordie accent. 'You're so welcome. Horst has always wanted to find the English family he's never known.'

'I've been trying to find out what happened to my father for more than a year. I've learnt a lot from his diaries, but only up to the time he left home – then nothing. Just a blank.'

Horst smiled. 'He's always been a great one for keeping a diary. Let's go through and have a drink.' They followed Horst through to the lounge. Mark and Gisela sat back and accepted glasses of wine. 'There's so much to talk about. I called Mutti this afternoon. She's so happy we're meeting. She's telling the rest of the family. But how is it you came looking for us now?'

'My mother died last year. We were clearing her house

and Ellie found these boxes of papers in the attic. Martina, my sister, tried to stop me but I couldn't resist going through them. I've learnt a lot since then. It wasn't a great marriage. I think Marty was already aware of some of the things we discovered.'

'Mutti has hinted that Papa's marriage was not so good, although she never quite said so.'

'I hadn't a clue why Dad left home until a couple of months ago. I wasn't quite five at the time and I hardly knew him. He was mostly away in the army before that and then he was just gone. It didn't seem such a big deal at the time.' He shrugged. 'That was just the way it was. But the more I've discovered, the more I've felt disappointed that he wasn't around when I was a kid. I'm beginning to realise now what I've missed.'

'This all must have very mixed emotions for you.'

'Yes, in a way.' He sipped his wine. 'It really started like a bit of academic research, but it's become personal. I feel I'm getting to know my father. But it must have been the same for you growing up without a father.'

'What do you mean? I didn't grow up without a father.'

'Did your mother re-marry? You must have been only a few months old when he died.'

Horst looked puzzled. 'I don't understand what you're saying. Papa, George Brown, my father, your father, is alive. He'll be eighty this month. Why did you think he'd died?'

Mark was stunned into silence. Gisela went over and sat on the arm of his chair and caressed the back of his neck. He looked at Horst in bewilderment. After a long pause he said haltingly, 'My mother sat us down about six months after he'd gone and told us he'd died in an accident. We had no reason to believe otherwise. When I was older, I asked her what had happened but she would only repeat that he had died in an accident. She wouldn't say any more.'

'But what about your family in Newcastle? Surely they told you this wasn't true.'

'We never saw them after Dad had gone. We've discovered now that Mum deliberately shut them out of our lives.'

'I'm so sorry. This must be opening up old wounds.'

Mark shifted uncomfortably in the chair. 'I suppose so. But they're wounds I didn't know were there until this last year or even this last minute or two.' He shook his head. 'Mum was a very private and controlling person. We didn't know anything of our father's relationship with your mother nor that they'd had a child until two months ago.'

Clara looked across at them. 'This must be very difficult for you. You should say if you want to stop or leave, though we hope you won't. We know some of what went on from Alice. She was very upset that she'd been cut off from you and Martina. She said she'd written to your mum many times. The replies she got were apparently very threatening, saying she would blacken your father's name and turn you against him if she or George tried to make contact with you.'

'I'm trying to take all this in.' Mark paused for a few moments to order his thoughts. 'Dad was in the army until 1947. He was only back for about six months before he left. Mum never spoke about him and there were no photos in the house. At first she said he'd gone to a job in the north and wouldn't be home for some time. Then nothing until she told us he'd died.'

'How did that make you feel?'

'I guess we were sad. He'd been fun when he was there – but it was for such a short time. Life just went on much as it always had done. We knew very little about the family in Newcastle although we did have a great holiday with them when Dad was home. There was so much we didn't know: what he'd done in the army, his friendship with your grandparents, about your mother.' He paused. 'I understand why you feel we might be upset. In many ways, I am. I'm just trying to process it all. I've learnt a lot about my mum since she died – a lot of it's not good. She and her parents tended to side-line Dad. Much of what she and they did must have been very hurtful to him.'

'Mutti's said that. Papa never said much. Mutti said their affair had ended and then she found she was pregnant. She told us she hadn't wanted to tell Papa but was persuaded to do so by my grandmother. Even then she was emphatic that they didn't want to break up his marriage.'

'We know that's right. We found the letters they sent. I'm sure he would have stayed with Mum, even knowing you were on the way. He said nothing to her but she found the letters and had them translated. She was very angry and felt he had humiliated her. That's when she threw him out and told him never to come back. And she insisted he should have no contact with us and, if he tried, access would be denied. The same must have applied to his family in Newcastle. I think she was very threatening.'

'She must have been very bitter.'

'I've now learned that he begged her more than once in the following month to reconsider but she told him she would contest any attempt to establish rights of access. I think he felt it would be very distressful for everyone and probably unsuccessful. Alice also tried – also without success. It seems at that point he decided to come to Germany and join your mother. I'm finding it difficult to forgive Mum for depriving us of contact with Dad and his family. We didn't have an easy relationship, particularly after I met Ellie. Mum was very anti-German but so were lots of others, so we didn't think it was that odd. After reading Dad's diaries, we've learned a lot about the relationship with your mother. But I'm still mystified as to why Dad didn't try to make contact with us directly or through Newcastle once we were adults.'

'He rarely mentioned you when we kids were around but I'm sure he talked a lot to Mutti.'

Anna had been listening throughout this exchange. 'So, are Oma and Opa your Mutti and Papa as well?'

Horst smiled at his daughter. 'It's a bit more complicated than that, sweetheart. Opa is my Papa and Mark's Papa but we have different mamas.'

'It's a bit difficult to understand.'

They all laughed. 'It's difficult for us too.'

Clara refreshed their glasses and then took Anna and Emilia off to bed, saying they should eat when she came back.

Mark was pleased to have a little time to think. 'This can't be easy for you either. Tell us about your family.'

'I should start from the present. As you know, our

government plans to re-establish Berlin as the capital. A number of us have already been relocated to make the necessary preparations. We've been here for six months. Before that we lived in Bonn.'

'How did you meet Clara?'

'That was simple. My grandmother spent time in England before the first war. She always wanted to go back. A few years before she died we all went over to stay with Papa's family. We stayed with your Aunt Alice and Uncle Joe. There wasn't room for all of us, so they arranged for me and my brother to stay with friends – Clara's parents.'

Clara had come back into the room. 'He was with us for ten days. We did one or two things together. Nothing serious. I didn't think much about it after Horst had gone home but then he started writing and sending me verses he had composed.' She laughed. 'They were quite awful and very sentimental. I'm afraid I behaved rather badly. I saw this as a challenge and started to send spoof romantic verses to him – in English. It was unfair. Despite his fluent spoken English, it was difficult for him to appreciate irony and parody in another language.'

They were all laughing. 'But how did you manage to get from there to where you are now?'

'Two things happened. First, he hadn't shown my poetic efforts to George and Hanny. After all, what twenty-two year old would show his parents what he imagined were passionate love poems from a girl? But one day he did as he was beginning to suspect I was taking the piss.'

'I did and Papa fell about laughing. But then he helped me compose a rhyme in a similar vein and I sent it off.'

'And?'

'It was quite awful,' Clara said. 'It went something like this:

I've found a stamp, my dearest Clare,
And thought that I had better
Pen a verse for one so fair
And send it in this letter.

Although through many, many a day
Your absence makes me fonder
My thoughts of love in every way
To you in Geordieland will wander

And if I cannot kiss you, Clare,
Remember I implore you
When old without my teeth and hair
That I will still adore you.

Clara continued through the laughter saying, 'I realised I'd been rumbled. But I also realised I'd been rather enjoying it and would like to see him again. I wrote a slightly more serious letter saying I would be inter-railing in Europe during my last long vac and it would be good to see him and his family again. They asked me to stay for a week and it went from there. We should eat, come on through.'

'Tell us more about our Newcastle family,' Mark asked when they were seated.

'We go over every few years. Joe died twelve years ago and Alice about four years ago so now our visits are mainly to my family. But we generally manage to see Ian and Aidan and their families.'

'And your family in Aachen?'

'My Uncle Bertie still lives there with his wife, Petra. One of my cousins has moved away elsewhere in Germany and one's in the United States. I have a brother and sister, Klaus and Birgit, who are still in the area. Klaus is married to Ursula and they have four kids. Birgit isn't married but has a long-term partner – Werner.'

'So what do they all do?'

'Klaus, like his grandfather, is a dentist – as is Ursula. They have three boys and a girl. Their ages run from three up to eleven. Birgit is an accountant and Werner an architect. They seem to spend most of their time travelling and having fun. But before we go on, what are your plans? How long will you be in Berlin?'

'I've one or two loose ends to tie up in our office here. We've arranged to take the rest of the week off. I don't have to be back until Monday. We were planning to go to Aachen to try to trace your family and then to Köln to see Ellie's mother. Now, I'm not sure.'

Clara looked at them. 'This has been a lot for you to take on board. You'll need time to reflect on this bombshell and talk to your sister before we talk more.' She paused, 'Or perhaps you would rather not talk more?'

'No, I do, but discovering my dad is alive has shaken me after so long believing he was dead.'

'I have a suggestion. You have a few days. You could still go to Aachen and meet George and Hanny. But I should tell you, your father's not as active as he was. He's had a heart attack and has a stent and his mobility is a bit limited. It might also be possible for you to meet Klaus and Birgit while you're there. Alternatively, you could check out of your hotel tomorrow and come and stay with us for a couple of days. It'll give you time to think about things overnight and give us all more time to talk. You can also talk to Martina. Even if she's not keen to meet, she should know her father is alive. That will still give you time to visit Köln at the weekend before you head for home.'

'Clara's right. I think it might be sensible to defer a meeting until you've spoken to your sister and Mutti has had a chance to talk to Papa. After what you've told us, all this will come as quite a shock to him.'

Gisela looked at Mark. 'I guess that makes sense.'

'Okay, if you're sure it's alright with you. I do need time to think and unscramble my mind.'

***

Back at the hotel, Mark and Gisela were lying on the covers of the bed, propped up on the pillows. Mark had his head down, lips pursed and hands clasped together on his chest. Finally, Gisela broke the silence. 'So, what do you make of your half-brother?'

'Seems a nice enough guy – obviously keen to get to know us. But finding out my father is still alive pretty well shut everything else out of my mind. There are so many questions.'

'Such as?'

'Did he know Mum had died?'

'Only he can answer that.'

'There are a load of things running around in my head. Would Dad have stayed with Mum if she'd been able to forgive and forget? I can't really see it. It would've been uncomfortable for sure. Would things have been different if he hadn't been thrown out in such an angry and summary manner? Had Mum just taken so strong a stand that she felt she could never backtrack? Or might she have seen this as an opportunity to consummate her relationship with Edna? Thank God that didn't happen.' Gisela reached over and took his hand.

'How do you feel now?'

'Sad that Mum couldn't have been more open and more flexible.'

'Your mum didn't do flexible.'

'And I'm angry she didn't consider whether Marty and I might want to know our father.'

'You'd built up an image of your dad – a hero with a difficult marriage. Then, when you found out about his affair, you became a bit more sympathetic towards your mum. Now you've found out she lied to you big time. Do you feel betrayed by her?'

'Yes.'

Mark got up and got himself a brandy from the minibar. He looked at Gisela. 'No thanks, I'm fine.' He returned to the bed. 'Do you still want to meet him?'

'This has totally thrown me. But, yes, I do.'

'To confront him?'

There was a long pause. 'There'd be no point. And you're right, my sympathies are now mainly with him.'

'I'd go along with that.'

'But what's still bugging me is why he didn't contact us once we were adults.'

'I'm sure he'd have done what he could to find out what you were up to. He'd have known something about you if he'd ever seen your paper.'

'I can see why he might have held back when we were kids after what Mum had said.'

'Don't you think that might have been true when you were adults as well?'

'Why?'

'Think about it. Your mum lied big, big time. If your dad or Alice had contacted you, that lie would have been exposed in nanoseconds. She would have had everything to lose if that happened. I would guess that her letters to Alice became increasingly threatening to forestall any approaches from your dad.'

'I guess you're right.'

'You should call Marty and discuss what to do next.'

'Yes, though I'm not looking forward to that. But whatever she says, I'm not backing off now.'

It was late before they turned out the lights. Mark found it difficult to sleep. Gisela's comments circulated endlessly in his mind. It was difficult not to accept that he had been betrayed by his mother. Thinking only of herself, she had calculatingly decided they should have no contact with their father and that there should not even be any reference to him. He had become a non-person in her eyes and she had been determined that he should be a non-person in their eyes as well. It was clear that she had retained George's diaries and the letters as weapons to shame and humiliate him in the eyes of his children should he ever try to return or make contact. He was not sure what role her parents or the rebarbative Edna had played in encouraging her vindictiveness.

Mark was finding it difficult to be too judgmental about his father's affair, given the circumstances in Germany at the time. But it was evidently more than that. George had sensed Joan's ambivalence about her sexuality. He had hinted as much to Hannelore – maybe he'd said more. They had shared confidences and her empathy had laid the foundations, as it turned out, for an enduring love. It was clear he had been and continued to be a loyal and loving father to his German family. Loyalty given and reciprocated, to family, colleagues and his men in the army, seemed to have been a key component of his personality.

But it was still difficult to understand fully his failure to make some sort of contact once they were adults. George could well have been apprehensive that they would react negatively to him. A meeting would certainly have been tense and unsettling, particularly as his mother's lie would have been instantly exposed. It would undoubtedly have led to angry discussions with Joan. His father could also have been anxious that they might be hostile towards Hannelore and his other children, who might be seen as having displaced them in his affections. Clara had been right. He needed time to reflect. His quest had started out of curiosity but this latest revelation had shaken him to his core. It had become deeply personal.

Mark called his sister the following morning before she

left for the hospital. She was as stunned as he had been by the news that their father was alive and that he had another family in Germany. But she was emphatic that she didn't want to meet him or his other family. Their father, she said angrily, had had an affair and then abandoned them. She wanted nothing to do with him. Mark was irritated by her intransigence and her lack of empathy. Finally, he persuaded her that at least he should let her know about any reunion that might take place.

He needed to meet his father and ask the questions which had haunted him throughout the night. It would take time to prepare emotionally for a reunion. He hoped George would be ready to talk but could not be certain he would, nor how open he might be. And he was conscious that time might be limited. A reunion might be stressful for his father, but it might be the only opportunity he might have. He was still finding it difficult to refer to George as Dad in his own mind. He had warmed to the man through reading his journal but the affection had little physical substance. It was akin to the positive feeling one might develop for a character in a novel. He worried, above all, that an approach after so many years might not be welcome. Mark cast his mind back to the conversation the previous day. Horst had said Hannelore was happy they were meeting but had not commented on his father's reaction. He had thought nothing of it at the time as the comment had been made before he knew George was alive. He needed to know whether his father would agree to meet and talk.

***

Mark called Clara and Horst and accepted their invitation to stay. It would be an opportunity to discuss arrangements for a possible reunion and discover if a meeting might be problematic for his father and for Hannelore. Mark needed time with Horst on his own and suggested they went for a walk. They strolled out to the Kurfürstendamm and headed towards the Zoo.

'I don't know how Papa will react,' said Horst. 'It won't be easy for him.'

'Are you suggesting we shouldn't meet?'

'Not at all. But he's always said very little when I've asked about his English family. He said he had given his word not to make contact and he wouldn't break it. I've challenged him more than once. I understood he was bound by his word but I felt we shouldn't be bound by it as well. His only reply was that it wouldn't be right. I could never get him to say why.'

'Do you think his attitude might have softened? How did he react when you told him we would be meeting?'

'I'm not sure he knows.'

Mark stopped and turned to Horst. 'He didn't know we were meeting?'

Horst looked a little uneasy. 'Let's go over there to talk.' He pointed to the Kaiser Wilhelm Church. 'The locals call it the lipstick and powder compact,' he said as they crossed the busy intersection. They stood for a moment inside the church admiring the intense blue light cast by thousands of stained-glass inlays in the honeycombed wall. 'I should have said this yesterday. I don't know if Papa knows we have met. I simply saw your name and decided that our generation should see if we wanted to get to know one another. I wasn't sure what Papa would say but I did tell Mutti what I was going to do, so she may have told him by now. She's always wanted to try to build bridges and reunite you and your father. Papa always seemed to be against it. He would say it was in the past and that it was best to let sleeping dogs lie and we should focus on the present. I think he feels very guilty that he let you down. I'm not quite sure how to say this in English but he is a very moral man. You may find that difficult, but he is. I think guilt has weighed very heavily on him.'

'Do you think the thought of a meeting, a reunion, will make him anxious?'

'I'm sure it'll be difficult. And he'll worry about how you might react to Mutti. You might feel she stole your father and that you'd be resentful and say things which would be upsetting for both of them. He is, as he always was, very much in love with Mutti.'

'And your mother?'

'She's worried about Papa. She said he spends a lot of time brooding about the past now he's older. He goes on endlessly about what was and what might have been and wasn't. She thinks a meeting will be painful but it might give him some peace of mind. She's worried – and sad that his time might be limited.'

Mark looked directly at Horst. 'Is that what you think too?'

'I think it's important for all of us. And I'd like to think your return today is a sign that it's important for you too.'

Mark nodded. 'Yes, but you should know that Martina

has rather different views. I spoke to her this morning. She was very emphatic that she doesn't want to meet our father. She can be very inflexible, a bit like our mother. How do you think we should arrange a meeting? I don't want to distress George or worse – particularly at his age.'

'Can I suggest we leave it to Mutti? She's very good at handling Papa. She's wanted this for so long. She may suggest she meets you first. I don't know how she'd play it but I do know she'll try to make sure everything goes as smoothly as possible.'

'And a first meeting – what can we do beforehand?'

'Exchanging some photographs and details of your lives and family would help.'

'And should you and Clara be there as well?'

'I think not. It could be too much for Papa and it could be embarrassing for him, which would make it more difficult. And I shouldn't steal a march on my brother and sister. I'll give your address and telephone number to Mutti and hers to you and then leave it to you two. I'm biased but I don't think you'll feel I've misled you in any way about Mutti's good sense. She's longing to meet you.'

'Where do you think we should meet?'

'I think in Aachen but not this weekend. Mutti will want time to help Papa prepare.'

'That sounds sensible. I feel I need some time too.'

'We should get back to Clara and Gisela.'

***

Horst spoke to his mother again who said she would call

Mark after he had arrived back home. There was little more they could do for now. Gisela and Mark stayed a further day and by tacit agreement they simply relaxed with their newly found brother and sister-in-law. The sense that the quest was nearing its conclusion was gratifying. That Mark would at last meet his father would be the natural final chapter in the search. But the discovery that he was alive had raised questions in Mark's mind as to where the boundaries of family might be drawn. Horst and Clara had been welcoming and there was the prospect of getting to know these other families and their children. This could be the start of an enduring family relationship. How close it might become would depend upon the bonds they might build, or fail to build, with their father and with Hannelore.

22

4 October 1990

'We're going out and we're celebrating this evening,' Hanny announced without preamble at breakfast.

'And what exactly is it we're celebrating?'

'First, my country, our country, has been put back together again. But there's something even more important to celebrate. I'm not going to explain now. I'll tell you everything this evening.'

George was not generally enthusiastic about surprises but agreed to go along with it. He was intrigued. There was some added gusto to Hanny's usual ebullience and positivity. His world had been closing in and his horizons had narrowed over the last few years due to his limited mobility. Her exuberance and knowing smile kept him wondering throughout the day.

A taxi dropped them off in a small street close to the cathedral. Hanny linked her arm in his and led him to a bar. 'I'm buying the drinks,' she said firmly. She whispered to the waitress as they were led to a table. The hubbub of conversation enveloped them as they sat. The place was crowded with office staff freed from their desks for the day. George looked around the stylish art deco bar. There was something vaguely familiar about it. Slowly, slowly it all came back to him. Despite the much-changed décor, the change in name and several make-overs during the past forty years, he knew this place. This was the first time they had been back since that evening that had changed his life, both their lives, forever. Memories of that bitter-sweet evening instantly invaded and laid siege to his mind. His past had never been far from his consciousness. His life had been shaped, defined and redefined by the complex interplay between his history and circumstances, by his desires and their consequences. His past was forever with him and with every act of recall the memories would change and evolve. But why had Hanny brought him here? Was it nostalgia and sentiment or was there something more?

The waitress was back a few moments later with glasses of champagne.

'You folks celebrating? Anniversary is it?'

Hanny nodded. 'In a way, yes,' she inclined her head towards George, 'But much, much more.'

'Enjoy and have a great evening.'

Hanny turned to George. 'Do you know where we are?'

'Yes,' he said sharply. 'I'm not gaga yet.' He took her hand. 'I'm sorry – I didn't mean it to come out quite like that. I was remembering how sad I felt that evening. I thought I was saying goodbye to you forever. It was here that I realised just how much you meant to me. In every way that mattered, you were already my lover and, as it's turned out, you have been so ever since.'

Hanny raised her eyebrows. 'Are you losing your British inhibitions in your old age?'

'No, you stripped me of those long ago. But there must be a reason why we've come here tonight.'

'There is. I also thought I was losing you. But that night has had so many consequences for both of us and it's the consequences we should talk about now. That's why we've come back here this particular evening.'

'What's this leading up to?'

'A lot. It's everything that's happened since that last day of February more than forty years ago.' George was about to say something but she put her finger to his lips. 'George, mein liebster Schatz, please, don't say anything until I've finished.' She drew a deep breath. 'The only thing I wanted back then was for you to know how much I loved you. I believed you loved me too but wouldn't and couldn't say so out of loyalty to Joan. I just wanted to create a memory of your love that I could hold close to me forever.' She gently caressed his arm. 'As it turned out, we created much more than a memory. I've had a wonderful life and not one but three children. I now have a lifetime of wonderful memories. I never believed, even when I was expecting Horst, that my life would turn out as amazingly as it has. It's a life I could never have imagined that evening when we first met in the ruins. And it wouldn't have happened if it hadn't been for Joan finding those letters.' She smiled. 'I'm sure it never crossed her mind when she excommunicated you that she would provide the basis for such a happy life for diese deutsche Dirne.'

Tears were welling up in George's eyes. It was some

time before he was able to speak. 'Hanny, my love, it's also given me a life I couldn't have imagined. It might never have happened but I'm happy it did.' He paused and looked hard at her. 'We're both getting very sentimental. What's this really about?'

'George, we have had a wonderful life – but it has come at a cost and that cost has been so much more for you than for me. There's always been a shadow over our lives. It's time to lighten that shadow.' Again she lifted a finger to stop him speaking. 'Please hear me out. I've been rehearsing this all day. I've always been sad that you've never been able to get to know Mark and Martina. It must have been as much a loss for them as for you. And it must have been very painful that Joan's anger denied you access or even much information about them. She deprived them of their father. I've always thought that was unforgiveable. And it's made me sad knowing I was the cause. I wanted to know them too. I suggested several times you should make contact when they were adults but you always said you'd given your word and wouldn't break it. I've always thought you were wrong about that.' She smiled. 'One of the many things I love about you, George Brown, is your integrity, even if you're infuriatingly pig-headed.'

'I tried and tried but Joan was very threatening. She said over and over again she would make sure the kids would have nothing to do with me if ever I tried to make contact. She said the same again when I wanted to divorce her in the seventies. But there's been nothing to stop them finding me. I've always hoped they would, but they haven't. It's been obvious they didn't want to know me.'

'George, that's not so.'

He looked at Hanny. 'Have you heard from them? Has something changed?'

'A lot has changed. There's a very good reason why Marty and Mark never tried to trace you.'

'What's happened?'

The noise in the bar was rising. Hanny moved closer to George and took his hand. 'Let me start with the reunification.'

'What the hell's that got to do with my kids?'

'Nothing directly but it could lead to a family reunification. Horst called yesterday from Berlin. He'd spotted that one of the foreign correspondents covering the ceremony was your son, Mark. He contacted him through the paper's local correspondent. They met yesterday and they're meeting again now. They seem to have got on well. And Mark's wife, Gisela, is with him – she is, or was, German.' Hanny paused for a few moments to let him take this in. George was totally taken aback and unsure how to react. 'Mark is keen to meet you and he's called Marty to let her know of the contact.'

'Horst shouldn't have done that. At least he should have called me first.'

'George, Horst is nearly forty-three. He did what he thought best. And I'm glad he did. As it turns out, we, you, might not have been in a position to meet Marty and Mark if he hadn't.'

'But it's obvious they've never wanted to see me. Why now?'

'Apparently, Joan told Mark and Marty a few months

after you came back to Germany that you'd died in an accident. They didn't know until a day ago that they had a living father.'

George turned and looked directly at Hanny. 'She did what? Is that really true?' She nodded.

'That's what they were told. I guess it was part of a plan to make sure you could never be part of the family again. As I've said, Joan's vengefulness is hard to understand. It was one thing to cut you out of her life but to totally deny her children knowledge of their father was unforgiveable.'

'I can't believe this. She knew I'd reluctantly accepted that I would have no contact with the kids. Why go further?'

'I can only think she had a very vindictive streak. But if Horst hadn't approached Mark we should never have known that, and Mark wouldn't have known his father was alive. But there's more. Joan died last year, as you know. When Marty and Mark were clearing her house they found your diaries and the letters Mutti and I sent. From those, they've learned much about you and your marriage and a lot of things they never knew about Joan. Mark's been trying to discover what happened to you ever since but kept coming up against dead ends.' She laughed. 'Sorry, that just slipped out. I guess "dead ends" is right as he's been trying to find out how you died.'

'This beggars belief. And they really want to see me?'

'Mark's very keen. He's read your diaries. I don't know what you wrote in them but, from what he said to Horst, he seems to have a lot of sympathy for you. I think his anger is mainly directed at Joan. Mark told Horst that Marty is more ambivalent. She's not so sure about meeting you.'

'I know Joan wanted me out of their lives. She made that very plain every time I tried to get in touch and in other ways too. As you know, I would get letters addressed to "Uncle" George, thanking me for the presents which Alice had bought for them with money I sent at Christmas and for their birthdays. I accepted that the "uncle" bit was simply to distance me. It never occurred to me it was a cover for the fiction that I'd died. Why ever did she feel she had to do that?'

'You must ask Mark but he may not know.'

Hanny signalled to the waitress. She came over and refilled their glasses.

'Mark and Gisela had planned to come to Aachen this weekend to try to trace my family and to find his half-brother, and also to find out how you died.' She raised her glass to George. 'I'm also celebrating the fact that you're alive.' George smiled. 'He and Gisela are staying with Horst until Saturday and then going home by way of Köln to see Gisela's family. They very much want to meet you. They've discussed how best to go about this. Mark hopes he and Marty might meet you together but he's not sure she'll sign up for that.'

George needed time to think. This was all happening so quickly – too quickly. He was apprehensive. A long period of introspection might make a reunion difficult – but it might be difficult anyhow. It would be particularly challenging if Martina was resentful and hostile. His thoughts went back to the daughter he had been so proud of. Even at the age of seven she had had a forceful personality. This was the fear which had haunted him over the years and had discouraged him from taking more active steps to contact them, either directly or through Alice. But his efforts had been met by ever more threatening responses from Joan. Now he knew the reason why. So many questions and concerns arose unbidden in his mind. Finally, he just said, 'How has it been left?'

'Horst and Mark have made a suggestion. The first part is that we should write with details and photographs of our families. Horst suggested that we, that is you and I, should meet Mark, together with Marty, if she can be persuaded to join him, here in Aachen.'

'And what then?'

'I don't know. That will be up to them and us but most of all up to you. We need to see how it goes. Horst did say that Mark was struck, after reading your journals, by what he's lost by never having had a father at home.' Hanny paused for a few moments. 'I think Horst provided quite a testimonial.'

George leant forward and was silent for a long time. Eventually he said haltingly, 'Hanny, you know how much I've always wanted to see them again. I've learned a little about them over the years but I've always been scared of meeting them. I did leave them fatherless and I did leave Joan. I know I was forced to but could I or should I have done more to try to stay in touch? But I was worried by Joan's increasing threats each time I or Alice wrote to her. Should I have done more to make contact when they were adults? Perhaps I should. But two things always held me back. The thought of having to face up to my own failures and guilt and handling the anger of my children. I also worried that re-establishing links might be seen as disloyal to you and our kids. I'd failed once. My family with you was too precious to risk. I'm sure you'll say there would have been no risk. Deep down, I'm sure you're right, but it worried me.'

Hanny took his hand and said very quietly, 'George, absolutely nothing could or would ever diminish my love for you and our family. You must do what's right for you.' She hesitated before adding, 'But you must also think about what's right for Marty and Mark now, as well as for Horst and Birgit and Klaus and for me. Everything's changed. Mark and Marty know they have a father for the first time since they were very young. And they know they have half-brothers and a half-sister. We can't turn the clock back; water can't be made to flow back under bridges again.'

'I know. And it seems, from what you say, that Mark would have found me sooner or later, perhaps even this weekend. I need time to think. I can see it might've been quite difficult if Mark had come to Aachen this weekend and found I was alive and we'd met without any warning.'

'George, my love, our life is so full of "ifs". We'll never know how our lives would have panned out if you had not rescued me, or if I had not been able to thank you in English, or if you'd not decided to learn German, or if you'd not become a family friend, or if you'd not played chess and come regularly to our home, or if we'd not fallen in love or if I'd not become pregnant, or even if Joan had not discovered those letters. There were so many points when our lives might have gone in entirely different directions. You can call it fate or chance or coincidence – maybe it's an amalgam of all those things. I just know I've been incredibly lucky to have you in my life, and so have the children. But thoughts of the harm I caused have always made me sad.'

'Hanny, you can't shoulder my guilt.'

'No, but I do share it. It's time to do what we can to repair some of the damage.'

'You're right. And, of course, I want to see Marty and Mark again – desperately.'

'Can I make a suggestion? That I contact Mark, possibly through Gisela over the phone, and arrange when we might get together. It might be easier for me to talk and arrange it with her but I think the timing should be left to Mark and he should decide if I should be there and if Gisela should be there.'

George nodded. In truth, he was relieved to have the arrangements taken out of his hands. He was worried he might say or do something inept. This was probably his one and only opportunity to make some amends to his children. He could not afford to fail again.

23

23 October 1990

Gisela was on the phone when Mark got home. She was speaking in German. He went through to the kitchen, made himself a cup of tea and idly thumbed through the Evening Standard. She came through a minute or so later and gestured that he should join her. 'How's Magda?' he asked.

She shook her head. 'It's not Mutti. It's Hannelore. She sounds lovely.'

Mark gulped, followed her into the lounge and took the receiver from her. For a few moments, he was lost for words. After a pause, the voice the other end simply said, 'I guess it was always going to be difficult to find the first words, for you and for me. I'm Hanny and I'm so happy Horst found you and we've found you too.' Mark choked. He could say nothing.

Gisela took the phone back. 'Hanny, he needs a moment or two. This has all been overwhelming. I'll put the phone on speaker. We can talk for a bit and Mark can join in when he's ready.' They talked for a few minutes in English while Hanny thanked her for providing details of the family and their lives.

Eventually, Mark was sufficiently composed to speak. 'Hanny, it's Mark. I'm sorry. Ellie was right. This has been overwhelming. I didn't quite know what to say.'

'It must be so difficult for you as you'd always believed George had died.'

'And George, Dad? How is he?'

'He's fine but we feel we should tread gently. I guess you do too. George asked me to call. He wasn't sure he would be able to control his feelings on the phone. And he's afraid he won't know what to say or that he might say the wrong thing.'

'Hanny, we've learnt so much since my mother died. There was so much I didn't know about my parents.'

'You had, have, a wonderful father. I'm so sorry you never had the chance to find that out when you were kids.' She paused before saying softly, 'And I'm even more sorry I was the cause.'

'Dad's diaries and letters have helped us understand some of what happened. But there's still a lot we don't know. I'm beginning to understand why Mum kept all those papers. I'm glad she did. If she hadn't, I might never have tried to discover what happened to my father. Although I guess I would've found out after Horst got in touch. But then I'd have been totally unprepared emotionally. Does George, I still find it difficult to think of him as my father, want to meet us?'

'Mark, we've not talked of anything much else for the

last three weeks. It'll be hard for him but yes, he's longing to see you.'

'I'm afraid Marty's not so keen. But I hope I can persuade her to come along.' Mark felt it would be easier to move the conversation on to practicalities. 'Does he just want to meet Marty and me, or just me if I can't persuade Marty to come? Would you be there?'

She paused. 'It's important for me too, but you should decide. You can meet him on your own first of all, with or without Gisela and with or without me.'

'I'll talk to Marty again. It's not easy just now with the problems she has. Where do you think it would be best to meet?'

'I think at home. Any neutral place would be public or semi-public. It will be easier to talk here, then we could all be freer with our emotions.'

'Not a problem. I'll talk to Marty before we make any definite plans. I might suggest she speaks to you but she may not feel able to do that.' They agreed to speak again the following week.

Mark called Martina after he had hung up. She was emphatic that she would not meet her father. 'You've pursued this mission without thinking where it might lead and what effect it might have on anyone else. He was my father as much as yours, although that word scarcely applies. He's my biological father – nothing more. Now you've made a commitment to meet him. What are you offering? Comfort and absolution despite all he's done and all he's failed to do?'

Mark was taken aback by the vehemence of her words but held his irritation in check as he responded as emolliently as he could. 'Marty, yes, he is your father and he's mine. And this would have happened anyway as Horst contacted me out of the blue in Berlin.' Perhaps, he thought, it would've been more straightforward if it had happened that way. Possibly Martina, having taken such a strong stance against his quest, was now finding it impossible to backtrack. It might then have avoided the tensions and recriminations which had marked the last twelve months. On the other hand it would have been extraordinarily difficult to have come to this point without all that he had gleaned from the contents of that hidden trunk. 'This is important for me,' Mark said quietly. 'I'm not taking a moral position or making any judgements. It just isn't possible forty years later to reach a balanced view of what happened back then. We'll never fully know the circumstances in which Dad worked and met Hannelore and we'll never fully understand the chemistry of his marriage to Mum.'

'I never wanted you to read those papers,' she said angrily, 'but you did despite Mum's express wishes. I might've known you would take such a relaxed view. Anything goes – that's always been your attitude. Our father had a fling with a tart and fathered a bastard and then two more from what you've told me.'

'Marty, that's not fair. She wasn't a tart and she's been his faithful partner for more than forty years.' He was about to add that his sister could hardly be regarded as an authority on marital harmony but thought better of it.

'How do you know she didn't engineer the whole thing? We only have her word for it. It could well have been planned as she thought she was onto a good thing.'

Mark paused before responding slowly. 'We also have our father's word for it. And her insistence that she was making no claims on him and that his life should be with us in England suggests otherwise – as does everything in his diaries.'

'How do you know she's not just highly manipulative and bloody devious? She may well have been waiting and planning to pressurise him once the child was born.'

'Marty,' he said wearily, 'all those things may be right but I don't believe they are. Ellie and I have spoken to Hannelore. We believe she's genuine. I'm as sure as I can be that what happened back then was not planned and that she was genuinely upset by what followed.'

'Well, I can't believe that you seriously think I would agree to meet this man and his mistress. I don't understand how you can be so accepting after he cheated on Mum and betrayed us.'

'Marty, there are two sides to this.' Mark was getting more and more irritated by his sister's intransigence. 'It seems the marriage was sterile and Mum betrayed us too. She deprived us of all contact with our father and then she fucking lied to us that he was dead. It's difficult to imagine anything more underhand than that.'

'Are you really suggesting there's a moral equivalence between the two?'

'She was having an affair of her own,' he said angrily.

'I don't believe that. That's simply a convenient supposition on you part.'

'Those letters and poems are quite explicit. You should read them.'

'Absolutely not. I'll respect Mum's wishes even if you won't.'

'Marty, you're in denial,' he shouted. 'You're just sticking your head in the bloody sand.' Gisela was sitting at Mark's side. She gestured with her hand for him to moderate his tone. He nodded and took a deep breath before saying as slowly and judiciously as he could, 'Marty, sadly we're not going to agree. On balance, and taking account of all the circumstances, if I were to apportion blame, which I'm not, I would place the greater part at Mum's door. But I'm trying to keep an open mind and not be judgmental.'

'You would,' she said angrily. 'And there's another big question. If he loved us so much, why the hell didn't he make contact, particularly once we were adult, and why didn't he speak to you himself on the phone?'

'I understand he did try but didn't approach us because he had given his word and felt guilty. He was also worried he might get a hostile reception. That was obviously justified,' he added pointedly. He went on quickly before she could say any more. 'Marty, I've had enough of this. Ellie and I are going to Germany to meet our father. I'll let you know how we get on. I just don't understand why you're taking such an unforgiving position.'

Mark was quivering with suppressed anger as he replaced the receiver. Gisela put her arms round him. 'Not good. I'm so sorry. It'll be difficult to reach an understanding with her.'

He shook his head resignedly. 'Probably impossible. I don't even feel much like trying just now.'

'Let the temperature cool a bit. Later on she may think better of the position she's taken.'

'Some hope.'

'Perhaps some of her anger comes from recognising that she has more of your mum's characteristics than she feels comfortable with.'

'Possibly. She has the same certainty that her view of the world is the only correct one.'

'Maybe her sadness that she couldn't have children and the impact that had on her own marriage partly lies behind her reaction. It must be difficult enough surrounded as she is by kids every day of her life at the hospital.'

Mark nodded. 'You may be right.'

Gisela thought for a moment. 'I guess, in a way, this is another long-term casualty of the war. You've found a father and a new family but, perhaps, lost a sister.' Mark nodded. She put her arms round him. 'But I want you to know how important this has all been for me. I've reconnected with my roots,' she paused and whispered in his ear, 'and with you.'

***

Mark arranged to meet his father and Hanny early in December. The prospect of the reunion had never been far from his mind since his return from Germany. They had all learned so much from the documents in the attic and, more recently, from Mo and Horst and Hanny. The uncertainties and ambiguities thrown up by his quest surrounding the absence (or death as he had believed) of his father had generated a degree of confusion in Mark's mind.

Hanny's words had implied that he and Marty had been harmed by their father's absence. But was that true?

His childhood would probably have been richer and less restrictive had George been around but had he been damaged by the absence of his father? He was not sure that was so. But was he the best judge of that? It was evident George had decided to remain within the family after learning of Hanny's pregnancy. He had seen that as an inescapable duty. But he would also have felt an obligation to maintain some contact and support for his child in Germany, difficult though that might have been. Maintaining a double life would have created intolerable stresses within him and even more within his marriage, as he sought to reconcile the irreconcilable. It was unlikely that would have been sustainable even if Joan had not found out about his relationship with Hanny. But she had and, even if she had been able to be more forgiving, there would have been considerable tensions if George had continued to have contact as an occasional visitor. Either scenario would have cast a pall over their childhoods. How might he have reacted in such circumstances against an inevitable background of antipathy and discord? Would a position of neutrality have been possible, manageable or sustainable? It seemed unlikely.

The question still remained as to why George had not tried to contact them directly. Possibly Horst was right. He had given his word and felt he could not break it. He might also have been held back by a sense of guilt and a degree of apprehension about the emotions which would be exposed if they were to meet. Any approach would have brought him directly or indirectly into contact and conflict with Joan. The emotional fallout from that was difficult to envisage – particularly in the light of what he had learned in the last few weeks. Perhaps he had hoped he and Marty would seek him out. He might have interpreted this omission as a sign that they had written him out of their lives. Was it possible that George had approached Joan seeking a divorce on the basis of separation when that became possible without consent in the seventies? Possibly he had but had been seen off again by threats and a degree of moral blackmail. His mother would have had much to lose if her lie had been revealed.

It was increasingly difficult to understand why his mother had accepted George as a suitor and husband. Had she simply regarded marriage and children as an integral part of a middle-class existence, a default position, an outward symbol of respectability? There was no doubt she had had a strong desire to have children and this had enabled her to overcome a distaste for sex – or at least heterosexual activities. He could envisage his grandmother advising her that she had a duty to meet her husband's needs, saying it was a price to be paid if she wished to have children. Her commitment to them had been absolute. Her inhibitions must have created difficulties after George had gone. To admit to separation or divorce back then might have led to a degree of social exclusion. Widowhood was a more acceptable status. That could also explain the banishment of Edna. The presence of a lesbian partner would have been more conspicuous in the absence of a man. It was clearly a source of concern and embarrassment to his grandparents. The rupture was probably encouraged, or even engineered, by them. Not only had his mother lost a husband but his departure had also led to the end of her relationship with Edna. This could only have added to her bitterness. Mark was unsure how Joan would have reacted if anything had occurred to fracture her cocoon of middle-class rectitude.

The unknown in the equation was Hanny. There was no doubt George had found comfort and respite through the hospitality extended to him by the Becker family. Mark was certain that the bonds between his father and Hanny had grown symbiotically. She had provided warmth, empathy and intellectual rapport and challenge which had been lacking in his marriage. Finally, she had offered the physical love and passion which had been absent from his life. Could he be certain that Hanny had been wholly confident she would not fall pregnant? Was it possible she had hoped a pregnancy would lead to a more permanent relationship? Mark was inclined to accept her assertion that they both believed the relationship was one without a future. He would never know how much pressure had been exerted on Hanny to assent to informing George that he was to be a father. Her later happiness must have been tinged with a sense of guilt that she was an unwitting cause of the rupture of his parents' marriage.

There were so many unanswered and possibly unanswerable questions – questions of choices, consequences and accountability for decisions made and actions taken. Mark had to ask himself one further critical question. Had he built up such an image of his father as a hero that he had become blinded to and an apologist for his faults and shortcomings?

24

7 December 1990

Gisela and Mark flew into Cologne/Bonn Airport and took the train to Aachen. They had planned to take a taxi to the house. Mark was surprised to hear his name called as they approached the exit. He turned to see the tall slim figure of Hanny, instantly recognisable from her photograph, waving to them. She hugged them both and suggested they should have a coffee together at the station.

She led them to a quiet corner of the buffet and was back a moment later with coffees and a packet of lebkuchen. 'I thought we should indulge as it was St Nicolas yesterday.' There was a pause. 'You're probably wondering why I'm delaying taking you to meet your father.' They waited, not sure what would follow. 'I feel I need to talk first. To be frank, I'm worried about George.'

'Is he ill?'

'Not as such, but his mind is in turmoil.'

'In what way?'

'It's not so easy to explain. He's not seen you for so long

and he only knew you as a kid. He had accepted that and, to an extent, come to terms with it. But there's always been an underlying sadness, particularly when he occasionally got news through Alice, mostly about you, Mark, from your paper. And there were high points, like when he heard you had won that press award. But so much has happened in these last two months. It's brought all his emotions to the surface. He's very tense. I know it's difficult for you, but I think it may be even harder for him.'

Mark nodded. 'Maybe – maybe not.'

'He's learnt so much more about you now and that's good. And a lot more about Joan – that's not so good. He gets angry when he thinks about her blocking contact with you and very angry that she lied so blatantly. He chunters on and then he suddenly switches and he's angry with himself for letting you and her down. It just keeps going round and round in his head.'

'And now?'

'He's also re-running our own history. When he first came back to Germany it was hard for him to settle. He was full of guilt. It was very difficult. I said more than once he should go back and confront Joan, apologise and try to rebuild the marriage. And I always felt he should insist on having contact with you.'

'And?'

'He did try. He wrote many, many times but, every time he did, the replies got angrier and angrier. That was mainly why he wouldn't go and confront her. He worried that would only harden her attitudes further.'

'It's difficult to think that would even have been possible.'

'You're probably right in the light of what we know now but that was the way he looked at it then. He also tried again years later to divorce your mother when that became possible after five years' separation. But apparently it couldn't happen without Joan being informed. He used a lawyer Alice knew. The petition, I think that's the right word, was served but he got a very nasty letter from Joan. She said she had preserved his good name with the two of you but if he went ahead she wouldn't hold back.'

'She would have been very scared, as the truth would inevitably have come out.'

'He became very depressed after that. He said he'd wanted to divorce so he could marry me. He muttered something about hell having no fury like a woman scorned. I looked it up – it seems to have been written by someone called Congreve.' Mark nodded. 'I had to say again and again that it wasn't important.' She smiled. 'Although it would have been nice. Only the immediate family knew we weren't married. I took his name. But it always upset George. He wanted to do things properly.'

'You're probably right. There's no knowing what Mum might have done if he'd tried to come back. She would have been terrified that her lies would be exposed. I can't even imagine how Marty and I would have reacted if she'd had to confess to lying to such an extent back then.'

'George was also desperately worried that making contact might make you even more hostile towards him than he believed you already were. That was why he didn't approach you later. He assumed your failure as adults to make contact meant you didn't want to have anything to do with him. That made him even more depressed. It was a bad time. Much though I loved him, I once even suggested he should think of moving out.' She paused and smiled sadly. 'I would have been devastated if he had but I felt I had to try to help him, whatever it might mean for me. I felt I had to give him a choice. As you know, if there's guilt, I'm as guilty as he.'

Hanny was struggling to control her emotions. Gisela got up and walked round the table. She pulled Hanny gently to her feet and put her arms around her. After a few moments she said something quietly to her in German. She turned back to Mark. 'Hanny needs a few minutes.' She dried Hanny's tears and kissed her on the forehead, saying something more in German. She smiled. 'I just said that even before we met, I knew she was going to be the stepmother-in-law I'd always wanted, even if I hadn't thought of such a possibility until October.'

'I'm so sorry,' said Hanny as she sat down again. She kissed Gisela's hand. 'I said all that very badly. But I've always felt a responsibility to help and stand by George. I loved him so much. I never wanted to turn him away, but I never wanted him to be separated from you either.' She smiled. 'It must seem odd to hear a woman who's nearly seventy talk like that, but I loved your father with a passion I'd never experienced before. That'll never change. But I'm anxious that this reunion should work for all of us and, Mark, you have a wonderful wife.'

'Hanny,' Mark said hesitantly, 'we're not here to confront George, Dad, or to accuse him in any way. What happened is past. It can't be changed. We know that.'

'I know. But I worry all the same. George is so tense. He so wants this to be a success. He's not sleeping well. Sometimes I hear him crying quietly in the night.'

'Hanny, this search for Dad has put a lot of things in perspective. It's made me feel somehow close to him – albeit at a distance. I know that sounds strange. I feel I'm getting to the end of a chapter in my life. I'm hoping there's a new one.'

'Me too. But hearing of your sister's reaction has been painful,' she said, her voice breaking as she did so. 'I never wanted to break up your parents' marriage.'

Mark stretched forward and took both her hands in his saying very gently, 'Hanny, we know that. Everything in Dad's diaries and your letters confirm that.' Hanny was becoming tearful again. Gisela got up once more and stood behind her chair, putting both hands on her shoulders. 'Dad's departure didn't seem to be such a big event in our lives. We knew so little of him when we were young and then he was gone. There was nobody there to say, "Your father's gone – sad but you must get over it". It sounds unfeeling, but there didn't seem to be so much to "get over". Now I know there was. But Mum was right about one thing. She did do nothing to blacken his name. She just didn't mention him.' He paused before saying very quietly, 'Hanny, this last year has been such a journey of discovery and I've learnt so much from Dad's journals and from what Ellie, her mother and you've told me. I can't be judgmental. And I'm in awe of what Dad did here.'

'Thank you.'

'It was a lucky coincidence that led to my first meeting

with Horst, and since then we've had time to think things through. I'm looking forward to meeting Dad. I'm just sorry I couldn't persuade Marty to be more accepting of what's happened. I'm sorry she's not here.'

'Sadly,' said Gisela, 'Marty's a bit too much like her mother. It makes me sad too. We've had enough conflicts in our pasts without creating new ones.'

'Ellie's right.'

'But what will this do for your relationship with your sister?'

Mark shrugged. 'Not a lot. But we've never been very close – particularly as adults. We don't fight. We just don't have a lot in common and we don't see each other very often. I think her own problems have contributed to that. But she does know I'm here this weekend.'

'We should get back before George begins to think we've been plotting.'

***

Hanny had recovered her composure by the time they reached the house. She led them through to the living room. Mark looked around. The family photographs they had sent only a few weeks earlier had been framed and were displayed prominently on a side table. George rose to his feet with a little difficulty, supported by a stick. The only real memories Mark had of his father had been of his cheerful good nature and his height. As George came slowly towards them, Mark was suddenly uncertain. How should he greet him? A handshake would be too formal but a hug or a kiss didn't seem quite right. Gisela sensed his dilemma. She stepped forward and took George's free hand in both of hers. 'I'm Ellie. We're so happy we're here. It's been a long journey.' She reached up, put her arms around him and kissed him on both cheeks. Mark went forward slowly – George extended his arm and embraced him. 'You've no idea how much this means to me. I'm so sorry it's been so long.' He paused. There was a catch in his voice and his eyes moistened. 'I've got so much wrong in my life. I hope you'll give me the chance to try and put some of it right.'

Mark was also in tears now and put his arms round his father. 'Dad, it seems strange to be able to say that after so long. I just want to get to know you and Hanny and your other children. That's the only thing that's important now.' They were both suddenly aware of the need to tread carefully and stood awkwardly for a few moments. An uncertain silence hovered in the air.

Hanny, aware of their unease, decided to take charge. 'I'm going to take you to your room so you can freshen up and I'll fix a drink while you do that. I think we all need one.' She put her arm around Gisela's shoulders. 'Ellie and I did some plotting over the phone. We both felt George and Mark should have some time together alone. She's going to join me in the kitchen. She can be my sous-chef.'

Mark rejoined his father in the living room. Despite his insights into the emotional challenges his father had faced, this was going to take time. He was finding it difficult to match the appearance of this eighty-year old with the impressions he had retained from childhood. He knew so much about him but was suddenly unsure if he really knew the man. He had developed an image of his father in his mind, an image which he had moulded and shaped progressively as he had learned more and more. But did that image he had created mirror the actuality? Did it truly reflect the personality, the nature and the essence of his father? Re-establishing a relationship, one which had scarcely existed previously, would be challenging.

George looked at him before starting to speak tentatively. 'I've thought so much about this moment. There's so much I want to say and now I'm not sure how to say it.' He paused. 'I just want to be sure I don't say the wrong thing. Most of all, I can't tell you how happy I am that you're here. I'd given up hope of ever seeing you again, though I often thought about you. I'm so sorry I let you down as a father and I'm so sorry I never knew you while you were growing up or since. There's so much in my life I've regretted but, more than anything else, it's been my loss of you and Marty.' George stopped. He was visibly struggling with his emotions as was Mark. They were both becoming tearful again. Mark went over, sat on the arm of his chair and put an arm round his shoulders. George looked up. 'I don't really know what I can do to make amends.'

'Dad, too much time has passed and too much has happened for recriminations. We are where we are. We've understood a lot from your diaries.' He laughed. 'I'm quite sure you never thought they'd be read by your children.'

He smiled. 'You're right. I'd like to see them again. I can't remember exactly what I wrote all those years ago. But I was very upset at leaving them behind. They were my outlet. I was probably more open in them than I ever would have been talking to anyone.'

'I suspect that's true. There's a lot we've learnt about you and Mum from them as well as from the other papers and letters we found. They're upstairs. We'll return them to you.'

'Perhaps I should have done more to get in touch when you were adults, but I was scared you would be resentful. I didn't think I could handle that. I'd always hoped you might come to me, but now I know why you never did until now. I don't know what possessed Joan to say I'd died or what else she might have said about me.'

'Almost nothing. She just didn't talk about you. All she would ever say was that you'd died in an accident and it was a consequence of the war.'

'But I don't understand how she was able to maintain that lie. I sent money each month. I only knew she'd died when her bank account was frozen after her death.'

'Marty had power of attorney for Mum after she had a stroke. I've asked her about that, Apparently the payments just came with an account number. She told Marty it was a widow's pension.'

'I also sent money for your birthdays and Christmas when you were kids by way of Alice. I couldn't once you were grown up as Joan wouldn't let me have your addresses once you had left home.'

'I don't remember getting anything.' He suddenly put his hand to his head. 'Oh my God – you were Uncle George.'

He nodded. 'You were always very meticulous about writing thank you letters – as your mother used to be. I accepted that the "Uncle" bit was Joan's way of distancing herself. But the letters did tell me a little about your lives.'

'That explains it. We sometimes asked about this mysterious uncle. Mum said he lived in Canada. We would write "George Brown Esquire" on the envelopes as instructed by Mum but she would always add the address.' He laughed. 'I imagine the letters didn't tell you very much. I, at least, said very little. I assumed I was writing to a distant relative I'd never met and probably never would. I guess, after creating this elaborate fiction, Mum would have found it more and more difficult to backtrack.'

'You're right. The letters were welcome but not very informative.'

'I do remember that we were encouraged to give some details of our lives and our achievements at school. I guess Mum felt that was the least she could do.'

'You shouldn't be too critical. I did pursue her. I thought the marriage would work out very differently. We were oddly matched. But I did let her down and she had every reason to feel angry and betrayed. All our lives would have been very different if I'd never met Hanny. But now I just want to try and catch up. I just hope it's not too late to get to know all about you and your lives, and for you to get to know my family here and in the north-east.'

'We've already met Horst and Clara and their girls. It would be good to get to know the others.'

'We've asked Klaus and Petra and their family and Birgit and Werner to lunch tomorrow. I hope that won't be too much all at once.'

'No, we're looking forward to it. And we'll make sure

we go to Newcastle. But there are others you should meet, your grandson Michael and your old friend Mo Burgess who sends her love.'

'Have you seen Mo? Is she still alive? That would be wonderful. I'd love to see her again. She was such an amazing friend. I lost contact when we moved a year or so after I came back to Germany. But what about your lives? You told me some things when you wrote. I knew you were a journalist as I occasionally bought the paper when I was in England. Once there was a photograph with your by-line. All I know about Marty is that she's a doctor in Birmingham. Tell me more.'

Mark hesitated. 'It's difficult. Marty's a paediatrician. She was very against my researching our family history – your history. And I'm sad she wouldn't come with us to Germany.'

'Perhaps later?'

'I hope so, but I'm not so sure. She believes the past is the past and that's where it should stay. I keep telling her it can never stay in the past, frozen in time. She's like Mum in some ways. Not easy to shift when she's made up her mind about something. I'll do my best but I'm not sure I'll succeed. She's also feeling quite fragile just now. Her marriage has come apart at the seams. It's not been a good year for her.'

George nodded. 'Tell me about you and Ellie. I know she's a successful sculptor and I know Hanny thinks she's wonderful.'

'Yes, she is.'

They were interrupted by Hanny and Gisela coming

back into the room, carrying glasses and a bottle of champagne. Gisela whispered in Mark's ear. 'Have you handed over what you brought for George?' Mark shook his head. 'I think you should as soon as we've got a glass of champagne in our hands.'

Mark slipped his hand into his pocket and brought out a small box and handed it over. 'Dad, you should have this.'

'What's this?' George opened the box and looked down in surprise. 'Oh my God, I'd forgotten all about this.'

'We knew nothing about it until we cleared the attic in Farnham.'

'What is it?' asked Hanny.

'It's my OBE.'

'Whatever's that?'

'An award for my mine-clearance work.'

'What do the letters mean?'

George laughed. 'Officer of the British Empire, not that there is an empire these days. More popularly known as for "Other Buggers' Efforts".'

'It's a big deal,' said Mark. 'The military version is an amazing honour.'

'Nothing like as important as seeing you and Ellie.'

It was time to raise their glasses. They had reached more secure ground. A sense of warmth and acceptance had been established. Mark and Gisela were experiencing the feeling that strangers sometimes have on meeting – that they have known each other all their lives. They had taken the first tentative steps towards re-creating a family – their own extended family. But it was a family which might never be wholly complete. Some rifts never heal.

War casts long shadows. Casualties occur even after the shooting has stopped. Absences and losses in the turmoil and chaos of war and its aftermath, particularly if unexplained, can generate uncertainties and ambiguities, conflicting passions and emotions leading to bitterness and rancour. Some wounds never heal, leaving indelible scars. There are countless unrecorded casualties of war.

DISCUSSION POINTS

The underlying theme of the novel is the impact of the ambiguities and emotional uncertainties which follow unexplained loss. The narrative highlights the challenges such losses can engender.

Unexplained loss can take many forms – enforced separation by external events, the unexpected disappearance of a loved one or death (or presumed death) without closure.

How do people face, deal with (or fail to deal with) and survive events which lead to unresolved grief? How important is it for people to experience seeing a body or observe funeral rites to validate the reality of loss? How does a lack of such verification create difficulties in adapting to the absence of a loved one? It is challenging to acknowledge that a loved one will never return – to do so is often felt to be disloyal and a betrayal. At what point does hope cease to be a positive sentiment and become an emotionally destructive one?

Healing can be a slow, uncertain and frequently incomplete process in the absence of certainty. How may unexplained loss impact on personal behaviour and on familial relationships? To what extent can recollections of past events, modified by additional insights learned later or subsequent external events, reshape embedded thought processes and behaviours?

Mark's search to discover his father's fate commenced as a curiosity driven project but, progressively, it became deeply personal. What impact did the absence of his father have on his childhood, emotional development and maturation and, later, his own perceptions of his role as a father? To what extent did his personal history and his quest impact on his relationship with Gisela and his sister?

The fate of Gisela's father was unknown. The abrupt rupture of a close-knit family with scarcely an opportunity to say farewell left her and her mother in an emotional vacuum. How did Gisela attempt to adjust? To what extent did her family life in England, her artistic endeavours, Mark's quest and political change in Germany contribute to her coming to terms with the loss of her father?

Sarah's husband was missing in action. She was buoyed up by the hope that he would one day walk back through the door, although this became increasingly unlikely the longer she was left without news. How do people come to terms with such emotional conflicts as they attempt to move on with their lives?

What is survivorship? It is customary to refer to those who have come through major periods of turbulence and turmoil as survivors. This word is most often used in a limited sense to refer to physical survival. As Gisela pointed out 'I'm only a survivor in the sense that I'm still here. None of us are really survivors. None of us are complete. None of us will ever again be the people we were or even the people we might have become. Just being alive isn't the same as surviving.'

How do people cope with emotional trauma as all around them others continue to pursue their everyday lives?

Regrets. It has been said[1] that 'what' and 'if' are two words as non-threatening as words can be, but when conjoined they have the power to haunt people for the rest of their lives. How do people live with the 'what if' and the 'might have been'?

The death of Mo's husband, Bob, while not unexplained was sudden and unexpected. She was devastated by the absence of an opportunity to say farewell. Her grief was overlain by speculation as to what might have been had he survived his injuries. In particular, she berated herself for her complicity in their agreement to defer raising a family until after the hostilities had concluded.

Memory. What is memory? How does it change in the re-

---

1   *Letters to Juliet*, Lisa and Ceil Friedman, Stewart, Tabori and Chang, 2010

telling? How do you get to the 'truth' of emotionally laden experiences and, ultimately, what is truth? In the words of Oliver Sacks[2], "... memories are not fixed or frozen .... but are transformed, disassembled, reassembled and recategorised with every act of recollection."

Memories are at the heart of the novel – the varied and somewhat disparate recollections of a shared childhood by Mark and Martina played a significant part in the development of tensions between them. Each recalled past events through their own unique lens and, for each, the shafts of memory were refracted in differing ways by their own life experiences and their differing assumptions of what Mark's quest might uncover. To what extent did their insights into the marriage of their parents play a role in reshaping their memories of their mother and their attitudes to the possibility of reconnecting with their father after more than forty years?

Finally, the novel reflects the current interest in ancestry. It touches on some of the reasons why many are driven to explore their family history, and some choose not to do so. Is it important to acquire knowledge of our parentage and ancestry beyond that which might have direct implications for our personal health or lifestyle?

For many, genealogical research appears to be driven more by romantic notions about the social status and achievements of their forebears than it is about genes. To what extent does

2   *Hallucinations*, Oliver Sacks, Picador, 2012

knowledge and perception of our family history play a role in shaping the beings we are? Does that knowledge have the same impact as culture, environment and the influence of our peers?

AUTHOR'S NOTE

The starting point for The Long Shadows of War is based on fact. It is a tribute to my father. He was absent for much of my early childhood serving in the Royal Engineers during the Second World War and was demobilised later than many of his contemporaries. I subsequently spent seven years at boarding school. He sadly died suddenly and unexpectedly during my second year as an undergraduate. There had been all too few opportunities to get to know him well as a child or as a young adult.

The suddenness of his death had a profound effect on us all, particularly on my mother who was to live as a widow for over fifty years. We felt it necessary in the days following his death to fill the time with practical tasks and decided to sort his personal effects. It was while performing this melancholy duty that we discovered several things which had been unknown to any of us. In common with many who served, my father rarely referred to the war after demobilisation. If he did so it would only be to recount some comical episode in military life. There was much of which we were ignorant. We learned, through finding his detailed notes, that he had volunteered for a mine-lifting and bomb disposal course. We also found amongst his papers a tribute to his leadership, prepared by one of the Mine Clearance Groups in the Aachen/Cologne area under his command and a German newspaper item publicly thanking him for his 'energetic support of all mine-clearers'. The mine-clearers were nearly all Germans 'recruited' from amongst former members of Pioneer Battalions. I have woven some of this into the narrative.

This background provided the framework for the narrative. The tale, however, is a work of fiction. That said I have made considerable efforts to portray the harsh realities of life during the final days of Nazi Germany and the period of occupation which followed as they were experienced by German people. There is little comprehension now of the level of destruction in Germany in May 1945, nor of the many millions of displaced, homeless and starving people in the country. The state of Germany today is a tribute to the resilience and enterprise of the German people during the occupation and following the creation of the Federal German Republic four years after the end of hostilities. It is also to the credit of the western occupying forces that, in general, they played such an effective role in rebuilding the various zones of occupation for which they were responsible. These efforts were even more remarkable as the administration and organisation was carried out, in most instances, by members of the forces over the four year period before parliamentary democracy was re-established in West Germany. The occupying forces had neither been trained nor been expected to undertake the role of civilian administrators. They received little support from the British

Government which was pre-occupied with the rebuilding of an impoverished Britain.

ACKNOWLEDGEMENTS
AND BIBLIOGRAPHY

The historical and political background to this tale has been derived from many sources. These include publicly accessible documents and archived newsreel and video clips (these are listed below). Further detail has been provided from my father's personal papers, my own interactions with German colleagues at the time of the fall of the Berlin Wall and reunification and the archives at the Royal Engineers Museum.

A dark and bloody ground, Edward G Miller, Texas A & M University Press, 2003

A defeated people, Directed by Humphrey Jennings, Crown Film Unit, 1946

After the Reich, Giles MacDonogh, John Murray, 2007

Aftermath, Harald Jähner, WH Allen, 2022

A history of modern Germany, 1800 to the present, Martin Kitchen, 2nd Edition, Wiley-Blackwell, 2012

Ambiguous loss – Learning to live with unresolved grief, Pauline Boss, Harvard University Press, 1999

Armageddon, Max Hastings, Macmillan, 2004

Austerity Britain, David Kynaston, Bloomsbury, 2007

Churchill's Secret Weapons – The story of Hobart's Funnies, Patrick Delaforce, Pen and Sword, 2015

Exorcising Hitler, Frederick Taylor, Bloomsbury Press, 2011

German Reunification – A short history, Deutsche Welle*

Germany 1945 – From war to peace, Richard Bessel, Simon and Schuster, 2009

Germany – Memories of a nation, Neil MacGregor, Allen Lane, 2014

Life in East Germany, BBC 2 – 1949 – 1990

Now the war is over, Paul Addison, BBC/Jonathan Cape, 1985

One year – Two Germanies, Deutsche Welle*

Overlord, Max Hastings, Michael Joseph Limited, 1984

Pathe news. Various contemporary cinema newsreels

Reconstituting German Society – http://germanhistorydocs.ghi-dc.org

Roller Coaster, Europe 1950 – 2017, Ian Kershaw, Allen Lane, 2018

The Berlin Wall, Frederick Taylor, Bloomsbury Press, 2006

The Impossible Peace, Anne Deighton, Clarendon Press, 1990

The Long Road Home, Ben Shephard, Bodley Head, 2010

The Naked Years, Marianne Mackinnon, Chatto and Windus, 1987

The Past is Myself, Christabel Bielenberg, Corgi Books, 1968

The Science of D-day, BBC 1 – October 2018

To hell and back, Ian Kershaw, Allen Lane, 2015

Tomorrow belongs to me, Peter Millar, Bloomsbury, 1992

Travellers in the Third Reich, Julia Boyd, Elliott and Thompson, 2017

War diaries – 1939 – 1945, Field Marshal Lord Alanbrooke, Weidenfield and Nicholson, 2001

What happened the day the Berlin Wall fell, Deutsche Welle*

When trumpets fade, HBO film – Directed by John Irvin and written by WW Vought, 1998

Winning the peace – the British in Occupied Germany 1945 – 48, Christopher Knowles, Bloomsbury Press, 2017

Winston Churchill's Toyshop, Stuart Macrae, Walker and Company, 1972

WW2 peoples War, BBC –

www.bbc.co.uk/history/ww2peopleswar/

In addition there are many film clips available on YouTube which graphically depict conditions in Germany in the final months of World War 2 and during the early years of the occupation.

I have benefitted from the guidance, advice and constructive criticism of Lesley Bryce, Jacqui Lofthouse and The Writing Coach throughout the writing of The Long Shadows of War.

I am grateful to Jörn Pusinelli and Nicole Mawdsley for translating an item from Rheinische Zeitung and for checking my German. The helpfulness of the archivists at the Royal Engineers Museum, Gillingham is gratefully acknowledged.

Finally, I am indebted to my wife, Sheila, for her encouragement throughout.